The

'Gareth didn't have any more . . . hallucinations?'

'Never. I doubt he even remembers them now. I've never told anyone this, Olwen. I tell you because it seems to me something similar is happening to you –'

'You think I'm hallucinating?"

'Are you? Do you see things that frighten you?'

Olwen feels the need to confide in him now, to share with him the vision of the woman in blue, to tell him of the enchanter and his possession of her grandfather. In time she stops herself . . . rather, something stops her . . . a voice, not her own, yet inside her: Careful, now. Don't show your hand. You'll ruin it all.

Grandfather?

Aye, aye, remember what I've always told you. Only us two. We don't want another in it.

Are you near then?

Nearer than you think, lovely girl. Nearer than you dream.

ROBERTA MURPHY

The Enchanted

A Mandarin Paperback

THE ENCHANTED

First published in Great Britain 1989
by William Heinemann Ltd
This edition published 1990 by Mandarin Paperbacks
an imprint of Reed Consumer Books Ltd
Michelin House, 81 Fulham Road, London SW3 6RB
and Auckland, Melbourne, Singapore and Toronto

Reprinted 1994

Copyright © Roberta Murphy 1989

A CIP catalogue record for this title
is available from the British Library

ISBN 0 7493 0482 0

Printed and bound in Great Britain
by Cox & Wyman Ltd, Reading, Berks

To My Father

Prologue

Once, when Olwen was seven years old, out for her daily walk in the Cwm Woods with her grandfather, she had asked him, 'Are ghosts real?'

Even then, when his mind was still sound and she the apple of his eye, the question had got stuck in her mouth many times before she dared ask it. He would want to know where she had heard of ghosts, since not from him, and when she told him, 'At school', he would be angry perhaps.

His rare fits of temper frightened her, and she had learned not to cause them, keeping in her head a list of subjects never to be mentioned in front of him. Alice, her mother, was top of the list – and easiest to avoid, for she had died before Olwen could know her. School was on the list only sometimes, depending. It was all right to tell him what she had learned in Welsh history (he liked to correct her teacher's interpretations) or to ask his help with arithmetic. It was not safe to repeat playground gossip (she was not supposed to listen) or to tell of the boys' teasing. When a boy had followed her to the bus stop, calling her, 'Ol, the china doll', she had told her grandfather, expecting his sympathy. Instead he had turned on her. 'And what did you do to encourage the little sod? Boys wouldn't bother you if you kept to yourself like I've told you to. Steer clear of them Pont Ysaf girls. You'll pick up no-good ways.'

So after asking him about ghosts, she had tugged at one of her plaits, hard enough to hurt her scalp, and looked away into the trees so she wouldn't see his face change. Anger always came on him like a seizure, and for a moment he would be unable to speak. In that moment, his top lip lifted over his teeth and his nostrils flared, showing the grey hairs inside. In a way, the harsh words that followed were a relief, shattering the mask that reminded her of the pictures of snarling ogres in her fairytale books.

I

One picture in particular leaped to her mind whenever he looked like that: a row of rosy, round-faced little girls, identical, with yellow braids, lay asleep in a big bed. An ogre towered over them, his fangs bared, a carving knife in his raised right hand. In the story the girls escaped, for one of them was clever and able to outwit the monster. Knowing this, Olwen still shivered and turned the page quickly each time she came upon the picture; and though her grandfather had never so much as lifted his hand to her, she felt a rush of fear whenever his face altered.

'Who's been talking to you about ghosts? From school this comes, is it?' His voice was not angry, merely irritated. 'A lot them teachers know! If they had any real knowledge, they wouldn't be stuck in a *twll* like Pont Ysaf.' As they walked down the winding path that led deep into the Cwm, he tapped his cane on the tree trunks. 'I send you to school because it's the law of the land. I have no hopes you'll learn much from them old biddies.'

'It wasn't a teacher. I heard some Standard Four girls talking in the yard.'

'Oh aye, and what did they have to say? Let's hear it.'

'They were just telling stories they'd heard.'

The older girls she had listened to, hovering near the bench where they sat on the edge of the playground, had been discussing a play they'd seen on television, but she didn't want to tell him this. Television was on the list in her head. It filled people up with nonsense, he said, encouraging nosey-parkers and wastrels.

'One girl told about this man whose wife died, and he got married again, only the first wife's ghost kept coming back and making trouble. No one could see her except the man.'

She remembered the big girls' laughter, which she, terrified by the idea of seeing a dead person, had not understood. For a week afterwards, she had dreamed every night of a misty, faceless creature who came wafting into her room to stand at the foot of her bed. This apparition, which she feared was her dead mother, held out its arms and said, 'Come to me, sweetheart.'

After a week of such dreams, she had asked her grandfather, 'Are ghosts real?'

After listening to the plot of *Blithe Spirit*, he said, 'Never more real than we want them to be. Ghosts have no power of their own. They can't come unless we bid them.'

2

'Why can't they?'

With the brass tip of his cane, he had pointed to their shadows on the path. 'Ghosts can't be, like them shadows can't be, without we make them. It's like them little cut-out figures you play with, see. Could they get up and walk about?'

She had laughed, thinking of the paper figures packed inside a Christmas-cake tin on a shelf in her bedroom. She imagined the lid flipping open, the figures tumbling out to run about the house, miniature knights, dragons, witches, in their brightly crayoned plumes and scales, rushing hither and thither, getting under her grandmother's feet in the kitchen, falling into the jam pot or the milk jug when they swarmed up the table legs to escape the broom Gwen would swipe at them with.

'No, they never could!'

'And why's that?'

'I made them, that's why. I make them do things.'

'Well, there you are. That's how it is with ghosts.'

Lying in bed that night, her grandparents still downstairs, one reading in the parlour, the other mending clothes by the kitchen fire (except for meals, they were rarely in the same room), Olwen had thought again about the cut-out figures. Imagining a mutiny inside the cake-tin prison, she saw them rise up, press their hands to the lid in unison, until it sprang open. Once free, they would creep across her carpet and crawl up the quilt to assail her, their jailor. Goose bumps pricked her arms as she lay in a parcel of blankets, listening intently for the click of the lid.

But on that summer afternoon, walking down the sunlit path in the Cwm, her hand tucked into her grandfather's, the idea that the paper figures might assume a life of their own had seemed absurd.

'What about the old enchanter, though?' she had asked, gazing into the shadowy places among the trees where he might, even then, be lurking. 'Did we make him up?'

'What do you think, *cariad*?'

Looking up into his blue eyes, she had slowly shaken her head. 'He's real,' she whispered.

'But he don't scare us, do he?'

On a bough above her grandfather's head, a squirrel leaped. Sunlight dappled the leaves and lit his hair. White for as long as she could remember, it spread like a cloud under his dai-cap,

3

framing his face, brown as the hazelnuts they gathered in the Cwm in September.

'He doesn't scare *us*,' she had repeated.

One

The Cwm Woods are bare on this pale Monday morning, the last day in March. From her bedroom window, Olwen looks across the barren garden and the lane to the leafless boughs, the grizzled trunks. Nineteen years old and recently bereaved, she seeks the one who has robbed her. He is in there somewhere. Wrapped in his cloak, camouflaged, he crouches close to the earth, watching the house, waiting to see the funeral party emerge.

Bracelets of ice hang from the branches of oaks and elms. Olwen, doubly hidden behind the lace curtain and a curtain of frost, knows that any two of those ice beads might be his eyes, piercing, sharp as needles, seeing her as she peers through spaces in the flowers of lace and frost. If she walked into the woods, he would leap on her, envelop her in the folds of his cloak. She would be easy prey, for she has the weakness . . . the disease invisible to all but him.

A victor, he grins now, baring his wolf's teeth. His lips and beard are spattered with blood. Years ago, on their rambles in the Cwm, her grandfather had told her about his insatiable appetite. As old as the woods themselves, he keeps himself alive, her grandfather said, by feeding off human desire.

'Whoever is infected with greed – and that's to say, whoever's heart is swollen up with it, fat and juicy with longing – *he* knows. That one he chooses.' Perhaps here her grandfather had sat on a fallen tree to rest his bad leg and drawn Olwen onto his lap. 'Say now, hundreds of years back, in the *Mabinogion* days, a royal hunting party comes riding into the Cwm after a stag. All of them, from the king down to the littlest page, wants something. Everybody wants something, don't they, *cariad*?'

'I want a bike this Christmas. Three-speed, remember?'

'And you shall have it, lovely. Did Grandfather ever deny you? That's a natural, ordinary desire for a little girl like you. But there's one in that royal party, so fine to see in their silk clothes on their high-stepping horses, who wants something *extra*-ordinary.'

'Like what?'

Here, he paused, perhaps, to light his pipe, to conjure up in smoke the prancing shapes of the ancient hunting party. 'Oh, it could be anything, but it's always too much, that's sure . . . something a human being is not supposed to want or have.'

'Like what, though? Tell me?'

'And that one he draws away from the others by magic enticement. Maybe he conjures up a pretty little doe that only the greedy one sees. So the hunter follows the doe into a lonely, far-off part of the Cwm. And there the old enchanter captures him and gobbles up his wicked heart.'

'It's wicked, to want something so much?'

'If it's the wrong thing – a forbidden thing – yes. Always.'

'But what would be a wrong thing, Grandfather?'

Stroking the part at the back of Olwen's head, where her grandmother had divided her hair into two plaits, he said softly, 'Nothing, *cariad*, that you can imagine.'

No one who had this desire ever escaped the enchanter, he said. Knights, vagrants, gypsies, courting couples, preachers, poachers had fallen prey to him. Only the two of them he let alone, Olwen because she was a child and innocent, her grandfather because he knew the secret of the enchanter's power.

'It's in his sleeve, see. He wears a great cloak with sleeves that trail on the ground. When he chances on a likely victim, he lifts his right arm and the sleeve falls and spreads like a curtain. He knows they'll look into the sleeve instead of into his eyes, and that's how he catches them. If they stared him straight in the face, he'd have no grip on them.'

'What does the sleeve look like?'

'Like the night sky, soft as velvet – not black, more indigo – embroidered with moons and stars in the finest silver threads. And in this sleeve he can show an image of whatever the heart wants most. Like in a dream. So the fool he's enticed steps right into the folds and the enchanter traps him.'

'I'd never look in his sleeve. Do you know what I'd do if I met the old enchanter? I'd stare him out.'

'That's the ticket. A pair of honest eyes would slice through his magic like a sword. Stare him in the face and he's as helpless as a robin redbreast.'

6

'Let's look for him now!' Here she must have bounded from her grandfather's lap and tugged at his hand to get him moving again.

'What? After all I told you? In't you scared, then?'

'No! I want to stare him out. Come on, Grandfather!'

'Well *daro*, you're a brave one. You got a lion's heart.'

And she had danced down the path, her grandfather limping beside her, but moving so fast that instead of impeding him, his right leg, gammy from an old pit accident, seemed to do a jig all of its own, the ferrule of his cane tapping out the rhythm, the brass horse's head on the handle flashing a warning to the evil enchanter. . .

Through spaces in the lace curtain Olwen searches the woods for a sign, a flicker of activity that will give away his hiding place, but she sees only melting snow, brown earth, patches of grey sky like a shredded banner among the boughs. Rain falls over everything, turning the snow to slush, making the icy trees weep.

A movement beneath her window distracts her. The coffin bearers have come out of the house. They stand on the garden path, their hands thrust into their overcoat pockets, their eyes fixed on the tips of their shiny black boots. All five of them she knows by sight. Ex-miners, they hang about Pont Ysaf High Street in the afternoons, waiting for The Bird in Hand to open. On trips into town with her grandmother, she must have spoken to them, heard their names, for Gwen would never pass an acquaintance without asking after health and family. But in their black Sunday suits, black coats and dai-caps, Olwen can't tell them apart. As alike as crows they are, and as commonplace. She has known only one extraordinary person in her life.

From the way they shuffle their feet and keep their heads down, she sees that the miners feel shy and embarrassed. They must know each other well, but they don't speak. They only cough and sniff. All of them, she guesses, have silicosis, their harsh, rasping cough a symptom of the disease. All of them, probably, are chain smokers, but they don't smoke now, out of respect. In the steady rain, in the dead garden, they wait to bear her grandfather – who never gave them the time of day after he retired from the pit.

The other mourners, her grandmother, Aunt Flindy, Dr Lloyd and his son Gareth, are still inside the house, in the parlour where the oak coffin lies. The undertaker and the minister are there too, and Morgan Pryce, the bus driver, who chauffeurs at weddings and funerals to earn a bit on the side.

The sixth bearer has not yet arrived. Unused to rising before noon, he has slept late. On purpose this morning, Olwen thinks, as a final insult to repay an old injury inflicted by her grandfather and nursed for years by their silent neighbour. Something must have happened to cause the cold courtesy and flashes of hostility her grandfather and Bryn Brewen showed each other. When Bryn came to their door and asked to be a bearer, Olwen was amazed, her grandmother's answer startling her even more than the request. Enraging her, too.

'I know John would want that, Bryn,' Gwen said.

'How could you lie!' Olwen shouted at Gwen after Bryn had left. 'He'd never want Bryn Brewen. He couldn't stand him. Go and tell him you've changed your mind.'

'Hush,' Gwen said. 'There are things you know nothing about. It's time to make amends.'

And she would not budge, though Olwen kept on at her for hours. This firmness surprised Olwen. She had always thought of her grandmother as compliant.

So that she won't be seen from the garden – or the woods – Olwen has drawn the lace curtain across her window. She has come to her room to escape the sorrowful looks and murmurs in the parlour.

'Never make a spectacle of yourself,' her grandfather said whenever Olwen, as a child, came home crying from some slight suffered on the school bus. 'People love to gossip and gape. Don't you give them the opportunity.'

In the parlour, she had kept a straight face and a straight back, moving away, mute, from anyone who approached her to say, 'There's a pity' or 'You'll miss him, Olwen *fach*.'

Then Gareth had arrived with his father. Although a Welshman by birth, the doctor is a newcomer to Pont Ysaf. After living in London for many years, he returned to Wales on the death of his wife, bringing with him his eleven-year-old son. His arrival, nine years ago, caused a stir in the town, and people flocked into his waiting room. At school, Gareth's English accent and correct grammar had made the children gape. 'Royalty has come among us,' her grandfather said. 'See all of Pont Ysaf *twti* down.'

Today, in their tailored London suits, charcoal grey for the doctor, dove grey for his son, they look like gentry, out of place among the miners in their worn and shapeless black, bought off the peg at British Home Stores in Cardiff or at the Swansea C & A. Save for the minister, the most distinguished mourner – and certainly the tallest, his well-brushed grey hair almost touching the moulded ceiling – Dr Lloyd seemed too tall for the Parrys' parlour, diminishing the rest of them, shrinking the furniture to doll proportions. At the same time, the closed coffin beneath the window had seemed to increase in size. In life, Olwen's grandfather and the doctor had treated each other with mutual respect and mutual disapproval. 'The doctor lived in London too long,' her grandfather would say. 'And he've given his boy London ways.'

Beside his father, Gareth, smaller boned and lacking his height, looked almost feminine. Blond, graceful, he reminds Olwen always of the androgynous figures in Pre-Raphaelite paintings. He had come to her side at once, not to offer sympathy like the others, not speaking at all, simply sticking to her as if they were a bridal pair. Unnerved, she had finally walked out.

In her small room with the door closed, she feels easier. Here, it's possible to believe that no catastrophe has occurred. Everything in the room harks back to the time when her grandfather was well. The pictures on the whitewashed walls – watercoloured landscapes, pen-and-ink drawings from fairytales – he chose for her, carving the frames from wood he cut himself in the Cwm. The bookcase is crowded with books he gave her and which they read by the fire on winter evenings, *The Mabinogion*, Hans Andersen, the Brothers Grimm. Even the fantastic shapes in the gnarled wood of the rafters exist because he created them. Sitting in the wicker chair by her bed, a book on his knees, he'd look up and say, 'Let's see if we can find the dragon in this story.'

Olwen, a little girl then, would put her head back on the pillow and look up too, her mouth open as if for a sweet.

'*Daro*, I see him! He's a big 'un, right enough.'

And as she lay cosy among the blankets, he'd make a dragon come to life out of the whorls and cracks in the wood. The rafters became inhabited with magical creatures, and although it's years now since the bedtime stories, the shapes remain, a fresco of the secret world they shared.

9

Her window, too, frames a memory picture. Beyond the garden gate and across Archer's Lane – filled today with cars from town – are the Cwm Woods where the two of them walked every day. At the end of the lane, opposite the last of the four cottages, she can see the entrance to the path they followed, the place where she took her first steps, he has told her.

She seems to remember, too, though vaguely, dreamily, a time before she could walk, when he had carried her into the woods. Her grandfather always insisted she did not remember this far back. 'A babe in arms, how could you? You only think you do, because I've told you so often.'

Someone else was in the woods with them, a woman – but not her grandmother or anyone she knows. She recalls raised voices, sudden movements, and a single cry, like the yelp of an animal caught in a trap. But all of this is blurred. Olwen can't picture the woman's face or make sense of the flurry that seems to accompany her. What she does recapture, always and vividly, is a sensation of falling – falling from her grandfather's arms – and colours – deep blue streaked with red, like the sky at sunset. She falls into this blue, is enveloped, suffocated. She hears her own stifled baby-screams, and then the scene blacks out, as if a curtain were dragged across a stage in the middle of an act. This part of the memory she never told her grandfather, fearing it would bring on one of his rages. He had not liked her to contradict him.

Standing at the window, looking at the woods in their March bareness, Olwen wishes this memory had not come. It casts a shadow over the little room, dimming the pictures on the walls, darkening the bright colours of the patchwork quilt. It's the shadow of a secret her grandfather kept from her, though he told her repeatedly, 'You're my heart's treasure, worth more than diamonds or rubies. No one in this world I love but you.'

Olwen shivers. The room is unheated and she wears a thin dress of black silk, a summer dress bought for the Upper Sixth leavers' dance at her grammar school last July. Her grandmother removed the white lace collar and floppy pink bow to make the dress more sombre. Still, with its soft pleats and scooped neckline, it seems frivolous to Olwen. Besides, her grandfather had disapproved.

'It's not befitting,' he had said, when she put on the dress to go to the dance. 'It's not modest.'

In the shop, Olwen had liked the dress. Black suggested a secret sorrow that struck her as romantic, and the colour had seemed to flatter her pale skin and dark eyes. Gwen had said, 'All the other girls will be in blue or pink, you watch. In this dress, you'll stand out.'

She had wanted to stand out. Knowing that Gareth, home from his first year at Oxford, would come to the dance, she had wanted him to notice her. In the silky dress with its floating skirt, she had felt the power to draw him. In the privacy of the curtained cubicle she had unplaited her dark hair (never cut above her waist because her grandfather despised 'cropped girls'), shaken it loose and run her fingers through it until it resembled the live tresses of the legendary women whose pictures she had admired in books. Then she had slowly pirouetted, her eyes fixed on her own reflection in the full-length mirror. Her body and legs, always too thin when she viewed them in her bedroom mirror at home, seemed slender and ethereal now, ornamented by her streaming hair and the fluid dress. She had thought of Tennyson's 'The Lady of Shalott', the illustration accompanying the poem in her text book, and remembered how, asked to read aloud by her Fifth-Form English teacher, she had thrilled to the words:

> A bow-shot from her bower eaves,
> He rode between the barley sheaves,
> The sun came dazzling through the leaves,
> And flamed upon the brazen greaves
> Of bold Sir Lancelot.

'Well done, Olwen,' Mrs Griffiths had said. 'Rendered with feeling indeed.'

Other girls in her class had giggled at the verses, and at the notes the boys passed, offering obscene parodies:

> A bow shot from above his knees,
> He did her in the barley sheaves . . .

But Olwen had read the poem to herself at home, responding powerfully, urgently to the sudden flare of passion ignited in the Lady at the sight of Lancelot. I want that, she had thought, I want to be swept into love, to risk everything . . .

Years later, charmed by her image in a dressing-room mirror, she had seen in her face the stricken beauty of the Lady of

Shalott, felt herself transformed by the magical dress . . . and bought it. After her grandfather's displeasure, she had never worn it again, but today she must.

To detract from the striking dress, she has pulled her heavy dark hair into a severe bun. The black lisle stockings and lace-up shoes she wears were part of her school uniform. Surely he will be satisfied that she has made every effort to appear reserved . . . modest.

In her left hand Olwen holds a long-stemmed rose. She has plucked it from the bunch her grandmother placed in a vase on her dressing table that morning. The card she handed Olwen read, 'To cheer you and help you through the day. Gareth.'

After giving her the card, Gwen had crossed to the wardrobe and taken out the black dress. 'I'll press it, shall I?' she said. 'And take off the decorations.'

Looking at the dress, Olwen had winced, remembering vividly her reason for buying it, and how she had danced in it with Gareth, forgetting her grandfather and his dislike of the doctor's son, betraying him to gratify her vanity.

('No one else I love but you . . .')

'He has a nerve!' Olwen had thrown the card to the floor.

'He sent them out of kindness,' Gwen said, 'and regard for you.'

'Out of arrogance, you mean. He thinks he can push himself in wherever he pleases, just because he's the doctor's son. Pont Ysaf aristocracy!' She had used her grandfather's words.

Now she holds the rose to her lips, inhaling the perfume, a scent as fragile and elusive as memory. Her grandfather grew roses . . . all kinds of flowers. In summer, his garden was abundant. The scent reminds her of the colours and perfumes in his garden.

More . . . as Olwen inhales, the scent seems to become imbued with a greater power than simply to evoke connections. She begins to sense his presence, as if he stood in the room, or down in the garden perhaps, and she fails to see him only because she doesn't know the right way of looking.

She thinks of the puzzle pictures she loved as a child, in which objects were hidden in a landscape, invisible if you looked at the whole picture. The trick was to focus on the parts, taking one section at a time. In that way, the objects revealed themselves, and once discovered, they remained. They could never again merge with the background. Even when she tried to lose them, they had stayed.

She begins to focus on parts of the garden, blocking out the patient miners on the path. There are no flowers; only the remnants of stalks strewn about the damp black earth. The chestnut tree is bare, the toolshed locked up. Down by the gate, delphiniums – his favourite flowers – cling, ragged, headless, to the creviced wall.

In this setting, he will be hard to see. The colours, black, brown, grey, peat green, will give him camouflage. He dressed in them, and they were his natural colours too, his face and arms brown from the weather, green stains on his hands, black earth under his nails. Grey was the colour of his skin during his six-month illness.

Dismayed, Olwen finds herself thinking of this time just past. As his body sank, her grandfather's mind had burgeoned with bizarre fantasies. Increasingly, as she sat by his bed, he spoke like an insane person, not to her but to someone he believed he could see – a woman in a blue dress.

'There's nice you look in blue, lovely,' his gaze fixed on a cloudless winter sky. 'Always wear that colour, won't you? It's the best one for you.' And then, his face altering, his eyes darting to a corner of the room, 'Don't give me lip, you little cow. I know what you are. Plenty have lifted that dress, haven't they? You'll alter your stroke or you'll come to a downfall.'

When Olwen put her hand on his shoulder and said 'Grandfather,' he sometimes snapped out of it. But sometimes, he'd knock her hand away and curl his lip. 'Leave me alone,' he'd say, 'or I'll ring your neck,' his fingers, emaciated, yellow, reaching for her. At these times, she'd run to the bedroom door and shout for her grandmother.

Over the months, he had changed into a person she feared. The man who lay in bed all day, grey and wasted, and who, at night, found the strength to rise and prowl the house, dragging his lame foot, she could not recognize as her grandfather.

'He might do you harm,' Gwen said, warning Olwen to lock her door when she went to bed. 'He's not himself.'

From this simple statement, Olwen had intuited what Gwen did not know: her grandfather was possessed. Clearly it must be so, for there were days when his old self emerged, when he talked to her as he used to, wise and lucid. On these days he was wont to say, 'I'm losing the will to fight, Olwen. He'll have the victory yet.'

13

And Olwen, nineteen years old, found herself believing again, with the naïveté and conviction of a child, in the enchanter of the Cwm. For she saw him, saw his black sleeve swirl deep in the irises of her grandfather's eyes, heard him speak out of her grandfather's mouth, listened to the swish of his cloak in the passage at night.

I'm mad, Olwen thought, to believe in such a creature. Yet, as her grandfather's sickness progressed, she grew more sure. One afternoon, just days before his death, she said to him, 'Is it the enchanter?'

He had looked at her with faded eyes. 'Aye, you've got it. I looked into his sleeve, *cariad*.'

'What can be done?'

She saw his face muscles strain, as if he were trying to remember something. Then he said, 'Stare him out or he'll get you too.'

'I will. I'll find him and make him leave you alone.'

Suddenly, he had clicked his tongue, changing moods. 'Hisht, that's old nonsense. Stuff I filled your head with to entertain a child. You're grown up now. If you want to comfort me, stay by my side.

On the last day, before he sank, he whispered in her ear, 'I won't leave you, *cariad*, so don't you leave me. Come to the Cwm in summer and we'll be together again.' Those were his last words to her. After speaking them he fell silent, raising his hand weakly to signal that she should move back from the bed, give him space, keep quiet. Olwen smoothed the counterpane where she had sat and moved to the window seat.

From there she watched him closely, searching for signs that he might be a little better than yesterday, than a month ago. 'Come to the Cwm in summer . . .' She wanted to understand the promise as proof that he meant to get well, to get up, cast off the mask of illness and resume his old, vigorous self. But his words had told her that they must part . . . and how could they be parted except in death?

He lay on his back, his arms stretched out, his hands open, a stick figure in pyjamas which seemed like hand-me-down clothes from a more robust, larger man. When he turned his head to gaze out of the window, the movement required great effort, and he wheezed, as he used to, sometimes, after hours of exertion in the garden.

Once, as a child, she had climbed onto his lap, pressed her fingers against his face and said, 'Grandfather, you're like a rainbow!'

He had misunderstood, laughed, and said, 'Not me, *cariad*. I'm a sober dresser. Aunt Flindy's the colourful one.'

But Olwen had meant his own colours, the ruddy tints of his skin, his blue eyes, the thick white hair filamented with gold, his arms, dark and solid as mahogany, his fingernails, streaked with mauve and green like rare shells . . . and the calf of his gammy leg. When he rolled up his trousers to soak his feet in a basin after gardening, all the hues in her paintbox were splashed across his left leg from knee to ankle.

Sickness had drained the colour from his face, jaundiced his eyes, and turned his white hair ashen. He lay in the bed inert, shrunken, his skin almost transparent, so that she could see the bones, and the irregular beat of his heart, as if a small, wild creature struggled in his pyjama pocket.

As she watched, he closed his eyes, slept. An uneasy sleep, she knew, for he breathed rapidly, the inhaled air rasping in his throat. Then, suddenly, his breath stopped and the commotion in his pyjama pocket ceased. Olwen saw that his features had stiffened, his lips drawn back from his teeth, his nostrils flared, his face resembling the brass horse's head on his walking stick.

'Grandfather?' She had reached out her hand to touch him, drawn it back again. Turned to brass . . . turned to stone . . . 'Nain!' she had cried, at the top of her voice.

Her grandmother came into the room and hurried to the bed, placing herself between Olwen and the strange figure, the impersonation, that lay there.

'He's gone, love,' Gwen said. 'It's over.'

Olwen lifted her hand and slipped the catch on the window. A cold March wind rushed into the room, chilling her to the bone. She opened her mouth and gulped in the rough, fresh air. 'It's over, over . . .' the wind cried as it bore her grandfather's spirit away to the Cwm. She had slammed the window shut and folded her body down onto her knees.

Olwen closes her hand tightly on the rose stem. She feels the thorns dig into her palm. Look for him, she tells herself, as he was before. She searches the garden for a clue – a flash of blue, a blur of white – a figure appears at the gate. Olwen starts, the rose thorns thrusting deep into the flesh beneath her thumb. At once she sees that the man coming into the garden is not her grandfather.

15

Tall and gaunt, his coarse black hair tied behind in a bushy tail, Bryn Brewen has always seemed to Olwen only half human. The dark semi-circles under his eyes are so prominent, his skin appears chalk white in comparison, reminding her of a badger's striped face. And indeed he has a stripe, an old scar reaching from the bridge of his nose to his jaw, neatly dividing his left cheek. In his long black coat, fitted at the waist, he looks like a highwayman.

A poacher, in fact, he comes out with the moon. Many nights during her grandfather's illness, she stood at her window and watched Bryn Brewen glide from his cottage next door. His lurcher at his heels, his sack over his shoulder, he slipped across the lane and vanished into the Cwm.

In the moonlight, the lurcher, a cross between a collie and a greyhound, appeared wolflike. His master named him Gelert after the heroic dog of Welsh legend – a nasty joke, it seems, on the ragged, obsequious mongrel who has skill but no courage, adoring Bryn, licking at his heels even when he kicks or curses it.

As he comes up the path, Bryn Brewen raises his black-rimmed eyes to her window. Olwen feels his gaze penetrate the lace and capture her. He lifts his hand, touches his cap, passes from sight beneath the stone wall of the cottage.

The miners are looking up. She steps back into the room. Now that the sixth bearer has come, the journey to the cemetery can begin. Reaching for the coat that lies across her bed, she sees scratches on the mound beneath her thumb. Spots of blood lie on the inside of her wrist like a bracelet of tiny rubies.

Two

Under a canopy of umbrellas the mourners file down the path in twos behind the coffin, Olwen and her grandmother, Aunt Flindy on Dr Lloyd's arm, the undertaker and Reverend Rhys, and lastly Gareth with Morgan Pryce. As they approach the black tarpaulin-covered toolshed her grandfather built at the bottom of the garden, Olwen sees a movement behind the square window, a flash of white across the dirt- and rain-streaked pane, as if someone had moved swiftly out of sight. She stares into the glass. It offers only a reflection of the chestnut tree on the lawn, its trunk distorted in the wet pane to resemble, at first glance, a crooked human shape. Yet she's sure she glimpsed something more.

Beside the locked door of the toolshed, guarded on either side by the empty stalks of last summer's sunflowers, Olwen and Gwen halt to allow the bearers to manoeuvre the coffin through the gate into Archer's Lane where the hearse waits.

'We should ask Mr Rhys to go in the front car with us,' Gwen whispers. 'It's only right.'

Olwen shakes her head. The minister would pat her hand as if she were six years old and tell her, 'Grandpa's in Heaven.' In the parlour, he had put his arm around her and said, 'He's joined the ranks, Olwen, so you mustn't fret.' His big moon face, boyish still though he's close to fifty, had beamed at her, as if he expected his words to cheer her up. Pont Ysaf's only minister, he officiates at so many funerals and weddings, he must sometimes confuse them, absentmindedly putting on the wrong demeanour, as Morgan Pryce has put on brown boots with his black suit.

'I envy John, I do,' Morgan had said in the parlour. Cap in hand, he had bowed his head before the minister. Strands of Brylcreemed grey hair lay flat on his nearly bald crown, reminding Olwen of withered eelgrass. 'This old world's a vale of tears, in't it, Mr Rhys? Lucky he is to be out of it.'

His words had startled her, and she had felt a rush of sympathy for the bus driver, seeing, for the first time, despair as well as age in his stooped shoulders. She had looked then to Mr Rhys, expecting him to offer comfort. Instead of compassion, she had caught revulsion on his face, caused, perhaps, by the stench of Brylcreem rising from Morgan's head. The next moment, a smile erased the disgust, and Mr Rhys said in his deep, pleasant voice, 'Now, now, Morgan, that smacks of blasphemy. Life is God's gift. We mustn't hanker to leave before He's ready for us.'

Cowed, Morgan Pryce had backed away. 'You're right, Mr Rhys, *wara teg*. My brains are in my feet sometimes.'

'Don't ask Mr Rhys,' Olwen says as she and Gwen go through the gate. 'He hardly knew Grandfather.'

When they reach the lane, Morgan darts in front of them, whippet-quick, and holds open the door of an ancient black Bentley.

'Aunt Flindy, then. She's our oldest neighbour, and he was fond of her.'

'We needn't ask anyone. There's plenty of room in the other cars.' Olwen nudges her grandmother's arm. 'Get in. It's pouring.'

'Shall I fetch Mrs Flinders?' Morgan Pryce says. 'She's just getting into the doctor's car.'

Olwen looks down the lane. At a distance, Aunt Flindy cuts a youthful figure, for she dresses as if she were twenty-five instead of close to eighty. Today she wears a black 1940's suit with a long, fitted jacket and a skirt that ends at her knees. On her head an elaborate hat sports feathers and a gauze veil. Around her neck she has draped a fox fur, the fox's head resting on her left shoulder. Close up, she had smelled of mothballs under the gardenia scent, as if the outfit has hung in her wardrobe for forty years, the length of time she has been a widow.

Opening the front door to her that morning, Olwen had stared at her garish make-up, purple rouge and lipstick, blue eyeshadow and mascara.

Aunt Flindy had laughed in her face. 'Don't look like you smelled a dead rat, dearie. I'm doing right by John. Giving him a proper send-off.' Then, leaning close to Olwen in the narrow hallway, 'I talked to him last night, and guess what he told me? "I wanted to escape, Flindy", he said.'

Olwen, cornered, had whispered, 'Escape from what?'

Aunt Flindy had nodded, her rhinestone earrings winking lewdly. 'Right up to my bed he came, like they all do, in the middle of the night. Cheeky buggers, the dead –'

'You didn't see my grandfather –'

'"Go on back, John," I told him. "It's all over now. No point dwelling on it." But he can't rest, y'see. He was hoping to find *her* over there, and he haven't. Something keeps them apart still –'

'I'm not listening.' Olwen had slid along the passage wall, Aunt Flindy stepping beside her, lurid as a figure in a nightmare. When they reached the parlour door, she had whispered, 'I can raise the dead without even trying. Remember that when you're in need.'

In the parlour, she had behaved as if the occasion were festive, flirting with the men, holding a glass of elderberry wine with her little finger cocked, as if it were champagne.

'Here's to John Parry,' she had said from time to time, lifting her glass. 'He got away from us scot-free!'

'Let her go with Dr Lloyd,' Olwen tells Gwen, who stands beside the Bentley, reluctant, for some reason, to get in. 'She'll enjoy herself more.'

'What a thing to say.' Her grandmother's eyes pucker, as they do when she tries to read without her glasses. 'Why would you think Aunt Flindy's enjoying herself?'

A slender thread of patience breaks inside Olwen. She snaps shut the umbrella she has been holding over them. 'I won't *have* the old bitch, that's all.'

Morgan Pryce's head jerks violently, as if pulled on an invisible string. '*Daro!*' he says under his breath.

'There's no call for that language, Olwen,' Gwen says, but she has lowered her eyes, and Olwen hears the defeat in her voice when she says, 'Could we get in the car now, please? It's time we went.'

So Olwen and Gwen share the back seat of the Bentley, enough room between them for a third person. The car moves slowly down Archer's Lane, Morgan hunched forward to peer through the rain that drives against the windshield, unimpeded by the rickety wipers. The lane is so narrow that branches knock the windows on the Cwm side. On the other side, the four greystone cottages stand in their barren gardens, curtains drawn across the windows. Olwen recalls that she did not draw her own curtains. But then she does not believe her grandfather is dead. He has passed into another state, yes . . . she will never see him again as he was . . . but she will see him. He promised her. It's a matter of learning how to look and where. 'In summer,' he said . . . but summer is months away. Watching the bare branches scratch across the window, she feels her heart swell, her breath snagging so that she cannot draw it up into her throat.

Gwen touches her arm. 'What's the matter?'

Olwen flinches and her breath comes out with a choking sound. 'Nothing. It's hard to breathe in here.'

'I'd open a window,' Morgan Pryce says, 'but it's raining so nasty. Not going to pass out, are you, love?' He tamps his Woodbine in the ashtray. 'Sorry if my smoking did it. Bad habit, I'm well aware. John was never a smoker, was he?'

'He liked a pipe,' Gwen says, 'on occasion.' She is looking at Olwen. 'You ought to get it out,' she says, too low for Morgan to hear. 'If you had a good cry, you'd feel better.'

You haven't cried yourself, Olwen thinks. But she knows her grandmother has no tears. She may even be glad it's over.

The Bentley turns out of the lane into Pont Ysaf Road. In one direction the road leads into the town it is named for; in the other it ends, like the Cwm, at the gates of the cemetery. On one side lie fields and a distant farmhouse, on the other the woods.

'Rain's letting up a bit,' Morgan Pryce says. 'With a bit of luck it may stop before we get there. I hope so, for your sakes. It's a tidy walk to the new graves.'

No one answers him, and he lights another Woodbine.

The big black hearse lumbers in front like an undersea monster – the Kraken, Grendel, or Jonah's whale. Her grandfather lies in the belly of a monster who came out of the Cwm Woods one misty morning, the hem of his cloak slithering over the damp earth, his eyes piercing as frost, his breath like winter.

'Why did you choose Cefn Heights, Gwen,' Morgan says, 'if you don't mind me asking? Aber Taf's a nice little cemetery and more convenient for visiting.'

'It was his wish to be near the woods. He was very fond of the Cwm.'

'And Aber Taf too near the town, I suppose. A real hermit

John became after he retired, didn't he? Kept to himself and never mixed much with his pit butties. When he did come into town, I'd pull his leg. "Have you let the Council know," I'd say, "so they can roll out the red carpet?"' The old man laughs, remembering.

'Mr Pryce,' Olwen says, 'would you please stop talking.'

Morgan Pryce hunches up, his skinny neck vanishing into the frayed collar of his overcoat.

Gwen looks reproachfully at Olwen and leans forward to press the driver's shoulder. 'We're a bit on edge, Morgan.'

When she draws her hand back, she rests it on the cracked beige upholstery in the space where another person might have sat. Olwen looks down at her grandmother's hand. On her fourth finger Gwen wears three rings: a gold band, a diamond solitaire, and a gold keeper, an intricate design of leaves and flowers. This ring Olwen covets, though she knows it is not a love gift, the seal on a marriage. Gwen bought it herself, thirteen years ago, at a fair in Pont Ysaf.

Her grandparents had dressed up for the day out, John with a paisley cravat tucked into his white shirt, Gwen in a yellow dress, her auburn hair loose on her shoulders. Ten years younger than John, she had been in her late forties then. To Olwen, they had both seemed glamorous and thrilling that day.

Stalls lined the narrow streets of Pont Ysaf, their striped awnings flapping like flags in the breeze. The air was raucous with the cries of the vendors, with the squawking, neighing, and bleating of animals packed into pens around the auction block, and with the voices of children demanding treats.

Through this pandemonium, Olwen wandered with her grandparents, her head bobbing as she tried to catch all the sights. The town had looked unfamiliar, exotic, a place where they might buy a flying carpet or see a genie pop out of a bottle of lavender water.

In the late afternoon, as they were making their way back to the bus, her grandmother had stopped at a jewellery stall. The gypsy who kept it wore a red waistcoat. Tiny gold studs pierced his ears. 'What do you fancy, missus?' he asked Gwen.

'Let me see the rings,' she said, and he had lifted the ring tray out of the clutter and placed it in front of her. Gwen had picked up the gold keeper she now wears.

'That's a bargain, that is,' the gypsy said. 'Thirty pounds.'

Olwen, attracted by the bright stones in the other rings, had not noticed the keeper. But when Gwen held it between her thumb and forefinger and she saw the tiny leaves and petals glinting in the sun, she was dazzled. 'Get it, Nain,' she said. 'It's a magic ring.'

'John?' Gwen said. 'You know I've always wanted a keeper.'

Olwen saw a look pass between her grandparents and understood, suddenly, that her grandfather was supposed to buy the ring. She didn't know why, but it was so. She looked up at him, sure he would pull out his wallet as he had many times that day when Olwen herself had hankered after some toy or bauble.

Her grandfather had turned away. 'I'm going to look at the garden tools,' he said. 'When you've finished here, I'll be ready to go. Bus leaves at six, so don't hang about.'

He crossed the street, and Olwen watched him stop at another stall. She could tell he wasn't interested in the wares. He simply stood there, on the edge of the crowd, his back turned to her and her grandmother.

'It's too dear,' Gwen said, holding the ring out to the gypsy.

'Try it on,' the gypsy said. 'If you like it, I dare say I can knock the price down.'

Gwen slipped the ring onto her finger. It moved snugly into place above the solitaire.

'Like it was made for you!' The gypsy had leaned across the stall. 'I feel a pull between you and that ring. You was *meant* to have it.'

Gwen had looked sceptical, the way she did when the butcher told her a piece of meat was fresh in that morning.

'It's yours for twenty-five.'

'I don't have twenty-five in my purse.' Gwen had turned her head to look at John's stiff back. When she turned round again, Olwen had witnessed proof of the ring's power. Her eyes glistening, her red hair fired by the sun, her grandmother had assumed a beauty she had seen previously only in pictures of queens in *The Mabinogion*.

'I can't give you more than twenty,' she said.

'Twenty will do,' the gypsy said softly, staring at Gwen. 'It's a shame if a woman like you don't have it.'

She's enchanted him, Olwen thought.

So the keeper was purchased, but on Gwen's finger it had not fulfilled its promise. Olwen had expected the ring to endow her grandmother with magic powers, making her always as beautiful and queenly as she had been when she charmed the gypsy vendor so that, like him, her grandfather, bewitched, would offer Gwen admiring glances and soft words. His brusque treatment of her grandmother had always made Olwen uneasy, but she had concluded it was Gwen's fault, some lack in her rather than in him, for did he not shower love on Olwen herself?

After the fair at Pont Ysaf, changes had occurred, but not of the magical sort. From that day, Gwen, never a strong presence in the house on Archer's Lane, had seemed to fade and become a figure in the background, easily ignored, like the good servant. And in herself Olwen had discovered a growing resentment towards her grandmother which increased in proportion to the ever-strengthening bond she felt with her grandfather. Sometimes, when she was with him in the garden or the house, absorbed in his company, she would glimpse behind his short but stocky frame the figure of her grandmother as she passed the parlour door or crossed the kitchen window, and vexation would seize her, as if Gwen had deliberately intruded. After the fair her grandfather had changed too. Never a demonstrative husband, he had seemed openly to spurn Gwen from that time, happiest when she was out of the house, or when he and Olwen were away from her, in the garden or the woods.

So the ring has not brought good fortune to Gwen. But that's because she doesn't know its value. It ought to be mine, Olwen thinks.

'We've come, Olwen,' Gwen says.

Olwen sees that they have reached the gates of Cefn Heights. Here the paved road ends, a dirt path, too narrow for cars, meandering up and down the slopes and valleys of the cemetery. In summer, when the trees are in leaf and wild flowers crowd the grass, it's a pretty enough place. Today, the trees and ground bare, it seems lonely and drear, the gravestones a host of grey spectres rising out of the mist to watch, broodingly, this intrusion of the living.

Without the veils of greenery it's possible, too, to see the terrible neglect many of the graves have fallen into, stones cracked and lopsided, tombs caving in, tumbled urns and broken statues littering the ground. This is not a place for her grandfather.

'It's shameful, the way the Council have let it go,' Gwen says. 'But Grandpa will be in the new part, not down here.'

'Rain's stopped,' Morgan Pryce says timidly as they get out of the car. 'I'm glad you won't get wet.'

Climbing the hill behind the bearers, Olwen keeps her eyes on the coffin. When it is lowered into the earth she fixes her gaze on it to shut out the other presences. But they won't leave her alone. Her grandmother, Gareth, Bryn Brewen, the miners . . . all of them, for different reasons, watch her.

Mr Rhys begins his sermon. 'Dearly beloved, we are gathered here to lay to rest John Parry . . .'

Olwen flinches, then digs her nails into her palms. 'Never make a spectacle of yourself.'

The five miners watch her for signs of grief. They think her unnatural, probably. ('She never shed a tear,' they will say later. 'His daughter's love-child, you'd think she'd show more feeling, more gratitude to the man that raised her.') Olwen has heard the name 'love-child' spoken behind hands in Pont Ysaf. No one would dare say the words to John Parry's face, but he must have overheard them too. It's why he avoided the town, surely, shunning the people who lived there.

'He do dote on that child. He'd put her in a glass case if he could.'

'Unhealthy if you ask me. How can she grow up normal?'

'Spoilt rotten.'

'Oh, you've said a mouthful there. You'd think he'd have learned his lesson the first time.'

'I see another bad ending.'

All this heard not at one time but in scraps as she walked along the High Street, or overheard at school, two teachers in a huddle, or inferred from the way mouths moved and eyes flicked when she was near.

The miners must not take it back to Pont Ysaf that they saw her cry.

'For forty-five years he worked underground. Those of you who knew him at Pen Colliery remember a man of principle. Remember how he joined you in your fight to improve conditions there.'

Obediently, the miners nod their heads, though Olwen knows her grandfather never joined them in anything. He took pride in his separateness, cleaving only to her, teaching her to value seclusion, to trust no one but him.

Olwen looks at Gwen. Their tie had excluded her, too. Without ever saying so, he had shown by example that a divided love was unacceptable. Frail and slender in black, leaning on the doctor's arm, Gwen looks across the grave at Olwen. Olwen looks away.

On Dr Lloyd's other side Gareth stands, his eyes green as new grass, his curly hair falling over his forehead. He has a feminine habit of shaking it away with a toss of his head, a mannerism that strikes her as vain, though once it charmed her. 'The young prince of Pont Ysaf,' her grandfather called him. Home from Oxford to attend the funeral, his father says, but Olwen knows differently. He's come because of what happened last summer at the Wen Pool, because of what she did to him there. When their eyes link, his irises darken as they did beneath the willow tree, compelling her to remember intimacy and cruelty. He'd like to see her cry now, an excuse to cross the grave and put his arm around her. She won't cry. She won't even look at him again.

Instead, she tries to rivet her eyes to the coffin, austere as her grandfather's face when he spoke of Gareth: 'Thinks he's cock of the walk. If I ever thought you'd keep company with such a one . . .' Yet, against her will, and of all the young men in Pont Ysaf, she prefers the doctor's son, the one her grandfather, disliking them all, despised most. Her eyes shrinking from the stern oak, Olwen looks up again.

Aunt Flindy raises a black-netted hand and waves to her. A witch, whispered the two children who lived in the first cottage on Archer's Lane when Olwen was little. A ball accidentally tossed into her garden had vanished instantly. 'Earth must've ate it up,' Aunt Flindy told the children when they ventured inside her garden to search. 'Don't step there, mind! That's deadly nightshade. You'll be covered in warts if that touches you.'

Olwen, hanging on Aunt Flindy's gate, had called, 'It won't hurt you. My grandfather planted it. It's just a flower that keeps insects away.'

(She had played with the children every day until her grandfather found out and forbade her. The boy was too rough, he said, the girl a liar.)

When she had contradicted Aunt Flindy, the old woman had shaken her fist and cried out in a rage, 'Bad luck to you, missie, for giving lip to your elders!'

Aunt Flindy has never liked her.

It's to spite me, Olwen thinks, that she's come to the funeral dressed for a fête.

Next to Aunt Flindy, Bryn Brewen watches Olwen. He is always cordial, but she sees mischief in his eyes whenever he looks at her. As a child she feared he would catch her in his sack and pop her into his pot like a rabbit. Now he disturbs her differently, but the images that give shape to her fear are connected still with abduction and assault.

'Be watchful,' her grandfather told her. 'Stay alert. Once you step outside this door, there's danger everywhere.'

On Bryn's other side Reverend Rhys is saying, 'John Parry loved the countryside and valued God's creatures. When he walked in the Cwm Woods, he heard the great hymn of Nature . . .'

Gwen must have told him about the woods, and now the minister takes a truth and distorts it to preach a sermon. As if to give the lie to his words, the poacher in his long black coat slouches and smirks at his elbow, like the devil incarnate with his wild hair and scarred face, his murderous hands folded against his chest in mockery, it seems, of Mr Rhys's posture. ('Old Nick loves cant,' her grandfather said, 'which is why he keeps company with preachers.')

Bryn wears a fancy muffler around his neck, white silk with long fringes, as if he has come not from bed, but from a night on the town, the black rings around his eyes symptoms of fast living, too many women and too much wine. She has never seen him with a woman . . . never seen him drunk . . . and yet there is something about him that makes her think always of de-bauchery.

She raises her eyes to his face. He cocks one black eyebrow. Then, as if she has asked him a question, he nods his head. It's a gesture so knowing, so intimate, that Olwen feels assaulted, as though he had thrust his hands into her clothes, or pressed his mouth on hers. He wants to hold her eyes, but she turns them to the minister, fixing on his pale, unploughed face.

'John was a gardener, too. He loved growing things. As a gardener, he knew that life continues. Barren winter gives way, always, to eternal spring. Like him, we must tend our earthly gardens in the hope that one day we shall be recalled to Eden, from whence we came.' The minister's moony face shines on

26

them all. 'Let us pray,' he says, and the dry-eyed mourners bow their heads.

Only Olwen keeps herself erect.

Suddenly her heart lifts, her pulse quickening. She senses it again – his presence. Turning from the grave, she looks down the cemetery path.

At the gates she sees him, as she knew she would. Leaning on his ash walking stick, he bends his body forward and tilts his head, as if to catch the words of the prayer. When their eyes meet, he winks, and though he is a good two hundred yards away, she can see the deep blue of his irises and every line on his face, ruddy with health again.

He is dressed in his best, the grey tweed suit he wore to walk with her on Sundays, the matching cap that has a blue lining of real silk. Sunshine bursting through clouds gilds his outline. His white hair gleams, the brass horse's head flashes, his body twitches with held-in mirth. He is laughing at the fools who have come to throw dirt on him.

'Grandfather,' Olwen says.

All the heads come up.

Her grandfather turns his back on her and limps across the road to the Cwm.

Olwen springs toward the path. She means to run after him, but at once she finds herself restrained. Bryn Brewen has moved swiftly. He grips her arm so hard, it hurts her.

'That's right,' Aunt Flindy screeches, 'don't let her escape!'

'Overburdened, poor child,' Mr Rhys says. 'She's borne it like a trooper, but it had to come out.'

Gareth comes beside her. 'Lean on me, Olwen,' he whispers.

Trapped between Bryn Brewen and Gareth, Olwen stares into the sunlit space where her grandfather stood. There is no sign of him now, though she can see deep into the woods. Her head swims and her legs give way. Bryn and Gareth prevent her from falling. They support her back to the graveside. Leaning on their arms, Olwen weeps as the minister hastily ends the benediction.

Three

Olwen dreams that she is pursued through the Cwm at night. The woods are different in this dream. Paths run off in all directions, like a maze, and she has lost her way. Her grandfather is in here somewhere, but she fears she will be caught before she finds him.

A shape flits among the trees ahead of her. She cries, 'Grandfather, wait!' The figure raises one arm and beckons. She tries to run faster and discovers that her ankles are chained. As her pursuer gains on her, she hears the swish of a long garment.

All at once the trees fall away and she stands on the edge of a clearing. An unnatural brightness floods this space, tinting the grass and leaves lurid shades of green, violet, and yellow, as if the clearing were a neon-lit stage. The figure is there, his back to her, enveloped in a flowing black cloak, shot with silver. He turns and Olwen sees glittering eyes, a knife-sharp nose, wolf's teeth gleaming through a beard that seems carved from ebony – features that do not coalesce into a human face.

Her grandfather's voice whispers in her ear, 'Stare him out. If you can do that, he's helpless.'

Olwen tries to hold the enchanter's gaze, but she can't. His eyes bore into her, a light darting from each pupil, like twin blades. Unbearable pain forces her head down and she looks instead into the voluminous folds of his cloak.

With a sweeping motion, the enchanter raises his right arm. His sleeve spreads like a great wing, and Olwen sees in it silver moons, stars, galaxies, and all the signs of the zodiac. Lovelier than the night sky, more magical than a medieval astronomer's map, seductive as a velvet quilt, the sleeve entices her. Mesmerized, she steps toward it.

A hand grasps her shoulder and stops her. In the fingers that grip her she feels a strength as powerful as the enchanter's and the spell breaks. She turns to confront her pursuer and looks into the face of her grandfather.

'Just caught you in time,' he says. Olwen falls on his chest. 'I knew you'd come back,' she says as his arms enfold her, pulling her up from darkness into sunlight.

She wakes among dishevelled sheets. Sunshine streams through the window. Closing her eyes again, she tries to get back to the dream, but scenes from yesterday intrude: she sees herself stumbling down the cemetery path, crying still, the mourners grouped around her like guards. When they reach the Bentley, Dr Lloyd gets in beside her. He sits between her and her grandmother, the third person Gwen wanted, and Olwen leans on him all the way home.

In their kitchen, while Gwen made tea, he spoke to Olwen in his large, cheerful voice. 'Now, my girl, you've got to pull yourself up. Your granny will give you a nice hot brew in a minute, and I've something in my pocket to help you sleep.'

'She hasn't slept well in ages,' Gwen said.

'I can see that. Hasn't been eating well either, has she? She's like a little bird lying in that chair.' Then he had sat on the footstool beside the paisley armchair where Olwen sprawled, clutching the box of tissues Gwen had placed in her lap.

'I know how it is,' he said, his grey eyes kind. 'I've been through it myself. Tomorrow I'll come round and have a talk with you, shall I?'

On the little stool the doctor had looked ludicrous, like a giant perched on a mushroom.

'There's nothing to talk about,' Olwen said.

'Then I'll come to make sure Gran's feeding you properly.' He had turned to smile at Gwen.

She stood at the table in the window alcove, pouring tea into blue and white willow-pattern cups. In her black merino dress she had looked fragile, but in a girlish not an aged way, her piled-up hair seeming too heavy for her small head. As she lifted the teapot, her arm curved gracefully. A shaft of sunlight from the bay window behind her brightened the auburn in her hair. Gold and silver needles flashed from her ring finger as if she were the seamstress of the sunshine that flooded the kitchen. She had smiled at the doctor and, for a moment, looked to Olwen as she had years ago at the Pont Ysaf fair.

Turning in the bed to lie on her back, Olwen thinks, She's free of her burden. All the time that he was ill she must have looked forward to this.

29

From the rafter above her bed gargoyle faces scowl at her, reminding her of her grandfather's face during his sickness, so often distorted – by anger, malice, or craft, depending on the drift of his fantasies. It was Gwen who had managed him then, bringing him back from whatever horrors he sank into with a firm word, a calm touch. Olwen had only made him worse.

She recalls a January morning when, in an attempt to cheer him, she had said, 'Spring will be here soon, Grandfather. We'll go walking in the Cwm again.'

His eyes on the frosted window pane, he had said, 'I won't see another spring, *cariad*. Before the snow melts, I'll be gone.'

She had held his hand tightly. 'You only feel that way because it's so dreary outside. In a month or two the primroses will be up, then the daffodils –'

His face had lightened, and in his eyes she had glimpsed the old, intense blue, as when a summer sky changes the colour of a lake. So, for a moment, she thought she had consoled him. But when he spoke, it was not to her.

'Put on your blue dress, then,' he said, looking past Olwen, as she clung to his hand, to a corner of the room where for him, apparently, the mingling of light and shadow created a mirage. 'We'll go into the Cwm like we used to. Remember how it was when we had our hearts' desire? We held it in our hands, didn't we? Roses, lilies . . . You always liked the wild flowers best, though. "Goldenrod," you said. "Pick me the goldenrod." And I did, didn't I? I never denied you.'

And then, his voice dropping to a mutter, 'Come into the Cwm and I'll give you what you deserve.'

His ravings, full of threats and innuendos, made Olwen afraid of the woods. Since his death, she has entered them only in nightmare.

Her grandmother taps on the door and comes in, carrying a tray. Her hair is braided, rouge dusts her cheeks, and under a flowered apron she wears a smart grey dress. When she sets the tray on the white wicker table beside the bed Olwen sees, in a pottery vase between the coffee cup and the toast rack, a handful of primroses.

'I found them in the garden when I threw bread out for the birds,' Gwen says. 'Spring has stolen up on us. I'd swear they weren't there yesterday.'

As she looks at the primroses, Olwen's eyes blur.

'Oh, love!' Gwen touches her shoulder.

On her wrist, Olwen smells lily-of-the-valley, a perfume her grandmother favours but has not worn in a long time. Rubbing her hand across her eyes, she says, 'You're dressed up. Why are you wearing scent?'

Beneath the rouge, Gwen's natural colour heightens. 'Just a fancy, I suppose . . . the lovely morning and all.'

'What time is it?'

'Nearly eleven. Dr Lloyd will be here soon.'

'I wish he'd leave me alone!'

'He wants to get you well, love.'

'Who says I'm ill, him or you?'

'You need building up, Olwen, and he's our doctor –'

'All right, all right.'

'I'll run a bath for you, shall I?'

'Yes,' Olwen says to get rid of her.

In the passage outside, Gwen's footsteps sound spry, unlike the stealthy night sounds she's grown accustomed to, the swish of her grandfather's long dressing gown against the skirting, the drag of his lame leg, the low muttering as he talked to himself, or – she sometimes thought – the murmur of two voices, conspiring.

The first time she heard him at night, she got up to go to him. When she opened her door, he was standing at the top of the stairs, about to go down. 'Grandfather!' she had called as she hurried along the passage. He had turned, and in the dim light, she saw his nostrils distend, his lip lift over his teeth. His face was the colour of ashes, his eyes yellow. So deathly he looked, so shrunken in the loose maroon dressing gown, she had not heeded the signs of rage, nor faltered when he growled deep in his throat. He seemed disoriented, and she had feared he might fall down the stairs. When she reached the landing, she opened her arms to him.

'Bitch,' he said through bared teeth and lunged at her. Olwen screamed. As his nails dug through the thin cotton sleeves of her nightgown and his head thrust toward her, Gwen had come running from her bedroom.

'Stop it!' she shouted.

He had released Olwen at once and cowered against the wall. 'I meant her no harm,' he whimpered. 'I'd never hurt a hair on her head.'

'I'll see that you don't,' Gwen said in a voice Olwen had

never heard. Her hand on his arm, she had led him back to his own room, docile as a sleep-walking child.

The incident was over in moments, but Olwen has never forgotten it. In those few seconds before Gwen intervened, she had known what he meant to do. She had seen his teeth descending towards her throat.

After that, though she sat with him all day, she never went to him at night. 'Leave him to me,' Gwen told her. 'When he's like that, it's not safe for you to be near.'

Forgetting the breakfast tray, Olwen lies on her back, her hands crossed over her neck. On the rafter, among the many shapes, there is one that resembles a woman with swirling hair. Unlike the others, it has not emerged from the grain with the ageing of the wood. Ten years ago, her grandfather put it there.

He had been reading Andersen's 'Snow Queen' to her by the parlour fire. Too big at last for his lap, she sat at the foot of his armchair, her arm resting on his knee, marvelling at the picture of the Snow Queen in her fur robe, her long black hair reaching to her ankles, her eyes like black gems in her imperious ivory face.

'No wonder she enchanted Kaye,' Olwen said. 'I bet he'd never seen anyone so gorgeous.'

'She's a bit on the pale side for my taste. She had no heart, see, and that's why there's no colour in her cheeks.'

'Still, Grandfather ...' She had studied the illustration. 'Nobody's as beautiful as that really, are they?'

'Some are. The rare one.'

'Have *you* ever seen a lady as beautiful as her?'

'More beautiful.'

'Where? Who was she?'

Instead of answering, he had pointed to the wreathes of smoke his pipe made. 'She had hair like that, full of ringlets. And so fair, it looked silver when the sun was on it . . . or the moonlight.'

'Like yours.'

'Aye, but my hair's silver because I'm getting on. She was young.'

'Who was she?'

'Never mind. She looked like an angel, but she had a wastrel heart. We won't speak of her.'

His tone warned her to ask no more, but when he took her up

to bed later, he said, smiling strangely, 'Now I'll make you a picture.'

Standing on her wicker chair, he had used his penknife to whittle an elfish face in the rafter above her head. An expert carver, he had worked swiftly, surrounding the face with long swirls of hair. The large, long eyes had a mischievous slant, repeated in the tilt of the thin lips. Olwen did not think it a beautiful face and wished he had not put it there.

'She's our prisoner,' he said when he'd finished, 'locked in a tower like Rapunzel. Only there's no prince to rescue her.'

Her grandmother had come in then to say goodnight, and so he had left. At the door, he winked behind Gwen's back and laid his finger against his nose, a sign that the face on the rafter was a secret not to be shared.

'You're so pale,' Gwen had said, sitting on the bed and brushing back Olwen's hair. 'Grandpa keeps you up too late. He forgets you have school in the morning. I made Welshcakes while you were reading. Shall I put a couple in your lunch?'

Olwen had clasped her grandmother tightly about the neck.

'Why, love!' Gwen had held her. 'Did something in those old books frighten you? They're only stories. Not a word of truth in them.'

Pulling away, Olwen had slid under the covers. 'Nothing frightened me. I'm not a baby.'

Gwen puts her head around the door. 'Bath's ready.' She sees the untouched tray and her face falls. 'You didn't eat your breakfast. Dr Lloyd *will* be upset with me.'

Olwen swings out of bed. 'You don't have to tell him, do you?' Snatching her dressing gown from the chair, she brushes past her grandmother.

In the bathroom mirror she studies her face, trying to see it as Gareth will when he comes with his father. Yesterday, she made herself plain. Today she wants to look well in his eyes. But this is not to be. She is pale from months spent indoors, thin from eating without appetite. Her heavy hair seems to eclipse her face. With feverish eyes, pallid skin and elf locks, she looks unhealthy, unnatural – demented. Surely she will scare him.

Sun pouring in through the little latticed window plays on the surface of the bathwater. So the Wen Pool shone last summer on that hot July afternoon. Olwen slides into the warm, sunlit water, puts her head back and closes her eyes. She thinks of Gareth, remembering his last year at school, the year she had fallen in love with him.

Lovesick, she had trailed him, all her happiness in gazing, sure no harm could come of it. In her navy tunic and white knee socks, her hair drawn into a plait, she looked like any of the other quiet, serious Lower-Sixth girls. She was not one of the stars who, with the rakish tilt of a beret or the peep of lace beneath blouse buttons undone too far, drew men's eyes even in school uniform. Anonymous, she could take pleasure in him, she thought, and remain safe. He would never see her.

Though she had no intimate friends at school, she had acquaintances with whom she went, once or twice a week, to the Mayflower Café – because Gareth went there. From her table, among half a dozen identically dressed companions, she watched him, learned him by heart, memorizing the details of his face, his body, his gestures.

Like all the Upper-Sixth boys, he wore a navy suit, but his jacket was cut longer and narrower than theirs, as if he belonged to an earlier, more elegant time, a misplaced Edwardian blade. With his long hair and light-footed walk, he had an almost seraphic grace. His mannerisms were graceful too – the way he tossed his head to shake back his hair; his habit of using his hands to embroider his speech, his fingers making agile, swiftly changing shapes. As if the air were his canvas, Olwen saw pictures when his hands moved. He must take after his mother, she had thought, watching him in the Mayflower. For in appearance and manner he was nothing like the big, solid doctor who reminded her of the bear in 'Rose Red and Snow White'. This femininity in Gareth she loved – the knights in fairytales were long-haired and slender – but she knew, too, that had he not been an athlete and a mixer, he might have been the laughing stock of Pont Ysaf Grammar.

On Saturday afternoons in winter, while her grandfather worked in his toolshed, she went to the rugby matches. The team's most constant fan, she learned nothing about tactics, seeing only one player, a young warlord decked in scarlet, his face and legs daubed with earth. In summer she watched him at cricket, immaculate in white, his movements as stylised as a dancer's.

Away from him, she dwelt on him so much that, seated at the

34

kitchen table with her homework or lying in bed at night, she would stare into a shadowy doorway or at a moonlit window and he would appear.

Her grandfather had taught her this conjuring trick, saying, 'Quick, Olwen, look in the trees yonder. It's the old enchanter.' Or, 'See that shadow crossing the wall? Sir Galahad himself. See the Grail in his hands?' And in the Cwm she would catch the flutter of a cloak among the trees; in the parlour see in the shadows thrown up by the firelight human – or inhuman – shapes.

When Gareth materialized she saw him in detail, as if he were really there. Her thumb nail pressed lightly between her teeth, she studied him like a sculptor, seeing the exact shade of his honey-coloured hair, dense with curls she longed to wear like rings on her fingers. His green eyes, the tiny white scar beneath the tail of his left eyebrow, his tanned throat, his skilful hands poised on his hipbones – every feature she contemplated in turn, until her gaze, embracing him, fastened on the elongated mound behind his jeans zipper, and the blood rushed to her face, her eyes were so wanton, so eager.

For it seemed to Olwen that here lay the source of his power. When she looked at him there she felt as she did in the Cwm, sensing a force, a vigour, that thrilled her. She longed to touch him, as she touched twigs in the woods, running her hand over their ridges, squeezing gently between her fingers the sticky green buds. Thrusting her thumb deeper into her mouth, she would suck on it, as she had in childhood, listening to her grandfather's tales.

When he left for Oxford, her pleasure had turned swiftly to pain. Unable to break the habit of watching, she had watched his absence, wandering down to the playing fields after school, lingering at the window of the Mayflower, or on the corner of Station Terrace where he always turned out of the High Street to go home.

At last, his truancy worked on her in a way his presence might never have. Sick of her one-sided love, she began to resent his ignorance of her. As if it were really unmindfulness, she felt misused, neglected. I'll make him see me, she thought. He should admit I'm on this earth, at least. He owes me that.

· So, to the Sixth Form party, which she knew he would attend (last year's Upper Sixth were always the celebrities at the function), she had worn high heels, make-up, the floating dress. It was the first party of her life. 'Compulsory,' she told her grandfather. 'You look like a tart,' he said, 'I'm ashamed to own you.' And Gareth had noticed her, danced with her, driven her home, and asked to see her again.

'I don't go out much,' Olwen had said, escaping from his car before he could ask why not. She hadn't the will to defy her grandfather further, nor the wish to deceive him. 'No boys coming after you,' he had warned her when she left to catch the bus. 'You're too young for that rigmarole.'

One day, not long after the party, she had gone into Pont Ysaf to buy a book. As she came out of the shop, she met Gareth. 'Olwen,' he said, and from the way he spoke her name she knew he'd seen her go in and had waited for her. His long fingers had closed lightly on her arm. 'Will you have a cup of coffee with me?'

In the Mayflower, at a window table, she had felt too nervous to be happy, shaking her head when he offered her food. 'Just coffee.' She sat up straight, her palms flat on the white linen tablecloth.

In a vase in the centre of the table the black eyes of sweet williams accused her. The click of the waitress's heels as she came for their order made her jump. Inhaling the aromas of coffee, chocolate, cinnamon, she had felt like a traitor.

Gareth, watching her, rested his elbows on the table and linked the backs of his fingers, the shape of folded wings. He talked about Oxford, and about the pleasures of coming home to the country, to his father, things he had not spoken of driving her home from the party. They had both been quite silent then, as if he were as surprised as she to find himself singling her out among the girls he knew, his old friends and old flames at Pont Ysaf Grammar.

'You're off yourself in October. Why Swansea, Olwen? You could have got into Oxford or Cambridge, you did so well in A-levels.'

'How do you know that?'

'My father told me.'

'I suppose my grandmother's been showing off.'

'Naturally – she's proud of you. I bet your grandfather's over the moon.'

'When your father mentioned my name, you must have asked him who he was talking about.'

'Are you kidding? I've lived in this town since I was eleven. We went to the same school.'

'But I was a year behind you, and –'

'You came to all the rugby and cricket matches when we had home games. We never had so many supporters that I wouldn't notice you. I thought about speaking – to say thanks and all that – but you were always so . . . remote.' His right hand had moved towards his shoulder as he said the word, his fingers curving as if to grasp something that wafted in the air beside his head. 'But at the party you smiled at me and I thought, "Well then, I suppose I can ask her to dance." He brought his hand down, resting it on the table near her own, his palm open. 'But that's not the whole story.' His thumb moved across his finger-nails in slow, rhythmic strokes.

Olwen, playing with a coffee spoon, had watched his hand, imagining his agile fingers undoing the buttons of her blouse to trace varied and thrilling patterns on her breasts.

'In that black dress, and with your hair loose, you were changed. It was like you'd taken off a mask and I knew you.' His thumb pressed against the nail of his index finger. 'I knew I'd seen you before, Olwen, a long time back.'

When she looked up, she saw his eyes were troubled, the white scar beneath his eyebrow distended by the pressure on the muscle there. 'I want to tell you about something that happened to me as a kid. Before I came here. It's something that concerns you.'

The intensity in his eyes had frightened her, and she had felt herself slipping into his gaze as if into a conspiracy. She knew he was about to reveal a secret, and if she allowed it there would be a bond between them. She would be fastened to him in some way she had not foreseen or desired. She began to shake her head.

He placed his hand on hers. 'It's about how I first saw you.'

'No,' she said, 'that's impossible,' and slid her hand away. 'You couldn't have seen me until you came here.'

For a moment they had looked at each other. Then Gareth shrugged. Leaning across the table, his fingers meshing, he said, 'Will you go out with me?'

Somehow she had managed to stand, managed to say, 'I can't, I'm sorry' and get herself out into the street. She had run all the way to the bus stop and gone home to her grandfather, not to tell him, but to recover, under his steady gaze, her own stability.

The next day, Gareth drove out to their house on Archer's Lane. She stood at the gate, talking to him, while her grandfather watched from the doorstep, sucking his pipe. After five minutes, he called, 'Olwen, come in now.'

'Tell that boy to keep away from here,' he said when she went to him.

'I did, Grandfather.'

'And you stay out of Pont Ysaf till he's gone back to his college. Anything you need, your grandmother can fetch.'

She had not seen Gareth again for weeks.

One afternoon, towards the end of a sultry week in late July, she had taken a pan from the kitchen and announced that she was going to pick blackberries. Turning down the lane, away from the road, she followed a path that led across fields to the Wen Pool where the young people of the town swam in summer, and where her grandfather had forbidden her to walk without him. She had meant only to watch Gareth from some covered spot, unseen. No more than that. Certainly she had not intended to harm him . . .

The bath water has grown tepid. Olwen shivers. As she dries herself, she decides that she will not go downstairs. Feigning nausea or fatigue, she will make the doctor come up and so avoid seeing Gareth.

Four

Wrapped in a white bath towel, Olwen stands behind the lace curtain, watching as the doctor's tan Morris draws up at the gate. Gwen must have been watching too, from the kitchen window, for she calls up the stairs, 'Olwen, Dr Lloyd is here.'

Spruce in his camel-hair coat, his battered leather bag in his hand, the doctor walks briskly up the path, a kind but determined look on his face. Gareth has not come with him.

'Hurry up, love! He has other calls to make.'

On her bed, Olwen has laid out a white angora sweater and pleated skirt, bought for college. Drying herself after her bath, she had changed her mind, meant after all to see Gareth, to say thank you for the flowers. She thrusts the new clothes back into her wardrobe and pulls out instead her school sweater and worn Levis. As she goes along the passage, she fastens her tangled hair with a piece of ribbon.

The uncarpeted wooden stairs lead down into a narrow rectangular hallway lit by a long window and by the two swirled glass panels in the front door. Beneath the window stands a rosewood table her grandfather made. On it, in a pewter jug, Gwen has placed another bunch of primroses. Outside the window a laurel bush grows, its branches spreading across the pane. Midmorning sun glistens on the broad laurel leaves and slants across the tabletop, burnishing the pewter, giving the primrose petals a sheen like fresh-churned butter. Olwen's heart lifts a little as she goes down into this sun-filled space. At the table she pauses to touch the flowers and look through the laurel leaves into the garden. It is the first of April, All Fools' Day. Is it foolish to believe that when the chestnut blossoms and the grass grows he will come again, unable to keep away from his garden in bloom?

Through the laurel curtain she sees the black toolshed. Squatting beside the garden gate, it has an air of expectancy, like a

39

living thing, a guard dog waiting for its master. The image is not a comforting one, for the creature she imagines has murderous fangs and a brutal, unstable temperament. Aroused, it might fail to distinguish friend from enemy, turn on her if she approached it, as she once saw a collie turn on a sheep, ripping its throat out before the shepherd could stop it.

Olwen shifts her eyes from the toolshed to the kitchen door, trying, too, to shift her mind from the dark fancies the shed evokes since, months ago, she locked it up at her grandfather's bidding.

'I don't want anybody nosing in my things,' he said. 'Remember that when I'm not here.'

Behind the kitchen door, ajar, she can hear the doctor and her grandmother chatting about the favourable change in the weather.

'You must get Olwen out in the sun,' Dr Lloyd says. 'She's been cooped up long enough.'

'I'll try, but I don't have much say with her.' Gwen sounds weary.

'That's because you allowed John too much influence. She's not used to listening to anyone else, but you have to assert yourself now, for her sake. We must bring her away from the notion that the centre of her life has gone.'

Pushing the kitchen door wide with the flat of her hand, Olwen enters the room. Her other hand on her hip, she confronts her grandmother and the doctor where they sit, drinking tea, at the table in the window alcove. It strikes her that a stranger entering the room would take them for a married couple breakfasting together. Gwen has taken off her apron. In her neat grey dress, a string of seed pearls around her neck, she looks a suitable wife for a doctor. She would keep his house cheery and restful, a place where he could lay his cares down.

It comes to Olwen that this idea of compatibility has occurred to both of them. Intent seems to permeate the air but, like dust motes in the sunshine, it is still ephemeral; unspoken, it has no solid shape. She knows (ahead of them, perhaps) because, since yesterday, her perceptions are heightened, as if her grandfather had bequeathed her second sight as a parting gift.

They have spoken to her and she has not answered. 'What?' she says.

'Dr Lloyd asked how you slept.' Gwen gets up and crosses

the kitchen to pour Olwen's coffee. 'I've made you a fresh cup, love. Will you have a piece of toast with it?'

'Nothing to eat, thank you.'

'Come and sit down, Olwen.' The doctor is pouring a second cup of tea, making himself at home. He has taken his coat off and slipped it over the back of his chair. A label sewn into the lining reads, 'James and Son, Tailors, Saville Row.'

'One of the crack-crack,' her grandfather said of Dr Lloyd, using the local word for people whose gentrified ways made them seem more English than Welsh. 'All them years in London, he's used to treating high-class diseases caused by too much drink and rich food. What do he know about a miner with silicosis?'

He never thanked the doctor for coming out to see him every other day. 'Don't bother to come back for a bit,' he'd say as Dr Lloyd left. 'I can manage without you.'

Olwen sits at the table. She puts her cheek on her fist and stares down at the blue-and-white willow pattern plate Gwen has set out for her, at the angry father chasing his daughter and her lover across a humpbacked bridge.

'*Did* you sleep well?' the doctor asks again.

Her head down, she glances at him sideways, looking as far as the lapels of his tweed jacket. 'So-so.'

Gwen places a coffee mug in front of her. 'She didn't touch her breakfast.'

Olwen glares at her grandmother.

'You need a brisk walk in the fresh air,' Dr Lloyd says. 'It will put a bit of colour in your cheeks and help you work up an appetite.'

'I don't want to go out.'

The doctor stands. An imposing figure, much taller and broader than her grandfather, he seems a man formed to inhabit spacious rooms. He'd never fit here, Olwen thinks.

'I'm not making a suggestion,' he says. 'This is a prescription, my girl. Drink up your coffee and put on stout shoes. The woods will be damp after yesterday's rain.'

Until he mentions the Cwm, Olwen has intended to refuse, to show him that, doctor or no, he can't give her orders. Now she sees that this is a sign. Her grandfather uses the doctor, speaking through him as spirits can, to tell her what she must do. Without a word, Olwen gets up and leaves the room.

Upstairs, she wraps her navy school scarf around her neck,

puts on woollen socks and ankle boots. As she ties the boot laces, her fingers falter. Something is not right. 'Come to the Cwm in summer,' he said, and now it is barely spring. Always a stubborn and steadfast man, never rescinding a promise or a decree, why has he changed his mind?

She remembers yesterday, his appearance at the cemetery gates, meant, surely, to give her hope and courage, to remind her he was still her protector, her champion. She had responded with a loss of faith, broken down in tears and cast herself upon the pity of others.

He must be angry.

If he calls her into the Cwm too soon, perhaps his purpose is to test and punish her. He could be hard in that way. After Gareth drove out to their house last summer, he had refused to speak to her for a week. And during his illness . . . how he had tried and tormented her, with abusive words, threats and, worst of all, exclusion.

What is she to expect then, in the woods, haunted by their murderous foe, the red-handed enchanter in his funeral cloak? Is it he who bids her, who holds her grandfather fast ('I looked into his sleeve, *cariad*'), and who seeks to draw her with false words and a false spring?

Olwen crosses to the window and looks out at the woods. Sunlight bathes the tree branches where only yesterday icicles hung. Crusts of snow still linger among the roots, but she can see, too, patches of primroses. Are the early flowers and the sunshine decoys, the enchanter's bait to lure her in?

She leaves the window and the room, goes slowly down the passage, her hands thrust into her pockets, her fingers clenching the cloth there. When she reaches the landing, she sees the doctor waiting in the hall, his coat on. He means to go with her. Relief overwhelms Olwen. This is a boon her grandfather has given, not a test after all. Letting her go into the Cwm with a companion, he helps her prepare for the day when she must go in alone. She manages a small smile for the doctor.

'I'll do a nice pork chop for your lunch.' Gwen hands Olwen her white lambswool jacket and opens the front door.

The jacket is warm and smells of lavender. Gwen has brought it from the airing cupboard beside the kitchen fire where she hangs the jacket after Olwen has tossed it on a chair or hooked it over the banister.

When they are out on the path, Dr Lloyd says, 'Gareth asked me to say goodbye for him. He drove back to Oxford this morning.' He holds open the garden gate. 'Between you and me, he wanted to put off going for another day and come with me. But I told him he'd best leave you alone for now. I was right, I think?'

'Yes,' Olwen says. As she goes through the gate, she glances at the door of the toolshed, covered in a sheet of black tarpaulin, a steel lock fastened to the latch. If Gareth had come, there would have been no signal.

They walk down Archer's Lane, the woods on one side, on the other the stone wall that bounds the four gardens, the Parrys', Bryn Brewen's, Aunt Flindy's, and the Millers'. Olwen looks over Bryn's gate to his house. In all four windows, the curtains are drawn. A folded newspaper sticks out of the letter box in his front door.

'Gareth's reading Physics at Oxford, did you know? I'm surprised really. He always seemed more inclined towards the arts. At one time I thought he'd be a writer . . . or a painter like his mother. He used to spend hours writing stories and illustrating them when we lived in London, but he gave that up when we moved down here. I always hoped he'd go back to it, though. He had talent, I thought.'

Aunt Flindy's downstairs windows are crammed with decaying herbs in cracked and grimy pots. A skinny orange cat peers through the rotting foliage in the parlour window. As Olwen and the doctor pass the gate, the cat, Cinders, arches its back and hisses.

'I must look in on Mrs Flinders before I go back to town,' Dr Lloyd says. 'She was very fond of your grandfather. I'm sure she's taking this hard.'

'He did a lot for her. Aunt Flindy was grateful, that's all.'

The doctor cocks his head at her. 'Are you suggesting she wasn't fond of him?'

Olwen flips one end of her scarf over her shoulder. 'Did you see how she dressed for the funeral? How she behaved? If she cared about him, why did she make a mockery like that?'

Dr Lloyd shakes his head. 'You've misunderstood, Olwen. Aunt Flindy's nearly eighty, nearing the end of her life. She wasn't mocking your grandfather, she was laughing in death's face. That strikes me as rather brave.'

43

They pass the last of the four grey-stone cottages and cross the ditch, filled with damp brown leaves. As they enter the path that winds through the Cwm, Dr Lloyd says, 'How do you get on with your new neighbours in Number One? They seem a nice young couple.'

'I've hardly seen them. I haven't formed an opinion.'

This is untrue. Since the Millers moved in in January, she has seen them frequently, watching from her bedroom window, hidden behind the lace curtain, as Rosamund and Alun (names supplied by Aunt Flindy) go off to work in the mornings. They walk down the path hand in hand. In the bright knitted caps and patterned sweaters she is partial to, Rosamund looks as if she is setting off for the ski slopes instead of the solicitor's office. She has a dashing air, as if her life were all risk and adventure.

Olwen has watched them come home in the evenings, too, their arms linked, Rosamund's cheeks glowing, her blonde hair flying out under a red or blue or turquoise cap. At the gate they always kiss, passionately, Alun wrapping Rosamund up in his arms, as though the walk up the path is too much to endure before they can embrace properly – make love. In her imagination, she has watched them do this too.

'You should get to know them,' Dr Lloyd says as they go down the twisting path. Olwen, looking into the woods, sees scattered among the oaks and elms, slender white birches, like naked bodies among the stouter trees. She shivers and slips her hands into the sleeves of her jacket, folding her arms across her waist.

'Rosamund Miller can't be more than half a dozen years older than you. You might make a friend of her.'

'She doesn't need a friend. She's got a husband.'

'Good lord, girl, marriage doesn't do away with the need for friends. Where in the world did you get that idea? A single attachment can't fill a life.'

Her head turned from him, Olwen seeks a sign among the trees. Nothing moves. The Cwm is as lifeless and silent as a cemetery.

Dr Lloyd takes a pipe from his pocket and pauses to fill and light it. Looking down as she waits, Olwen sees that his suede shoes, camel like his coat, are soaked and muddied. His feet must be wet and cold, yet his face shows no sign of discomfort. When he blows out the first puff of smoke, she inhales the tobacco scent. It's not the brand her grandfather used, but suddenly she feels his presence. The sensation is so keen that, almost, she expects him to appear.

Eagerly, Olwen looks again into the woods, but she sees only charnel-house images in the frozen trees, their limbs twisted and deformed, as if they were victims of a torturer. Patches of melting snow lie among the roots, grey sky shows through the branches, and in between, emptiness. Her grandfather's presence recedes. Or perhaps he was never there and she judged amiss, fooled by the scent of tobacco and her own longing. She has read falsely then. There was no signal in the doctor's order. It's too soon.

Dr Lloyd touches her arm. 'Let's go on. It's cold for you to stand about.'

She walks beside him, silent, looking down the narrow path, seeing its twists and turns, hidden in summer by the rich foliage, brambles, and undergrowth. In winter the woods have no magic. Nothing can happen here until the Cwm comes to life again. Yet even as she thinks this Olwen senses something, some invisible being, not her grandfather, that accompanies them. It's a thing composed of frigid air and vast space, casting its presence over the woods, gathering the trees, the doctor, and herself into its folds. Above them and around them, it hovers.

Olwen looks up, fancies she sees in the fretwork of branches an immense face, part-hawk, part-human, the face of the enchanter. He grins as he plays hobgoblin games with her mind, showing her corpses among the oaks, transforming the white birches into fleeing figures, their arms thrust out, their screams congealed into black holes.

To escape him, Olwen reaches out to the doctor. 'What kind of stories did Gareth write?'

'H'm?' He has been watching her, she sees. Swiftly, he wipes the worry from his face. 'Oh, the same sort that he liked to read – adventures and mysteries. He used to give us readings – his mother and me – at dinner. He liked ghost stories, too, I remember. Where we lived in London there were no children his age, so he filled his time at home with writing, reading, and drawing. Partly, he was imitating his mother, of course. She worked at home and he was always with her. After she died and we came to Pont Ysaf, there were plenty of boys his age and he gave up those pursuits for rough and tumble. I must say I was relieved. I'd worried that he'd have problems fitting in after such a solitary life. But he took to the boys' games like a fish diving into water. As if he'd been gasping for breath, you know, all the years that we'd thought he had everything he needed.'

'I'm sure he did have everything when his mother was alive,' Olwen says. 'He wouldn't have wanted other company if she'd lived.'

The doctor removes his pipe and looks at her under heavy brows. 'Perhaps not, but would that have been a good thing?'

Olwen stares back at him. 'One person *can* fill a life,' she says, 'if it's an extraordinary person. That's what no one understands. Because it's so rare – so special – everyone thinks it must be wrong. You talk as if there are rules for what's healthy and what's not. But where are the rules written down, and who made them, and who's proved them? Can you prove Gareth's happier with lots of friends and without his mother? You say he doesn't write or draw any more. Is that a gain or a loss? And my grandmother – she knows loads of people in Pont Ysaf, and she has her sister and her nieces, but I don't see her so happy –' Olwen stops short, surprised by her own outpouring. 'How do you *know* it's wrong to be exclusive?' she says on a rush of breath.

'From my own experience.' The doctor's eyes are intent on her. As if an invisible thread attaches their gaze, Olwen can't look away. 'I tell you what I've learned to be true.'

'True for you. For me, it's a lie. I heard what you said to my grandmother in the kitchen. Well, he *was* the centre of my life, and he still is. I don't want to be drawn away from him.'

'But he's dead, Olwen.' Dr Lloyd's voice is softer, gentler, than she's ever known it. His eyes pull hard on the thread. 'A dead person can't be the centre of anything.'

'You say he's dead. Everything is only what you say, Dr Lloyd.'

The doctor's pipe is going out, for he forgets to puff on it. She sees by the shape of his mouth that he clenches the stem between his teeth. When he removes the pipe, a last wisp of smoke rises, twists into a frail curl, like a snipped lock of hair, and disperses. 'I think you'd better tell me what happened yesterday. What upset you so much? I don't mean to sound callous – it was your grandfather's funeral. But up to that point, you'd been very calm. And then, all of a sudden –'

46

'I broke down. Because I *was* upset. Is that abnormal?'

'Grief is very normal indeed. It's how we deal with it that may sometimes be harmful.' The doctor cups the dead pipe in his palm, frowning into the bowl, as though he were reading tea leaves in a cup. Then he turns his eyes on her again. 'Let me tell you what I've learned about feelings. All the dark ones – grief, fear, anger, jealousy – thrive in small, airless spaces. Confined, they grow strong and fierce, until they become more powerful than the person who harbours them. When that happens, strife breaks out. If you think of the mind as a country, it's like civil war when you have to fight your own emotions. There are ways to prevent such a war.' He turns the stem of the pipe toward her, like a finger. 'Just confiding in someone helps, believe me.'

'You think we make it happen to ourselves, don't you? You think it's like a nervous breakdown,' Olwen says. 'That's why you call it civil war. Not everyone would share your view, though.'

'I take it you don't?'

'I'm just saying there are other ways of seeing it. Someone who was – who *wasn't* a doctor – might call that strife possession.'

'Possession?' The doctor's eyebrows lift. 'Well . . . that's the old, superstitious concept of a fragmented psyche, yes.'

'You don't believe a person can be possessed?'

'By a demon?' His quizzical expression reminds her of Gareth, of his scarred eyebrow shaped into a permanent question mark. 'No, I don't. Not unless it's a demon of their own making.'

'So you don't believe in evil?'

'What do you mean exactly?' Dr Lloyd takes a matchbox from his pocket and leans against the trunk of an oak to light his pipe. Positioned so, with his back to the woods, he seems to create with his own large body a barrier between Olwen and whatever might be lurking among the trees.

'Evil in the form of spirits,' she says, her eyes on his top coat-button, large as an owl's eye. 'People have seen such things.'

'People have hallucinated.' He sucks audibly on his pipe. '*You* thought you saw your grandfather yesterday, didn't you?'

'I never said that.'

'You don't have to. Before you ran, you said "Grandfather" in just the way a person would greet another whom she saw. You spoke, Olwen, as if he were there.'

Olwen shakes her head, her eyes still on the button. In its centre the gathered black threads stare back at her like a pupil.

'It's what I was trying to tell you, my dear. Strong emotions suddenly unleashed can cause a sensitive person to hallucinate. Your grandfather suffered in that way before he died. He thought he saw someone he knew. Spoke to her, even. Your grandmother told me how it distressed you. But that person wasn't there, Olwen. It was all in his mind.'

'My mother. He saw my mother.'

'Alice. That was her name, wasn't it?'

'He never called her by her name,' Olwen says swiftly.

The doctor has broken a taboo and a new, rapt silence seems to fall over the woods, as if an eavesdropper, invisible but near, holds his breath and listens intently. Smoke rising from the pipe becomes swirls of drifting hair, as though the air were water and the body of a drowned woman floated slowly, gracefully, to the surface. Then, deep in the trees, a noise starts up, a muffled roar like the collision of distant ice floes.

Olwen looks at the doctor to see if he hears.

Puffing on his pipe, he watches her, concern in his eyes but no fear. He senses nothing, seems not to notice that the long smoky strands entwine her. The roaring swells and advances. Engulfed in the din, Olwen sees the trees topple and feels the earth split under her feet. Dr Lloyd catches her, his arm like a joist against her back.

She closes her eyes and leans on him. When she rests her head on the soft cloth of his coat the uproar ceases as suddenly as it began.

The doctor strokes her head with his free hand. 'Tell me,' he says.

Olwen stiffens and draws away. 'I felt a bit faint. It's passed off now.'

'That's what happens when you don't eat. We'd better get back and put some food into you.' He puts his arm over her shoulder and turns her in the direction they came. 'The Cwm is bleak at this time of year,' Dr Lloyd says as he propels her along the path. 'Silly of me to bring you.'

Olwen, looking away from him into the trees, sees among the withered and broken creepers a black shape that glitters and undulates like a hula dancer as it keeps pace with the two of them. It's a monstrous shape, yet without bulk, like a shadow

48

thrown up on a wall, and it moves with excessive grace, as if to mock her own awkward steps.

'When my wife died,' the doctor says, 'I couldn't stay in the house we'd shared for fifteen years, though we had both loved it. London – the entire city – became a memory chest. I saw her, sensed her, everywhere. I know what it is, to be obsessed.'

Hurry, Olwen wants to say to him. Hurry! The enchanter is upon us. But of course he can't see. He thinks it's only recollection that disturbs her.

'Eventually you'll have to go away as I did, to recover. You'll be off to college in October. A good thing. New friends, a new environment. Perhaps that's all the tonic you need.' He speaks loudly, confidently, as if he is aware after all of the creature who stalks them and tries to subdue it with bluff.

But the enchanter is not deterred. Like a jester, he capers among the trees, his elongated silhouette performing impossible contortions, as if to parody in his twists and bends and caprioles the gyrations of Olwen's heart. He is a shape-shifter indeed, for he can assume the forms of thunder, earthquake, and deluge, of shadow and illusion, and mimic the living or the dead.

'We don't betray those who loved us by living,' the doctor says, as they come to the edge of the Cwm at last. 'Quite the opposite. By seizing life, we strengthen our devotion. It's passivity, not action, that infects and withers love.'

Now the enchanter stops, throwing up his hands in fake despair. His new game is to pretend he has lost his quarry. He wraps his arms over his head and strikes a moping pose. Motionless, he is hard to see, and as Olwen watches he fades away, becomes the shadow on the trunk of an oak tree.

'Come along,' the doctor says. 'It's warmer out of the woods. See how bright the sun is?'

As they step over the ditch into Archer's Lane, Olwen says, 'What did my grandfather tell you about my mother?'

'Nothing at all. He didn't like or trust me enough, as you must realize, to make me his confidante. I only know what I've heard from your grandmother.'

'Do you know that she died giving birth to me? That's why I came to live here. My grandfather went up to London and brought me back.'

'She was very lovely, I hear.' The doctor's hand presses her shoulder. 'Three generations of good-looking women in your family, eh?'

'I don't know what she looked like.'

'Don't you have a photo?'

'There aren't any.'

'I see,' the doctor says.

In the garden Gwen is throwing crumbs for the birds. She waves and calls to Dr Lloyd, 'Another cup of tea?'

'Too many calls to make, thank you.'

Olwen sees her grandmother's smile slip. It reappears when he says, 'I'll look in again soon, though.' To Olwen, he says quietly, 'Try to talk to her.'

'About what?'

'Ask her about your mother for a start. You must have a lot of questions, and you're entitled to answers.' He touches her shoulder, salutes Gwen with a raised palm, and turns in the direction of Aunt Flindy's.

Olwen opens the gate and goes up the path.

'You weren't long,' Gwen says. 'I haven't started lunch yet. Did you have a talk with Dr Lloyd?'

Olwen tilts her chin. 'Was I supposed to?'

A muscle quivers in Gwen's cheek. 'I'll put the pork chops in the oven,' she says. 'And I'll make some coffee to warm you up.'

When her grandmother has gone into the house, Olwen crosses the strip of lawn to the chestnut tree. Leaning against the trunk, she surveys her grandfather's garden. Like all four gardens in Archer's Lane it is rectangular in shape, divided by the path and bordered by a high fence on one side separating it from Bryn Brewen's property. On the other sides, stone walls enclose it, the stones cemented unevenly. In summer moss grows in the crevices, and clusters of tiny blue flowers.

Every summer the garden was crowded with flowers – dahlias, phlox, gladioli, a paintbox of colours. Sweet peas clambered profusely over the fence, roses perfumed the air and golden sunflowers ringed the toolshed. Against the far wall, between the gate and the fence, he had grown his favourites, tall blue delphiniums, stately as princesses, their stems loaded with blossoms like gems.

This summer his flowers will thrive again, for she will tend them. She will do this as an offering to her grandfather. Softened by her dedication, he will, perhaps, allow their reunion to take place in the garden instead of calling her into the Cwm where, she knows now, something more terrifying than she has ever suspected waits. In there she had felt her strength drain away as the loops of hair twined around her and the enchanter thundered through the trees. Alone, she might never have come out.

'Coffee's ready,' Gwen calls from the doorstep.

As Olwen goes towards the house, she remembers the doctor's words. 'Ask her about your mother.' But she won't. She already suspects more than Gwen could ever tell her.

Five

All through the capricious days of April, in sunshine and shower, Olwen works in her grandfather's garden. She digs and plants, hoes and weeds, clearing and purifying the earth for the new seeds, and for the bulbs she buried in autumn, when her grandfather still directed her, calling instructions from the window of his sick-room. Absorbed in these tasks, her vision fixed in the future, she hardly notices the weather. It's all one to her if rain or heat soaks her shirt and plasters her cheeks with strands of hair loosened from her braid.

'I wish you'd come in when it's wet,' Gwen said at first. 'You'll catch cold, love. April is so treacherous.'

'Nothing outside will hurt me,' Olwen answered her. 'It's only in this house that I feel ill.'

By May, the ache in her muscles has ceased, and each morning, once she is out in the open, she feels as sturdy as the chestnut tree, bursting now into flower. When she touches the shell-pink petals, or walks barefoot across the lush grass, or waters the shoots on the other side of the garden, her heart casts off the stone that weighs her down at night, when she sinks into the whirlpool of memory, the quicksand of dreams.

One windy morning in mid-May Olwen opens the front door and steps into a carnival. Clouds cavort like clowns across the blue sky, the chestnut twirls its boughs like a juggler, peonies, asters, tulips, sporting round, conical, or bell-shaped hats in yellow, blue, red and purple, dance to the wind's rambunctious music. Beneath the chestnut tree the strip of grass is a rich green carpet, the two deckchairs twin thrones awaiting the guests of honour . . . Olwen and her grandfather.

So she fancies, as she stands in the doorway, her spirits lifting in response to the festive morning – a sign surely – a promise from him that he is coming to make her heart glad again. And looking towards the toolshed, where the heads of the guardian sunflowers are already striped with yellow, she believes it possible that *this* morning, when she opens the door and goes inside to collect the garden tools, he will be there, waiting for her, his arms spread wide.

'You did right,' he will say as he enfolds her. 'Everything pleases me, *cariad*.'

Yet on this merry morning, as on every other morning since she began her work in the garden, she hesitates. For something in the toolshed's posture forbids her, its roof, its single-paned window, and the nailed-together sheets of tarpaulin all tipping forward towards the path, as if the shed were closed in on itself, suspicious and hostile as her grandfather when he lay in his sickbed, his legs drawn up, his arms wrapped around his chest, his eyes turned inward. Impossible for her to proceed boldly to the shed, as one entitled to enter; instead, as usual, she takes a circuitous route.

First, she lingers by the laurel bush. Its leaves drape the hall window in a green mantle through which the sun glitters in geometric shapes, as if the glass were a pictograph, a sheet torn from a book of spells. Fingering the shiny leaves, thick as parchment, she remembers something her grandfather told her when they walked on the Roman road on the other side of the Cwm: 'The Romans put laurel wreaths on the heads of their generals when they marched through the city in a victory parade. Laurel was a sign of nobility for them. For us, it's a symbol of shame. A lot of the prisoners in those parades were Celtic chieftains in chains.'

'Then why did you plant a laurel bush outside our window, Grandfather?' Olwen asked him.

'It's good to remember shame,' he said. 'Shame's a better teacher than victory.'

From the laurel, Olwen crosses to the luxurious chestnut, its lower branches trailing the ground like a woman's long skirt. She moves into the branches until they envelop her. Leaning against the trunk, she rests her cheek against the cool, rough bark, a texture like her grandfather's palm when he touched her face. Through the leaves and pink blossoms she looks across the lawn to the toolshed.

Squat-shaped, its tarpaulin sides bulging and blistered from the heat of many summers, it reminds her always of a great black dog, one of the hunting dogs in *The Mabinogion*, grown too old for the chase, sleeping out the remainder of its days but able, still, to bare its fangs and raise its hackles at the whiff of game.

She had spent many hours playing in the shed, sitting on the floor with a pile of wood shavings, shaping the pieces into patterns while her grandfather worked at his bench, the sounds of the saw or lathe as reassuring as his voice – his other voices, in fact, for he was a master-carpenter who used his tools as adroitly as if they were his own limbs. Only since his death has the shed assumed an ominous aspect.

Olwen moves out of the chestnut branches and crosses the grass to the shed. Behind it, just beyond the garden wall, the Cwm towers, the trees covered in deep green foliage. At the gate she pauses to look across the lane. With the resurgence of leaves, creepers, undergrowth, the woods look majestic again. Deformities in the trunks, distortions in the branches, are hidden now. The earth massed with growing things, the secret places recovered, the Cwm is magical. Deep in the trees a cuckoo sings.

Leaning on the gate, Olwen feels the power that emanates from the woods. Leaves rustling in the wind seem to whisper 'Come'. Through the tiered boughs she glimpses sunlit places, the golden rooms of a great palace. It's as if, today, her grandfather's spirit predominates there as it did when they walked together and he told her not to fear the other: 'That old enchanter, he's all trappings and show. If we meet him, just you get behind me. I'll look him in the eye and he'll be off, quick as a wink.'

As Olwen reached her teens he spoke less and less of the enchanter's guile, warning her increasingly of human trickery. In her last year at school, when she was applying to universities, his warnings became so frequent that she took to working on her applications in secret, seeing how it distressed him when she spread the forms and brochures on the kitchen table. Yet he didn't want her behind the counter of a Pont Ysaf shop either, or in an office in the Town Hall. He wanted for her the education he had not obtained. So he never forbade her. If he had, she would have obeyed.

She applied to the three universities nearest home: Swansea, Cardiff, Aberystwyth. When all three accepted her, her grandfather's face shone with pride. 'Go to Swansea,' he said, choosing the closest. She sent off her acceptance before he could change his mind, say, 'Well, let's think a bit . . . Would it hurt to take a year off?'

Months before, she began to dread her departure. Although he had walked with her to the post box to mail her acceptance, the moment the letter slipped into the slot, he grew morose. 'We never considered,' he said as they walked home. 'We never discussed the pros and cons. Act in haste, repent at leisure.'

When she and Gwen returned from a shopping trip to Cardiff to buy new clothes, he refused to look at her purchases. 'Aye, aye, you spent like there was no tomorrow, I dare say,' he said and walked out into the garden, leaving Olwen standing at the kitchen table where she had spread her packages.

Sometimes it was hard to understand him, he contradicted himself so. Much of the money he had received as compensation for his pit accident was in a trust fund for her, 'to have when you're twenty-one,' he said, 'in case you want to go in for something higher. A Ph.D. I'm thinking would be a grand thing.' At the same time, he seemed unable to cope with the fact that in October she would be fifty miles away. 'I might have a telephone put in,' he said, 'so you can ring me every day.'

As it turned out, she had stayed at home after all. Her grandfather, a sufferer from silicosis, collapsed in the garden one August evening when he was pruning the delphiniums. She wrote to Swansea. The Admissions Office wrote back: in view of the circumstances and her superlative examination results, they would offer her a place the following year. She had shown him the letter, meaning to spare him anxiety on her behalf.

'It don't matter one way or the other,' he said. 'You and me will be parting sooner than that.'

Gazing into the Cwm, she thinks now without enthusiasm of the option Swansea has offered her. She has no desire to leave; new places, new experiences, have lost their glamour. She wishes only to recapture the old, to find, somehow, the border line between memory and evocation and cross it into the world where her grandfather still lives.

So . . . she must complete the task she has set herself. When his garden flourishes, he will return and take her with him to whatever place he now inhabits. In her mind, this place is a green country bathed in sunlight, like the landscapes of her childhood.

Olwen turns from the gate to the toolshed. From her pocket

she draws the old-fashioned iron key and fits it into the lock. Opening the door, she enters the shed. Inside, everything is as he left it. She has touched nothing save the tools she takes out and replaces daily.

Sun falls on the wooden carpenter's bench beneath the window, and on the steel last beside it. Like a miniature tree, the last sprouts three branches, the end of each shaped to a human foot, a man's, a woman's, a child's. He repaired their shoes on the last, and sometimes made new ones for Olwen from the softest leather he could find, in jewel colours, scarlet, midnight blue, ivory with the sheen of pearl, sling-backs, peep-toes, button-straps – party shoes, though she never went to parties. At school, the other girls made fun of her, calling her 'show-off' and 'Milady'. But she saw the envy in their eyes and didn't care.

Where had her grandfather learned cobbling and carpentry? Was his father a shoemaker, perhaps? She knows little of his early life, for he never spoke of the past except to dismiss it. Unable to imagine him anywhere but Archer's Lane, she has come to imagine his life as, in a sense, beginning with hers. Often he said to her, 'You're the sole reason I'm on this earth, *cariad*. Nothing else could keep me here.'

Shavings litter the wood floor of the shed, giving off a musty scent that reminds her of the Cwm. Against the end wall lie pieces of his unfinished work, segments of a desk he said she would need when she became a college student, wood cut for picture frames, a kitchen chair wanting legs. Draped in shadow, the pale, stripped wood assumes the colour of flesh, the legless chair, tipped on its side, vaguely resembling a human torso. Olwen bites her lip, distressed, perplexed that this image should present itself to her. Perhaps it is the tools on the carpenter's bench, the sharp-toothed saw, the claw hammer, the long knife he used to cut leather, that remind her of carnage.

Often in these past weeks her imagination has wandered into dark places. At night she dreams of him frequently. Sometimes in these dreams she is a child again, sitting in his lap by the parlour fire, or skipping beside him in the Cwm. More commonly, though, she dreams of flight and pursuit, of endless paths and corridors, and of dark corners where she hides but never escapes. In his long robe, he looms in front of her, his face twisted into an ogre's grimace, his hand wielding a knife, or his own nails, sprouting like talons as he reaches for her.

Olwen turns her eyes from the carpenter's bench to the shelved wall opposite. Here are cans of nails, screws, bolts, tins of varnish and paint, seed packets, clay pots, and much else he amassed over the years. He was not one to throw things away, though many of the objects are rusty and useless. Most of the top shelf is taken up by a long, narrow metal box with rusted clasps and a brass ring at either end for lifting and carrying. It has lain there as long as she can remember, never taken down, never opened. It contains, she guesses, tools broken or forgotten. In the corner between the shelves and the door stand the shovel, the rake, and the hoe. Olwen collects them and leaves the shed.

Outside in the fresh, breezy air, her spirits revive. As she drives the shovel into the rich, damp earth, turns the soil and breaks the clods, she feels strong and hopeful again. No wonder her grandfather loved to garden; it braces the injured heart.

'I'm going into town,' Gwen says as they eat breakfast. 'Can I get you anything? Or would you like to come?' This last question she asks tentatively.

'I've too much to do in the garden.'

'Well . . . tomorrow I thought I'd take a walk to Cefn Heights again. You haven't visited Grandpa's grave yet. We could take some asters and tulips?'

'No,' Olwen says, 'I don't want to go there.'

Gwen looks down at her hands. Slowly, methodically, she rubs her fingers across the knuckles of her left hand, across the rings there. Every fine Sunday since the funeral she has visited the cemetery. She must do it for show, since it can't be for love.

She lifts her head and smiles. 'I'm glad you're doing the garden. I'd have missed the flowers this year.'

Olwen, buttering toast, nods briefly. Her grandmother likes to have flowers in the house. She recalls how her grandfather begrudged every one she cut, saying, 'Mind you only take the full-blown. Don't go lopping off the buds.' He got no pleasure from the sight of cut flowers in vases. 'They're dead already,' he told Olwen. 'She might as well buy plastic ones in Woolworths and leave mine be.'

'He prized his garden,' Gwen says. 'I'm glad you're keeping it up for him.'

Her grandmother speaks as if she, too, believes that he still lives. Is she thinking as a good Christian? Gwen goes to service at Harvest, Christmas, and Easter, when one or other of the

57

members of Hebron Chapel drives out to pick her up. As a child Olwen went too, wanting to see the chapel filled with great baskets of fruit, vegetables, and flowers at harvest time, candlelit and hushed on the Sunday before Christmas, decorated with greenery on Easter Sunday when the congregation sang 'Rock of Ages', one of the hymns her grandmother often sang at home back in the days when her grandfather still worked at the colliery. But she has never thought of Gwen as a deeply religious woman. Surely she can't believe he's in heaven?

'Do you think there's another life after we die?' Olwen asks her now.

'I don't know, I'm sure.' Gwen twists the keeper between her thumb and index finger. 'I believe in God, but I can't claim to know His intentions for us. Mr Rhys would be a better person to ask than me.'

'You don't need a divinity degree to have an opinion. Even a madwoman like Aunt Flindy –'

'Aunt Flindy isn't mad, Olwen. She's just getting a bit *twp* –'

'She thinks she can speak to the dead. She's spoken to Grandfather, she told me.'

'To John? Never! When did she tell you that?'

'The day of the funeral. She said he came to her in the night. A lot of dead people come to her when she's in bed.'

'Poor old dab, she dwells in the past. She never saw Grandpa, Olwen, nor anyone else either. It's all in her mind.'

'That's what you think, but you can't *know*, can you?'

'I don't believe in ghosts,' Gwen says firmly.

'So what do you believe? Just now you said you're glad I'm keeping up the garden for Grandfather – as if he'd be aware of that. Do you think he's in heaven, then? Or in hell, maybe?'

Gwen closes her hands around her teacup. 'Your grandfather made his own hell. I hope he's at peace now.'

Olwen pushes away her plate and stands up. 'What hell did he make?'

'The same one all people make who wish for things they can't have. We should live the life we know, not pine for a different one.'

'What if we don't *like* the life we know?'

Gwen stands too. Her face is flushed. 'Then we're ungrateful. And if you're speaking of yourself, all I can say is, you haven't given life a chance yet. First, because you weren't allowed to, and now because you won't.' She begins to stack the breakfast dishes, making a loud clatter with the cutlery.

'You couldn't stand him, could you?' Olwen says. 'And the feeling was mutual, so I'm sure you'd prefer to think he's rotting in the earth.' She walks out of the house, slamming the front door.

When Gwen comes out an hour later, she is clearing dead sweet-pea vines from the latticed fence they share with Bryn Brewen. Her grandmother is dressed for town in a grey coat, a cloche hat, Cuban heel shoes. She has a handbag over one arm, a shopping bag on the other. She looks neat but dowdy, the coat a trifle long, the hat too large, both emphasizing her shortness. Slowly, she comes down the path. Olwen turns away, busying herself with the vines, but Gwen says her name and she is forced to look round.

'Will you meet the two o'clock bus and help me carry the shopping?'

'Yes,' Olwen says, laying an armful of vines in the wheel-barrow.

'Is there anything you need?'

'Nothing, thank you.'

'Well . . . I'm going then.'

Olwen watches her walk down the path. From the back she looks like a child in dressing-up clothes – or like a much older woman whose body has shrunk. She wonders why her grand-mother's smallness has never struck her so acutely before. Then, as Gwen goes through the gate, she sees what it is. She is holding herself in an unfamiliar posture, her shoulders hunched, her head down, as if she expects a blow. Olwen turns away and rips at the vines.

In a few hours she has cleared the fence and staked the new plants. Through gaps in the trellis she can see into Bryn Brewen's garden, and until the sweet peas grow profuse he will have a clear view into theirs. Realizing this, Olwen feels anxious. Ever since she can remember, Bryn has vexed her.

If he chanced to be in his garden when she came home from school, he'd hurry out into the lane, stand in front of her, barring her way, and ask foolish questions about lessons and teachers. All the time he spoke, his dark eyes fixed her like rivets, pushing into her skin. Mumbling a brief reply, Olwen would step round him and run to her own gate. These encounters happened so often, she came to believe he watched for her.

Now she remembers something he said to her one afternoon last spring: 'Step into my house for a minute, will you, Olwen *fach*?'

'I can't,' she had said. 'I don't have time.'

'I've a thing to show you inside – when you've got a minute to spare,' he said as she swerved past him. And as she walked swiftly on, 'Don't tell Grandpa, mind.'

She hadn't told. Her grandfather hated Bryn to talk to her, so she kept quiet about the meetings in the lane. She worried, though, believing that their next-door neighbour meant her harm. Bryn has never married, never been seen with a woman; yet she knows, whenever he comes near, that he needs a woman desperately. She reads it in his eyes and in the tremors of his body, which he tries to hold so still. Living close to him is like looking through the bars of a lion's cage. Except, no bars restrain him, only – so far – lack of opportunity.

Raising her eyes from the fence, Olwen looks up at his house. In one of the upstairs windows he stands watching her. He wears only a vest and underpants – just risen from bed probably – and Olwen sees that his body, like his head, is covered in thick, black hair. It coats his muscled arms like fur, rises out of the V of his vest like a bush, and sprouts from the crotch of his underpants. The hair on his head is loose, wild as brambles; on his face, a crafty, gluttonous smile, as if he has been eating up the sight of her.

Olwen stares back at him a moment. Then she sprints across the garden into the house, slamming and bolting the door behind her. Trembling, she goes into the kitchen, runs cold water and bends her head to drink, her throat parched. Suddenly, she wants to immerse herself in water. Turning off the tap, she goes upstairs to bathe.

At the top of the stairs, the bathroom opens off a small landing. Two steps lead up from the landing to a narrow passage, three doors on one side, Gwen's bedroom, Olwen's, and, at the far end, the box room where her grandfather slept. Olwen has not entered this room since he died there. Looking at the closed door, she feels an urge to go in now. She climbs the steps and goes down the passage. Her hand on the door knob, she falters.

Go on, she prompts herself.

Turning the knob, she pushes the door wide, her heart clenching. Whatever she feared, or hoped for, is not there. The room is neat, clean – empty of any presence. Under the window, his bed is made up and covered with a bright candlewick bedspread the colour of daffodils. Yellow gauze curtains waft in a breeze from the open window. The few bits of furniture, a bedside table and chair, a chest of drawers against the wall, give off a fresh scent of beeswax polish. In the afternoon sunlight the cheerful room retains no hint of death, or of the grim suffering that preceded it.

Dazed, Olwen moves towards the window. The cheeriness of the room shocks her more than the dark remnants she anticipated. Last time she stood here, her grandfather lay among dishevelled sheets, his white hair spread on the pillow, the fine, silky locks tinged with yellow like his eyes, which were turned to the window. On the table, his pipe spilled tobacco and made the air reek. Books she had brought in to read to him cluttered the floor, medicine and tablet bottles stood on top of the chest of drawers and towels hung from its brass knobs. The white china handle of a chamber pot jutted from beneath the bed, and on the window ledge a ewer of tepid water waited. Last time, it was a sick room she entered; now it might be a room in a hotel, so bright, so impersonal it seems.

It strikes her that Gwen has eradicated all signs that he ever inhabited the room. But her disappointment goes too deep for anger. As she moves into the space between the bed and the window she feels bereft, as if he had in reality promised to be here and then failed to appear.

Olwen pushes back the gauze curtain and sits in the window seat. This was her place every day while he was ill. She left it only to eat, to take a breath of air in the garden, to plant bulbs, to attempt sleep. Here she read to him, or to herself while he napped, and here, too, in the last, dreadful months, she listened to his crazed, fragmented monologues:

'She's down in the garden. I see her there, by the toolshed. Why don't she come up? Don't she know I'm going fast? She'd come if she cared a whit.'

Or, speaking directly to the spectre, his voice buttery, 'Lily white . . . white as the lilies, my lovely girl . . . red as rosebuds, too, I know, don't I? . . . But blue is our favourite colour always.'

The gauze curtain, caught on an upsurge in the breeze, flies out of the window. Leaning out to catch it before it snags on the casement, Olwen sees a movement among the trees on the edge of the Cwm. Transfixed, her left arm still extended, a fold of the curtain between her fingers, she sees, staring through the leaves, a face.

The moment she spots it, the face vanishes. Only a fluttering of leaves as a branch settles confirms that it was there. It was a woman's face, she's sure, for she glimpsed a delicate bone structure, wide eyes like a doe's, wistful, yet seductive too. She had seen these qualities in the eyes clearly, as if the creature's gaze diminished distance with its intense longing. Mingled with the greenery that framed the face like a wreath, Olwen had seen, too, swirls of long silver hair.

Rising from the window seat, she shuts the casement and leaves the room. Did her grandfather see such apparitions as he lay in bed looking towards the Cwm? If he did, no wonder they drove him to frenzy. The face, though fragile, feminine, had something terribly ominous in it. She had felt, in that moment when the eyes linked with hers, as if cold, graceful fingers circled her throat. As she goes down the passage she thinks that perhaps this was one of the enchanter's masquerades. Or, possibly, the face of a victim? Another question occurs: did she catch the creature off-guard, or was she meant to see her?

In her own room, Olwen undresses for her bath. As she lifts her arms to pull off her T-shirt, she raises her head and her eyes focus on the rafter. There, among the many shapes her grandfather created, is the face he carved with his penknife – an exact replica of the face Olwen has just seen peering through leaves in the Cwm.

Six

As Olwen turns out of Archer's Lane into Pont Ysaf Road, the bus rushes past on its way back to town. 'How do, love!' Morgan Pryce calls through the open window and lifts his hand off the wheel to touch the peak of his driver's cap. Leaping playfully over potholes, the bus veers off towards the hedge on the opposite side of the road. Morgan grabs the wheel and prevents a plunge. Back on course again, the rickety red bus charges down the road, Morgan dwarf-like up front, as if the vehicle were a monster bearing him off in its jaws.

Olwen watches its progress, thinking of Morgan's cheery salute, what he risked to give it to her. He bears her no ill will for the snub she gave him at the funeral. '*Dwp* as they come, Morgan Pryce,' her grandfather used to say. 'A baby could trick him.' Her grandfather would never forget an insult. 'Daft to take two cuts from the same knife,' he used to tell Olwen. 'Anybody who stabs you once will stab you again.' Yet she can't scoff at Morgan. In her heart she's grateful.

Her grandmother is coming down the road from the bus stop. Their new neighbour, Rosamund Miller, walks beside her. Gwen waves. Rosamund waves, too, though she and Olwen have never spoken.

Today Rosamund wears a cream-coloured linen suit, expensively cut, the skirt falling in soft folds to her calves, the long, loose jacket open to show a silky emerald blouse. Her blonde hair swings as she walks. With one hand she pushes a collapsible canvas shopping cart, brightly striped like a beach umbrella. She manages always to suggest that she is in transit, bound for more exotic places than Pont Ysaf.

Gwen's shopping must be in Rosamund's cart, for she carries only her handbag. Her step is sprightly again. She has lost the dowdy, cowed look of the morning.

As they come towards her, Olwen, against her will, stares at

Rosamund. Her easy, fashionable clothes move fluidly with the rhythm of her body, her legs in sheer stockings flashing in and out of the folds of her skirt. Her mouth and cheeks are red and shiny as apples, her breasts and hips like fruit too – melons, Olwen thinks of, or grapefruit.

'I could eat you up!' Welshwomen say to a comely child. A man could feast on Rosamund Miller. Her husband must always be ravenous for her. Watching her, Olwen feels scrawny, unkempt – unsexed.

'I'm a bit late,' she says when they reach her. She looks at Gwen. 'I'm sorry.'

'Oh, it don't matter, love. I met Rosamund in town and she's got all my shopping in her cart.' Gwen smiles at her. She, too, is the forgiving sort, a habit she must have acquired from living with a man who lived as if he were single.

'We haven't met.' Rosamund holds out her hand.

Olwen touches her fingers briefly.

'It does seem odd, doesn't it? Imagine, we've been here four months and never come to see you. That's not a bit like me, really, but Mrs Flinders told us of your trouble, and Alun said I shouldn't intrude. I always told your grandmother though when I met her in the lane, "If there's anything I can do –"'

Gwen touches Rosamund's sleeve. 'You did, and I appreciated it.'

'I want to be a good neighbour. I was brought up that way, Alun too. But we've only been married six months, so we're still in the honeymoon stage. It's easy to get wrapped up in each other.' She gives Olwen a brilliant smile. 'When you're married, you'll know what I mean.'

'Rosamund treated me to lunch at the Mayflower,' Gwen says as they reach the Millers' gate. 'Wasn't that kind?'

'Oh no, it was nothing. I want you both to come for dinner soon. I'll talk to Alun and we'll make a date.'

As if he's been looking out for her, her husband appears at the front door. He is a tall, thin man with close-cropped dark hair and a goatee beard, dressed today in black jeans and a black turtle-neck sweater. Olwen is reminded of a pirate, or a soldier of fortune, for there is an air of dash and daring about him. It's hard to imagine him as a history teacher at Pont Ysaf Grammar, a replacement for old Mr Hopkins, the grey-haired patriarch who gravely and pedantically taught Olwen and her peers. All the Sixth-Form girls must have a crush on Alun Miller.

As he hurries down the path, the look on his face sews up Olwen's heart, there's so much desire, so much exclusiveness in it. His eyes, fixed on Rosamund, don't see Olwen and her grandmother; they are outside the boundaries of his private world.

Alun comes out into the lane and immediately attaches himself to his wife. His arm around her waist, he draws her so close her hair brushes his cheek.

'I hope I haven't kept Rosamund out too long,' Gwen says. Olwen sees that this display delights her. She is smiling all over her face.

'Oh, he can't get on without me for a minute.' Rosamund tips her head towards her husband's shoulder and gives him a coquettish look. The way he looks back at her makes Olwen feel as if she has witnessed an intimate gesture.

'Alun, this is Olwen, Mrs Parry's granddaughter.'

Alun holds out his hand. When Olwen gives him hers, he grasps it tightly, wrapping her fingers in his. His eyes, turned on her now, still hold the look that belongs to Rosamund, and Olwen is shamed by the response that leaps inside her. Withdrawing her hand, she says to her grandmother, 'We'd better get the shopping home.'

'I'll help you,' Alun Miller says.

'No need, thank you.' Gwen takes her shopping bag from Rosamund's cart and hands it to Olwen. 'There's just this and a plastic bag. We have most of our goods delivered, but I do like to go to the bakery on Saturday, when everything's fresh. And a trip into town makes a change, doesn't it?' She lifts the other bag from the cart. 'Thank you so much, Rosamund.'

'It was a pleasure, Mrs Parry. And don't forget you're coming to dinner soon. We'll ask Mrs Flinders too. She's all alone, poor thing.'

'Great,' Alun says, but Olwen sees that he is simply being polite. His mind is on Rosamund, on getting her into the house. Even as he speaks, he draws her through the gate.

'What a nice couple,' Gwen says as she and Olwen walk up the lane.

When they reach Aunt Flindy's, the old woman is at her gate. She wears a turquoise shot-silk dress, ripped under the left armhole, and her lipstick and eyeshadow are smeared as if she has just returned from a riotous party. Her skinny orange cat, its fur matching the shade and texture of Aunt Flindy's hair, perches on the top bar and hisses at Gwen and Olwen.

'Oh, hush, Cinders!' Gwen waves her hand in the cat's face. 'Hullo, Aunt Flindy. Are you all right, then?'

Aunt Flindy offers her syrupy smile, batting her stiff blue lashes. 'I seen you talking to the couple next door, Gwen. Nice little 'oman, she is. Very friendly and obliging.' Her eyes slide towards Olwen, then back to Gwen. 'Went shopping with her, did you? There's nice for you, to have a bit of company at last.'

'We met in town by accident. I've got your lardy cake and bread here. Let's go in and make a cup of tea, shall we? I'll sit with you a bit.'

'Lovely.' Aunt Flindy's eyes slip back to Olwen. 'I don't suppose you're coming in, dearie?'

Olwen shakes her head. 'No, thanks.'

'Olwen has to unpack the shopping.' Gwen takes a sticky lardy cake wrapped in wax paper and a cob loaf from the baker's bag and hands the bag to Olwen.

'She never do come in my house. Rosamund next door, now, she pops in all the time to see if I need anything. And *she* has prior obligations, too.'

'Olwen's not much for visiting, you know that. Get away, Cinders!' Gwen pushes the snarling cat off the gate and Aunt Flindy aims a kick at it with the toe of her button-up boot. 'Grizzling little devil. She don't give me no peace. I've a good mind to put her to sleep.' Her blue eyes glitter at Olwen. 'Spoilt rotten, she is. Well, you'll come when you have a need, dearie, won't you?'

'Let's go and put the kettle on, then.' Gwen takes Aunt Flindy's arm and shakes her head at Olwen, signalling that she should pay no attention to the old woman's remarks.

'Why don't you cook supper today?' Aunt Flindy says over her shoulder. 'Since you'll be at home with nothing to do. It would be a rare treat for Nain, wouldn't it?' As she goes up the path on Gwen's arm, she says loudly, 'Are you still waiting on her hand and foot, Gwen?'

'Old cow,' Olwen says under her breath.

Inside the house, she unpacks the bags and puts the shopping away, her mind on the Millers. Rosamund Miller is the good girl everyone likes. She's also the kind of woman who draws men, makes them fall in love with her. It's not just her looks. Olwen looked well enough herself before her grandfather's illness, but except for Gareth, no boy has ever chased her. It's her embracing manner; Rosamund behaves as if she has love and solicitude to give away like pennies. She must come from a large, close family. People as free and open as she are never only children.

Olwen feels envious again. Yet when her grandfather was alive she had never longed for other relatives. It was hard enough to leave him to visit the relatives they do have, Gwen's sister and her family in Swansea. Now, standing in the empty kitchen, she wonders what it would have been like had her mother lived, married, had children.

What is it like, she wonders, to be married to a man like Alun Miller? To have a man with intense eyes and strong hands come out of the house to meet you, to see gladness in his face – and desire – to go inside with him and close the door . . .

When all the shopping is put away Olwen goes up to her room. She kicks off her shoes and lies down on her narrow bed. A breeze from the open window fans her hair and lifts her shirt. Gareth looked at her once as Alun Miller looks at Rosamund. Ah, but that's different. He had desire, she saw that; but his eyes turn on many. His gaze is not exclusive like Alun's.

Now, perhaps, Rosamund Miller lies on her back as Olwen does, the breeze playing on her melon breasts which fill her husband's hands as he kneels between her legs, engaging her eyes as he will soon engage her body . . . she has seen that too, the expression on a man's face when he has uncovered a woman and prepares to cover her again with himself . . .

She had taken a pan from the kitchen that afternoon last summer, saying to Gwen, 'I'm going to pick blackberries.'

Gwen, preoccupied with some chore, said, 'That's nice, love.'

Out on the lawn, his gardening finished for the day, her grandfather sat in a deckchair under the chestnut, reading the *South Wales Echo*.

'I'm going for blackberries,' Olwen told him. 'We haven't had a blackberry tart this year.'

'Too hot for all that scrounging about,' he said. 'Wait till after tea and I'll go with you.'

'I want to make the tart for your tea.'

'Well, no need to go far. Plenty of ripe ones in the lane. I seen them myself.'

He was right. In the opposite direction from Pont Ysaf Road

the lane ran through fields, and the hedges there were crammed with blackberries. But the ripest grow by the Wen, Olwen thought, and kept walking. The sun was so intense that afternoon, she could feel the heat of the path through the thin soles of her sandals. Heat lay heavy on her bare arms and legs and collected under the waistband of her denim shorts and at the nape of her neck. As she walked through the simmering afternoon towards the Wen Pool, she frequently lifted her hair with the back of her hand or flapped the ends of her gingham shirt against her midriff, but these actions did not cool her.

The lane ended in an arm of the Cwm. Here the wooded hillside sloped down to the River Taf and the broad, deep pool called the Wen. As soon as she entered the trees she heard the boys' voices, the splashes as they dived into the water. A little farther on and she could see them through the bushes. There were four, all boys she knew from school, and Gareth was one of them.

He stood on a platform of rock jutting from the steep ground on the other side of the river, a golden figure in the glaring spotlight of the high, white sun. Sunlight glowed on his body and burnished his hair. He was poised to dive. Two boys sat on a rock nearby, a third backflipped in the green water, dense with reflected leaves. None of them wore swimming trunks, as they would have if girls had been present. They had simply stripped to their white briefs.

A hot blush rose to Olwen's face. She felt like a voyeur, seeing them like that when they thought themselves unobserved. Unchaste she felt, too, as if she had come with promiscuous intent, to offer them turns at her. Still, she couldn't move away. The sight of Gareth transfixed her.

He dived, arrow-straight, his fingertips reaching the water first, then his arms, then his body, his feet in a perfect arch. Like a fish, he slid into the pool, hardly raising a ripple, it seemed to her, yet the sound of the splash rang clear as a bell in her ears; pure, thrilling, it sliced the oppressive air and swept over her like a cooling draft, making her skin shiver.

He surfaced, trod water. She watched his hands stroke and part the water, his beautiful hands that made shapes like pictures when he spoke.

'Great shot,' one of the boys on the rock called. 'Champion.'

'Ah, you angled a bit when you went in,' the other said.

68

Gareth raised his right hand, two fingers shaping an obscenity.

Olwen flinched.

The other boy laughed. 'You aim straighter when you do that, I hope, boyo!'

Gareth laughed too. Raising his arms, he flipped over in the water, came up near the fourth boy, put his hands on his head and ducked him. The boys on the rock dived in – imperfectly. Meeting in the middle of the pool, the four of them played like children, splashing and ducking each other.

Olwen knows she should leave but can't. She wants to stay where Gareth is. To give herself an excuse, she begins to pick blackberries. The bushes are so crowded, she could fill the white enamel bowl where she stands. Yet, as she picks, she wanders closer to the bank. She keeps her head averted from the pool, her eyes on the bushes.

The boys in the pool are silent suddenly. She knows they have seen her.

'Olwen!' Gareth calls.

She lifts her head.

He leaves the others and swims across to her. When he reaches the shallows, he wades to the bank. Water drops sparkle on his shoulders and chest, a diaphanous cloak. His damp hair clusters in tight curls about his head, bronze like a sculpture.

Olwen watches him rise from the pool, the enamel bowl cupped in both her hands. She forces her eyes away from his tanned thighs, away from the white briefs moulded to his hip bones and the long shape that lies between them.

Knee-deep in water, he looks up at her. 'Give me some blackberries, Olwen. I'm thirsty.'

The other boys watch silently.

Silently, she holds out the pan.

He puts in his hand, scoops up berries, and tilts his head back to tip them into his mouth.

'Juicy,' he says. 'But not enough. Can I have some more?'

She offers the pan again. He dips in several times, then wipes his hand across his mouth. 'I've finished them off, so now I have to help you pick, don't I?'

He climbs out of the pool and stands in front of her. Smiling, he shakes himself violently.

Olwen jumps away. 'You've soaked me!'

'Doesn't it feel grand? Don't you want to swim?'

She glances at the boys in the pool and shakes her head.

'I'll send them away.'

'No.'

'Can't you?'

'What?'

'Swim?'

'A bit . . . not well.'

'I'll teach you.'

'No.'

'We'll pick blackberries, then.' He takes her hand, leads her into the bushes. Behind them, the boys hoot.

'Idiots,' Gareth says.

For a while they pick in silence, side by side, but Olwen spills more berries than she gathers, squashing or dropping them.

'Butterfingers,' Gareth says softly.

They come to a willow tree. He parts the branches like a curtain, points to a smooth, flat stone they conceal. 'Let's sit for a bit and cool off. Then I'll fill the pan for you.'

Olwen puts the pan down on the grass and goes through.

Gareth follows, letting the curtain fall. 'Sit down,' he says in an easy voice, as if she were a visitor, he the host.

She sits on the cool stone, smooth and white as a sheet. Gareth stretches out, lying on his side, his chin propped on his hand. 'Did you know about this place?'

She shakes her head, drawing up her knees, clasping them in her arms.

'I like to think nobody knows. If those fellows came up into the woods,' he jerks his head towards the pool, 'they'd think we'd gone.'

Olwen, looking past him, can see through the willow branches, the distant Wen and the boys cavorting there.

'How did you find it?' she asks. At the bottom of her field of vision, she sees his brown body, shining where the sun slants on him through the long willow leaves, the muscles in his arms and thighs, the fine golden hairs on his shins.

'Years ago, when I was a kid. When we first came here. I liked to scout around in the woods and find hideouts. I know other places like this.'

'I used to do that too – with my grandfather. Not in this part of the Cwm though. You never showed it to anyone?'

'You're the first, Olwen.'

She tries to imagine herself and Gareth as children, playing in the woods. What would it have been like to have a companion her own age? But the image won't come. He is not a boy now. She is not a girl. They are a man and a woman, twenty and eighteen.

'The Welsh don't like their children to grow up,' she says, as if they have been talking about this.

'Some don't. But they do grow up all the same.'

'Maybe.'

'You have.'

'I don't know.'

They are silent again. Until he says, 'Olwen.'

'No,' she says at once.

'At least look at me.'

Slowly, dreamily, she brings her eyes to his face.

His head on his hand, he watches her intently.

She moves her eyes down his body, looks at the long hard shape in his crotch, the wet cloth moulded to it, golden hairs curling out like the tendrils of a flower.

Olwen can't help herself. She puts out her hand and touches him there.

Gareth's breath comes swiftly. He shudders but doesn't move. He keeps his eyes on her face, narrowing them, catlike.

She closes her fingers on him, rubs her palm against the ridges she feels through the cloth.

He's up then. His arms fastening her, he pulls her against him, thrusts his tongue into her mouth. She tastes blackberries, feels his hands under her shirt, pressing her shoulder blades. It's as if he wants to draw her into him, pull her through his skin, still damp and cool from swimming. She doesn't resist; she wants to be immersed.

One hand on the back of her head, woven into her hair, he holds her mouth to his while he unhooks her brassiere and cups her breast. Olwen shivers. Still she keeps her hand on him. When he unbuttons her shirt, she slips her hand inside his briefs.

In the flesh, it is sturdy, nubbed. It feels as she expected, like the thick, green-budded stalks in the Cwm. She makes a tube of her hand, close-fitting, and moves along the length of it. The way it springs up delights and thrills her.

'I like it,' she says in his ear.

71

He thrusts his body against her when she says this and becomes rigid, rock-hard in her hand. Unfastening the clasp of her shorts, he pulls the zipper down, pushes his hand between her legs. For a moment she feels his fingers on her. Then she struggles.

The change is so swift, she has the advantage. She's on her feet, fastening her clothes, before he reacts

'I won't do that,' she says when he sits up.

'I thought you wanted to.'

'You don't know what I want. It's not *that*.'

'All right. I'm sorry.' His voice is placating, but his hands are rolled into fists, his arms taut. In his eyes she sees pain. His pain makes her angry.

'That's all you want from girls, isn't it?' she says. 'I know it is.'

'Olwen,' he says quietly, opening one hand, holding it up, as if to show her the shape of emptiness, 'you started it.'

'No, you did, when you said my name. You told me to look at you. I don't want to look at you. Why don't you leave me alone?'

She pushes through the willow boughs, snatches up the bowl, and runs out of the Cwm and across the fields. Where the hedgerows end, she stops, quickly fills the bowl, throwing in green berries with the black ones, and hurries the short distance to her house.

'There's a state on you, girl,' her grandfather says when she comes into the garden. 'You look like you been pulled through a hedge backwards.'

'It was hot,' she says.

'Aye, well I told you that. Next time you'll heed, maybe.'

Lying on her bed, remembering, Olwen has unbuttoned her shirt and unhooked her brassiere. She puts her hands on her breasts, strokes her nipples as Gareth did.

She had cheated on her grandfather that day, lied to him.

But she stopped Gareth in time. Before he went too far, she'd remembered her grandfather's warning: 'He's up to no good, that lad. I can read it in his face. I hope you'll hold yourself above him.'

Her right hand slides down to the zipper of her jeans. How would it have felt inside her, the golden stalk that rose and thrust in her hand, the thick stamen of a lily? As her hand slips into her

72

opened jeans, her eyes focus on the rafter. The face that looks down seems altered, the mouth twisted into a mocking grin. Is it a nub in the wood, or does the tongue protrude from the tilted lips?

Olwen stares at the face. What she sees, or seems to see, chills her. It appears now more male than female and has a wrathful yet lascivious cast. This is how a man might look, it strikes her, if he were about to rape. But the image doesn't stick. The face is too demoniac to be human.

Fastening her clothes, Olwen rises from the bed. Looking up at the face in the rafter, she says aloud, 'I didn't do it. You know I didn't. I never will.'

Seven

One morning early in June, Olwen, rising later now that the garden demands less time, comes down to the kitchen to find Gwen reading a letter at the table. She looks up over her reading glasses. 'From Aunt Pridwyn.'

Olwen crosses to the other side of the kitchen and pours coffee into the mug Gwen has set out for her. 'How is she?' She leans against the sink to sip the coffee, fearing that if she sits at the table Gwen will launch into a lengthy account of the most recent events in the lives of Pridwyn's daughters, Gwyneth and Gwyneira. These events are repetitive: the christenings, birthday parties and illnesses of Gwyneth's three children; Gwyneira's saga of boyfriends found and lost.

Eight years younger than Gwen, Pridwyn married and bore children late, so Olwen's cousins are six and three years older than her. As a child she played with them on the beach at Swansea and joined in pillow fights and dressing-up games in the big seafront house turned into a guest house after their father died. But, growing up, Olwen has grown away from them.

'Ninnies,' her grandfather called his nieces. 'Nothing in their heads but fluff. I never could abide them even when they were little 'uns. That's why I don't go there. Come the day you won't want to go either.'

Olwen had known that he wished she would stop her visits, but in this one thing she had not obeyed him. She couldn't bring herself to refuse Gwen her company for those August holidays, the only two weeks in the year when she did something specifically to please her grandmother.

Besides, her great-aunt always welcomed her so warmly, embracing her the moment she stepped off the train, holding her against her heart, as if the year's separation from her great-niece had really pained her. When they reached the seafront house she would settle Gwen in the parlour with Gwyneth, Gwyneira, and the tea trolley, and, linking Olwen's arm, take her on a tour of the rooms to show her the changes she'd made and to ask her opinion. Often during the two-week stay she would take Olwen off like this, to walk along the shore or to shop in the town, singling her out from her own sister and daughters and saying, when Olwen asked, 'What about the others?', 'Leave them be, I've had them all my life and you so rarely.'

Always, she kept Olwen close to her physically, holding her by the hand or the arm or about the waist, as if she treasured the connection, as if Olwen were her own, adored child. And Olwen, knowing she was won over by her aunt, felt guilt keenly. Gwen, who had hugged and kissed her when she was a child, ceased as soon as Olwen showed reluctance. And when she grew too old to sit on her grandfather's lap, he had stopped touching her of his own accord. With her great-aunt, Olwen looked forward to the embraces she would no longer permit her grandmother and which her grandfather no longer attempted. So she would go each year to Swansea and write to him every day of her absence, letters he never answered.

'She's worried about Gwyneira,' Gwen says. 'That medical student broke up with her. Remember we met him last summer? He seemed a nice, steady young man, too. She doesn't have much luck with boyfriends, Gwyneira.'

'Why's that, do you think?' Olwen dips her hand into a cream-cracker packet lying on the side.

'Shall I boil you an egg?'

'No, thanks. This is all I want.'

'At least butter it.'

'Why do you think Gwyneira has no luck with men?'

'I don't know, I'm sure. She's a nice girl, a pretty girl –'

'But they always leave her, don't they?'

'Poor thing. She's taking it hard, Pridwyn says.'

'What does she do wrong?'

'Olwen, I don't know.' Behind the glasses, Gwen's eyes are perplexed. 'It might not be anything she does. Something could be amiss with the men.'

'All of them? This has been going on for ages. She's had a dozen that I can count, and sooner or later they've all gone off her.'

'Young men can be fickle –'

'Some people just have no power in love,' Olwen says. 'That's what I think.'

Gwen takes off her glasses and lays them down beside her cup. 'What do you mean?'

'Rosamund Miller has it.'

'What?'

'The power to command love and keep it. But in our family, we don't. Not the women, anyway. I'm going into the garden now.' She drains her cup and crosses the kitchen.

'Auntie Pridwyn's invited us for a weekend.'

Olwen stops at the door.

'She thinks a little break would do us good. We're going to Rosamund's for dinner next Saturday, so I thought the weekend after?' Gwen moves her body forward when she says this, her shoulders dipping, as if to draw closer to the letter in her hand. (It's a posture Olwen has seen before, when her grandmother asked her grandfather for something: a walk on a Sunday evening, a trip into Pont Ysaf to buy some household item. 'You go,' he always said, 'if it appeals to you.' He never objected to anything she wanted to do; he simply refused to do it with her.) 'Will that be all right, Olwen?' says Gwen.

'I can't go before August. I've too much to do in the garden.'

'Surely you could leave it for a few days?' Gwen rubs her thumb across her ring finger and narrows her eyes, making the pattern of lines around them more prominent.

'Not before August.' Olwen steps into the hall to escape the look on her grandmother's face. Then, as she puts her hand on the door knob, it strikes her like a lightning bolt – Gwen must go on the trip, of course. If she is alone in the house he will come to her. Her grandmother's presence is the deterrent. He holds off from coming near her, as he avoided her in life. Olwen steps back into the kitchen.

'Aunt Pridwyn didn't come to the funeral –'

'She couldn't, Olwen. Gwyneth and the children were all laid up with the flu.'

'I know, I'm not criticizing. But don't you think she wants to make up to you for not coming? She'll think you're offended if you don't let her.'

'Pridwyn knows me better than that. My own sister –'

'Well, she'll be hurt anyway. And why don't you go? What's to stop you?'

'I'd worry, leaving you on your own.'

'I'd *like* to be on my own for a bit.'

'Oh,' Gwen says. Then, slowly, 'Yes, I know that, I suppose. You're like him in that way. He was always glad to see us go off for two weeks.'

You, Olwen thinks, never me. 'Write and tell her you'll come then.'

'I'll think about it. Don't push me, love.'

Olwen leaves the kitchen and goes out of the front door. Standing on the step, she surveys the garden. The sight of it makes her heart lift. All the flowers are out now, blooming as abundantly for her as they did for her grandfather – showy dahlias and phlox, striped lilies and ruffled gladioli ranged in rows like the bright, primary colours in a child's paint box. Sweet peas cluster among their sprawling vines, and Gloire de Dijon roses flood the garden with their seductive perfume. On sturdy, upright stalks, golden-helmeted sunflowers guard the toolshed. In a row against the end wall, between the gate and the fence, her grandfather's favourites, the temperamental delphiniums, have opened in a blaze of blue, stately, arrogant, yet coquettish, too, when their bells wave in a breeze. Already they are five feet tall.

Shimmering in the morning sun, the garden reminds her of the picture on the lid of a box of chocolates her grandfather once gave her. In that picture, a thatched cottage looked over a garden. Packed with flowers, the garden was empty of people. No one stood on the crazy-paving path, or looked out of a window, or gossiped over the clematis-covered fence. And she had liked this absence of figures. Uninhabited, the garden was hers. She could imagine herself the sole occupant, as she was the exclusive possessor of her grandfather's love. When the chocolates were eaten, she had cut the picture off the lid and kept it, looked at it often, transformed it, in her fantasy, into a real garden, created by her own hand and known only to her. Even her grandfather had no knowledge of its existence; it was her private place. On wet or snowbound days she often sat on her bed with the picture in her hand and slipped into this garden. As she walked there, she conjured up shrubs and trees and flowers, making them spring into life as she named them. Uninhibited by climate or soil conditions or boundaries, she mixed the exotic with the common, creating palm trees and orchids and parrots if she fancied a tropical flamboyance, or, in a different mood, an avenue of magnolias lit by the moon, a marble fountain as ornate as the Trevi fountain, trailing ivy and wistaria.

In this garden she gathered all the wonders she had seen and read about in books and made them her own. She never told her grandfather, sensing that he would find fault with her, though she could not say why. Now, long after she has put the picture away, Olwen understands that in the extravagance of her imaginary garden he would have seen dissatisfaction . . . ingratitude even.

Stepping into the sunlight, she crosses the lawn to the chestnut and sits in one of the deckchairs, stretching her bare legs, already tanned. She can't recall another year when she swapped jeans for shorts in the first days of June, or when the garden came so quickly into full bloom. It's a good omen, signifying that her grandfather is pleased with her.

Half closing her eyes, she focuses on the delphiniums, which dissolve into a blur of blue. Something stirs deep in her memory, something the exact shade of these flowers, an object that once filled her vision as they do now. She concentrates, but the image refuses to attach itself to a past event. Bluebells in the Cwm come to mind, armfuls she gathered as a child; the blue silk lining of her grandfather's Sunday cap which he let her stroke, saying, 'See, I've got a bit of the sky on my head.'

But the memory she strives for is connected to another thing, not these. Olwen feels her body stiffen; her hands grasp the wooden arms of the deckchair as if preparing for a physical shock. The event, whatever it was, had been laced with pain then – and with fear.

Among the delphiniums, a strange thing happens. One of them, the centre flower, grows taller as she watches. Its shape alters, the separate flowers merging, the green stalk receding. For a moment, she is looking at a sheet of blue suspended in the air, transparent as chiffon, wafting like a blown curtain. Then this too changes, fills out and becomes more substantial, assuming the shape of a human body, a young woman's body, curved and slender, graceful as a flower.

She wears a blue dress that reaches to her calves. The dress fits snugly over her breasts and hips, then flows out like water into a full skirt, a style called the H-line, fashionable twenty years back. Beneath the billowing skirt, her legs and feet are bare. Olwen cannot see her face. Her head is bent, a wealth of silvery hair tumbling onto her breasts. Her arms hang loose at her sides, the fingers dangling like a marionette's.

In a minute she'll lift her head, Olwen thinks, and I'll know her. She sits rigid in her chair, compelled by the life-sized, lifeless figure that hangs suspended among the delphiniums.

Slowly, the head moves, begins to lift. A scream rises in Olwen's throat. A premonition, a chill clasp at her heart, warns her that this, after all, is not a face she is ready to confront. Yet she can't move, can't shut her eyes.

Deftly the figure flicks her head to one side as she raises it. The long, tumbled hair rearranges, falls across her profile, hiding it from Olwen's sight. In the same instant, her body springs to life and she glides towards the gate, her feet seeming to skim the grass.

Delicate, poised, she should be pleasing to watch, but the sight of her fills Olwen with horror, for a sickly-sweet scent accompanies the apparition, overwhelming the perfume of the flowers. Cloying as the rotted rose, but tinged with something sharper, acrid, the aroma wafts across the garden, enveloping Olwen, making her nauseous. If malice had an odour, it would surely be this.

Her back to Olwen now, the figure stands at the gate, her hands resting on the top bar. Olwen judges her to be about her own age, then changes her mind, for there is a confidence – an arrogance even – in the way she holds herself that Olwen has never felt. She has the bearing of a woman accustomed to admiration and compliance, the air of one who picks and chooses at will, and whose will has never been thwarted. Much taller than Olwen, and formed on a grander scale, she resembles the female figures in myth and fairytale, a woman born of man, as Diana leaped from the head of Zeus.

But then, as she watches, the creature climbs onto the gate as a child would, and the majestic images shatter. One bare foot on the bottom rung, she pushes herself off with the other and swings out into the lane, her long hair streaming. Pulling the gate back, she swings out again, just as Olwen used to do, waiting for her grandfather to come home from the pit.

She picks up speed, swings faster, kicking the earth so hard to push off that dust flies up in clouds. Each time the gate cracks to a halt, the shock jars her body with a force that could snap a bone. The hinges whine in protest. The girl–woman leaps to the ground, drags the gate back. It crashes into the gate post and the latch snaps off, peeling the wood into jagged strips.

Now she hurls her body against the top bar, falling across it as the gate swings out. If the hinges break, she will be thrown like a rider from a bucking horse. The gate stops. The woman jumps off, pulls it back, prepares to mount again.

'Stop it!' Olwen screams.

The figure stops at once, her head poised as if she has heard. Olwen expects her to turn and braces herself. Footsteps sound on the gravel in the lane. A quiver runs down the creature's back. This is what she hears, not Olwen's cry.

She leans one arm on the gate, slips her other hand into the folds of her skirt, as if reaching into a concealed pocket. The footsteps are near now, heavy, male . . . in a moment, the visitor will come into view. The creature's hand emerges from the voluminous skirt. She lifts her arm, as if in greeting, but her hand is not empty. In her clenched fist, in the bright sunlight, a knife flashes. As her arm arcs gracefully in the clear air, the visitor reaches the gate. Red mingles with blue as the knife descends, blurring Olwen's vision.

Dr Lloyd does not falter – he walks straight into the knife's path – and through it. For a moment, the two bodies merge and Olwen sees the doctor enveloped in a blue haze. Then the haze evaporates and he comes towards her, unharmed.

'Olwen, what's the matter?' He stands over her, his familiar brown leather bag in one hand, the familiar look of concern on his face. 'You look as if you're going to pass out, my girl.'

Olwen struggles to compose herself. Lifting her hand, she rubs it across her forehead and feels the stickiness of sweat. 'I must have fallen asleep,' she says. 'I had a dream . . .'

The doctor sits in the deckchair beside her, placing his bag between his feet. He wears Oxford brogues this morning. Yellow socks show beneath the cuffs of his camel trousers. 'Would you like to tell me about it?'

Olwen flicks her eyes to the gate. The latch is intact. Against the wall, the delphiniums rival the sky in their blue intensity. But they are merely flowers.

'Have you been seeing things again?' His voice is soothing, unsurprised, as if he is asking about a stomach ache.

'It was a dream, I told you.'

The doctor rests his elbows on his knees and makes an arch of his fingers. His face reminds Olwen of sculptures she has seen gracing the walls of ancient cathedrals in art books. The powerful bone structure and deep crevices replicate the endurance chiselled into those stone faces. But the doctor's eyes are not hollows; they are alive with kindness and humour. His mouth is always ready to smile or to speak encouraging words. He is a good man; everyone in Pont Ysaf speaks well of him. Even her grandfather, harshly critical of most, had nothing to say against him except that he had become too much the English gentleman, and that he spoilt his son.

'Gareth used to hallucinate when he was younger,' the doctor says.

Olwen startles. 'How?'

'It was after his mother died – about a year after. During the time that we still lived in our London house. He must have been ten or eleven years old then.'

'Did he see his mother?'

'No, nothing so easily explained.' The doctor's eyes grow distant, focused somewhere beyond Olwen, beyond the garden where they sit. She recognizes the expression. He is looking back into the past, as she has so often done herself.

'What then?' she prompts him.

For a moment he says nothing, and when he speaks it is not to answer her question. 'My wife was an artist, not a famous one, though she could have been, *would* have been, I'm sure, had she lived. She had great talent, a true eye for form and colour – and something more. Genius.' He smiles shyly, not at Olwen, but as if he had offered this word to the woman he speaks of and she had laughed and shaken her head.

Olwen sees his grey eyes brighten with love, as if the woman stood, now, just behind her. Almost, she glimpses her reflection in the doctor's eyes, senses her presence, light, teasing, like the flutter of a scented handkerchief. She wants to turn her head, but the doctor continues:

'Art, however, requires dedication, and Sarah was dedicated already to Gareth and me. She put us first.' He smiles tenderly, rubbing his chin across his hands, as if gently reproving his wife for her generosity. 'She'd never have seen it that way, though. Never felt it, I'm sure. I felt it for her – and, selfishly, did nothing. I found too much happiness in her company. How we claim the lives of those who love us! We excuse ourselves, promising we'll repay, make them take their share, knowing quite well they'll never call in our debt.' The doctor falls silent. The lines at the corners of his eyes tighten. He's right, Olwen thinks. I have a debt to pay for all I was given.

'You said Gareth saw things?'

'Yes, but I must explain how it came about, so bear with me. Sarah illustrated children's books, fairytales. Gareth loved to watch her work. Some of the pictures – his favourites – she made copies of and he hung them in his bedroom.'

'What were they? What kind of pictures did he like?'

'Adventure scenes – like all boys, I suppose. Knights jousting or fighting dragons – anything with movement, action. She was very good at capturing movement. You could feel, looking at her drawings, that they were about to spring into life. One he had showed a knight battling with an evil spirit. It was quite terrifying, not the stuff for children, I thought, but Sarah said, yes, children love that sort of thing.' He cocks his head, as if he hears his wife's voice saying this. 'She must have been right for she never lacked commissions – swamped with them most of the time.

'Another of Gareth's favourites showed a young girl on a great horse. She was fleeing from something, though the picture didn't show what. And that was the core of Sarah's genius – what she was able to suggest. The way the horse leaped over the ground, the strain in its body, the girl clinging to its mane – and a great turmoil in the landscape. You got the sense that the pursuer was on their heels, just outside the picture, and that it was something monstrous.'

Olwen leans closer to the doctor. 'These were the pictures he put on his wall?'

'Oh, and others, but they were his favourites. Until they began to work too forcibly on his imagination.' Dr Lloyd stops, his grey eyes worried. Slowly he shakes his head. To Olwen he seems sunk in a waking dream whose content he cannot fathom. Although he answers her questions, he doesn't look at her. Other scenes, other people fill his vision, the past blurring the present. Observing him, Olwen feels intense excitement, for his behaviour confirms her own belief. Flimsy as a net curtain, the division between 'then' and 'now' can be torn down if grasped by a resolute hand. The doctor, though, only gazes through the curtain without attempting to lift it. Memory gives him pain, and pleasure, but no hope.

'What did the spirit look like – in the picture of the knight?'

'Fearsome. A great bearded creature rising out of a swirling mist with his arms thrust out like the wings of a gigantic crow. Some sort of cloak he had on –'

'An enchanter? Was he an enchanter?'

The doctor's eyes focus at last on her face. He rubs his chin, smiling in his normal, wry fashion, back in the present again. 'Could have been. I'm not too well up on magic. My parents were pragmatic folk. The lives of great men, my father bred me on. Didn't do me any harm, I suppose – but it turned me into a factual person. I don't have much imagination, Olwen. Not of that sort, anyway.'

'The girl on the horse. Did that picture belong to the same story as the knight?'

'I couldn't say. You'd have to ask Gareth. Which reminds me of my point. I've digressed, I see. After his mother died, Gareth had waking nightmares – hallucinations, as I said – and saw those pictures come to life.'

'You mean he saw the enchanter?'

'Or whatever it was. He saw the girl too. She stood by his bed and asked him to help her escape.'

'What did he say about the enchanter?'

'He was never very coherent about him. Too frightening for a child to articulate, I'm sure. We moved down here shortly after these things started. It seemed to me that the hallucinations were part of Gareth's distress at losing his mother – a child's way of showing grief and fear. But I was afraid too that he was developing a quality Sarah had, a certain sombreness – melancholy, if you will – that struck me as dangerous. We left the house and came to this part of Wales because my wife grew up here.'

'Here? In Pont Ysaf?' Olwen knits her fingers.

'Over in Maes-Y-Coed, on the other side of the Cwm. I'm a Cardiff chap myself, but Sarah loved the country. It seemed to me that here I could help Gareth form a healthier connection with his mother. Treading the paths she trod and all that, you know. I suppose, like Wordsworth, I believe that nature restores. Seems to have done the trick. Gareth *is* a normal, healthy young man, I think.'

'What happened to the pictures?' Olwen, her mind on the mother, finds no interest, for the moment, in discussing the son. I'd like to see them,' she says.

'I packed them away, hoping Gareth wouldn't ask for them in a new place. And he never did. I have them in a box somewhere, but I couldn't put my hand on them without a great deal of searching.'

'Gareth didn't have any more . . . hallucinations?'

'Never. I doubt he even remembers them now. I've never told anyone this, Olwen. I tell you because it seems to me something similar is happening to you –'

'You think I'm hallucinating?'

'Are you? Do you see things that frighten you?'

Olwen feels the need to confide in him now, to share with him the vision of the woman in blue, to tell him of the enchanter and his possession of her grandfather. In time she stops herself . . . rather, something stops her . . . a voice, not her own, yet inside her: Careful, now. Don't show your hand. You'll ruin it all.

Grandfather?

Aye, aye, remember what I've always told you. Only us two. We don't want another in it.

Are you near then?

Nearer than you think, lovely girl. Nearer than you dream.

Instead of joy, a chill runs through Olwen. The voice is his and yet not his. Faintly menacing, it's the voice that emerged during his illness to tease and taunt her, to say, 'Come to the Cwm when summer's here.'

The doctor is looking at her gravely. Dissemble, dissemble, Olwen thinks. Don't trust him. 'I don't see things. I've never seen anything like Gareth did.'

'But when I came through the gate you *looked* as if you'd seen a ghost. If not, what frightened you?'

'Nothing. Just a fancy. When I was little I used to listen for my grandfather coming up the lane from work. I heard your footsteps and thought –'

How easy guile is! She tells the half-truth without faltering and the doctor nods his head, accepting it.

'I left my car outside the Millers. I paid them a call first.'

'Is one of them ill?'

'No indeed. They're in the best of health, as young people should be. Just a routine visit. I like to keep in touch with my patients. I hear you've been invited to dinner on Saturday? I'm glad of that. I hoped you and Rosamund would become friends.'

'It's my grandmother she likes.'

'Oh, you too. She said so. By the way, Gareth will be home on Sunday.'

'So soon?'

The doctor smiles. 'I won't tell him you said that when he asks about you.'

'Don't send him to see me either, please.'

'My dear girl, I don't *send* him anywhere. He does as he chooses.'

'I meant – would you tell him not to come?'

'I'll pass on the message. I can't promise he'll listen. He's foolhardy sometimes. All those stories his mother told, you know – knights and their quests – have affected him. I think he imagines you are *his* quest!'

The doctor lays his hand on her shoulder. 'Never mind. It all passes. Shall we go in and see how Nain's doing? She'll give me a cup of tea, I dare say. Rosamund's a fine young woman, but she can't brew up like your grandmother.'

Eight

Olwen sits cross-legged on her bedroom floor amid old shoe boxes. All the lids are off and the contents dumped out, the treasures of her childhood strewing the blue carpet. From a heap of shells gathered on the beach at Swansea she takes a speckled cowrie the texture of china. Aunt Pridwyn gave her this fancy shell. 'In case you miss the sea at home,' she said, lifting Olwen's hair and placing the shell to her ear. 'Hear the waves roar?'

Listening now, Olwen hears the breakers crash on the rocks at Mumbles Head. She sees Aunt Pridwyn's big white house on the seafront, the verandah where they sat in the evenings after Aunt Pridwyn had served dinner to her paying guests. The five of them, Gwen, Olwen, Pridwyn, Gwyneth and Gwyneira, would draw chairs into a circle around a low table where Aunt Pridwyn lit a little oil lamp, a bright flame dancing inside a fluted porcelain cup on which she had painted sprays of forget-me-not. Gwen knitted, a sweater or a scarf for Olwen, and Pridwyn told stories of their younger days, the girls egging her on, half-enchanted, half-amused, the swish of the sea like bitter-sweet music in the background, as if, Olwen thinks, they were watching an old-fashioned melodrama, hilarious, but heart-rending too:

'Remember Glanville Morris, Gwen, the night he serenaded you with a ram's horn?'

'Come again? A ram's horn? Are you serious? An old Welsh custom, was it, or couldn't he afford a guitar?' Gwyneth had rounded her eyes at Olwen and Gwyneira.

'He was a student at the agricultural college and he borrowed the horn from there. He was mad in love with Gwen, but she wouldn't give him the time of day –'

'Oh, that's not true, Pridwyn. I didn't want to encourage him –'

'She had so many courting her, Glanville couldn't get a look in. It was Emrys Owen you fancied then, wasn't it, Gwen?'

'Emrys Owen? Never! He was too wild for me, a gambler and a mountain fighter –'

'What's a mountain fighter?' Olwen asked.

'In them days, young men would go up on the mountain and box, bare fist. Emrys was the South Wales champion and all the girls in Swansea thought he was God's gift.'

'I didn't. All that money he won and he couldn't keep a penny in his pocket. There was something unsteady about him. Besides, I didn't hold with the fighting. A man who'd do that must have a violent nature, I always thought.'

'Oh, you had a soft spot for him, don't deny it. What about that Sunday afternoon he turned up unexpected and you ran upstairs to put on your new hat with the tulle flowers? When you came down, our Dad said, "Have you been invited to a garden party, Gwendoline?" and you turned as red as the roses on your hat. And Emrys, dressed to the nines himself, in a fancy suit and a black trilby, the two of you sitting in the parlour stiff as mannequins, and Dad in his shirt sleeves, looking over the Sunday paper at Emrys's two-toned shoes and saying, "Where are you employed now, Emrys? A good-paying job, is it?"'

'I love the clothes you used to wear in those days,' Gwyneira said. 'All that lace and chiffon and crêpe de chine. No wonder the men were so romantic.'

'What about the ram's horn?' Gwyneth said. 'Tell us about that. Very symbolic it sounds.' She was eighteen then, in her first year at Swansea University, studying literature. She left a year later to get married. Gwyneira was fifteen, Olwen twelve.

'Late one night – we were all asleep – Glanville came to the house and stood under Gwen's window blowing this horn. I never heard such a horrible noise, worse than a factory hooter or a ship's siren. I put my head out of the window, and there was Gwen with her head out, and Dad and Mam, too. Dad was playing the bear, shouting and swearing, but Glanville just blew the horn and didn't pay him any notice. It was like he was drunk, wasn't it?'

'Drunk with passion,' Gwyneira said.

'What did Grandpa do?'

'He went down to take the horn away, but Glanville wouldn't give it. "I'm sick in love with your daughter, Mr Roberts," he said, "and nothing can cure me." "A boot in the arse might," Dad said, "and I'm about to give you one if you don't clear off." Glanville had nerve, I must say. Our father wasn't a small man, or a patient one either. But you had that effect on men, Gwen – like an enchantress. I can see you now, leaning out of your window, your hair hanging down like Rapunzel's, in that nightgown with all the ribbons and tucks –'

'Oh, go on with you. That boy had something seriously wrong with him, I'm sure.'

'Men *were* more romantic in those days, weren't they?'

'How did you get rid of him and his horn? *Did* Grandpa kick him?'

'I ran down and whispered in his ear, "My sister's in love with Emrys Owen and he's in love with her. He'll kill you if he hears." That put the wind up Glanville and he went, quiet as a lamb. Emrys used to fight for Gwen up on Culvert mountain. Challenged any fella that came near her.'

'My God, it's like the cinema,' Gwyneth said.

'No, like a fairytale.' And Olwen had looked curiously at her grandmother. How did Grandfather win you away from all those men, she'd wanted to ask. But John's name was never mentioned in the Swansea house, and he never figured in Aunt Pridwyn's stories, so she had kept her mouth shut. Lying in bed later, thinking about it, she had reshaped the question. It began, she realized, not with 'how' but with 'why'. In this form, it has recurred throughout the years since her aunt's stories ceased, the circle broken by Gwyneth's marriage, Gwyneira's boyfriends, and Olwen's rejection, as she grew older, of all activities that excluded her grandfather.

Now, as she cups the speckled shell in her palm and holds it to her ear, she sees herself as a little girl in a ruched bathing suit wading into the sea with her grandmother and her aunt. The women's skirts are tucked into their knicker legs, their stockings removed, though from the waist up they remain decorous, each in a long-sleeved lawn blouse fastened at the neck with a brooch. Their long hair blows free, whipped from its fastenings by a strong breeze. Her aunt's hair flies out like dark wings, her grandmother's a spill of copper coins. She hears the women's laughter, sees their flushed faces, as they hold her hands and lead her into the waves.

'Lie on our hands, love,' Gwen says. 'We'll teach you to swim.'

'Don't be afraid,' Aunt Pridwyn says. 'We won't let go of you.'

Trusting them, she had learned to keep up in the water, though her stroke was all wrong, for her instructors, self-taught, had shown her a method that was really only a struggle against going under. They taught her as they had taught Gwyneth and Gwyneira, and none of them ever went out of their depth in the sea at Swansea.

Her grandfather had not known about the swimming lessons, nor about the evenings on the verandah. She wrote to him daily, but kept to factual statements: 'We had pork chops for dinner and trifle for dessert. It rained so we couldn't go to the beach,' and so on, each sentence carefully scanned in her mind before she wrote it down for words that might suggest she enjoyed herself without him.

Olwen lays the shell among the others.

Another box contained dozens of paper figures, copied from pictures in fairytale books, coloured with crayons, and cut out – knights in plumed helmets, princesses with long ropes of hair, a king in a gold crown larger than his head, dragons, giants, elves – and, yes, here is a black-cloaked enchanter, a scribbled beard hiding half his face. Holding the figure between her thumb and forefinger, Olwen remembers how she played with these cut-outs for hours, her grandfather away at the mine, her grandmother gratifyingly inattentive when Olwen talked to herself in many voices, or, in the thick of an adventure, knocked over an ornament, toppled a chair.

How safe she had felt then, the enchanter just a plaything like the other figures, taking his turn when she needed him, lying forgotten in the box when he had no role in the game. Now the paper image unnerves her. She lets it drop from her fingers onto the pile, then quickly pushes it to the bottom and turns to other items.

Lucky charms, Christmas ornaments, and old costume jewellery discarded by Gwen litter the rug, together with coins, keys, dominoes, dice, coloured discs for Ludo. What a collector she had been. Nothing thrown away, yet the one thing she wants, feels sure she put in a box for safe keeping, can't be found.

One box gave her hope when she began the search. Crammed with folded papers, it seemed the one in which she would most likely have put the chocolate-box picture. All the papers are out and unfolded now, and they are paintings she did in infant school, or at home on wet afternoons. Paint, slapped on thick, flaked from the sheets as she unfolded them, showering into her lap like confetti. The paintings show a sameness: three beachball figures stand on a green line, a blue line above their heads, sometimes a vermilion sun, a tree, flowers, a bird. Simple pictures, they suggest a child secure and loved, never spurred or troubled by fancy because there was nothing to wish for or dread.

Olwen glances again at the pile of cut-outs heaped on the rug like victims of a tiny mayhem. She remembers the violence that sometimes figured in her play. In an imaginary battle, she tore off paper arms and legs, severed heads, and cast the remnants into the parlour fire. These atrocities, performed by ogres, evil knights – often by the enchanter, singlehanded – never frightened her as she roamed her make-believe world, her grandmother only steps away, poised at the edge of her vision, respecting the boundary until Olwen needed her to say, 'Put those things away now. It's nearly teatime.'

But at night, when she lay in bed after her grandfather had told her a story and left, the terrors came. Pale knights with drawn swords emerged from the shadows, witches with red malice in their eyes sidled toward her bed, harpies hovered under the rafters, a gorgon head stared out of the mirror on her dressing table. And somewhere, unseen, lurked an even more ominous presence, the puppet-master who made these monsters move. She sensed him always, though she did not know then that he was the enchanter.

Olwen frowns. Something in this memory strikes her as wrong. The childish paintings, too, seem to misrepresent. All of them contain three figures, always in the same grouping, two smiling beach balls on either side of a smaller circle, its stick arms reaching out to both of them. Was there a time when she loved them both equally? A time when her grandmother's presence meant as much to her, comforted her as much, as her grandfather's?

More, possibly?

Fiercely, Olwen rejects this notion. She has always loved him best. He was the one who went to London to bring her home on the train, a baby. His were the first arms that wrapped around her. Alice had never held her.

'I was the first,' he told her.

She has always known this, so what causes the doubt – the lie – to spring into her mind?

Swiftly, Olwen looks around the room, then over her shoulder to the window. It is filled with blue sky, nothing more. Sunlight streams into the little room, lighting all its corners; there are no shadows, no dark places.

Yet something has entered . . . something stealthy, invisible, plants this thought. It's a thought akin to those her grandfather must have had during his illness when he betrayed her, choosing Alice, the mother Olwen can't love. It was she, of course, who appeared in the garden. She came to taunt me, Olwen thinks, because he's gone where I can't reach him. Where she can, perhaps? Yet, if so, why did she display such rage? And how could her grandfather have doted on a creature so arrogant, so wilful? How could he prefer Alice when she, Olwen, loved him so entirely, never questioning or disobeying?

Olwen stops these thoughts. They, too, verge on betrayal. He did not love her mother more. It was only the enchanter's guile made it seem so when he threw up visions of Alice to deceive her grandfather, weak and weary from his long illness. She has read of hypnotists, Svengalis, who make fools of their victims, causing them to speak in many tongues, to bark like dogs and howl like wolves. And she has read, too, of demons who possess afflicted humans, reducing them to minions, mouthpieces for their own horrid, obscene utterances. Many a winter evening, she and her grandfather read such tales and mulled over the diversities and deceptions of the magic realm and its denizens.

'They got tricks up their sleeves, all right,' he told her when he was well and hearty, 'and only the vigilant can outwit them.'

The enchanter was master of mesmerists, emperor of eidolons. 'We got to stand together, stand firm. He can't beat us unless he divide us first.'

As he assailed her grandfather, so he attacks her now, his weapons, doubt and jealousy, craftily chosen from his vast armoury as the ones most likely to vanquish her.

Olwen gets up, crosses to the window and looks out at the Cwm, splendid in rich, trailing greenery. Somewhere in its midst they wait for her, her grandfather and his adversary – now, perhaps, his keeper – and, grotesquely, his accomplice in this one matter: both want her to enter the woods.

Gwen comes out onto the garden path, her shopping bag over her arm. It is Saturday morning. Seeing her, Olwen thinks of the boxes she has just explored, their contents still heaped on the carpet behind her, and she is overwhelmed by feelings she can hardly decipher.

'Nain!' she calls.

Gwen looks up.

'I'll go with you as far as the bus stop.' Olwen slips on her sandals and runs downstairs, out of the house into sunshine.

'Rosamund's not going to town this morning,' Gwen says as they go through the gate. 'Too busy cooking for us, she said. I told her not to go to any trouble. What shall we take, Olwen? Should I buy a bottle of wine in town? I don't know what's what, though. Maybe a bunch of flowers from the garden –'

'Wine's better,' Olwen says quickly. 'You can ask someone at the off-licence what kind.'

When they reach Bryn Brewen's gate, they see him in his garden, tying up tomato plants.

'Morning, Bryn,' Gwen says. 'You're up early. Doing a bit of gardening?'

Gelert sits on the path, close to his master. When he sees Gwen and Olwen, he thumps his tail and makes little noises in his throat, more like a lap dog than a hunter. The dog always greets Olwen eagerly, surprising her, for she has never shown him affection. His lack of ferocity surprises her, too. She has seen him run away when Aunt Flindy's cat, Cinders, appears, arched and hissing, on top of the common wall. She can't imagine him pouncing on animals in the Cwm, though he does, presumably, or why would Bryn keep him?

'Just doing what I have to, nothing fancy.' Bryn comes down the path, rubbing his palms on his army pants as if preparing to shake hands. His wiry hair is pulled back and fastened behind in a badger's tail. 'I'm not fanatical like Olwen here.' He rests his arms on the gate. 'Been working in that garden as if your life depended on it, haven't you, love?' Below his grimy, rolled-up sleeves, his arms are hairy, tough as leather. 'Off to town, is it?'

'Just me,' Gwen says. 'Olwen's giving me company as far as the bus stop.'

'Nice that you're company for each other.' He cocks his head towards his right shoulder to give Olwen a sly, sideways look. 'I expect you have a lot to talk about, too.' His voice is soft, smooth, unmatched to his leathery exterior. Like the wolf who put butter on his tongue. 'Myself, I don't yearn for company – not any more. I'm not a big talker.' His eyes shift to Gwen. 'I keep my mouth shut unless there's something needs saying.'

Olwen sees her grandmother's face flush. 'That's right,' Gwen says in a tight voice, as if he's offended her. 'Idle talk serves no purpose.'

'I could say a lot, though, if I'd a mind to.'

'No point,' Gwen says. 'Let sleeping dogs lie, isn't it? Olwen, I'll miss my bus if we don't move.'

Hurrying beside her grandmother, who is stepping out smartly, Olwen glances back at Bryn's grey face, his bushy hair like briar, his black eyes watching her.

Swiftly, she turns away. 'What did he mean, he could say a lot?'

'How should I know? He wants to bring up some old trouble with your grandpa, I dare say. You know they didn't get on.'

'Why would he want to do that?'

'People like to tell their side of things, that's all. But there's no use talking to us. Nothing we can do for him.'

'Why did he and Grandfather fall out?'

Gwen turns her head to look into the woods where bluebell patches show among the trees. Beside the ditch, cowslips, foxgloves, tall buttercups, and wild orchids crowd the grass.

'He had a fancy for your mother once. Your grandpa didn't like it.'

They have reached the turning into Pont Ysaf Road. Olwen stops. 'My *mother*? Bryn Brewen?'

'Is that such a shock?'

'I never thought of them knowing each other.'

'Of course they knew each other. Bryn's lived next door for over twenty years, since he was a young man.'

The truth, Olwen realizes, is that she has never thought of her mother as a real person. Whenever Alice crossed her mind – swiftly to be dismissed – she drifted, barely visible, across an anonymous scenario of tall buildings and busy streets Olwen thought of as 'London'. She has never pictured her in the house in Archer's Lane, a child playing in the garden, running along the path in the Cwm, sleeping in one of the bedrooms, doing first all the things Olwen has done . . . her mother as a girl growing up into a woman . . . and her grandfather treating

Alice as he treated Olwen, loving, protecting, instructing her . . . all this, she cannot imagine.

'Wasn't he too old for her? Is that why Grandfather didn't like it?'

'Bryn's forty-eight. If your mother had lived, she'd be forty-one. That's not such a big age difference. Your grandfather was ten years older than me.'

'Did *she* fancy him?'

'She went off to London when she was nineteen.'

'She couldn't have cared about him then, could she?'

'Here's the bus.' Gwen sounds relieved. She waves to Morgan Pryce as he passes them to make a U-turn. 'I'll see you at quarter past two. I hope I don't make a mistake with the wine.'

Gwen gets on the bus. Today she wears a grey silk dress scattered with pink flowers, a straw boater perched jauntily above her bun. She takes the seat behind Morgan Pryce and smiles at Olwen through the window, happy to be going among people. Morgan, already talking to her, touches his cap to Olwen.

When the bus disappears round a bend, Olwen stands looking down the empty road. For as long as she can remember, her grandmother has dressed in her best on Saturday mornings and gone off to town as gladly as if she were setting off on a holiday – or for a rendezvous. Much younger, Olwen often stood on the bottom rung of the gate and watched Gwen go down the lane, high-stepping over puddles and potholes, her auburn hair hanging down her back like bullion pouring from a pirate's chest. She had made up a game, pretending that her grandmother was meeting a secret admirer – she hadn't known the word 'lover' then – who lived in the white farmhouse, visible in the distance from the road where she now stands. Olwen knows the family who own this farm. The husband delivers their milk, the wife breeds horses, the children went to school with her. But in the story she invented, this was not so:

Instead of going to the bus stop, Gwen crossed Pont Ysaf Road every Saturday morning and pushed open the gate into the fields. She waltzed through the waving corn into the arms of a big, red-faced farmer who wore Wellington boots and smelled of hay. In the farmhouse he had a feast spread for her, and he sat beside her, kissing her hand, as she ate strawberries and cream and fresh-baked scones. When it was time for her to leave, he packed her bag with cheese, butter, sausages, bacon rashers, and apples and pears from his orchard – everything she might have bought in town – a carton of brown eggs on top, and a bag of toffees for Olwen. Gwen always brought her sweets.

When her grandmother came home and tumbled her purchases onto the kitchen table, she'd talk to Olwen about events in Pont Ysaf. 'There was ever such a long queue at Milwood's,' she'd say. 'I was afraid he'd sell out of pork chops before my turn,' or, 'I got a lovely cream sponge in Howfield's. Mrs Pugh saved it for me special. She knows your grandpa's weakness for fresh cream.'

Olwen, sitting at the table, her chin cupped in her hands, would smile at these alibis. When Gwen handed her the paper bag filled with toffees, she'd pop one in her mouth, giggle, and say, 'I know they're from a shop, but they *taste* homemade.'

Standing in the road now, Olwen wonders why she invented a lover for her grandmother, and why she had felt no guilt, making up stories in which her grandfather was betrayed. Had she felt sorry for Gwen? Or had she done it out of wishfulness, willing her grandmother to leave so that she, Olwen, could have her grandfather all to herself? But he had always been hers – 'Only you I love in all this world, *cariad*.'

She wonders how he behaved when he courted Gwen. Surely he must have been kind, treated her well, or why would she have fallen for him with so many men after her? So how had the change occurred? Did something happen between them that she doesn't know about, something before her birth? Or could her grandfather love only one person at a time, first Gwen, then Alice, then Olwen, but never all three of them?

Olwen feels a weakness in her legs and sits down in the grass among the tall rosebay willowherbs that grow so profusely. She crosses her legs and her arms, making herself compact, and the red willowherbs enclose her. 'The most common flower round here,' he told her, 'and the truest. See, they're like spears with blood on them. Our history's in them flowers,' and he would talk about invasions, Roman, Norman, English, foreign soldiers sent to subjugate the Celtic tribes, soldiers of the realm ordered to subdue striking miners. 'Wales never had a chance. We had no peace till they broke us.'

Olwen snaps the stalk of a willowherb and plucks the red petals, one by one, laying them in a row along her thigh. In the hedge across the road bees hum drowsily, drunk on honeysuckle and wild rose. The flower she strips has no perfume. Only a faint, bitter scent rises as she digs her nails into the sap. Tiny, colourless drops run down the stem from the cuts and trickle into the well of her fingers. Transparent circles form where the sticky drops congeal on her skin. When the line of petals has reached her knee, she begins another beside it. Bent over her task, she feels the sun on the crown of her head, like a warm palm cupping it, as if he stood over her, watching. Often, in her childhood, absorbed in some game, she would become aware of him in this way. He would come quietly so as not to interrupt her play, and place his hand on her head or her shoulder, saying nothing, only letting her know he was there, that he waited. She would discard her game at once, glad for the interruption, preferring his company to any pastime.

Olwen drops the willowherb stem. Brushing her fingers across her thigh, she scatters the petals. Like a child believing in the efficacy of charms, she says aloud, 'Grandfather, come,' and repeats the words over and over, her head drooping towards her clasped hands.

Something in the air – a change in the motion of the breeze, a sharpening of the light – alerts her. Hopefully, fearfully, she lifts her head. They are coming down the road towards her, from the direction of Cefn Heights. At first they are insubstantial, airy, like the woman in blue as she emerged from the delphiniums. Hues of the roadside flowers, scarlet, mauve, ochre and shades of green, show through their transparent bodies, as if they are dressed in carnival colours. Rapidly they come, as if borne on a strong wind, kaleidoscopic figures that, as they draw nearer, assume solid shapes.

She sees his flowing white hair, his green and brown dog's-tooth cap and jacket, his brown face and hands. The child's dark plaits bounce as she trots beside him, her hand tucked into his. The skirt of her pink cotton dress flips on the breeze like a flower petal as she pumps her legs to keep up.

Olwen, watching behind a fence of rosebay willowherb, sees that above their hurtling bodies their faces are immobile, as if the man's were carved from wood, the child's from wax, his eyes painted blue, her cheeks tinted, to resemble life. As they pass by her, the air changes, intensifies, becomes redolent with the scents of musk and camphor; as though she were shut in a closet, she fights for breath. The figures hurry on, oblivious of her, towards Archer's Lane, their haste suggesting lateness or pursuit. Yet the road is empty. No one waits or follows.

Olwen scrambles up and runs after them. Turning into the lane, she sees they have reached the path leading into the Cwm. The child leaps lightly over the ditch, the man crossing it with one long stride. He has no walking stick, no limp. She sees then into a time before his accident, a time when she was very young, four or five years old.

Stopping at the ditch, Olwen looks down the long, sunlit tunnel overhung with boughs and sees them go along it, hand in hand, at great speed. If she crosses over, catches them up, she senses that time will unravel further, alter somehow, allowing her to merge with the apparition of herself and become a child again. But, rooted as the oaks, she can't move. As she watches, the figures lose substance, become a composition of light and shade, and vanish into the trees.

At the sound of gravel scuttering behind her, Olwen swings round. A few yards off, Bryn Brewen stands grinning, tugging at a lock of his wild hair. He has crept up on her, the way he creeps through the woods at night.

'Nice morning for a walk in the Cwm.' His eyes swerve to the path behind her. 'Quiet and peaceful in there. Private.'

The expression on his face as he looks into the woods alarms her. But she needn't fear him here, in broad daylight, the Millers' cottage only a stone's throw away. The pumping at her heart slows and she looks him in the face. He has very white teeth, the two front ones larger than the others, slightly protruding. In contrast his skin looks grey. His is the miner's complexion. Her grandfather got rid of it in fresh air and rain after he retired. Bryn, laid off for years, has it still. The black smudges under his eyes are the colour of anthracite, as if the coal has left a permanent stain. Gwen suspects a case of creeping silicosis, but to Olwen he looks as if he has been shut up in a tomb.

'I'm not going for a walk,' she says. 'I'm going home.'

'Why don't you go to town with Nain never?'

'I've work to do.'

'Like the old man, you are. He wouldn't go nowhere with Gwen, would he? And you take after him. You're not like *her* in your nature. She was never a home bird.' He shuffles his feet on the gravel. His hobnailed boots are caked with dried mud. His hands, thrust into his trouser pockets, make two lumps, as if he had stones there.

'It's just that she likes to shop and I don't.'

'I didn't mean your granny.'

'Who then?'

'You're like her in her face though, right enough.'

He means Alice. Revulsion rises in Olwen. She can't bear to think that her mother had anything to do with this man who frightens and sickens her. 'I have to go.' She looks pointedly up the lane, barred by his body.

'I got something to show you.' His eyelids flicker, a nervous twitch. 'I could have shown you before, but you wouldn't come in. Not when he was there. Now you can. It's time you saw it. If you'll just stop in a minute . . .?' He speaks softly, ingratiatingly, as if he were wooing her, his head turned towards his shoulder, as though to hide his face, his intentions, in the bush of hair.

Olwen realizes what she dislikes so intensely in his voice. It's sticky-warm like the toffee she ate as a child. If she chewed too large a lump, it stuck to her teeth, giving her a panicky feeling, as if with her mouth so full she would choke.

'I can't. I don't have time. Let me pass, please.' She steps towards him, but he doesn't move out of her way.

'You ought to see it. You ought to know. You're old enough.' His eyes flicker over her body. 'A woman,' he says. 'A young woman.'

'I don't want to, I said.'

She's level with him now, smelling his grass and earth scent. She moves to sidestep him. His right arm shoots out in front of her, like a bar at a railway crossing. 'Come in the house with me.'

Ducking under his arm, Olwen runs up the lane, gravel spraying under her feet, her hair flying. When she reaches her own gate and puts out her hand to the latch, it's not there. A strip of jagged wood shows where it has been torn from the post. A sob rises in her throat and she feels her knees give. But Bryn still stands in the lane, looking after her, so Olwen pushes open the gate and stumbles up the path.

Nine

'Stay away from Bryn Brewen,' her grandfather warned her. But how can she unless she never goes out? And what of the woman in blue – the apparition of Alice? How can she protect herself from her mother's ghost and the spite and rage it manifests? Twice the latch has been torn from the gate. The first time, Olwen felt herself to be an accidental witness of the destruction, the spectre's malice bent on another. This time the broken latch seems menacing, a portent of harm, a warning that she has a part in whatever foul purpose conjures the dead woman from her grave.

Slowly, Olwen climbs the stairs. It's clear now why Bryn has always watched her, why he stops her in the lane, his eyes slipping over her greedily. She reminds him of her mother. Whom he loved, apparently. Olwen flinches at the word. Not love, surely. A man like Bryn could never love. Whom he wanted, then. Having failed to get Alice, does he want to get her instead?

On the landing Olwen stops and leans against the wall. Wrapping her arms around her waist, she thinks about her next-door neighbour. In the fairytales she read with her grandfather, a handsome prince often masqueraded as a beast to test the heroine, throwing off the disguise when he'd won her heart. With Bryn, the pattern seems reversed. He is like a wild, dangerous animal pretending to be human, his golden-syrup voice and deferential manner tricks to lure his prey.

Once Olwen, out with her grandfather, had seen a collie turn on a sheep and savage it. The shepherd had immediately clubbed the dog to death. As he led her away from the fence where they'd stopped to watch the collie driving the herd, her grandfather said, 'A bad 'un, and that fella should have spotted it before he lost a sheep. There's always signs if you're alert.'

He must have seen the signs in Bryn Brewen. It's why he

warned her. If he had known, why didn't he do something to protect her from harm? They could have moved from Archer's Lane. True, he hated the town, but couldn't he have put up with it for the sake of her safety?

No, that's unfair. He never knew how Bryn harassed her. Fearing a row, she'd never told him of the encounters in the lane. To him, their neighbour was detestable but not dangerous. Besides, he believed he could keep her safe anywhere. He hadn't foreseen leaving her so soon.

Olwen looks up the passage to the closed door at the end. A need to enter that room stirs again, though she knows she will not feel closer to him there. Nowhere in the house now is there a place where she feels his presence. Yet, alive, he had filled it. Surely it should be as Dr Lloyd said: a beloved person's spirit – essence – should pervade the home he shared?

Olwen climbs the two steps to the passage. At Gwen's door she pauses to look into her room. The double bed is covered with a quilt of deep rose, the rug and curtains dusty pink. A vase of Gloire de Dijon roses stands on the dressing table, their perfume mingling with Gwen's lily-of-the-valley scent. It's the room of a woman who sleeps alone, tasteful, gracious even, but entirely feminine. For as long as Olwen can remember, her grandparents slept separately. So her grandmother's room is not the place to seek memories.

Leaning in the doorway, Olwen looks at the room in a way she never has before, her eyes lingering on each item. Gwen, she sees, likes to create and possess beautiful things. The dressing-table runner, the scalloped pillow cases, the plump cushion on the basket chair are all intricately embroidered. Pink rosebuds, tiny yellow daisies, and blue loveknots edge the runner and the pillow cases; full-blown red roses on long, curving stems grace the cushion. Countless evenings, she has seen her grandmother seated by the kitchen fire with her sewing basket, a length of material across her knees, her needle flying; and she has seen, without remark, the results of her work, chair-backs and doilies and cushion covers, the patchwork quilt on her own bed, the broderie anglaise on her dressing-table skirt and on the petticoats she wears. She has seen and accepted Gwen's work without thought. Sewing was simply something her grandmother did, a skill that Olwen, trailing her grandfather about his garden, did not consider or feel any desire to learn. Now, looking for the first time at Gwen's bedroom, she sees how her grandmother used her needle and thread to weave enchantment for herself. It's the room of a woman who dreams a life she has not lived, who has distilled her dreams in order to endure the life given her.

'My grandmother's room,' Olwen thinks, and, gazing at the rose-coloured quilt, imagines until the images blur her sight. Pressing her fingers to her eyelids, she thinks of other rooms in the house, conjures them up behind her closed eyes to see if she can discover in any of them, legacies of her grandfather, objects so infused with his spirit that they will move her as her grandmother's possessions do now.

The kitchen, of course, was always Gwen's domain. He never entered it except for meals. The copper pots above the stove, the willow-pattern china on the dresser, the spotless surfaces, all bespeak her grandmother – her faultless, cheerful housekeeping. Even the sun filling the bay window connects, in Olwen's mind, with Gwen standing at the table to serve meals, pour tea, arrange flowers.

The parlour, then, where they spent so many hours? She pictures the room she has hardly entered since the funeral: the leather armchair by the fireplace, his favourite seat in winter; against the wall behind the chair, a bookcase holding the books they shared. What else? The sofa, the grandfather clock, the knick-knacks, all must have been chosen and purchased by Gwen. She was the one who bought things for the house. At her request, he made small pieces occasionally, but really he had no interest in furnishing the cottage.

So the parlour is not his room either. When they sat there, the place they inhabited took shape from his own fancy, from his stories and conjurations. Its props were ephemeral – the play of shadow and light on the walls, the flickering flames of the fire, the grey carpet becoming a stormy sea, rocking the arm-chair boat, the sofa an island, the long shadows . . .

'The alligators are all around the boat, Grandfather!'

'Aye, I see them. Quick, pull up your legs before they nip your toes. *Cwtch* up to me now. We'll be on the island soon, sucking pomegranates, happy as monkeys.'

It was a place of the mind . . . and of the emotions. She remembers the sweet terror as she snuggled in his lap, made a nest of his body, eagerly complicitous in the adventures he spun.

His deep coal- and tobacco-roughened voice and strong, embracing arms, the scent of Havana, the beat of his heart against her cheek – these are the things she associates with him, not the fixtures of the parlour, which he never seemed to observe, never referred to, except to turn them into something else.

Her own room then? Olwen takes the two steps from her grandmother's door to her own and stands in the doorway, recalling how, on the day of the funeral, she thought she sensed John's presence here. It should still be so, for almost everything in the room has come from him as gifts to her. He gave her the pictures, books, knick-knacks, made her a bookcase, shelves, and the little table for her bedside lamp, and all to her tastes, which he knew well – as he should, for he shaped them. Yet they are her possessions, not his.

And perhaps there lies the source of his absence. In this room, as in all the rooms in the cottage, there is nothing that he chose for himself, not a single book or piece of furniture he prized, no object of which she might say to herself, 'My grandfather loved this.' How could a person live in one place so long, all his married life, upward of forty years, and leave no tangible imprint?

Olwen raises her eyes to the rafter above her bed, to the carving he fashioned there with his pocket knife. Viewed from this angle, it is unrecognizable as a human face. To see it as such one would have to stand directly under it, or lie on the bed. Even then it might be impossible to perceive among the knots and whorls if one did not know it was there.

Of late Olwen has purposely avoided looking at the face. Now it strikes her forcibly that the one thing in the house which he chose, brought into being from his own desire, is a thing that disturbs her deeply.

Yet he could not have meant to frighten her. If he could be faulted for anything in his raising of her, it would surely be for over-protectiveness. She recalls the circumstances preceding the carving, the story of the Snow Queen who froze hearts, and her question, 'Have you ever seen a lady as beautiful as her?' Believing him a competent judge in all matters, she had hoped he would say that *she* would possess such beauty when she grew up. Instead, he had spoken of a woman he'd known once, and out of that memory the carving had come.

Jealousy sharpening need, Olwen moves away from her own

door to the one at the end of the corridor. She turns the knob and goes in, the cheerful colours, the cleanliness shocking her afresh. She crosses to the bed and lays her hand on the yellow satin quilt, cupping her palm over one of the stitched, foam-filled mounds, firm as young flesh, pliant under her fingers. Outside the window, in the hazy afternoon sunshine, the woods and garden assume an idyllic aspect. Yet how dreary they must have appeared to her grandfather as he lay here through the winter months, watching rain drip from the branches of the chestnut.

One afternoon, deep in December, a day of drizzling rain and melting snow, he had talked to her as she sat in the window seat of his time at the Pen Colliery on the other side of Pont Ysaf.

'I wanted pit work because the money was good,' he said. 'I had some daft notion as a young feller that I could earn a small fortune in no time and be a free man. I walked all the way from Porthmadoc, like a gypsy, buying my food as I went, sleeping in the fields – in a barn if the weather turned nasty – never so happy in my life as I was on the road, sorry in my heart when I came over Maes-Y-Coed Mountain and saw the Pen Colliery. But I told myself, "Just a few years, boyo, and you'll have money to travel the world." When I came south, I didn't dream what those pay packets would cost me. I thought it was just muscle and backbone the job required. Too late when I found out I had to give my lungs and my heart. I thank God for my accident. The cave-in crushed my leg, but I got my life back.'

'Why did you stay in the pit if you hated it, Grandfather?'

'Because in no time at all after coming down here I made a yoke for my neck out of another foolish notion.'

Olwen had known he referred to Gwen, whom he must have met soon after his arrival. She dearly wanted to know about their courtship. Simple things, like how they had met. Had he taken a day trip to Swansea one Sunday and seen her walking on the promenade in her hat with the tulle roses? How had he managed to speak to her, and what had he said? And there were difficult things she wanted to know, too – about the forces that must once have bound her grandparents and how their love died. But she dared not ask these questions. Instead, she had covered his hand with hers.

His head turned towards the window, he gazed at the snow, rapidly turning into grey slush. 'The colour of them pit ponies. I felt sorrier for them animals than I did for myself. At least I could always come up at the end of a shift. The ponies spent their lives underground, born under there some of them. Never seen daylight nor felt the sun on their backs. Didn't know what it was to gallop across a field or chew the fresh grass. *Daro*, that was a shame! It broke my heart.'

And then, as happened so often in those last months, his mind had leaped. 'I wanted to get her a little pony. She loved to ride. Used to take her on a Saturday, oh, many a time, over to Powell's Farm. We'd hire two horses and ride for an hour. "I wish I had one of my own," she'd say, but I couldn't afford it then. And now look, I got this hefty compo from the pit. I could get her anything she wanted, and it's too late. Why couldn't I have had the accident thirty years back?'

Alice. Tears in his eyes remembering. And jealousy, a needle pricking at Olwen's heart, sewing resentment. He never took me riding. I never knew till now it was something we might have shared. He never wanted to buy me a pony.

Her fingers knead the quilt. Impulsively, she throws herself down on the bed, clutching the satin cover with both hands. You didn't love me best, in spite of everything I did to please you. I loved *you* best, but you never put me first. It was all pretence.

At once jealousy gives way to guilt. Again she is doubting her grandfather, believing things he said when his body and mind were sick. Forgetting the years of devotion, she plays into the hand of the enchanter, whose trump card is suspicion.

Laying her head on the lavender-scented pillow, Olwen wills composure, concentrating on the sun-warmed satin under her body, the sleekness of it against her bare arms and legs. Slipping her hands under her head, she closes her eyes and lets her mind drift.

The hot sun is like a physical weight, an embrace. Sliding her hands to her waist, Olwen lifts her body towards the heat. As if an invisible hand strokes her back, her spine quivers, and she arches up. Then a violent trembling seizes her, and her body thrusts repeatedly, her limbs out of control, as though she suffered from St Vitus' dance. The spasms terrify her, but she can't stop them, can find no connection between her will and her jerking limbs. Tears flow freely. She hears herself sob. The sobs snatch her breath away and she thinks, 'I'm having a fit.

People die like this.' Then she thinks of her hands, focuses on them and pries them away from her waist, rolls them into fists and pounds her stomach until nausea overwhelms her and the spasms cease. Exhausted, she sinks back onto the quilt. Sun-warmed satin, the texture of skin, enfolds her. Queasy, frightened still, she thinks, 'I'm safe. I saved myself.'

Unbidden, an image flits across her mind.

Olwen's eyes fly open. She leaps from the bed and runs out of the room. Down the stairs she races and out of the front door, down the garden path to the gate. Leaning her arms on the top bar, she stares into the Cwm, trying to catch a glimpse of him – for surely he is near. It was he, no other, who put the image into her mind as she lay on her grandfather's sick-bed. Among the trees, she sees no sign of life, but now she grasps the extent of his power. She has looked into his evil heart. Terror and shame make her feel faint and she grips the gate with both hands.

In this part of the lane the trees of the Cwm grow close, their branches intertwined and meshed with creepers. Saplings that have tried to push up under the great oaks have found no space and become stunted and withered. Their deformed branches, bare of leaves, are hung with dead tendrils like long grey beards. One of these latecomers managed to grow several feet taller than its peers before it was forced to halt. Turned back on itself, the trunk has curved so that it vaguely resembles a hunchbacked figure. Its covering of creepers sweeps the ground like a long cloak. Beneath one of its limbs, a smaller sapling has sprung up, as if the hunchback rests on a walking stick. Of this formation, her grandfather liked to joke, 'That's a statue of the old enchanter. He set it there himself to tease us.'

'But he looks like a dwarf, Grandfather. I thought he was gigantic?'

'Oh, that's just one of his disguises, not how he really looks. Trying to make us sorry for him, he is. He's no different from most people in that, though he's not human. Many like to make you think they're small so you'll feel pity and let them take advantage.'

Olwen notices now that the limb resting on the smaller sapling has a gnarled grey finger. The finger points towards the garden wall. She turns her head. It points through the mossy stones to the toolshed, which her grandfather, claiming nothing indoors, built for himself.

In the kitchen Olwen takes the key from the hook and shuts it into her palm. She pauses on the doorstep and looks across the grass to the shed. Glistening in the sun, the black, bulging tarpaulin seems to sweat, like a great dog lathered from the hunt. Behind the sunflowers the little window has a sly gleam, as if the dog watches her, warily.

As she crosses the lawn the image becomes so real in her mind she can almost hear the creature pant, but she knows it's the beat of her own heart. Through the broad leaves of the sunflowers the window reflects a blue sky marred with grime. Behind the glass, a white face looks out.

Olwen stops, her hand leaping to her mouth. Then she recognizes her own face, imprisoned in the window. Catching her breath, she goes on. From the corner of her eye, in a blur of blue, she sees the delphiniums, hears them rustle as if they watch and whisper. At the shed door a sunflower, taller than she, stands guard. Olwen fits the key into the lock and turns it. Creaking, the door swings open.

She is on the threshold of her grandfather's place.

Sun filtering through the window lights the shed with a muted glow, casting the back wall into shadow, sharpening the outlines of objects in the foreground, the workbench, lathe, and shoemaker's last, as if this were not a real place but a still-life in oils. In here, everything he collected over the forty-odd years since he built the shed remains intact.

As soon as she steps inside, she senses him. Her eyes move over the workbench and along the shelves crowded with tins and jam jars to the long box that fills the top shelf, and she feels his presence. In the mingled scents of wood and turpentine, boot polish and linseed oil, his aura wafts, hovers, as if at any moment he will take shape, show himself to her.

When she narrows her eyes, tilts her head at a certain angle, there he is.

He leans over the bench, a knife in his right hand, intent on the piece of wood in front of him. She can see the lines on his face, the creases in his shirt where he has pushed up the sleeves, his brown sinewy arms braceleted with fine silver hairs – even the faint blue-green markings on his nails, like tinted marble, are visible to her. His long hair, tucked behind his ears, clouds over his neck like dandelion down.

'Grandfather,' she says.

At the sound of her voice, no more than a whisper, the image evaporates, becomes simply a sun-filled space where dust motes dance.

Olwen blinks, focuses again . . . but now she cannot bring him back. Instead, her eyes light on the bench, on the objects there, the knife he held, the silver blade flecked with rust near the handle, and beside it, something flat, rectangular. She had thought it a piece of wood. Slowly, dreamily, she recognizes the picture she cut years ago from the chocolate box he gave her.

She steps towards it, her eyes on the brightly painted flowers. As her fingers reach for the picture, a cloying perfume fills the shed, so overpowering in its sweetness that Olwen's head swims. She turns. In the doorway stands the woman in blue. With one hand she holds her long silver hair across her face like a veil, only her tilted eyes visible, glittering, indifferent as ice.

Olwen screams and jumps back, flinging herself against the shelves. Cans of nails topple and cascade over her, stinging her bare arms. The woman springs past her and snatches up the knife. Crouching in a pool of nails, Olwen watches the blade flash, sees it rip through the chocolate-box picture.

The apparition is a whirlwind of fury. Her blue dress and silver hair swirl and eddy as if liquefied. Again and again she slashes at the picture, her back to Olwen cowering beneath the shelves. When the cardboard is in shreds she stops, slips the knife into a hidden pocket in the folds of her skirt, and glides towards the door. The moment she steps over the threshold she vanishes, leaving only her sickening perfume, tinged with the bitter scent of aloes.

Ten

'Imagine yourself suddenly transposed,' Alun Miller says, 'from Pont Ysaf to – oh, say a remote village in India. Think of the culture shock – the strange tongue, the unfamiliar customs, the hundred-degree heat. Ordinary things, necessary to your comfort and well-being, would be unavailable. I'm not speaking of luxuries, mind, like a car or a telephone or a TV –'

I don't have any of those anyway, Olwen thinks.

'– I mean no running water, no electricity, not even toilet paper –'

'No toilet paper!' Aunt Flindy's false eyelashes skitter. 'What do they use then? Do they have to make do with newspaper like we did in the War?'

'They wash themselves, Mrs Flinders.' Alun sips the dry martini Gwen bought in town and watches Aunt Flindy, a smile twitching his mouth.

Aunt Flindy has a martini, too, and a cigarette in a long black holder. Olwen has never seen her drink alcohol or smoke before, but she manages both like an habituée. This evening she wears a purple taffeta dress with padded shoulders and an elaborately draped skirt. Her lipstick and eyeshadow match the dress; her rouge complements the artificial pink rosebuds in her corsage. As always, the effect is startling and unsettling. Olwen wonders what Alun Miller makes of Aunt Flindy; he behaves as if he finds her charming. Since they arrived, he has treated all three of them, Aunt Flindy, Gwen, Olwen, with great courtesy, making no distinctions . . . except his eyes contract and darken when he turns them on Olwen.

'*Wash* themselves?' Aunt Flindy lifts her plucked eyebrows.

'Instead of using toilet paper, which isn't available, but which they would regard as a dirty habit anyway, they use water and their left hand. Never the right hand. That's used for eating and performing religious devotions.'

'I don't believe it. He's pulling my leg, isn't he, Olwen?' Aunt Flindy turns to Olwen, seated at the other end of the dark green Victorian sofa, her hands wrapped around a glass of shandy. The base rests on her knees which press tightly together under the folds of her black dress.

Alun has seated himself in the wing-chair beside Olwen, just one ornate leg of the mahogany coffee table between them. His legs crossed, he angles his lean body towards her, as if to catch every word she says. In fact, Olwen has hardly opened her mouth since she arrived half an hour ago. Alun's close attention unnerves her. Now she forces herself to ask, 'Have you been to India?'

'Indeed. After I got my degree I went around the world with a couple of friends and a backpack. It's the best way to get an education, believe me, especially for a historian. I lived in an Indian village for six months and helped the government build a road.'

Olwen nods. She can see him as a world traveller. Even seated, he seems filled with intense, highly-strung energy – not a person to stay in one place for long. She wonders how long he'll stay in Pont Ysaf Grammar.

'Rather you than me,' Aunt Flindy says. 'I can't get over it – no toilet paper! Olwen, in't you glad you was born in Wales instead of some outlandish place like India?'

'Well, that's my point exactly, Mrs Flinders. That's what I'm trying to get across to my Ancient History class at the grammar. What it felt like to be a Roman soldier in Britain. They felt just as you would in an Indian village – worse, because the natives were hostile and they had to fight every step of the way. And they weren't just soldiers, either. They were builders, too, carrying the empire on their backs, so to speak. That's why I worked on the Indian road project. It was the closest I could come to living the experience of the common soldier of Rome.'

'Who asked them to come, though? Had no business in Wales, did they?'

'They wanted to extend their empire and civilize the world, Mrs Flinders. Olwen, you must have seen the Roman road on the other side of the Cwm woods?'

'Of course.' She had walked there often with her grandfather but, unlike Alun Miller, his sympathy had lain with the tribal Welsh. She wants to tell Alun this, to say that Aunt Flindy, old witch though she is, has a point. But she can't put the words together. Sitting so close to him, forced to endure his gaze and his attempts to draw her out, she feels tongue-tied and witless. She remembers again what she has put out of her mind for many months: that she never could speak easily to boys at school, or to any man not significantly older than she. The eyes of young males, turned on her, make her jumpy. At the sound of their voices addressing her, however trivially – 'Lend me your compass, will you?' 'What page are we on?' – her stomach knotted, her throat dried up, and blood rushed to her cheeks. As if she harboured some bad secret and must avoid discovery, she cast her own eyes away, moved off, whenever a young man approached.

Since she left school, no young man *has* approached her, save Gareth, whom she fears differently. Now here is Alun Miller, and with him her disability is worse, for his eyes insist, his voice thrusts upon her as no schoolboy's did, and she can't escape.

In the kitchen she can hear Rosamund and her grandmother chatting. 'As if they had a bell on every tooth,' her grandfather would have said. Gwen laughs frequently. At home she never laughs, but only now, away from it, Olwen realizes how silent their cottage is.

'I took my students to the road last week. We marched on it – though we were carrying lunch packs instead of shields. I asked them to imagine that at any moment a pack of wild men in woad and skins might come pouring out of the woods or down the mountain, whooping, cursing, brandishing spears – a terrifying sight to emerge from the swirling mists. Wales was the worst place for the Romans. It was in the grip of the Druids. Tell us who they were, Olwen.'

He makes her feel as if she sits in a classroom again. But she's used to this role. Teachers often called on her; she could be trusted to know the answers.

'They were the priests. All the tribes were afraid of them, they were so fierce. They made human sacrifices and were believed to have supernatural powers.' Her long, accurate response pleases her.

'Human sacrifices in Wales? Never!'

'Wales was barbaric, Mrs Flinders. Whereas the soldiers came from a highly advanced part of the world. They didn't come to plunder and destroy like the Vikings. Look at the viaducts, the villas they left. Have you been to Caerleon, Olwen?'

Olwen shakes her head.

'What? Never been and it's so close! Doesn't history interest you?'

'John was never one for going on trips,' Aunt Flindy says, 'and Olwen never went nowhere without him. Stuck to Grandpa like a toffee dab, didn't you, love?'

Olwen glares at her.

Alun Miller leans closer to Olwen. 'In the museum at Caerleon there are two paintings that capture the dichotomy of war. One shows Roman soldiers on the march. Heavy rain, bitter cold, the soldiers wrapped in their cloaks, stark misery on their faces – some of them no more than boys. One young fellow is about to give up. You can see by his face, he's telling the centurion, "I can't." And the centurion has his club raised, ready to beat him senseless if he stops.'

'*Ach-a-fi!*' Aunt Flindy wrinkles her heavily powdered nose. 'I thought you said they were civilized.'

'Yes, but it was war, you see. Now, in the next picture there are those same soldiers resplendent in their breastplates, driving their knived chariots through the enemy. And who are the enemy? Backward, poorly armed Silurians and their helpless women and babes. You see?'

He stops, stares at Olwen, his eyebrows raised. He might be a Roman himself, she a doomed Silurian, for he strikes terror into her heart, and now he expects her to respond with an intelligent remark.

'Of course,' he says after a moment's silence, 'the Druids were another story. Had the Romans quaking in their thonged sandals. Do you believe in magic, Olwen? With eyes like yours, you must, surely? Perchance you even know some?'

'Dinner's nearly ready.' Rosamund stands in the doorway, her face flushed, blonde hair in fetching disarray. 'Will you open the wine, Alun?'

Alun gets up at once. 'Excuse me,' he says, but absently, his attention switched to his wife. He crosses the room as eagerly as if . . . as if she were inviting him to make love, Olwen thinks. As they go out, he slips his arm around her, his hand resting intimately on her hip. Olwen, wretched, feels as if she were some item he had picked up in a shop, examined, and discarded. He didn't even wait for her answer.

'I do like to see a young couple head over heels,' Aunt Flindy says. 'Takes me back to my own married life. My Idris was every bit as moithered by love as that young feller. Couldn't be parted from me for a minute.'

'Didn't he go to work?' Olwen speaks sharply.

'Course he went to work. Put in long hours at the Pen Colliery. How do you think we raised two strapping boys – on air?'

'You said he couldn't be parted from you.' It was as if she had ceased to exist the moment Rosamund appeared. Of course, he entertains them just to please her, counting the hours, probably, until he's alone with his wife.

'It's a manner of speaking, that's all. Idris couldn't *bear* to be parted from me is what I meant. You'd have understood that if you was in love yourself. But you'll have to alter your stroke, my lady, if you hope to be courted. No young feller's going to fall for a girl as sour as week-old milk.' Aunt Flindy fills her glass from the bottle on the coffee table. 'That may be a blessing for others, I dare say. The Parrys never did bring much joy where they cast their fancy.'

Olwen, who has turned her head away, swings round. 'What are you talking about?'

'About your Mam and your Grandpa. You come from people who can't love what's not blood.'

Olwen stares at the old woman. 'You've no business speaking about my grandfather like that. How dare you!'

Unperturbed, Aunt Flindy lifts her glass and takes a long swig. 'They couldn't love others, neither of 'em. Want 'em, yes – I seen that – but never love. I'll tell you what, though, I'm in touch with Grandpa and he's sorry in his heart now it's too late. He asked me to tell you not to follow in his path. He came out of my bedroom wall a few nights back and said, "Flindy, tell Olwen not to bring ruin on herself like I done."'

She's a lunatic, Olwen thinks, I mustn't listen to her.

'Dinner is served.' Alun reappears, all warmth and charm again. 'Now, Mrs Flinders, let's do this in style. Give me your arm.' He smiles and winks at Olwen. When she does not respond, his smile fades, but his eyes linger on her face.

Olwen stands at her bedroom window looking over the moonlit garden. Although it's a cool night and she wears only a sleeveless cotton gown, she has opened the window wide. After a fitful sleep, she is wide awake, hot and jittery, as if she had a temperature.

She and Gwen left the Millers' at ten-thirty, Aunt Flindy sitting on for more lemon mousse, more Irish coffee, more attention.

'I hope she doesn't keep you up till all hours,' Gwen said as she passed through the gate Alun held open for her. 'Poor old dab, it's her first night out in years.'

It's ours too, Olwen had thought.

'And she does love company. When she was younger she belonged to all sorts of clubs in Pont Ysaf – the Pensioners, the Spiritualists – but she can't travel far from home these days.'

They had started along the lane, Alun walking between Olwen and Gwen, carrying a flashlight. 'What about her sons? Don't they ever take her out?'

'One's in Australia, and the other the Lord knows where. She's been on her own for donkey's years.'

'That's too bad. Neglect of ageing parents is the second most unforgivable family crime.'

'What's the first?' Olwen asked.

'Child abuse, of course.'

At this point a frightening thing had happened. Olwen had seen a dark shape crouching near Bryn Brewen's gate, its glittering eyes fixed on her. At the same moment a shrill whistle sounded in the woods. The shape streaked across the lane, right in their path, and Olwen had screamed.

'Why, Olwen, it's only Bryn's old dog,' Gwen said as Gelert vanished into the Cwm.

'You're high strung,' Alun said softly. Then, amazed, Olwen had felt his arm come round her, felt herself drawn so close that the sides of their bodies touched. He held her like that until they arrived at the Parrys' gate.

'We had a lovely time,' Gwen said. 'Thank you indeed.' In the dark, she couldn't see Alun's arm around Olwen's waist. Slowly – reluctantly, it seemed to Olwen – he released her.

'Your latch is broken,' he said, shining his torch on the gate, intending to open it for them.

'Yes, I don't know how it happened, I'm sure.'

'Perhaps Olwen banged it too hard in a temper!'

'Oh, she gave it a good hammering when she was little. Liked to pretend the gate was a horse, didn't you, love? But it stood up to all that, and now . . .' Gwen's voice trails off, mystified.

'I'll fix it for you,' Alun says. 'It will give me an excuse to call.' He had touched Olwen's arm lightly, as if to suggest a secret – but humorous – meaning in his words.

Olwen had gone straight upstairs, refusing the cup of tea Gwen offered, saying, 'I'm too tired.' Gwen would have liked to discuss the evening, she knew. But I never discuss anything with her, she had thought. She must be used to it.

For a long time she couldn't sleep. She lay on her back, staring at the moonlit window, thinking about Alun Miller. Or rather, asking herself unanswerable questions about his behaviour. As they talked before dinner – as *he* talked – why had he given her such intimate looks, and why had his conversation about the Romans seemed to her to be fraught with some deeper significance that she inferred but could not fathom? She had been reminded of literature classes at school, when the teacher demanded that they explore the 'subtexts' of the works they read. But Olwen had been good at that. Always quick to interpret metaphor and symbol, she had delighted in unravelling hidden meanings, the text a shining, slippery skin of words which she peeled away until she had uncovered the fruit.

Life was different from books, however, and lying in bed thinking of Alun's embrace in the lane, she couldn't imagine his motive, or even understand her own response, half ravished, half repelled, unable to draw away though it had felt wrong that he should hold her like that, as close as a lover.

When, at last, she fell asleep it was to dream and wake and dream again. The dreams had an odd structure. Instead of narrative fragments, she had dreamed a collage. Faces, bits of scenes flicked by, often juxtaposed in an absurd fashion, as if she were being ridiculed by her own subconscious. Thus, her grandfather's face, intent on something she could not see, dissolved into the bubbling lasagna on Rosamund's dinner table; Alun's arm, reaching for her, became a branch waving in the Cwm from which she snapped a twig to roll in her palm, only, when she looked down, it was her grandfather's pipe she held.

Then Rosamund and Alun, side by side at the candlelit dinner table, like a portrait. When they turned to kiss, the candle flame leapt between them and became the woman in blue, whirling in a mad dance. And behind all these scenes, a lithe brown body dived repeatedly into water, so that the sound of splashing accompanied the pastiche like music.

Standing at the window, her arms wrapped round her, Olwen thinks of Gareth. Perhaps, if she wanted, he would hold her as Alun Miller had. Surely it must be pleasant to walk entwined like that on a summer's evening, as she has seen lovers walk up Archer's Lane. And to hold hands by candlelight at your own table must be pleasant, too, with food and wine and guests – and laughter – knowing that later, when the guests were gone, you would lie together.

Gareth will be home tomorrow – but he won't come to see her. His father will tell him she doesn't wish it. And perhaps he has changed his mind about her anyway.

'Sour as week-old milk.'

Olwen recalls a poem read at school in which the narrator willed his beloved to come to him by the force of his desire. Could that happen? Tonight Gareth is her beloved again, the focus of her thoughts, the nub of her wishes, a lodestar that guides her longing. If she concentrates, can she call to him, stir his sleep, wake him and waft him from his own bed to hers . . . ?

The sky is spread with stars, silver threads on deepest indigo, impossible to tell which light shines brightest.

The sleeve of the enchanter . . .

'Don't look into his sleeve.'

'Whoever has the forbidden desire, *he* knows. That one he chooses.'

Olwen turns from the window. She has no guide.

Only a meteor, a trail of incandescent dust, marks the space where his star fell from the heavens and shot to earth, deep in the Cwm Woods, where a path winds all the way from Archer's Lane to Cefn Heights.

Eleven

'The Council ought to give me a new bus by rights,' Morgan Pryce says as they climb the steep road that runs over Abernath Mountain into Pont Ysaf. 'This one have got more ailments than me. Hark at it wheeze! I put in a request a year back. Went to the Town Hall and told them straight. "It's a scandal," I said. "If that bus conks out when it's full of people, you'll have a lot of trouble on your plate."'

'What did they say?' Olwen, seated behind Morgan, watches the valley drop away as they climb the mountain, the slopes littered with sheep.

'Fobbed me off with an excuse and a promise. What do they care? I been asking them to move me to another house for a dozen years, ever since my mother passed away. The one I got now is so damp you could grow mushrooms in it.'

'I don't remember your mother.' Olwen looks down at the long, green arm of the Cwm curving around the valley.

'No, well you wouldn't.' Morgan plucks a Woodbine from behind his ear and lights up. 'She was bedridden a long time, since before you was born. You'd never have seen her in Pont Ysaf.'

'What was wrong with her?' Far below she sees the gleam of water where the Taf winds among willows and rocks. Behind a rocky hillock, the Wen Pool lies, shining, gemlike, hidden in willows and giant ferns. She imagines how the ferns' thick stems curve toward the water, their massive fronds thrusting towards the surface where willow branches trail like tendrils of sunlit hair. In the blackberry bushes, among the delicate white flowers, hard green berries are beginning to ripen. In the grass, she sees a white enamel bowl; behind a willow curtain, a sunwarmed stone.

'Dropsy she had. That's a wasting disease. She got so bloated she couldn't rise from bed, and lying in that upstairs room day in, day out, the damp got into her bones and her chest and killed her eventually. She was so full of water when she died, she looked like a balloon.'

Olwen bites her lip, an image of Morgan's swollen mother blotting out the Wen Pool. 'Do you miss her still?'

'It was a lot of trouble for me, looking after her all those years, and it's taken a toll, too. I haven't been right myself since. It wears out the whole system, tending to an invalid. All that lifting and carrying and listening and watching.'

'Watching is the worst part.'

'Still, I don't regret it. She was a good mother and I did my duty. I'm glad I didn't put her in the hospital the way some do. Many times I thought of it, mind, more shame on me – specially getting up at night and climbing those stairs. She was always bad at night when the water ran down to her legs. I'd have to massage them. Legs like tree trunks . . .' Morgan's short neck slips into his collar as he hunches his shoulders and drags on the Woodbine between his lips. 'I could hardly lift her legs. Sometimes I'd hurt her and she'd scream out.'

'How long was she ill like that?'

'That bad, only the last year, but it seemed like twenty. I got real run down, and straight after the funeral a dose of pleurisy knocked me off my feet. Now that you might recall. Your granny came to see me. Every day for two weeks she came out on the bus, in the middle of winter, too. Do you remember that? You came with her once.'

'Yes,' Olwen says, 'I do.' She sees herself, a child of seven, going with her grandmother into Morgan's house, a narrow one-up and one-down on a terrace in Pont Ysaf. Morgan lay on the sofa, covered with army blankets, his head tied up in a woman's scarf. Gwen made her sit in the wooden armchair by the empty fireplace while she heated soup and chatted to Morgan. Olwen vividly recalls the smell of that room, musty, like the darkest parts of the Cwm. Morgan, crouched under the blankets, had looked like a toad, and Olwen had longed to go home. She remembers, too, the bare stone floor, the sparse furniture, the damp stains on the walls, reptile shapes, and whispering to her grandmother, 'Nain, when can we go?'

'Every day she brought food and lit the fire for me. I'd have died of cold or starvation without her. My mother'd fallen out with our neighbours in her well days, so none of them lifted a finger to help. I've made up with them since, of course, but I hadn't had time when the pleurisy hit me.'

'They sound mean,' Olwen says.

'No, indeed. They're good enough. They just thought – I'd be like my mother was, see. Thought I'd cut them like she did. I had to show them I wouldn't by making the first moves. I did that as soon as I was better and every one of them gives me the time of day now when I pass down the street. Mrs Jones on my one side brings me a bit of supper now and again, and Mrs Davies on my other told me to knock the wall if I'm ever taken bad like I was with the pleurisy. It's nice to know you can count on people when you live on your own. I sit in my chair at night and think, "There's people I'm friends with on the other side of them walls," and it gives me a lot of comfort.'

Olwen imagines Morgan sitting in that wooden armchair where she sat to wait for Gwen, surrounded by the emptiness of his house. No wonder he talks so much! The words that flood from him whenever he's in company must build up inside him during the long evening hours when the silence is a stone around his neck. He's a man who should have married (unlike her grandfather), but he chose duty instead. Olwen ponders this.

The bus has reached the crest of the mountain. The Mountain View Inn sits up here, a low, eighteenth-century building with dormer windows and sloping, slate roofs. Hanging baskets, bright with flowers, decorate the grey stone walls. In the courtyard a group of young people in hiking boots and shorts stand around a wooden table drinking lager from glass mugs. They are talking loudly, animatedly, in German. One young man rests his arm on the shoulders of a girl who wears her hair in a thick braid hanging almost to her waist. As the bus passes, he raises his arm and waves. Olwen makes no response but finds herself wishing, suddenly, to be the young woman he embraces.

'Must be doing good business,' Morgan says, jerking his head towards the inn. 'Plenty of tourists this time of year.'

In front of them the road swoops down into Pont Ysaf. The bus plunges like a car on a roller coaster, throwing Olwen's behind off the seat. Her stomach dips and she clutches the rail. Wind whipping through the windows makes her hair fly and lifts her paisley skirt. 'I wish I were a tourist,' Olwen shouts in Morgan Pryce's ear, infected by the unexpected life in the old bus as it leaps into Pont Ysaf High Street. 'I wouldn't mind seeing a bit of the world.'

Morgan stops the bus at the terminus, a glassed-in shelter at the top of the High Street. 'That's right,' he says, pulling the crumpled packet of Woodbines from inside his jacket. 'Go you on while you're young and healthy. I wish I'd done things when I was able. Now I got a bad back and a bad chest and I don't know what else.' He takes a cigarette from the packet and tamps it against his palm.

Olwen stand up. 'Well . . .' she says, 'I hope you feel better.'

Morgan looks surprised. 'I won't,' he says, putting the Woodbine in his mouth and fishing for matches. 'Not now. But I thank you for the kind wish.'

She starts to get off the bus, then turns back. 'Mr Pryce, I'm sorry I was rude to you.'

Morgan takes the Woodbine from his mouth. 'Rude? When, love?'

'The day of the funeral.'

'I don't recall –'

'When you were driving us in the Bentley and I asked you to stop talking.'

The old man's eyes open wide. 'Oh, that,' he says. 'Bless your heart, I'd forgotten all about it.' Then his face fills with concern. 'I hope it haven't been on your mind all these months?'

'I thought –' Olwen steps off the bus. 'Goodbye, Mr Pryce. Thank you,' she says and walks rapidly down the street.

The road is empty of vehicles and there are few people on the pavement outside the shops. Weekdays are quiet in Pont Ysaf. On the steps of the red-brick town hall a tabby cat stretches in the sun. Behind one of the big bay windows a man in a dark business suit waters a yellow geranium. As she approaches the Public Library, Olwen sees that the benches beneath the ash trees are all occupied, as usual, by old men. Arranged in a semicircle beneath a statue of Lloyd George, and shaded by the trees, the benches face the road. It's a good place to sit and watch passers-by. Neatly dressed in tweed caps and jackets, pastel shirts and ties, the dozen or so men seem posed for a camera, so quietly they sit, their hands resting on their knees or on the handle of a cane. Among them Olwen recognizes the five miners who came to her grandfather's funeral. She nods and they nod back in unison. The moment she passes, they begin to talk about her.

'Know who that is, don't you? That's John Parry's grand-daughter.'

'Never! I thought she went to London years back.'

'You're losing on yourself, Dafydd. That was the mother. *Daro*, she turned out a wild one – there was no holding her. If the young 'un have got her ways –'

They don't lower their voices, as if, once she has passed them, she ceases to exist. Or perhaps, she thinks, old men, hard of hearing, don't realize how their voices carry. She stops a few yards from them and looks into the window of Jeanne's Paris Fashions. Mannequins in summer dresses stand knee-deep in sheer blouses propped on bulging plastic breasts amid gaudy slacks, their legs pinned wide apart. Though Jeanne surely could not have intended it, her window dressing is porno-graphic.

Among the mannequins she sees her own reflection, her sun-darkened skin, her shoulders bare save for the narrow satin ribbons of her white halter-neck top, her hair long and loose on her shoulders. Beneath her paisley skirt, her legs are brown and lithe. Surely he will like her again?

She hears the name 'Bryn Brewen' and tilts her head towards the old men on the benches. 'Couldn't have been Bryn. She never had looks on him. Some London feller no doubt.'

'The girl don't resemble him neither.'

'That don't mean nothing. Do she resemble Alice? No, she don't. Haven't got Alice's build nor her fine features.'

'And what about her hair? Beautiful head of hair she had.'

'No wonder John doted on her.'

'Ran away from him though.'

'You can't tame a wild thing.'

Olwen, her face burning, even though after all these years she tells herself she should be used to it, walks on swiftly up the High Street. When she reaches Boots the Chemist she turns left into Station Terrace. Passing the station and the post office, she enters a narrow lane flanked by high stone walls overhung with lilac. Behind these walls stand the fine houses of the town's wealthy, the 'crack-crack' as her grandfather called them. The lane opens onto a shady square around which stand half a dozen houses fronted by driveways and wrought-iron gates. The houses are elegant, Georgian. Into this cul-de-sac Dr Lloyd moved ten years ago, a widower with an eleven-year-old son.

Gareth's red MG stands outside the house. Olwen hesitates. What if he answers the door? Will she be able to speak without her tongue tripping over the words? And even if she doesn't meet Gareth, will his father tell him at dinner everything she says in the consulting room? What will he think when he finds out she hasn't come because she's ill but because she fears she is losing her mind? He surely won't want anything to do with a mad girl.

Olwen reaches the steps. At the front door she pauses to think over what she must tell the doctor. Last night, the night after the Millers' dinner party, she saw the woman in blue again. But before telling Dr Lloyd this, she must talk to him about his own son, enlist his help in unravelling Gareth's role in the hauntings . . . for before seeing Alice, she had seen *him*, a vision called up by the force of her longing.

All day she had anticipated him as she pottered in the garden or tried to read in the deckchair under the chestnut. Helping Gwen prepare the Sunday meal, she had peeled extra potatoes, cut a fluted paper trim for the leg of lamb, and polished the cutlery (activities Gwen made no comment on), in case he should arrive during lunch. After lunch, from late afternoon until dusk, she had wandered repeatedly down the garden path to lean on the gate, expecting at any moment to see his red car pull into the lane. 'We'll go for a walk,' she thought, 'perhaps, as far as the Wen, and he will put his arm around my waist . . .'

When she went, at last, into the house, when the moon was out and the night had grown chill, Gwen came to the kitchen door to say, 'Why don't we go into Pont Ysaf tomorrow and have coffee and cakes at the Mayflower? That would be a nice little outing, and you might see some of your school friends home from university.'

'I don't have any friends in Pont Ysaf,' Olwen had answered as she climbed the stairs.

Standing at the window in her nightdress, she had looked at the dark Cwm and the tall trees there had seemed like the massive wall of a castle, shutting her in. A memory of fairytale princesses sequestered in tower rooms had induced a vision of Gareth, sword in hand, hacking a path through the woods, his armour gleaming in moonlight. A fanciful and ludicrous vision, it had made her cheeks burn even as she indulged it. I am not a princess . . . he didn't come . . . he doesn't care for me. Sour as week-old milk. You'll have to alter your stroke, my lady . . .

A movement in the garden had distracted her. As the dream of Gareth faded, out of the delphiniums the woman in blue had emerged, her figure swathed in a long, hooded cloak. Beneath the hood, which hid her face, only a few ringlets of the marvellous hair were visible. Her carriage, as well as her clothes, were different. As she moved towards the gate, her steps seemed heavy, earthbound, with no vestige of the grace and liquidity that she had hitherto possessed even during bouts of violence. Under the long cloak, her legs jerked oddly, awkwardly, as she stumbled across the garden.

At the gate she stopped, placing one hand on the top bar, slipping the other into the folds of her cloak. Familiar by now with the creature's malevolence, Olwen worked her fingers into the flesh of her crossed arms. In that hidden pocket lay a knife. The woman's hand had already closed on its handle, her index finger testing the sharpness of the blade. Soon footsteps would sound in the lane. But whose? For whom did she wait in the silent, shadowy garden?

In Archer's Lane a crunch of gravel, a low whistle . . . out of the Cwm comes Bryn Brewen, Gelert loping beside him. On Bryn's shoulder the bulging sack shows he's had luck tonight. For a moment, Olwen thinks that Bryn is separate from the waking dream in which she sees the woman. She expects him to cross the lane, go up the path to his house. But he stops, heaves the sack to the ground, and turns in the direction of the Parrys' house. For a few seconds he is out of sight behind the garden wall. When he reappears, Olwen gasps. He has transformed himself. The man she sees in the moonlight is years younger, prouder and straighter of bearing, more handsome than Bryn. His clothes are smart, urbane – a black suit, white shirt, black bow tie – clothes for an elegant dinner party . . . or a wedding. The bushy hair, cut and combed, reminds Olwen of the sleek mane of a racehorse. And it is this hint of the animal, albeit a thoroughbred, that confirms for her that the man *is* Bryn Brewen.

As he approaches the woman, his face clear in the moon's light, Olwen sees that he is in thrall. The blinding flame that leaps in his eyes dazzles her and alters the beat of her heart, excitement driving out fear. She almost cries out, as if she were the beloved, the sole object of this sightless, unmindful desire. Paintings, visions, dreams, coalesce for Olwen as he reaches out his arms and empowers her imagination, which plunges eagerly, willingly forward to what will happen next ... he will slip the cloak from her shoulders as he draws her into the lane, lift her dress, swing her off the ground into his arms, her only support, and make her ride ...

A sudden alteration in Bryn's behaviour halts Olwen's fancy; she sees him stiffen, his face changing, fervour giving way to horror as the woman raises her arm. The knife flashes, blood spurts, Bryn's face becomes a hideous flower, redder than any rose. The woman lifts the knife again, aims for the heart.

Bryn springs away. On his swift robber's feet he runs down the lane, appears at his own gate where the lurcher waits. His hands pressed to his face, blood pouring through his fingers, he rushes up the path, Gelert whimpering at his heels. The door slams on the poacher and his dog.

In the garden, caressed by moonlight, the woman stands motionless, her hands, empty now, loose at her sides.

Leaning out of the window, Olwen calls, 'Who are you? Why have you come?'

The woman turns, shaking off her hood. Silver hair spills about her shoulders as she raises her head and looks up. In the full moon's light Olwen gazes into a face she has known all her life.

Slowly, the apparition lifts the hand that bore the knife and fastens it in her long hair.

Olwen, incredulous, murmurs, 'Don't ...' Then, as the creature tugs at her shining hair, she screams and cannot stop.

Her bedroom door opens. Gwen, still fastening her dressing gown, comes swiftly to her. She pulls Olwen into her arms. Dropping her head onto her grandmother's breast, Olwen sobs.

'For God's sake,' Gwen says, 'get yourself to Dr Lloyd tomorrow. If you don't, I'll go into town and bring him here myself.'

Twelve

'We make our own ghosts,' her grandfather had said, 'out of our fears and wishes.' If this is so, she must be a monster. Olwen drops her hand from the brass knocker. Why did she imagine that she could speak to Dr Lloyd of matters so private . . . so shameful?

Turning from the door, she runs down the steps, down the driveway, with its laurel and rhododendron border. When she reaches the gate, she hears the house door open, hears Gareth call her name. She doesn't stop or look back. Across the leafy square and down the lane to Station Street, she runs.

At the end of the High Street the bus terminus is deserted. Collapsing onto the wooden bench, she closes her eyes and drops her head onto her hands, pressing her palms to her forehead. Behind her eyelids a disc of colour forms, blood red, spinning like a vortex. Into this whirlpool, she, the fearful swimmer, feels herself sucked.

As she spins in the eddies, nightmarish forms rise from the depths – the dark enchanter, pale Alice in her wafting blue gown, and her grandfather, baleful, his nostrils distended, his lip curled. Frozen thus, his face suggests a death mask, or the paralysis of unyielding rage. Alice droops on his shoulder, her eyes vacant as a doll's. Beside her, the enchanter grins and flicks his wrist, a showman exhibiting his freaks. Like figures on a carousel, they go round and round, stretching out their hands to Olwen, wanting to catch her and drag her down.

A hand grasps her shoulder and she cries out.

'Olwen?' Gareth Lloyd says.

'Go away,' she says behind her hands. 'Leave me alone.'

'I can't.' Gently, he massages her shoulder. Sensations of warmth and comfort flow from his fingers. His hand draws her up out of the whirlpool. She opens her eyes and looks at him.

Gareth brushes back her hair. 'Come on,' he says, and holds open the passenger door of his MG, parked at the kerb.

Olwen stands shakily. He slips his hand under her elbow and helps her into the car. When he is in the driver's seat, he says, 'You don't want me to take you back to see my father, right?'

She shakes her head.

'Home?'

'Not yet.'

'Good. It's my choice, then.' He starts the car, makes a U-turn in the empty road, and drives down the High Street out of Pont Ysaf.

Olwen sits pressed against the door, her arm resting on the open window, her face turned from Gareth.

They climb the mountain road, the car flying up the steep slope like a bird. When they reach the crest, a couple of mountain ponies appear and run beside the MG.

Startled, Olwen draws back. Gareth touches her arm. 'It's all right. They're after food, that's all. They've got used to people throwing stuff from cars.'

'I wasn't afraid,' she says, as the car outdistances the ponies, 'just surprised.'

'You must have seen them often. Wild ponies are all over these mountains.'

'I've seen them from the bus. That's different – not so close.'

'Haven't you ever walked up here?'

'Never.' They had confined their walks to the valley, mainly to the Cwm. She wonders, now, why that was so.

'I used to come up here all the time when I was a kid and try to catch them. A gang of us boys from the town used to do it. Except I kept trying long after the others gave up.'

'Why? I mean, if you wanted to ride so much, your father could have afforded riding lessons, couldn't he?'

'It wasn't lessons I wanted.'

Olwen turns her head and glances at him curiously. She looks away again when he returns her glance.

'I wanted to ride like the wind – like Bellerophon, you know! I had this idea that if I rode hard enough, if I was fearless enough, I could somehow ride out of this world.'

Olwen turns to him again. 'Out of this world?'

Gareth smiles, flicking his right hand, the palm open, as if he were tossing something into the air. 'Go up – into the sky. Like

I said, I was just a kid.' His tone is dismissive, self-mocking, but Olwen recalls suddenly his father's story, the drawing of the girl on the great stallion that he kept on his bedroom wall, how he had dreamed of the girl, or imagined her – or *seen* her, perhaps?

She feels her pulse race. She wants to ask him about this but doesn't know where to begin. 'That was when you first moved here? After your mother died?' She speaks softly, tentatively.

'Yes.'

She waits for him to go on. When he doesn't, she says, 'So what happened? Why did you stop trying to catch the ponies?'

'I grew out of it. It's part of growing up, isn't it?'

'What is?'

'Learning what you can and can't do. Making compromises.' He pats the steering wheel. 'I settled for a sports car. It's not a bad substitute – gets me where I want to go.'

'Where *do* you want to go?'

'A long way.'

'Out of this world?'

'Not any more.'

Olwen turns her head to the open window. The wind whips her hair and for a moment she imagines that she sits astride a great horse, galloping madly. The creature's hooves pound the earth and drum in her ears. But where would she be going? She has no destination far away. What she seeks is right here, in the Cwm Woods, and in her own garden. My destination is behind me, she thinks. I have to go back to reach it.

In the ferny grass beside the road sheep graze, oblivious to the passing car. Far below, on the valley bed, the Taf glints, appearing and disappearing among trees and rocks, like pieces of a broken thread. Beside it runs the ancient road, little more than a footpath really, but paved, and wide enough, she supposes, for chariot wheels and ox carts.

'There's the Roman road,' she says.

Gareth looks over. 'And legions of ghosts marching on it,' he says lightly.

Olwen starts. It is something her grandfather would have said. "Why do you say that?"

He shrugs. 'Just a fancy. The river makes me think of their helmets and breastplates, the way it flashes down there.'

'I used to walk on the road with my grandfather. Not this part. Farther down, beside the Cwm. He used to make up stories about the soldiers –' She stops. How to explain to Gareth that with her grandfather she *had* gone out of this world? With him, moving through time and space had been a daily occurrence, normal as breathing.

'He was everything to you,' Gareth says quietly – sadly, it seems to her.

'He still is.'

'I used to feel that way about my mother. Did you know that she came from round here?'

'Your father mentioned it.'

'When we lived in London she used to tell me about this area, about the Cwm and the Roman road and the Wen – she even mentioned Archer's Lane. After my father and I moved here, it was strange, discovering these places – like slipping into a dream or a story. I'd thought of them as make-believe, you know, they were so mixed up in my mind with the landscapes of the legends and tales she used to tell me.'

'I was raised like that too,' Olwen says slowly. 'When you grow up on fairytales, you tend to half-believe in magic.' This she says warily, unsure how much to tell but wanting to lead him into talking about his mother.

'For a while I believed she would come back by magic – especially here, in one of the places she'd told me about – the Cwm, or the Wen. I'd go to them a lot on my own, and often – when I just sat quietly, waiting – it did seem as if she'd appear in the next minute. I thought I could . . . sort of sense her.'

'*Did* you ever see her?'

'Of course not. The dead can't come back, Olwen.'

They have reached the Mountain Inn. 'I'd like to buy you a drink,' Gareth says. 'And lunch, if you'll stay a bit.'

Without waiting for her answer, he parks the car in the courtyard. The Germans have gone now, but there are several parked cars with English number plates. Tourists, Olwen thinks, as they cross the yard, and wishes, briefly, that she and Gareth were on holiday, travelling together to places she has never seen.

They go through the inn door, passing from bright sunlight into the pleasant gloom of the oak-panelled bar-room. As he pushes open the door, Gareth's arm touches her shoulder. For a moment, she feels his skin against hers. Swiftly, she moves away, stepping in front of him.

'We can sit in the garden,' he says. 'Go on out. I'll give our order.'

He walks to the bar and Olwen crosses the empty room. A high wall draped in ivy encloses the small garden behind the inn. Of the half-dozen tables on the terrace, Olwen chooses a corner one next to a trellis covered with sweet peas and shaded by a laburnum tree. When she sits in the wicker chair she feels ennervated, as if she has been too long in the sun. Being with Gareth has this effect on her. She feels as she did coming out of an examination at school, drained by the long effort to do well, to form careful, correct answers.

She thinks of him now, sitting beside her in the car. He drove with one hand, using the other to gesture, or to tap his thigh when he spoke of things that, she guessed, evoked painful memories. From the corner of her eye, she had looked at his legs, hard and muscular, a covering of blond hair on the shins, scars on his knees – a sportsman's legs, a game-player's. His white tennis shorts (he must have been setting out to play when he opened the front door and saw her running) accentuated the tan of his thighs where the skin was smooth, supple, like fine suede. He smelled of soap and fresh air and, very faintly – like a secret – of himself, his maleness.

Olwen crosses her legs, uncrosses them, smooths her skirt over her knees. She feels, still, the sensation of his arm against her back, the warmth of his skin. His fingers have left an ache, like a bruise, on the round of her arm, just above her elbow. She presses her own fingers to the place, kneading the flesh there as if to ease a sore muscle.

The brilliant hues of the sweet peas hurt her eyes, their fragrance makes her drowsy. She thrusts her hands into her lap. Soon Gareth will return, sit near her, look at her, speak to her, expect her to answer.

He comes across the terrace with two mugs of cider.

'I've never drunk cider before,' she says.

'First time for everything. But sip slowly. They make a potent brew here.'

Olwen raises her glass, tastes the cider. It is cold, bitter and sweet at the same time.

'They'll start serving lunch in about an hour. Can you stay?'

She shakes her head.

'Olwen, do you ever say yes?' His voice is teasing, but his eyes when she looks into them are serious. The colour of spring, of the tender new grass, of the Wen Pool, they mesmerize her. If she looks into them too long, she will drown. She has always known this. She recalls, too, how they can darken, turn the colour of ivy leaves. She raises her glass and takes a long drink. The cider goes to her head at once. She drinks again and feels the liquid bubble inside her, like laughter.

'Look at our glasses,' she says as she sets hers down. 'They're winking at each other.'

'Like attracts like,' Gareth says.

'You mean they're both full of cider!' Olwen laughs. 'It must be easy to show off when you're drunk. See, she thinks she's irresistible!' She places her finger on the side of her glass, sparkling in the sunlight. 'But really she's just short and stout.'

'Not to him.' Gareth nods at his own glass. 'To him she's shapely and shining. It's how he sees her that counts.'

On impulse, she leans across the table and clinks her glass against Gareth's. 'There, she kissed him.'

Gareth rests his chin on his fist, his head tilted to one side, his scarred eyebrow cocked at her.

Olwen laughs, blushes, puts down her glass and looks away across the courtyard. 'I'm a bit tipsy myself,' she says.

'If you won't have lunch, how about a sandwich to go with that cider? Pork pie? Bag of crisps?'

Olwen shakes her head, drinks again.

'Pheasant? Caviar? Lobster? Golden apples, silver plums? Tell me what you want and I'll get it for you.'

She turns her head. Through an airy, glowing haze she looks at him, and sees the wish in his eyes.

'I don't know what I want,' she says softly.

His eyes wait. She lifts a strand of her hair and tucks it behind her ear.

'Are you sorry for what happened last summer at the Wen Pool?'

Gareth's face alters. His eyes narrow, the scar contracting, a dot at the end of a question mark. 'I'm not sure what you mean by "sorry". Sorry as in regret – "I wish it had never happened" – or "Sorry, I apologize"?'

Olwen says nothing. She meant, she realizes, a different question. But what she wants to know, she can't ask.

'I don't regret it,' he says slowly. 'Except how it ended. If you want me to apologize, though, I will – if it means we can start with a clean slate. I'm sorry, Olwen.'

'You don't sound as if you mean it.'

'Olwen –' He spreads his hands. 'Look, if you've been avoiding me because you think I'm a sex maniac, I can promise you I'm not. I won't rape you if you go out with me. I won't even touch you if you tell me not to.'

'You have a reputation.'

'As a sex maniac?' His eyebrow cocks differently, amused.

'For wanting sex from the girls you go with.' She lifts her glass and drains it.

At first he simply looks surprised. Then anger darkens his eyes. 'Who says so?'

Olwen lowers her head. 'Never mind.'

'But I do mind – a lot. I'd like to know who's told you lies about me.'

'No one *told* me anything. I heard rumours.'

'So who was spreading the rumours? Name me some names.'

'Why?'

'I want to confront whoever it was. Take you with me and ask them to say it to my face.'

'I don't know why you're making such an issue of it. All sorts of rumours go around a school. Especially a small school like ours. It doesn't mean anything.'

'This rumour meant something to you.'

'Why should you care?'

'Because I want you to trust me. So . . . who was it?'

Olwen feels her cheeks blaze. 'I forget,' she says. She dearly wishes she had never spoken, that she was far away from Gareth and this moment.

'I'll tell you what,' he says, 'I don't believe you heard this at school. I think it was your grandfather said it.'

'You know nothing about my grandfather!' Olwen feels the heat of embarrassment turn swiftly to rage.

'I know he didn't like me.'

From the open windows of the inn, music suddenly blares across the terrace. Someone has come into the bar and put money in the juke box, a Beatles song.

Olwen and Gareth stare at each other like enemies, a glove thrown down, a knife blade thrust into the table between them. It's true, she thinks, Grandfather didn't like him, didn't want me to be with him. Yet here she is, sitting with the young man he forbade – a few minutes ago she was flirting with him.

'I'm sorry,' Gareth says, 'but it's better to get the truth out. I'm not blaming him. I can see why he thought that way, but he was wrong. You ought to give me a chance to show you that. It wasn't just me he disliked, Olwen. He would have detested any boy who showed interest in you.'

As he speaks, Olwen feels her anger transform, heat giving way to cold, as if an icicle had entered her heart. Say nothing, she counsels herself. Wait till you can thrust deep and really hurt him. She shrugs, taps her foot to the Beatles song.

'Do you dance in Oxford?'

Gareth frowns. For a moment, she thinks he is going to say more about her grandfather, and thinks, If he does, I'll strike him.

'Sometimes,' he says.

'Do you go to a lot of parties there?'

'Not a lot. I work quite hard.'

'But you do go to them.' She imagines him dancing with a woman she has never seen, pressing his body against hers.

'Yes, on a Saturday night. So will you.'

'No, I won't. I don't like dancing.'

'You liked it at the end-of-term party. There's nothing *wrong*, Olwen, with doing things that you like.'

'I always do what I like. I don't need you to tell me.'

'Look, why don't we stop arguing? There's a dance here every Saturday. Will you go with me this weekend?'

How can he ask her this, suggest another meeting, after what has passed between them? He has no scruples. Self-interest drives him.

'I can't. I'm doing something else on Saturday.' It is the weekend Gwen goes to Swansea. She will be alone in the house.

'That's not true.'

'You think I'm telling a lie?'

'I'm sorry,' Gareth says. 'Again.'

'For calling me a liar?'

'Christ. Yes. For whatever you like. For whatever you think I should be sorry for. Don't you know how long I've –'

'I'd better go home now,' she says. When she gets up, her head swims and she staggers. Gareth catches her under her arms.

131

'My head is going round.'

'You shouldn't have drunk so fast.'

She frees herself from him and walks rapidly across the terrace, bumping into chairs. When they enter the bar, she sees a group of young people, three men and two women, sitting at a table near the juke box. Olwen recognizes them from school. They had been in Gareth's year. Their faces are surprised. One of the girls freezes, her drink halfway to her mouth, her eyes fixed on Olwen. When Gareth stops to speak, Olwen keeps walking. At the door she looks back. The girl with the glass in her hand is staring after her. The other girl has stood up and has her arm around Gareth's waist. She wears a candy-striped sun-dress, the material tight over her high, round behind. Her laughter, and Gareth's voice, follow Olwen as she goes out.

She crosses the courtyard and stands beside Gareth's car, her back to the inn. She feels light-headed, but the flint is still in her heart. Myra Talbot is one of those Gareth went out with at school. How easily he had linked himself with her again, how smoothly he slipped into the group. Life would always be like that for him – a hospitable place, a welcome home. What does he know, really, of wishing to escape the world?

When she hears him cross the courtyard, calling her name, a sharp pain rips through her, as if her body were a piece of cloth.

'Why did you walk out?' He comes beside her. 'Why didn't you stop to talk? You know them all.' He opens the passenger door and she slides into the seat.

'I don't know them,' she says when he gets in.

Gareth sighs. 'You make yourself seem unfriendly.' He starts the engine.

'I am what I seem.'

As the car moves onto the mountain road Olwen puts her head back and closes her eyes. Immediately, her grandfather appears. She is with him, deep in the Cwm, watching as he plaits a wreath of laurel and bay leaves, weaving in bluebells, ragged robins, daisies. When it is finished, he places it on her head and makes a fancy bow. 'Queen of the Cwm,' he says. 'What is your heart's desire, Your Majesty?'

The scene shifts and she's at her bedroom window again, watching the woman in blue, seeing the woman's face as she lifts it in the moonlight to look at Olwen –

Her eyes fly open.

'All right?' Gareth says.

'I'm fine.'

'Why were you coming to see my father, Olwen?'

'I didn't feel well over the weekend.'

'You should talk to him. He can help you, I'm sure.'

'I'll go back sometime,' she says, to quiet him.

They are driving beside the Cwm towards Archer's Lane. Tree branches thrust out into the road, brushing the car like long fingers. The sound they make is like a whisper, 'Come'.

When they turn into Archer's Lane, Gareth pulls over to the side, just below the Millers' cottage, and switches off the engine.

'Why have you stopped here?'

'Because your house is just steps away, and I know that as soon as we reach the gate you'll jump out and run.' He turns to her. 'This afternoon was the first time I've seen you laugh.'

'The cider made me silly. It's worn off now.'

He has parked the car at the entrance to the woods. Looking out of the window, Olwen sees the familiar path, the great oaks lining it like sentinels, their branches crossed swords. It's easy to imagine the path as a royal road, leading to the palace of some great monarch, the bright sunshine beyond the boughs suggesting a wall of gold. And indeed she had felt queenly, rambling in the Cwm with her grandfather.

Countless times they walked this path, all the way from Archer's Lane to Cefn Heights, where it ends at the cemetery gates, spinning tales and dreams as they went. Yet now, gazing into the silent woods, Olwen senses a lack there, its gold and green luxuriance failing to appease the need that rises in her. Wild flowers, lavish in the grass, like gems carelessly spilled, taunt her with images of lost wealth.

She turns slowly to Gareth. He has been watching her, she sees, his green eyes a reflection of the woods, the expression in them as enigmatic as the Cwm itself.

'I've seen you before, Olwen,' he says dreamily. 'With just that expression on your face . . . a long time ago.'

It occurs to her as she looks into his eyes that she has lost all sense of direction, as if she wanders in a maze. And as if he is a stranger who happens by, she catches at his arm.

'Kiss me,' she says, 'like you did at the Wen.'

His mouth makes her shudder with delight. She opens her arms and wraps them around him. Closing her eyes, she forgets that they are in Archer's Lane, in broad daylight. She arches her back and thrusts her body against him.

'Come into the Cwm, Olwen,' One arm around her, his other hand on her breast, Gareth sits up to look at her.

His hair is tousled, his eyes glistening like ivy leaves. But when he breaks their embrace, Olwen's desire shrivels. Looking down at herself, she sees her skirt risen to her thighs, her legs spread, the crablike shape of his hand under her top, and revulsion overwhelms her. She thrusts her palms against his chest and pushes him away. Pulling down her skirt, she leaps from the car, slams the door behind her, and runs round to the other side where Gareth, dishevelled, grasps the steering wheel.

'My grandfather was right about you,' she says. 'From now on, don't come after me. Leave me alone, do you hear?'

'You're a tease and a bitch, Olwen,' he says.

Tears sting her eyes. She turns on her heel and walks swiftly up the road. It's not until he calls her name that she sees Bryn Brewen leaning on his gate.

'I saw,' he says.

Olwen stumbles and stops, caught by his eyes as neatly as if he had set a snare for her.

'Never you mind, lovely girl,' he says in his warm-toffee voice. 'I was watching out for you. Won't you come in and sit down a bit?'

Olwen finds her voice. 'You leave me alone, too.' The words come out harsh, fierce.

Bryn flinches.

She smiles at him, a baring of her teeth. 'If you don't, I'll kill you.'

For a moment she sees shock in his face. Then he says, smoothly, 'No need for threats, Olwen. I meant no harm.'

Turning from him, she looks back down the lane. Gareth still sits immobile at the wheel of his car.

'I won't brook interference any more,' she says, and goes on up the lane.

As she walks, Bryn Brewen and Gareth fall from her mind like a discarded burden. Weightless, a blown leaf, she drifts towards her own gate. When she reaches it and places her hand on the top rung, a breeze comes suddenly out of the Cwm and enfolds her, soft and soothing as velvet against her skin.

Thirteen

Gwen has left a note beneath the blue and white sugar bowl on the kitchen table. Olwen reads:

> 12:30
> I'm just slipping down to Aunt Flindy's to give her a hand in the house. Salad and ham in the fridge for your lunch. Alun is coming about three to mend the gate.

She is glad her grandmother is not there to ask about her visit to Dr Lloyd. I'll tell her the waiting room was too crowded, she thinks, as she goes upstairs to change her rumpled clothes. When she has put on shorts and a shirt, she goes into the garden to sit under the chestnut.

Under the trailing boughs, voluminous as a hoop skirt, Olwen plucks at leaves and tries to make sense of her behaviour towards Gareth.

He had promised he wouldn't touch her, and then . . . But she knows at once that this is unfair. It was she who started it, today, and last time, at the Wen.

'You're a tease and a bitch, Olwen.'

The names make her smart. She is not those things. How could she be? She has never had boyfriends, never been with anyone but him. The rules and rituals of love, the procedures and the boundaries, are as foreign to her as the Orient. With Gareth, she feels like an ill-prepared traveller, instinct and fear her only guides, one urging her on, the other crying halt.

Neither of her grandparents had ever spoken to her directly about sex. Gwen had vaguely explained menstruation as connected to the future, not the present, to a distant time when Olwen might want to marry and have babies. John had issued warnings that boys wanted only 'one thing', implying something shameful incurring endless remorse.

But in the stories they read, in the books he gave her, she had sensed a different significance . . . Kaye ravished by the Snow Queen; Lancelot enthralled by Guinevere; Odysseus fastening himself to the ship's mast to resist the Sirens' song . . . Even the places she had grown up in, the wild Cwm, the lush, fragrant garden, fostered a delight in sensuous pleasures. Yet he always forbade her –

It was not his intent, then, but her response, something in *her*, a thing she was born with, that slanted the inferences she drew from books, pictures, plants, the tools he used to teach her. A hereditary warp, passed on from Alice . . . the woman in blue, voluptuous and bloody. To have had a mother like that! To have sprung from a woman so lustful, so murderous! Olwen feels her heart beat harder. Fear and anxiety web in her chest; at the edges of her mind, the red vortex swirls.

'Stop it!' she says out loud, sharply. Then, softer, as if she spoke to a fretful child, 'No need to be frightened.' Hadn't he told her that years ago when she asked him if ghosts were real?

'They're like them little cut-out figures you play with. They have no life of their own.'

Called up by the enchanter, Alice is not as she was in life, but merely his plaything, performing deeds he dreams up, manipulated by him as the cut-outs were commanded by Olwen.

The explanation does not hold. What she saw on Sunday night, the revelation that drove her to Dr Lloyd's door, points to a mystery deeper than the enigmas the enchanter spins, to a separate, prior evil that emanates from within her own house on Archer's Lane.

Unless it was a trick of the moonlight? A self-deception? Longing for what she has not yet earned, perhaps she had allowed her heart to deceive her and had imagined, not seen, above the collar of the blue cloak and framed by Alice's silver hair, the face of her grandfather.

Out in the woods, the enchanter waits and plots confusion. 'Once he sets his heart on someone,' her grandfather said, 'he brooks no interference. His pride is too puffed up for him to suffer a single loss. Why, if that happened, it might destroy him.'

Above the garden wall, the Cwm rises. The massed leaves of the giant oaks and elms shiver under a sky that has filled with clouds while Olwen has sat pondering beneath the chestnut. The sun, still high, fringes the clouds with gold, but in their gloomy centres she sees the threat of an approaching storm. It's time. The heatwave has lasted weeks. Despite her daily waterings, the lawn shows specks of brown, the flowers have begun to droop.

Soon it will be midsummer. Those who wait upon her – her grandfather and his arch-enemy – grow impatient. In the Cwm, she will find them both. She must settle on a day, make the decision firm, irrevocable.

'I will go on Sunday,' she says.

After all, it is the most appropriate day. On Sundays she and her grandfather would put on their best clothes for their walk in the woods as if they were dressing for service, though neither of them were chapel-goers. Their Sunday walks had assumed a different tenor, too, from their weekday ones. How, exactly, she can't fathom. Had the clothes they'd worn made them more subdued, more reverent? Surely he'd had a reason for the ritual of dressing up, though it had never occurred to her then to question.

His best cap with the blue silk lining . . . a blue sky . . . blue ribbons in Olwen's hair. His favourite colour. One Sunday – it must have been a Sunday – they had discovered a jay trapped in a thicket. He had plunged in his hand and rescued it. The bird lay petrified in his palm. She had touched its feathers and looked into her grandfather's eyes, bluest of all.

'Is it dead?'

'Not it!' He had laughed and flicked his wrist and the bird had soared from the nest of his cupped hand and vanished through a break in the leafy boughs that arched high above the path where Olwen stood with her face upturned.

The gate whines. Olwen looks up, expecting Gwen, but it's Alun Miller who stands there, handsome ('debonair' is the word that leaps to her mind) in a grey pinstripe suit. At first she notices only the fine cut of his clothes and a wild thought occurs – he has dressed up to visit her. Then she sees the toolbox in his left hand, the hammer in his right. He has come to mend the gate, of course, and he wears a suit because he has come straight from school.

As she crosses the lawn he watches her, his eyes moving over her body, her bare legs. 'You look charming,' he says when she reaches him. He gives 'charming' a slight emphasis, as if she had asked him for reassurance. 'Only girls and *very* young women look well in shorts. Here, hold the toolbox, be my helper.

Twenty-five, I think, don't you agree, is the cut-off. Rosamund has one more year, and then I shall forbid her to wear shorts.'

Olwen, holding the toolbox in both hands as if it were a gift, stares at him. Is he serious or pulling her leg?

'Of course she looks marvellous in all clothes. It won't be a hardship for her to give up one type of outfit with so much to choose from. Put the box down, Olwen, and open it. Hand me the pincers.'

Alun pulls out the two nails remaining in the gate-post. 'What have you been doing to this gate? Look how you've stripped the wood off.'

'I didn't do that.'

He raises an eyebrow at her.

'Did you mean what you said, about telling Rosamund when to stop wearing shorts?'

He laughs. 'Not quite. But she does take my advice. I have good taste in women's clothes. Rosamund dresses differently now than when I first met her – differently and better. Pass me four nails.' He picks up the hammer. 'Can you hold the bracket in place while I knock these nails in? I won't miss, I promise.'

To do as he asks, Olwen must move closer to him. He hammers in the nails, millimetres from her fingers, his head almost touching hers. The pounding of the hammer reverberates along her nerves.

'There, that's firm, I think.' 'Now give me the latch I bought in town and hand me some more nails.'

She reaches into the toolbox and holds out the shiny new latch.

'Bring the gate in.'

Olwen jumps up and pulls in the gate.

'Ready to hold again?'

Again she stands beside him, her body close to his, keeping herself steady, unflinching, as the hammer pounds.

'Okay, now we'll test it.'

Olwen closes the gate. The latch clicks neatly into place.

'We make a good pair. We both have strong nerves. Like the knife-thrower and his lady accomplice. Do you want to run away with me and join the circus?'

Olwen feels herself blush. Now that her hands are no longer useful, they dangle awkwardly at her sides.

Alun smiles. 'You have dirty knees.'

She bends to rub her knees with her palms.

'Don't worry about it though. You're charming, as I've already told you.'

His mocking tone riles her suddenly. '*I* could have mended the gate!' she says.

'Why didn't you?'

For this, she has no answer. How can she tell him that the broken latch has not figured in her mind as an object to mend but as something more sinister, a symbol of the evil that besieges her. Standing in front of him, aware of her hot cheeks and her stained knees, she says only, 'I didn't think of it.'

Alun puts his hands on his hips. 'I expect there's a great deal you haven't thought of yet,' he says in what she imagines to be his schoolteacher's voice. 'You haven't, for example, thought of offering me a drink. Anything cold will do nicely.'

Olwen goes swiftly up the path. With effort, she keeps herself from running. In the kitchen, pouring lemonade into a glass, she thinks, he *meant* to embarrass me. He enjoyed it. She can picture him in the classroom, disconcerting students with his arrogant gaze and derisive comments. He has made her feel like a schoolgirl – crushed. As if she had a crush on him.

When she goes out, he is sitting in a deckchair, lounging elegantly, his long legs stretched out, crossed at the ankles. Olwen hands him the glass of lemonade.

'Where's yours?'

'I don't want any.' It had not occurred to her to pour herself a glass.

'Still, it would have been companionable of you to join me. At least you'll sit down? Or should I drink up and go?'

She moves in front of him, stepping wide to avoid crossing over his legs.

As she sits, he says, 'Very fey. Elfish,' and raises his glass to her before drinking.

'Selfish?' Olwen startles.

'Possibly you are – but I said "elfish". You look as if you've strayed out of those woods.' He nods toward the Cwm. 'As if they were your real home. Why are you perched on the edge of your chair? Do you want to run away?' He smiles lazily. 'I won't let you escape, so don't try.'

Olwen knots her fingers. She knows he's teasing her, enjoying her confusion, but she can't quell the alarm rising in her chest.

As on the evening of the dinner, when he spoke of Roman conquests, she feels ensnarled. She wishes he would go away . . . and she wishes he would hold her.

'Wispy, secretive creature. I love your tilted eyes.'

Her fear takes a different shape, his words suggesting associations that horrify her – the face in the woods, the image carved on the rafter, the apparition at the door of the toolshed, the tilted eyes indicative of a tipped mind – he has touched the core of her terror.

Above his spruce beard his mouth smiles, a row of even white teeth. His black eyes, too, are evenly spaced, hard as cobnuts on either side of a stemlike nose. His good looks spring from precision, as if a controlled and expert hand had shaped his features to correspond to a mind incisive as a razor.

'My eyes are not tilted,' she says, her voice wavering.

'It's the first thing I noticed about you, that curious tilt. In Ancient Britain, in the days of the Druids, it was a feature regarded with awe. The possessor was supposed to have psychic powers – be in touch with ghosts and all that.' As he speaks – lectures – he drops his teasing tone. His gaze, no longer fixed on her, becomes alert, seeking; his own eyes assume an obsessive cast. Watching him, she intuits at once that his first love is not, after all, his wife, or himself, but history. 'I'm not sure what reasoning informed their belief, but all cultures in all ages seem to have been sensitive to the specialness of the eyes. Eventually, they came to be regarded as the mirror of the soul. That was long after the Druids' time, of course, but I wonder whether people then made a similar connection – so that the tilt would represent a skewed perception – madness regarded as visionary, divine –'

'My eyes aren't tilted.'

Alun sets down his glass and leans toward her. 'I'll show you. Close them.'

With the tip of his little finger he traces the crescent of her eyelid, close to the lashes. When he reaches the outer corner of her eye, his finger makes an upward movement.

'Feel that?'

'I felt the way you moved your finger.'

'I simply followed the curve. Of course, if you refuse to accept the evidence –' He sits back in his chair and cocks his head at her. 'Your hair, too, when it's loose like that . . . dangerous hair, you have, Olwen. A fellow could get all tangled up in it.'

For a moment, they stare at each other, Alun relaxed, wry, tongue in cheek. Olwen sits stiffly, her hands between her knees.

'Well,' he says at last, 'you won't be led, I see.' Bending, he picks up his glass and drains it. 'I must be off. Rosamund misses me. We miss each other. Neither of us manages separation well, though we manage it differently. Will you walk to the gate with me?'

As they cross the grass, Olwen, glancing towards the toolshed, fancies she sees, behind the dusty window, a face. This time she feels no tremor. It's as if she glimpsed herself, unexpectedly, in a mirror, catching sight of an expression she never knew was hers – the look of a gazer, a voyeur.

She opens the gate and Alun steps out into the lane. Olwen clicks the latch shut and stands with her hands on the top bar, her eyes cast down so he will not see the distress she feels.

'What's up?' he asks softly. 'You look like a lost child. I feel compelled to stay and comfort you. Should I?'

'I'm fine, thank you.'

'You're a firm one, Olwen – under that wispiness – a hard nut to crack, as the saying goes.' Slipping a finger under her chin, he forces her head up. 'Some fellow will crack you one day, though. It's the fate of all young women.' He touches his forehead in a mock salute. Then he turns his back on her and goes whistling down the lane. She watches him until he reaches his own gate, but he doesn't look round. His thoughts leaping to Rosamund, no doubt, he has dismissed her.

She turns from the gate and crosses the lawn again. Standing beside the deckchair where Alun sat, she looks up into the crisscrossed boughs of the chestnut, the jigsaw pieces of sky. All the pieces are grey. Rain is coming. She feels the stillness that precedes a storm. The green leaves might be painted, they're so motionless.

Her hands find the crossbar of the deckchair and grasp it. He is taking his wife to bed right at this moment.

Yet is it love that drives him? Minutes ago he was flirting with her. Had she behaved differently, shown confidence instead of the fear he seemed to misinterpret as stubbornness, he would have pressed further, seduced her, she's certain. Believing her a 'hard nut', he's gone home to his passionate wife. In his haste, he has forgotten his toolbox.

If he had pressed, I would have let him, Olwen thinks. She sinks into the deckchair. Behind closed eyes she sees her grandfather's stern face, hears his voice: 'They want one thing only.' But he was wrong. It is she who wants it.

The latch clicks. Gwen comes up the path, her hair tied in a yellow spotted kerchief, her arms full of bluebells.

'Hello, love. Alun mended the gate, then? What did Dr Lloyd say?' She sits in the other deckchair and lays the bluebells in her lap.

'There was a queue so I didn't wait.'

'Oh, Olwen –'

'I'm all right now, anyway.' Olwen takes one of the flowers by its long slender stem. 'So many. How did you manage to find all these in the lane?'

'Oh, there's none to speak of in our lane. It's too dry and sunny. I picked them in the woods.'

Olwen's heart jumps. 'You went into the Cwm?'

Gwen smiles shyly. 'It sounds funny, I know. I was coming out of Aunt Flindy's, thinking you might like sausages for tea and I'd better thaw them, and all of a sudden the fancy took me. I looked at the Cwm and thought, "I haven't been in there for years, not since Olwen was a baby," and my feet just started to move. Perhaps it was memories that pulled me.'

'What happened in there?'

Gwen looks at her in surprise. 'Nothing *happened*. I just walked for a bit, enjoying myself, and then I saw the bluebells and I started to pick. And I couldn't stop! Long after I knew I had enough to fill the house – and how will I carry them and where will I find all the vases, I said to myself – I kept on gathering. And the funniest thing, Olwen – the more bluebells I picked, the more there seemed to be. It sounds daft, I know, but I swear they were springing up right under my nose!'

'But –' Olwen begins, and wonders how to go on. Thinking of Gwen walking unprotected in the Cwm, anxiety consumes her, but how can she say so when she can't tell her grandmother the reason? 'Did you meet anyone?'

'Who would I meet in the woods? Do you know, I think I'll start walking in there again, regular, while summer lasts. I'd forgotten how nice it is.'

'Don't!' Olwen cries, and bites her lip. Quickly, she says, 'It might not be safe. Bryn Brewen goes in there.'

142

'Only at night. Besides, Bryn's not dangerous, Olwen. Surely you don't think he'd harm us?'

'Next time you feel like going for a walk, tell me. We'll go together.'

'That would be lovely.' Gwen's smile lights her face and pierces Olwen's heart. How unkind, how neglectful she's been to her grandmother. How glad she is that Gwen has come out of the Cwm unharmed. Looking down at her grandmother's hands, resting on the stems of the bluebells, she sees the gold keeper, the ring she has always believed to be magical. In the failing afternoon light, the tiny intertwined leaves and flowers gleam softly. Like a compass, it must have guided her grandmother through the woods, keeping her out of evil's path.

'There's a storm brewing,' Gwen says. 'I didn't come out of the Cwm a whit too soon. I shouldn't like to be caught under them oaks with lightning about.' She sighs. 'I'm tired, too, after all that bending, though I felt spry as a girl doing it. Still, I ought to slip back down to Aunt Flindy's and get her extra blankets out of the tallboy. It might turn cold and I don't like to think of her climbing on a chair to reach them –'

'I'll go,' Olwen says.

'Will you? I can get supper started if you'll do that. Of course, I haven't thawed the sausages. Will Welsh rarebit do?'

Her grandmother's face, a faded flower, touches Olwen deeply. 'I'll help you carry the bluebells in before I go.'

As they go up the path, Gwen says, 'Rain will do the garden good.'

'And when the bluebells die, you can pick flowers here. You needn't go into the Cwm for them.'

'I thought you wouldn't like me to take from the garden.'

Olwen slips her free arm through her grandmother's. 'Take as many as you like. They're yours too.'

'Thank you,' Gwen says. 'I appreciate that, love.'

As they go into the house and close the door, the sky darkens. A sudden harsh wind from the Cwm rattles at the gate. The new latch holds, but the wind rushes through the bars and tears across the garden, bending flower stalks, tossing the chestnut boughs, shrieking like a thing in fury.

Fourteen

Aunt Flindy's garden is consumed by weeds. Docks have sprung up there like the beanstalk in the fairytale, their broad leaves meshed in a gloomy awning. Inside the dock forest giant dandelions and vicious clumps of purple thistle strangle the grass. Remembering how her grandfather had tended this garden as well as his own, Olwen feels ashamed. It has not occurred to her that she might carry on his work here too.

He had planted vegetables and herbs – thyme, mint, rosemary – because they were what the old woman wanted.

'I have no looks on flowers,' she told him. 'Can't put them in broth to give it a bit of flavour, can I? Sweet william won't make the Sunday mutton taste no better. Don't be bothered with flowers, John.'

But to give the garden colour, he had nailed trellises to the walls and trained the briar rose. Now, as if to spite Aunt Flindy, the rose runs amok, stifling the gooseberry and blackcurrant bushes, spreading a net of thorns across the path. Olwen scratches her bare feet and burns her legs on nettles thrusting out their stinging leaves. But going up the path she smells the fresh, clean scent of mint. Herself a gardener now, she could clear this jungle in a week . . . if she had a week to spare Aunt Flindy.

She reaches the doorstep and raps on the blistered door. Yellow paint flakes and powders her knuckles like pollen, the only response to her knock, although behind the dingy curtains a light gleams in the parlour. Olwen knocks again, then tries the doorknob. The knob turns and the door opens on a glittering white figure standing motionless in the dark passage, its arm raised like a javelin-thrower's, a long, silvery weapon poised in its fist.

Olwen's heart lurches.

'It's not manners to walk into a person's house uninvited,' Aunt Flindy says. She lowers the steel-tipped walking stick.

'I knocked – twice.'

'And never waited for an answer. I was coming. Takes time. I'm not a slip of a girl like you.'

Olwen sees that she is draped in a long, lamé shawl, the metallic threads sparkling like stars in the dim light that seeps from the parlour. Beneath the shawl, she wears a calf-length, black brocade skirt, on her shoeless feet, a man's red and white striped rugby socks. Her son, Albert, Olwen recalls, played rugby for the county before he took off for Australia.

Aunt Flindy turns and goes back into the parlour, beckoning Olwen to follow her. 'Lucky you didn't get a clout over the head with Idris' stick,' she says over her shoulder, 'coming in the way a thief would.'

In the parlour she shoves the ginger cat out of the rocking chair and lowers herself into it, both hands pressed on the knob of the stick, her body arched forward until her behind meets the cushion. 'Sit 'ee down.' She points her stick at a three-legged stool on the other side of the threadbare hearthrug.

Olwen sits. Beneath a cavernous chimney the empty blacklead grate sits between them, a giant squatting toad. Olwen thinks of small boys – Hansel, Tom, the chimney sweep. 'I can't stay long –'

'Never thought you could. I'm flabbergasted you've come at all.'

Olwen shifts the stool out of the draught that whistles down the chimney. From the brass fender where it has perched itself, the cat hisses at her.

'Shut your face!' Aunt Flindy casts her stick within inches of the cat's back. The creature leaps across the room and springs onto the dining table, covered with a long, deep-red, moth-eaten chenille cloth. Gold tassels trail on the floor like the hem of an old-fashioned opera gown.

'Cinders don't care for young 'uns,' Aunt Flindy says. 'She's accustomed to bad treatment from 'em. Stone-throwing and that. Nearly lost her right eye by a young 'un and she've never forgot. Got long memories, cats.' She stares at Olwen accusingly, as if she had been the stone-slinger.

Olwen looks around the parlour, where she has not been for years. Besides the table and four dining chairs, the rocking chair and the stool, a glass-fronted cabinet is the only piece of furniture in the room. The cabinet shelves are crammed with dusty dishes, its top massed with framed photographs. More framed portraits decorate the walls and crowd the mantelshelf, men and women and children in sepia-hued clothes, their faces deadly serious. To Olwen, the parlour looks like a missing persons' bureau. She shivers.

'Cold?' Aunt Flindy says without solicitude. 'You got thin blood, I expect. Been raised too soft.'

'There's a storm coming,' Olwen says. 'Nain sent me to see if you need more blankets on your bed.'

'She's a good 'oman, your nain. I hope you know that.'

'Yes.'

'No, you don't. Never have appreciated her. You was always too much for him. Mind you, John was good too. To me, he was. I don't say he was good to everyone. There's some that's glad he's gone, I dare say, and you needn't look beyond Archer's Lane to know who. But he always did for me, and I miss him terrible.'

Olwen winces.

Aunt Flindy tosses her head, a mannerism that might have been called perky in a young girl. 'Can't stand to hear him spoken of, eh? We all got to learn to take that, miss.'

'It's just –'

'I lost three men. Idris died, Emlyn disappeared, and then Albert went off to Australie. How do you think *that* feels? All I got are photos, and a letter now and then. When I see an envelope with the Australie stamp, I say, "Here's another from the picture-man, Flinders. *He* might as well be dead."'

'I don't think it's the same –'

'Don't ye? Why not? I never see him, same as you don't see Grandpa.'

'He could come back, couldn't he?'

'Tell you what, I thought I saw him the other night. Sunday must have been 'cause I was saying my prayers.'

'Who?'

'Who're we talking about? Lloyd George? Twasn't John, though. Know who it was? Bryn Brewen! What do you make of that?'

Olwen's patience snaps. Oppressed by the eyes that stare at her from the walls and mantelpiece, she longs to leave. 'I don't make anything of it. I can't follow you at all. Shall I get your blankets?'

'Course you can't follow me. You don't know about night

146

goings-on. Sleep like a princess, I expect. But I have trouble nodding off since Albert left. I put the light out and skimmed-milk faces float out of the walls, jibbing at me. They get cheeky when a woman lives on her own. I got Cinders, course, but I wish I had a telly so I could see some real faces. The Council ought to lay the pipes for telly out here. Not a bit of care, have they? Too busy lining their own wallets to give the old-aged a thought. My pension's hardly gone up in years. And there's him next-door, strong as an ox, living like a lord on the dole. Is that fair?'

'Did you say Bryn Brewen came here on Sunday night?' Out of Aunt Flindy's meanderings, Olwen snatches, suddenly, a connection with her own Sunday-night vision of Bryn, his face torn and bloodied from the knife.

'Not him! I wouldn't have him through my gate. Wouldn't look nice, him a bachelor and me a widow. There'd be talk. 'Sides, he's a criminal.'

'Did he commit a crime? What was it?'

'Oh, hark at her!' Aunt Flindy rolls her eyes back, a chilling vision of how she will look laid out among lilies. '"Did he commit a crime?"' She imitates Olwen's voice. 'God bless the innocent. Only every night of his manhood, dearie.'

'You mean *poaching*.'

'Yes, I mean *poaching*. In't that a crime no more, then?'

'No one pays attention to that. He supplies the Pont Ysaf police force with rabbits. Grandfather told me.'

'Is that so? Shows how much Grandpa knew, lovey. If it wasn't a bobby after him Sunday night, it must've been Old Nick, and it wasn't Old Nick 'cause him and Bryn are best butties. He had his hands up to his face, too, like he was trying to disguise it.' She covers her own face and peeks at Olwen through her fingers. Her nails are the colour of blood.

Olwen grips the stool to stop the trembling that has begun in her arms.

'He was running down the lane like old boots. Galloped up his path and dived into his house with that useless dog of his right behind. Had a good fright somewhere, both of 'em. He was in such a state he didn't even see me, though I was leaning out of the window in full moonlight. I thought it was John, see, come back as they do when they've no peace, and I intended to advise him like I did twenty years ago. He listened to me then –'

'You think my grandfather's not . . . peaceful?'

'I don't claim to be a medium like old Mrs Jacobs, but they do come to me – unasked – so I thought it was John coming down the lane.'

'You said he has no peace?'

'Beg your pardon, I never. I said I *thought* not – but it wasn't John, I told you. It was Bryn Brewen.' Aunt Flindy's lashes fly up like twin fans. 'Has Bryn died, do you think? Have you seen him recently? I hope I haven't been speaking ill of the dead.'

'He was alive and well this morning, Aunt Flindy. What time was it on Sunday that you saw him?'

'Missy, you sound like one of them wireless detectives on *Dick Barton*. It was half past two, thereabouts. I hadn't long gone upstairs –'

'Was it only Bryn you saw? You didn't see a woman too?'

'A woman with Bryn?' Aunt Flindy hoots. 'Chance'd be a fine thing. He'd be running into the house with his trousers down then, I dare say, for it must be years . . . Only one 'oman ever had looks on him and she not for long. He's not the type 'omans fancy, is he? Too shifty, and no steady work.'

'Who was she? The one that did?'

Aunt Flindy hoods her eyes. 'Nobody you'd know.'

'It was my mother, wasn't it?'

'He asked me once, could I call her up. About a year after she died, it was.'

'Bryn did?'

'Your grandpa.'

Olwen's heart strikes the wall of her chest. 'Why, Aunt Flindy?'

''Cause he knew I had the gift.'

'I mean, why did he want to?'

'Why do you think?'

'He missed her, of course.'

'Oh, he missed her all right.'

'Did you do it?'

'No, I never. That's the devil's business. I gave him good advice instead. "Leave Alice rest," I said, "and tend to the baby she left. Your hope lies in that child, John." He listened to me, too, didn't he? Too well, I think sometimes, but he never had much looks on you before, so I do take the credit.'

'That's not true! He went up to London to get me when my mother died.'

148

Aunt Flindy rocks, smiles, and says nothing. She's lying, of course. Olwen regrets her outburst, for it has given spiteful pleasure to the old woman, who has never liked her.

'I'd better go,' she says and starts to rise.

Aunt Flindy, rocking, begins to hum. Olwen recognizes the tune, an old nonsense rhyme her grandfather used to sing to her. It's a shock, hearing it after so many years, and she sits again, clasping her hands.

Aunt Flindy murmurs the words:

> Ha, ha, ha, hee, hee, hee,
> Elephants nest in the rhubarb tree.

'Stop it.'

'Mrs Jacobs used to ask for the deceased's favourite song, and she'd sing it before she called. She had a fine voice, I'll say that for her. Hearing the song put the departed in a consenting mood, she believed. But if singing didn't work, she had other tricks up her sleeve.'

'Where does she live? In Pont Ysaf?' Olwen tries to speak calmly, so Aunt Flindy won't detect a reason behind her questions.

'Used to, but not any more. She's had an address on the other side for donkey's years, but she never gave it to me before going. Someone'd have to sing to her now.' Aunt Flindy neighs, making Olwen jump. Then she leans forward, serious. 'You want to call Grandpa, don't ye?'

Olwen stares at her, distressed to hear her half-formed idea spoken. 'Shh!' she says, and glances around the room at the dead faces.

'You can do if you want. Don't need a go-between if you know the method and you're not afeared. I never believed Mrs Jacobs really did it anyhow. It was her husband, is my opinion, dressed up in the deceased's clothes what she always asked for before she gave a seance. When it was an 'oman, he wore a wig, and they used dolls for the babies. I know that for a fact, 'cause one fell off the chair once and I heard the china head crack. She switched off the torch quick and told some cock-and-bull story about how the sight of its mam and dad had given the baby a fit. Now, I know the method and never use it. They come to me of their own accord, the power's so strong. It's in you, too. I can tell by your eyes. You got the look, like me.'

'How?' Olwen says. 'How do I do it?'

'You know best.'

'But you said there's a method.'

'That's right, and if you know the person, you know the method. Different fish, different bait. *You* know where he's most likely skulking, and you know the words to bring him out. Go where he waits and say what he wants to hear, that's all.'

Olwen rises. 'I have to go now, Aunt Flindy.'

'Surprised you stayed so long. You'll find the tallboy in the front bedroom. Stand on the cane chair not the brocade. Two blankets will do nicely.'

Outside, the light has changed. It seems unusually clear to Olwen, greenish, as if she looked into a limpid pond. In this light, each weed and blade of grass in the garden is clearly defined. The briar rose petals, the bramble thorns, the veins on the dock leaves are so distinct they might have been etched by an artist meticulously attentive to detail.

At the gate she turns right instead of left and walks down the lane to the opening into the Cwm. When she crosses the ditch the dirt path is soft as velvet under her feet. No tangled undergrowth or jutting branches impede her. Oak and elm leaves gleam in the strange light like satin ribbons hung out at a fête.

As she moves deeper into the woods, following the illuminated path, it widens into a glade she does not remember, except in dreaming. She pauses to look back. Perhaps the path has changed behind her, too, like the insubstantial, shifting scenery of dreams.

The path is the same – but someone else is entering the woods. Darting behind the trunk of an oak, Olwen drops to her hands and knees. She peers through the foliage to watch them come, the man with his odd, crooked walk, the skipping child with long, swinging braids. The man holds the child's hand, his other hand wrapped over the brass horse's head on his walking stick. They make no sound, and their faces wear the same rapt, oblivious expressions as when she first saw them near the bus stop in Pont Ysaf Road.

As they pass her, Olwen holds her breath and keeps her body rigid. Yet she knows caution is needless. If she had stood in front of them they would not have seen her. About to crawl out of her hiding place and follow, she instinctively looks again down the path. Sauntering along it, several yards behind the man and the little girl, comes Alice in her blue dress.

Her step is light and easy, unselfconscious as a child's, but her body is womanly, her breasts like large, ripe fruits on a slender tree. As she walks, she swings her hips, her hands reaching out to pull a leaf from a branch, a flower from a bush, and then toss it away with a graceful, indolent gesture, as if the act of plucking and discarding is done only to show off her round arms and seductive shoulders.

Her face is hidden by the curtain of hair that falls across it, and no matter how she turns her body she keeps her head averted, so that even when she passes in front of her, Olwen cannot glimpse her features. She is singing, softly, a song Olwen hears for the second time that evening:

> Ha, ha, ha, hee, hee, hee,
> Elephants nest in the rhubarb tree.

Olwen crawls out and follows the apparition. She must move swiftly for although the woman seems to amble she is already a good distance down the path. The man and the child have entered the glade. Soon they cross it and vanish into the trees on the far side. Fear envelops Olwen, as if the spectres were her charges, as if she is responsible for their safety. She wants to run, to catch them up, but she dare not pass the woman in blue, who has stopped at the opening to the clearing.

Olwen stops too. Several yards behind the woman, she senses her anxiety. She has ceased singing and holds her body motionless. Olwen knows, as if she knew the creature herself intimately, that her torpor signifies loss of will. She has not the courage to enter the glade.

For some moments everything is so fixed and lifeless – the woman, the trees, the unwavering light – that Olwen feels part of a tableau. Then, suddenly, the woman shatters the silence. In a thin, childish voice, she cries, 'Father! Father! Where are you? Why don't you come? Don't leave me here! I can't live if you leave me!'

On the other side of the glade the trees begin to sway, as if the woman's shrieks have set them in motion. A wind rises, the boughs swing and dip, and from deep within the woods something approaches. All her senses alert, as if she were more animal than human, Olwen stands poised, listening.

The trees around the glade rustle, and behind her, and all through the wood, the noise is taken up, as if a great crowd clapped or chanted in unison. And then, abruptly, the atmosphere alters. Her heart beats harder. Terror locks her limbs. The thing approaching the glade is monstrous, fatal. She hears the crash and thresh of its progress, as if it snapped trees like twigs. The earth pounds as though a herd of elephants are rampaging. In the clearing the brilliant green light evaporates, plunging the woods into deep gloom. All around Olwen hears the scurrying of animals, the squawking of birds. And again the woman cries out: 'Father! Come, Father! I'm ready for you.'

Without warning, a deluge comes crashing through the trees, turning the earth under Olwen's feet into a swamp, throwing an impenetrable curtain between her and the scene that has transfixed her. She turns and runs down the muddy track to Archer's Lane.

As she sprints up the road, the rain lashing her body, she is overcome with shame. She has abandoned them all – her grandfather, Alice, herself – to the enchanter. 'But I couldn't stop it,' she says aloud. 'I didn't know how. He never told me the words.'

Tears mingle with the rain on her face.

Fifteen

In the dressing-table mirror, Olwen examines the shape of her
eyes. Last night, coming in from the woods, she had not dared
to look, avoiding her reflection as she stripped off her sopping
clothes. Preparing for bed later, she had still kept her gaze
averted from the glass. Distressed by what she had seen in the
Cwm, she could not have borne to discover, in her own features,
a resemblance to the mad, glittering eyes of Alice as she stood at
the toolshed door. It is Alice's face her grandfather carved on
the rafter; her face Olwen saw from the window of his sick
room. And she had dreaded to see the hereditary tilt in her own
mirror.

So she went quickly to bed and lay sleepless under the covers,
comforted by the thought that Gwen slept in the room next
door – Gwen, the wearer of the gold keeper, who had gone
alone into the Cwm and come out unscathed with an armload
of bluebells. Nothing bad can come into this house while she's
here, Olwen told herself repeatedly ... and realized that this
was so. Nothing *had* entered the cottage. The apparitions, the
frightening events, had all occurred outside, in the garden, the
toolshed, the woods – the places she thought of as her grandfather's domain. Gwen, immune to evil, made the house a safe
place. At last Olwen had fallen asleep.

In the morning sunshine, she looks into the mirror. And sees
that her eyes are oval – like her grandmother's. Their hazel
colour comes from Gwen too.

Why, then, did Alun Miller insist that her eyes tilted? He was
teasing her, yes ... but something more purposeful lay behind
his words. 'You have ...' he said, and 'You are ...', all his
statements declarative, as if he could not be wrong in his
perceptions. As if, by saying she was this or that, he could make
her so. As if he were making her up to suit himself, like a dollmaker giving shape to his fancies from the materials at hand.

Troubled by this insight she does not fully understand, Olwen crosses from the mirror to the open window. In the rain-cleansed garden the flowers glow. On the fence the sweet peas are like jewels in a necklace of many strands. Roses, rhododendrons, hollyhocks cascade from the bushes, and all along the path a border of tiny forget-me-nots, as lovely in their simplicity as the showier flowers, the flamboyant tiger lily and the gorgeous phlox. The golden sunflowers give the garden grandeur . . . and the delphiniums . . . Olwen stiffens, forces herself to look at them. They dazzle her eyes and beguile her senses, but the anticipated terror does not stir. Her mind remains quiet as she gazes. Celestial flowers this morning, their colour reflects the sky. Dew sparkles on the azure petals like tears. An odd and whimsical thought occurs: if God were a gardener, He would grow delphiniums.

And all these flowers Olwen has planted and nurtured without partiality, delighting in their diversity. Her grandfather had planted his garden like that; the greater the variety, the more it pleased him. 'So many flowers in the world, *cariad*, and I want to raise them all.' Yet he had thought differently about people. In humans he had valued conformity, narrowing his acquaintance, limiting his love to one or two – herself and her mother, the only beings on earth whom he could shape in his image. Olwen hesitates, pulls herself up mentally, as if she had strayed too near the edge of a ravine. But the question has formed: was her grandfather, like Alun Miller – like all determined men, perhaps – a dollmaker, too?

'Olwen!' Gwen calls from the bottom of the stairs. 'Breakfast!'

A car pulls up in the lane. Olwen sees the doctor open the gate. The sight of him lifts her heart. Everything about Dr Lloyd – his physical frame, his large-boned face, his old tweed hat and jacket – reassures her. The battered leather bag in his hand, the pipe bowl peering like a large, round eye out of his breast pocket are emblems of his kindness and wisdom. Wherever he goes, he brings cheer . . . and sanity.

Strolling up the path, pausing to look at her flowers, he seems a man untroubled by apparitions, unharried by dark forces. As he stops to sniff the roses Olwen thinks, he is content with life. He wants nothing more than he has. Yet once he had a wife whom he adored. Like her, he knows what it means to lose the person loved most. Somehow he has come to terms with that and found peace.

Dr Lloyd vanishes beneath the window, raps the knocker. Olwen leaves her room and runs downstairs, reaching the hall just as her grandmother opens the door.

In the kitchen the doctor sits at the table with them, accepting tea and toast, admiring the bluebells Gwen has arranged in a cut-glass vase.

'I picked them in the Cwm yesterday,' Gwen says.

'I didn't know you liked to walk in the woods.' The doctor's tone and the look he turns on Gwen suggest great interest and pleasure, as if she has revealed some extraordinary talent. His expression reminds Olwen of Alun Miller's, gazing at his wife . . . but it is different too. In Dr Lloyd's admiration, there is nothing proprietory.

'I haven't walked in there for years,' Gwen says, 'but I was telling Olwen, I think I'll start again. I used to love the woods. When Olwen was a baby, I'd push her pram in there every fine day.'

Olwen startles, a vision springing out of the bluebells – her own hands, baby hands, clutching at them, her grandfather pulling the stems towards her so that her fingers could grasp the flowers. 'I thought it was Grandfather did that.'

'Grandpa used to take you, too, of course. But when you were a baby, he was still working, so it was mainly me then.' Gwen turns to the doctor. 'After John retired, he took Olwen for walks every day, so there was no need for me to bother . . ' Her voice trails off, leaving questions in Olwen's mind: Why didn't you come with us? Did he make you stop?

Olwen wonders if these questions occur to the doctor. His face shows sympathy, but no surprise. Having known John, he knows the answers. As Olwen herself begins to.

'I'm off on a jaunt this weekend,' Gwen says into the silence. 'Going to visit my sister in Swansea for a few days.'

'Wonderful! A trip to the seaside will do you both good.' Dr Lloyd smiles at Olwen.

'I'm not going,' she says.

'Ah . . . well, you'll go in August as usual, I expect.' She is glad he doesn't ask her reason. Instead, he attends to Gwen. 'Now, when are you leaving? Saturday morning? I'll come out and give you a lift to the station.'

Gwen's cheeks colour up, a heightening of the rouge Olwen has noticed she wears every day now. 'That would be too much trouble for you. I can catch the bus.'

'No, I won't hear of it. You'll have a suitcase to lug. What time is your train?'

'I thought I'd catch the twenty-five past one. It will get me into Swansea by three. There's a ten o'clock, of course, if that's more convenient —' Her grandmother is flustered, like a girl invited on her first date. Her sudden shyness and the bright hue of rose in her face suggest the young woman sitting on the porch of the Swansea house surrounded by suitors.

'What if I pick you up at noon,' the doctor says, 'and we have a spot of lunch first?'

Gwen looks at Olwen, her eyebrows raised, as if she seeks advice – or permission.

Olwen touches her grandmother's hand. 'Great,' she says, and winks her left eyelid, surprising herself. She cannot recall ever having winked in her life, though she often saw that secret communication pass between girls – and boys – at school.

Gwen stares, surprised too. On her ring finger, the gold keeper boldly returns Olwen's wink.

'Walk to the car with me, Olwen,' Dr Lloyd says as he gets up to leave. 'I've something to give you I forgot to bring in.'

As they go down the path, he says, 'Your grandmother's an exceptional woman.'

'I suppose she is.'

'And I've been lonely for a long time.'

At the rose bush where he stopped to sniff the blooms Olwen breaks off a red rose and holds it out to the doctor. 'For your buttonhole.' She slips the stem into his lapel.

'Thank you,' he says, 'for understanding,' and, as they walk on, 'You're changing, Olwen.'

'Am I? How?'

'You're beginning to show your good heart.'

'You mean I haven't been very nice up to now.'

'Not at all. You've been withdrawn, guarded –'

'I've been unkind. I know that.'

As they go through the gate, he says, 'The thing about love, I've discovered, is that it's a renewable resource. Perverse as we humans are, it takes us a long time to accept that fortunate fact. By the way, have you seen Gareth since he came home?'

'Once. It didn't go well.'

'I'm sorry to hear that. I ask because I was talking about you at dinner last night. I was telling him of the conversation we had about his mother's drawings, the ones he hung on his wall. Do you remember?'

Olwen nods.

'I said I thought you'd like to see them and that he might hunt them out to show to you. He didn't seem very eager, so I guessed you weren't on good terms still. Then, after dinner, he went straight upstairs and when he came down he had the drawings. I must say, I was surprised. He came back so soon, he must have known exactly where they were. I thought I'd packed them away, but no, he's kept them to hand. I imagine he still looks at them from time to time – or often, perhaps – and keeps in touch with his mother that way. If that's so, then she was still raising him, in a sense, all the time I thought I was doing it alone. Can you understand why I find the idea comforting?'

'Yes,' Olwen says. She sees how Gareth's mother, the imaginative parent, must have nurtured in her son certain qualities the good, capable father might have neglected – even, unwittingly, repressed. 'It's important, isn't it, not to have just one influence when you're growing up?'

'Exactly. We raise our children to see the world as we see it, to behave in it as we behave. It's good to have another voice, another vision, so we don't clone ourselves.'

'My grandfather was very different from my grandmother.' Olwen looks off into the woods.

'Certainly.' Dr Lloyd leans against the bonnet of his Morris and takes his pipe from his pocket.

'And a much stronger influence.'

'Possibly.'

'No, he was. I'm much more like him than like her.'

From another pocket the doctor takes a tin of tobacco, flips it open with his thumb and fills his pipe. 'Do you want to be more like him?'

'I love my grandmother!' The words come spontaneously, and Olwen is surprised at the force in her voice. Looking into the woods, green, still, silent, she feels as if she has hurled a declaration into the trees.

The Cwm makes no response.

'But *he's* dead . . .' Her voice, a wail now, reminds her of Alice crying 'Father!' at the edge of the glade.

The doctor strikes a match and lights his pipe. 'You can be

157

like both your grandparents, you know. It isn't a betrayal of one to have qualities of the other. And most important, Olwen, you can be yourself, which is different from either of them.'

'Yes,' she says slowly. 'I want to be myself. I'm not sure how to begin, though.'

'Just go on opening – as this flower did.' He touches the rose in his lapel. 'Just as naturally.'

She catches the subtle compliment and smiles at him. Then, swiftly, she says, 'I'll never let anyone wear me in his button-hole!'

'Good for you. Wear yourself, my dear. And may flowers spring where you walk, as they did for your namesake in *The Mabinogion*.'

'I thought you weren't familiar with fairytales!'

'My wife educated me. I listened when she read to Gareth. Which reminds me –' He opens the back door of the car, reaches in and takes from the seat two large squares of white card fastened with a thin ribbon. 'Before we got sidetracked, I was telling you that Gareth found the pictures. Here they are.' He holds out the card parcel. 'They're yours if you want them, he told me to say.'

'I can't keep them!'

'Well, sort that out with Gareth. I'm merely the messenger. Let's see if I can repeat the message verbatim: "Give these to Olwen as a gift, if she'll take them. Tell her to look carefully at the faces and she may understand something." Now that's cryptic, isn't it? Well, I must be off. Morgan Pryce is waiting for me to give him another new cure for the oldest of all diseases.'

The cardboard squares pressed against her chest, Olwen asks, 'What's that?'

'Loneliness.' The doctor shakes his head. 'It's a sad case, for there's no medicine to treat it in this brown bag.' He opens the car door, tosses the bag onto the passenger seat, and gets in.

'Why did he never marry? Was it his mother's fault? He looked after her for years, didn't he?'

Dr Lloyd looks up at her through the open window. 'She might have been to blame. Or she might have been his excuse. He may have let his chances pass . . . or he may never have had any. In short, Olwen, I can't answer a question like that!'

'But what can I do for him?'

The doctor smiles. 'Just be kind. That's the best you can do for anybody.' He starts the car, lifts his hand, and backs down the lane. 'See you Saturday!'

Olwen raises her hand, watches him until he's out of sight. What would it have been like, she wonders, how would she have been different, if *he* had been her closest relative?

In her room Olwen unties the ribbon and lifts the top sheet of card. The picture that lies beneath takes her breath away. It is the drawing of the knight battling the enchanter. Into the sweeping black ink strokes, a knowing and skilful hand has infused powerful and frightening emotions. She sees stupendous energy and malice in the black cloak that whirls like a maelstrom; in the great beard, a tidal wave, destructive, greedy, engulfing. His hair, intricately curled, swells like a swarm of locusts; under writhing brows, his eyes blaze; his pointed teeth are so lifelike that, almost, she can hear them gnash. So potent is this figure, filling three-quarters of the page, that the viewer's eyes must inevitably fix on him, missing at first the much smaller figure to the right.

Olwen sees him now. A young knight, slender-waisted, but with muscular arms and a well-shaped head. He wears only a short tunic (why did she not give him armour?), a round shield in his left hand, a sword in the other. The edges of the enchanter's cloak lap at the knight, threatening to swallow him up.

Olwen marvels at the woman who created a picture so terrifying and bleak, and wonders, too, at this reproduction, perfect in every detail, of her own image of the enchanter of the Cwm. In the lineaments of the face, there is something else that seems familiar . . . Olwen tries to grasp and shape the thought, but it evades her.

She shifts her gaze to the knight again . . . and sees at once what she missed before. The face and hair, though highly stylized, are Gareth's! It's as if the artist, the mother, had seen in the child's features the man he would become – and the terror he would have to confront. Deeply shocked, and with a sense of revulsion too, Olwen, who has bent over the picture to study it, straightens up, draws away. Did the woman fancy herself psychic? And if she did, and had this vision, how could she translate it into a drawing, an act that seems acquiescent in the danger she foresaw for her son?

She looks at the picture again, and again sees something

unnoticed before. The knight is repelling his foe. His sword aimed at the heart, his eyes looking straight into the eyes of the enchanter, he drives him back. Yes, she sees now that the enchanter's frenzied movement is a backward one, missed at first because, filling so much of the paper, the enchanter-figure appeared insuperable. But it is the knight who stands upright and firm, the enchanter who shrinks away.

Understanding, Olwen sighs. The mother had seen some terrible future battle for her son and had created this picture as a charm to protect him, as if, by depicting the outcome, she could effect it. Yet so many questions remain. Perplexed, she lays the illustration aside to look at the one beneath it.

At once, she cries out and presses her fingers to her lips.

The great stallion and the girl on its back show the same frantic motion as the first picture. She sees the lathering of the horse's flanks, the panting breath that comes in a cloud through its distended nostrils, hears the pounding hooves. Urgency floods the drawing in the streaming mane, in the girl's flying hair and arched back, her arms flung around the horse's neck, her bare legs pressed to its glistening hide. It is another picture of extreme emotions: anxiety, terror and, oddly, exhilaration too – all stylized, exaggerated, yet lifelike. Olwen sees all this at once, but cries out for another reason. The girl's face, shown only in profile, is unmistakably her own.

Sixteen

Olwen stands on the path and watches her grandmother decorate the grave. Kneeling in the grass, a pair of scissors in her right hand, Gwen selects flowers from the wicker basket they filled in the garden, snips the long stems of gladioli and asters and fits them into slots in a marble urn. There are four urns on the grave, one in each corner, and a marble headstone with gold lettering. The grave is one of the showiest in the cemetery. Knowing Pont Ysaf will judge the strength of her feelings and measure her 'rightness' by it, her grandmother has chosen the costliest headstone and ornaments in the mason's catalogue. Olwen tries to understand and forgive. Gwen has always cared about the opinions of others. A Welshwoman, she has been brought up to see virtue in keeping up appearances. In a different way, her grandfather, too, put on a front and required Olwen to do the same. Still, she can't dismiss the idea that, with all this show, Gwen celebrates her husband's death.

She had not wanted to come to the cemetery with her grandmother. 'I'd rather not,' she said, when Gwen asked her that morning at breakfast.

'But Olwen, love, you've never been. For months I've gone on my own, and whenever I meet people from the town, they always ask where *you* are. "It still hurts her too much," I say, and they say, "Naturally. It do take time. She was that fond of him." But that's not what they're thinking, I know.'

Olwen had understood then that for her grandmother private affection was not enough. She needed the town to see them arm-in-arm at the graveside. Wishing to please, to make up for years of neglect, she had said, 'All right, then. But just this once.'

Now she regrets giving in. Profound anguish, and anger, have gripped her at the sight of the grave. With a seething heart she turns and walks down the path. Longing to run, she forces herself to go slowly, as if, bored, she is simply taking a stroll. There are other mourners in the cemetery this Friday morning and they are not too grief-stricken to look about.

At the gates, where her grandfather appeared on the morning of his funeral, Olwen stops. She looks across the road to the Cwm. In the morning sun leaves shimmer, tree trunks shine as if powdered with gold dust, a hazy light enshrining the woods. She knows the Cwm so well, she could find the places where bluebells grow thickest with her eyes closed, the hazelnut grove hidden among the oaks, the best spot for blackberries, the nests of various birds, too, and the trees they favour. She had often gone bird-nesting with her grandfather. Not to tamper with or steal the eggs; he had taught her the wrongness of that: 'In these woods, you don't take nothing that belongs to someone else.' They had gone only to see and admire. He would lift her into a tree and she would scramble up to the nest, crying out in delight upon discovering the eggs, brown or pastel-coloured or speckled, in their neat twig-baskets.

'Don't you touch, mind,' he'd call to her, and though she longed to hold one of the eggs in her palm, she never disobeyed, so strongly had he instilled in her a respect for the creatures who inhabited the Cwm.

Sometimes they would come upon a trap. In a fury, he would kick it shut, snatch it up and carry it home to dispose of it, ranting about 'that murderer and his hound of hell,' his savage rage frightening her.

Remembering these things, Olwen feels her anger at Gwen evaporate in the hot love that envelops her. Loving her grandfather, his justice and his rage, his violent fits of temper as well as his goodness, she loves her grandmother again. Like him, Gwen is imperfect. Like him, she wants to be best-beloved. Indeed, like Olwen herself, who cannot bear to think that he might have preferred Alice. Gazing into the Cwm, aching for a glimpse of him, she sees that, henceforth, she must try to be gentle, patient with those who love her, presently and in the future, to make up to them for what they can never be – the best-beloved. And to herself, also, she must be kind for the same reason. That's what the enchanter knows about human weakness, she thinks: Grandfather didn't get it quite right. It's not different desires but the same in everyone, the wish to be the heart's first choice.

She hears footsteps on the cemetery path and sees Gwen

coming, the empty basket over her arm. 'Shall we walk back through the Cwm instead of catching the bus?' she says. 'It will be nice and cool under the trees.'

Olwen hesitates, then says, 'If you like.'

As they go along the path, she links arms with her grandmother and finds, at last, the courage to ask, 'Why did you and Grandfather marry?'

She feels Gwen's arm stiffen. The question is abrupt. She might have broached it more tactfully . . . but it's out, and she's glad.

After a moment, Gwen says, 'I can see why you'd wonder about that. It will be hard for you to credit, but we did care for each other once. When he courted me, he was different, more like he was with you. He made me feel prized at first.'

'A lot of men must have made you feel that way. All those suitors Aunt Pridwyn talks about.'

'Yes, I was popular. But *I* never felt anything – not anything deep – till I met him.'

The path through the Cwm widens and narrows at intervals. They have come to a narrow stretch and Olwen goes in front, holding back branches so that her grandmother can pass unhindered. When they can walk side by side again, she says, 'How did you meet?'

'In Pont Ysaf at a fair. I'd come up for the day with some girls I knew. We were out for a good time and all of us had dressed to the knocker, intending to show off and break hearts among the locals. We were silly and flighty and thought ourselves city girls with airs and graces, you know, that would bring the boys to our feet.' Gwen clicks her tongue softly, then forgives herself with a smile. 'But we *were* young. I remember exactly how I was dressed. I had on a new frock, ivory chiffon with an inset of lace flowers around the neck. My skin showed through the lace and I felt very daring and sophisticated. I had ivory shoes and stockings, and my hair done up very stylish in a French knot.' She raises her hand to make the shape of a figure eight behind her head. 'Very complicated. Pridwyn helped me, holding the pins and that. She loved to see me put my hair up fancy. I wore a picture hat, a ring of white satin roses round the brim. I had this notion that all the light tones would set off my red hair. It was my most striking feature, and I *was* vain about it. Sitting on the train, I kept primping and preening in my compact mirror, spreading my skirt so it wouldn't crease, the other girls just as bad. The four of us took up a compartment to seat eight. People would open the door and look in, and we'd stare back, brazen, and refuse to make room, not in words but by our attitudes. When they moved on, we'd laugh and make hoity-toity comments – as if we owned the train.' Gwen stops. Her face, lit with pleasure as she reminisced, sobers. 'Such foolishness! We thought we were the cream. I've come down a peg or two since then, and I dare say they have as well.'

The sudden harshness in Gwen's voice jolts Olwen. Her picture of the young girls on the train, careless as butterflies in their flimsy dresses, recedes, and she sees again the sun-gilded leaves of the Cwm, hears the birdsong and the scuttering of squirrels. Passing under the brilliant foliage, her arm through her grandmother's, she thinks, she couldn't compete for long. None of us can.

She thinks, too, of Aunt Flindy and her outmoded fashions, her camphor-scented brocades and satins, her foxfur stole, her beaded and frilled and padded dresses. Every day she dresses and makes herself up gorgeously, then sits in her rocking chair, looking at photographs, or walks to the gate to see what neighbours are about.

'It's hard, isn't it,' she says, 'for women? Getting older, I mean.'

'Oh, it's hard for everyone,' Gwen says. 'But then, it's not so bad either.' Her voice lifts. 'Not so bad,' she repeats, and Olwen guesses she is thinking of the doctor.

Tenderly, she presses her grandmother's arm. 'Go on. You haven't told me how you met him.'

'I got separated from my friends. Pont Ysaf was heaving. You know how it is on fair days. Remember the time the three of us went, you and me and Grandpa?'

'Yes,' Olwen says, and sees herself standing beside Gwen at the jewellery stall, looking across the road at the stiff back of her grandfather. 'It was the day you bought the keeper.'

'I've always been partial to jewellery. On that day, too, it was the jewellery stalls that drew me. I stopped to look at brooches. The other girls wanted to see the fortune-teller and they kept nagging me to hurry up. "Go you on," I said, "and I'll meet you there in half an hour." I bought a brooch – it's that peacock one in my jewel box, blue and green stones set in gold. I knocked it down to a good price, too, after a lot of haggling. I slipped it in my purse and set off to find my friends but, as I said, the town was heaving and I wandered down this street and that one, all packed with stalls and people, and couldn't find the fortune-teller's booth anywhere.' Gwen pauses for breath.

'Shall we sit down for a bit?' Olwen says.

'That would be nice. I don't have the puff I used to.'

Gwen sits on a tree stump, as Olwen's grandfather often had, stretching out his gammy leg to ease it. She spreads her flowered skirt as she must have spread the ivory chiffon on the Pont Ysaf train. Olwen sits cross-legged in the grass at her feet. 'You were lost,' she says.

'Yes, I didn't know my way around the town in those days. I came at last to the place where they were auctioning the animals. There was a beautiful horse up on the block, I remember – a roan it was. A lot of farmers were standing round, and some gypsies too – a rough crew, and I thought I ought to give *them* a wide berth, but that horse was so fine I stopped to look. That's when I saw John. He was on the other side of the ring, right in the front, and he was watching that horse with such a look on his face ... He was a handsome man, blond and blue-eyed like a Swede, rare colouring in these parts – not tall, but very strong and compact-looking. It was his eyes, though, that affected me. "If a man looked at me like he's looking at that horse," I thought, "I'd be done for." And right then he did look – caught me staring – and his eyes didn't alter, and I fell for him.'

'Love at first sight,' Olwen says, 'like in fairytales.'

Gwen sighs. 'It's not like they say in books. Not for me it wasn't. I didn't feel on top of the world or anything. It was more like he'd killed me, really. All my strength went and I was scared out of my wits. I know that's not romantic, but that's how it was. I wanted to run away – and I did manage to move at last. I shoved through the people, saying, 'Excuse me, excuse me,' but when I tried to get past the gypsy lads, they wouldn't allow me. They came round me in a circle and started jibing, asking would I go off with them and that. Next thing I knew, John had pushed in and taken me by the arm. "Where've you been, love?" he said. "I been looking for you all over." Those boys just fell back like skittles and we walked off together, arm in arm. I remember thinking, "Well, this is it. He's claimed me, and I'll go anywhere with him now."' Gwen smooths her skirt. 'It was another terrible feeling – not a lovely one, as you might expect. I was always a wilful girl, but with him I had no will, right from the first.

'I spent the day with him, never thinking of my friends. We didn't talk much, and I don't recall what we did either. Funny, how everything before is so clear in my memory and so hazy after. He just led me about, I suppose, like I was his prisoner – no, that's not right. I *could* have left him at any point. It was more in me than in him. I was –' Gwen lifts her hand, as if reaching for the word.

'Subjugated?' Olwen says softly.

'Enchanted,' Gwen says. 'He'd enchanted me.' She smiles, her colour rising. 'There's foolish I feel, a sixty-year-old woman talking like this. Shall we walk on? It's turned a bit cold.'

Olwen gets up. While they've been sitting, the sun has moved behind clouds and the air in the woods has grown chill.

'We met every Sunday after that,' Gwen says as they go along the path. 'At first he came to Swansea, but that soon changed. We'd run into my friends wherever we went and he didn't like it. He was jealous, though he'd no reason to be. I had no looks for anyone else, and I often told him so. But he made such ructions each time a young man spoke to me, so I started coming to Pont Ysaf where I knew nobody. He wasn't allowed to entertain in his lodgings, so we'd catch a bus and come out here to walk in the Cwm.' She shakes her head. 'It's not good for young people to be alone as much as we were. Feelings run ahead of sense. Of course, your grandfather wasn't a youngster – but I was barely twenty then and mad for him. He didn't talk much, as I've told you, and never about the two of us – never said he loved me – but he did show it. At least –' Gwen falters, '– when you're a slip of a girl, it's easy to mistake passion for something deeper, and I made that error. Even before we married I knew there was something not right in him. He could hardly wait to get me off the train on Sundays, it's true. As soon as it pulled into the station, before it had stopped properly, he'd be on board, rushing down the corridor, looking for me. But then, at the end of the day, he seemed glad enough to see me go.'

'Yet the two of you married,' Olwen says. She speaks softly, affected by a change in the atmosphere of the Cwm. With the disappearance of the sun, the birdsong and animal noises have ceased too. A deep silence wraps the woods.

'Yes, we married, and you're old enough to know why. You have a right to, I suppose. We were forced to wed, Olwen, because your mother was on the way. I suppose that's what turned him off me sooner than later. To his way of thinking, I'd trapped him.'

'That's an old-fashioned idea,' Olwen says, 'that the woman's to blame.'

'It was an old-fashioned time. People believed it was up to the woman to hold the man off. I believed it myself, and I'd always refused other, younger men. With John I had no will, only feelings so powerful I couldn't deny them.'

Olwen looks at her grandmother's averted face, trying to imagine the quiet, soft-spoken woman as a headstrong, amorous girl. So it's her I've inherited it from, she thinks, and him, too. It's not just Alice.

'How did he feel,' she says, 'about . . . my mother?'

'He didn't want her till she was born. Then, from the minute he saw her, he worshipped her. The two of them were like you and him, except –'

'Except what?'

'I don't know . . . too much. Well, I always thought he kept you too close, but with Alice it was worse. I made her go away to London. She listened to me, for there was often bad feeling between her and her father as well as love. She wasn't for him all the time, like you were. I told her, "You better get away from here before he ruins you," and she went. He didn't know my part in her going, but he had his suspicions, of course, and it didn't make things any better between us.

'She went to London and lived there like a thing let loose. The letters she wrote . . . I believe she wrote them to taunt him, but he never read one after the first.'

'Where are the letters?'

'All burnt, done away with. He'd carry them straight from the postman to the fire. If I managed to get hold of one and he caught me reading it, he'd snatch it out of my hand and rip it up. The ones he didn't get, I had to rip up myself, soon as I'd read them.'

'And she never came back?'

'Only once. About two years after she went away.'

'What for?'

'To bring you to us.'

Olwen starts. 'I thought –'

'Your grandpa made me promise to hold to the story that she died having you, and it was him who brought you here. He said it would be easier on you than the truth, and I believed him then.'

'What is the truth?'

In the stillness before Gwen answers Olwen senses a presence, a listener who stalks them on silent feet, who has created this hush in the woods so that he may eavesdrop. Looking over her shoulder, she sees nothing but the trees bent over the path, shutting it behind them. She strains to hear a footstep, a snapping twig, the sweep of a long garment against the low-hanging boughs, but no sound confirms her suspicion. And though several times she imagines a face looking at her from the foliage, it is only a trick of light and shade, or the petrified eyes of an animal.

'The truth is that she brought you to us when you were four months old,' Gwen says, 'because she couldn't take care of you. She stayed a few days, but they had rows all the time, and finally he turned her out. She meant to come back for you when she was better off.'

'Why didn't she?'

'Because . . . she died soon after. That part's true enough.'

How did she die? Olwen wants to ask. But an image leaping into her mind prevents her: the woods in another time, the harsh voices, the colours – blue stained with red – and herself falling, choking, and the screams – her own and another's. The image suggests something so horrible, she cannot grasp words, thoughts evade her, the red flood sweeps through her mind, threatening to unhinge it. At the same time, the roaring she has heard before starts up in the trees. She halts on the path and a violent trembling seizes her.

'Olwen!' Gwen's arm comes round her shoulders.

'Listen!' Olwen says. 'He's coming. Dr Lloyd couldn't hear him, but *you* can, can't you?'

'I don't hear anything, love.' Gwen's arm pushes against her back. 'Let's get home.'

Olwen manages a few steps then gives up. 'It's no use,' she says, for the woods are exploding again, the roars of the enchanter ripping through the trees like cannon shot. 'I can't escape. He'll get me this time for sure.'

'Nobody'll get you if I have any say. I'll clout whoever tries with this basket.' Gwen urges her forward. 'See, Olwen, there's the opening to Archer's Lane. Only a bit further.'

The hue and cry rages through the Cwm as birds scream and squawk and small animals rush for cover. The trees shake and the earth cracks under her feet as her grandmother hastens her on. Behind the thunderous voice of the enchanter she hears another inhuman sound – which could be the wind, or the howl of a creature caught in a trap – but she knows it's a woman shrieking in terror.

'Just a few steps,' Gwen says.

A hand falls on Olwen's shoulder. Sharp nails dig into her flesh. A voice, coaxing, obscene, whispers in her ear, 'Come back, Olwen.'

Gwen drags her across the ditch, pulling her up when she trips on the damp stones, half lifting her over the bank. When they stumble into Archer's Lane, the clamour ceases just as it did before, the only discordant sounds her own and her grandmother's panting.

'There,' Gwen says. 'See? It was nothing. You had a funny turn, that's all.'

'Didn't you hear it too?'

'There was nothing to hear, love – except the thumping of your own heart, I expect. But you looked so ill, I thought I'd better get you out of them woods fast. What gave you such a fright?' She raises her hand and strokes Olwen's hair from her face.

And now Olwen, too, in the quiet of the summer's afternoon, wonders if what she heard was real or self-made. She catches her grandmother's hand and feels, under her fingers, the solidity of the embossed keeper. Her eyes on the ring, she says, 'He wouldn't buy it for you, would he? Why not? Why did he make you buy it yourself?'

'A keeper's a seal on a marriage,' Gwen says, 'and he never wanted to be married. It was foolish of me to ask him for the ring.' She links Olwen's arm. 'Let's get home, love. I fancy a nice cup of tea.' As they go up the lane, past the whispering trees, she says, 'I don't know why, but sometimes the Cwm *does* give me the creeps.'

Seventeen

On Saturday morning, passing her grandmother's door on her way downstairs, Olwen looks in and sees Gwen riffling through her wardrobe.

'I don't know what to wear, I'm sure.'

Olwen goes in and stands beside her. 'The green linen. Green is a lucky colour.' The dress she takes from the wardrobe, a shirtwaister with a long, full skirt, is a muted, tender green, the colour of shoots and leaf buds . . . of the Wen Pool in the early morning, before trees cast their shadows across its surface . . yes, and the colour of Gareth's eyes, too, when they are quiescent. Olwen's heart contracts as she remembers the pain that darkened his eyes the last time they parted.

Gwen pats her arm. 'You've fallen into a daydream. I'll wear this, then.' She takes the dress from Olwen and lays it across her bed.

'And why don't you do your hair differently today, in a French knot or a chignon?'

'It's been so long.' Her grandmother's smile is wistful. 'I'm not sure I even remember how to do those styles.'

'I'll help you, like Aunt Pridwyn used to.'

Olwen touches her grandmother's hair. Loose, it hangs to her waist, red and silver mingling, like shot silk. What pleasure for the doctor, releasing it from its pins! Not today, of course, nor even soon, possibly, for her grandmother and Dr Lloyd will proceed politely, cautiously. But at some point in the future Gwen will give and receive again the pleasures she has so long done without.

'I'll make breakfast,' Olwen says. 'You have your bath.'

Later in the morning they sit at the kitchen table, waiting for the doctor. Gwen sips the tea Olwen has made and looks at her suitcase beside the door.

'You'll be packing yourself soon.'

'Yes, we'll go to Aunt Pridwyn's together in August.'

'I didn't mean that.' Gwen raises her left hand from the table and studies it. 'In a few months you'll be off to university. I'll miss you.'

'It's only Swansea, no farther than you're going today.'

'Will you stay with Pridwyn?'

'I don't know. I'll have to think about it.'

'I don't want you to be lonely.'

'I won't be. I'll make friends.' The statement thrills Olwen as she says it. To be part of a group instead of an outsider . . . is that easy or hard, if one is willing? Willing, but shy . . . and fearful. Course work, exams, give her no anxiety, but can she manage a few friends, a few attachments? Dr Lloyd's words come to her: 'Just go on opening, naturally.'

'I won't be lonely,' she repeats, to reassure herself as well as her grandmother.

A car sounds in the lane.

Gwen's left hand flies to her chignon; her right hand clatters the empty cup into its saucer.

'And neither will you.' Olwen gives her grandmother an arch look.

'Oh, I won't do anything hasty.'

Olwen laughs. 'I know you won't. You've reached a sensible age.'

'Yes. I'm sixty. Who'd have thought –'

Suddenly, as the car engine dies away behind their garden wall, Gwen slides the gold keeper off her finger and holds it out in her palm. 'You'll be twenty in two weeks. I meant to give you this for your birthday . . . but I don't want to wait.'

Olwen stares at the ring.

'Take it, love. You've always liked it.'

The gate clicks. They hear the doctor's footsteps on the path. Gwen takes Olwen's right hand and slips the keeper onto her third finger. 'It's a bit big. We'll have it altered when I come back.'

Dr Lloyd raps at the knocker.

'I haven't been out to lunch with a man,' Gwen says, 'in over forty years.'

Olwen goes to open the door.

'All set?' Dr Lloyd comes in, cheerful as the sunshine that follows him. He smells of tweed, tobacco, and, Olwen notices, a hint of cologne.

171

In the kitchen, Gwen has composed herself. Seated beside the table, her hands folded in her lap, her legs crossed, she looks calm and poised. The wide skirt of the green dress cascades in wavelike pleats.

'Well,' the doctor says, gazing at her from the doorway. 'That's a chic dress. A new hairstyle too, eh?'

'No, an old one. I used to wear my hair this way.'

'Old or new, it becomes you.'

Olwen sees her grandmother's hands flutter.

'Dr Lloyd,' she says, 'would you like a cup of tea?'

The doctor pulls himself together. 'No, we'd better be off.' He bends smartly and picks up Gwen's suitcase. 'Join us for lunch, Olwen?'

'Thank you, I can't.'

He doesn't insist.

As they go down the path, Gwen says, 'You'll be all right, love?'

'Olwen can take care of herself,' Dr Lloyd says. 'And if there *is* a problem, she can ring me from the Millers'. I'll be out like a shot.'

When Gwen is in the passenger seat of the car, Olwen follows the doctor as he walks around to put the suitcase in the boot. 'The drawings are wonderful,' she says. 'I want to thank Gareth.'

'Why don't you? He's been away for a few days, camping with a pal, but he'll be back today. I think he'd be glad to see you.'

'I'll come into town . . . soon.'

The car backs down the lane. Olwen stands at the gate waving until it vanishes.

Archer's Lane is empty, no sign of any neighbours. Across the way the Cwm glitters, but there is no evidence of life there either. Instead of the elation she has expected to feel at this moment, Olwen has a profound sense of isolation and, beneath it, anxiety, scratching at the edges of her loneliness like a persistent cat.

She goes into the house, sees the keeper lying on the kitchen table, and slips it on. The beauty of the ring delights her, its unaccustomed weight on her finger comforting, but she has no sense of the potency she once ascribed to it. Power does not surge into her limbs, nor courage well in her heart. She thinks of

Gwen, who brought her safely out of the Cwm yesterday, who wandered there alone, picking bluebells, and suffered no harm. When she needs it, the power will come, perhaps. However, the ring is too big.

For safe-keeping, Olwen carries it upstairs and lays it on her dressing table. Then she leaves the empty house to sit in the garden.

Under the chestnut tree, her legs stretched out to the sun, her body within the green embrace of boughs, she tries to still her anxiety. This is the time she has longed for, the time when she can, at last, expect her grandfather. Many mornings, afternoons, evenings, she has sat here, looking down the path, imagining his appearance.

Dressed for the occasion in his grey tweed jacket and Sunday trousers, and the cap with the silk lining, blue as the sky above the chestnut leaves, he'd raise his hand to greet her as he opened the gate. Up the path he'd come, his gammy leg jerking in the odd, witty dance that seemed to suggest that here was a humorous man, one who turned accident to advantage. The sun would glint from his blue eyes, flash from the brass horse's head on his cane, and glitter through his cloudy hair. And he would be smiling, glad in his heart to see her again.

And then what?

Then he would say, 'Ready, *cariad*?' and she would answer, 'Yes, Grandfather,' and he would take her with him into whatever world he now inhabits, a world without loss, or jealousy, or any other human travail.

Olwen grows cold. She had wished to die then, like him. But how could she – young, healthy – *die*? By what means would death come to her? Had she fancied it some magical transformation? That he would simply take her hand and lead her into it, the way characters in the old childhood stories passed from the human world to the faerie?

But she is not a child now. And she wants life, activity, companions, a world beyond the one she has known with him. How will he brook such a change in her? If he comes – when he comes – will he be angry, hostile . . . violent?

She remembers the night during his illness when she left her room to go to him as he prowled the passage. He had sprung at her, his teeth bared, and dug his nails into her flesh.

The other, older memory swims up from the red pool forming

173

behind her eyes. The Cwm, the voices, red stains on blue. *How did Alice die?*

Olwen leaps from the deckchair and begins to pace the lawn. Her pacing brings her to the toolshed, to her own reflection, an image framed by white clouds and blue sky as in a child's painting, except that her face is unsmiling, her mouth drawn. Behind her face, beyond the sky, dark shapes rise, the hoard of an inveterate collector. If there are clues, answers, this is where she will find them.

She runs across the lawn to the house. In the kitchen, she snatches the key from its hook and races back to the shed. Thrusting aside a sentinel sunflower, she fits the key into the lock. Her hand trembles, the key slips from her fingers. She retrieves it, tries again, and opens the toolshed door.

Inside, the shed is sunlit, tranquil, a still life executed with loving, attentive brushstrokes – nothing fearful presents itself today. The bench, the last, the lathe, shimmering in the diffused light, soothe her wildly beating heart. The man who worked here, fashioning beautiful things, was surely incapable of a foul act.

Her eyes, roaming the shelves, come to rest on the long, rectangular box, never opened, never moved. As she looks at it from the doorway, it seems a stain on the canvas, the ugly black tin misplaced among the smooth natural woods, its surface rejecting the sunlight that suffuses the cedar, oak and pine. The box disrupts the harmony of the composition. It is shaped, she realizes with revulsion, like a miniature coffin.

Olwen enters the shed, picks up the stool under the bench and places it next to the shelves. Standing on the stool, she can reach the box easily. Its lightness surprises her. It feels empty. She lifts it down and places it on the carpenter's bench.

Her fingers on the rusted metal clasp, she pauses, looks round to the door. Across the path the delphiniums turn their blank, lovely faces on her. Among their ranks nothing stirs, no apparition hovers there, about to materialize from azure petals and gauzy sunshine. If the ghost of her mother watches, it is acquiescent, or indifferent . . . or, perhaps, if spectres are capable of fear, trembles as Olwen does.

Olwen releases the clasp and lifts the lid. Beneath it lie sheets of yellowed newspaper, the *South Wales Echo*, dated November 20 in the year of Olwen's birth. She lifts off the top sheet, then another, and a third – under six sheets of newspaper she finds a layer of blue cotton, the colour of the delphiniums, a soft covering, she supposes, for whatever object the box protects.

Gathering the material in her hands, she pulls it out. As it rises from the box, filling the shed with the sickly-sweet odour of stale perfume, an odour familiar to her, she sees that the material is not a covering, it *is* what the box contains. In her hands she holds a long blue dress, the front ripped apart from bodice to hem. From the long rent, brown stains spread across the cloth, which feels brittle to her fingers, not soft as cotton should be.

For a moment Olwen, numb, stares at the blood-stained dress, an exact replica of one she has seen before, on the apparition of Alice, her mother. Then terror surges up, making her nauseous. She drops the dress onto the box and steps back towards the door. Her hand gropes for the opening, she moves through it, out into the bright afternoon.

Sickened, she runs, stumbles, back to the house. In the kitchen she leans her arms on the cool aluminium sink, rests her forehead against the steel tap. Only dry, wrenching sobs come from her throat. Yet she wants to empty out her stomach, her heart – whatever organs rack her body now. She would like to be an empty thing, unable to comprehend what she knows.

Neat rows of Savoy cabbages border Bryn Brewen's path. Their pale green heads have a translucent gleam, like giant moonstones. Behind the cabbages, the leaves of potatoes and carrots spring in dense, dark green bouquets, and beyond them, the graceful fronds of tomato plants curl up over the fence as prettily as Olwen's sweet-pea vines. In the kidney-bean arbour outside the kitchen window, among the long, pointed leaves and swollen bean pods, scarlet flowers blaze, set on fire by the evening sun.

Olwen goes up the path slowly, her resolution, formed from need, faltering as she nears his door. On the threshold she looks over her shoulder to the gate, imagining herself opening it and stepping, still safe, back into the lane. But then she would never know if the horror story she has told herself repeatedly through the long afternoon is true or another tale. Thus, though the bloodstained dress is shut back into the box and the toolshed locked up again, there is no real safety beyond the gate. She raises her hand and raps on the door.

Inside the house Gelert barks. She hears Bryn say sharply, 'Shut!' and the dog ceases at once.

The door opens and he stands staring at her, in his vest and army trousers, a razor in his right hand. At the sight of the razor, Olwen jumps. Then she sees the streaks of shaving cream on his face.

'I've come –'

Bryn nods. 'I knew you would, sooner or later.' He opens the door wider. 'Come on, then. You've caught me shaving, but I'll be done in two ticks.'

Olwen steps into the passage and he closes the door behind her.

His kitchen, to her surprise, is neat and spotless. Like Gwen, he keeps a table in the window alcove, but not the traditional scrubbed-top family table. Bryn's is a little café affair covered with a red and white checked cloth. In the centre stands a wooden bowl filled with russet apples.

At the other end of the room Gelert lies on a woven hearth rug at the foot of his master's chair, a dark-brown barrel-back. He thumps his tail and gazes at Olwen with melancholy eyes. One word of greeting, she guesses, would bring him drooling to her side.

Against one wall a small oak dresser stands, a pendulum clock and a pair of china spaniels on its polished top shelf, a forest of fishing tackle beside it, and several steel traps. Olwen flinches at the traps. Yet, save for these, the kitchen is one such as any Welsh country bachelor might keep, spare in furnishing, but cheerful and homely.

While she looks around, Bryn stands silent, just behind her. When she turns to him, raising her eyes reluctantly, his own swerve away and he motions towards the chair by the fireplace. 'Will you sit down?'

Olwen sits in one of the two cane-backed chairs drawn up to the table, a chair she can spring from easily, within steps of the door.

A smile flits across Bryn's foam-streaked face. The vertical lines of shaving cream remind Olwen of war paint.

'Shall I put the kettle on?'

'No, thank you.'

'Not a tea drinker? Well, I've some elderberry wine in the cupboard. You shall have a glass in a minute, soon as I clean off my face.'

He crosses to the sink, an old-fashioned *bosh*, attached to the wall opposite the oak dresser. A cooker stands next to it, a huge iron pot on top (to boil the rabbits, Olwen thinks); above the *bosh* and cooker, a row of cedar cupboards. His back turned to her, Bryn runs water and scrapes off the shaving cream, looking into a square of unframed glass that hangs from the whitewashed wall by a brass-link chain.

Olwen watches the movements of his right arm, the muscles there round and firm as the russets in the glass bowl. Through his thin vest, she sees the V of his back, the back of a man accustomed to exertion.

Gelert has slunk across the room. He thrusts his muzzle against Olwen's thigh, sniffing at her. She pushes his head away and says, 'Stop it!'

Bryn swings round. 'Damn you, get back over there,' he tells the dog, pointing to the fireplace. 'He's like me, poor dab,' he says, turning back to the *bosh* as the dog sidles away. 'We have the same complaint.'

His hair, tied behind with a shoelace, lies on his neck like broom, like the bushes in the Cwm into which, as a child, she would sink her hands, delighting in their roughness that tickled but did not hurt.

He stands with his legs apart, and when he bends to splash water on his face she sees the shape of his buttocks, lean and hard in the close-fitting trousers.

Olwen picks up an apple and rolls it in her palm.

'Eat it.' A white flannel in his hand, Bryn smiles at her as he dabs his face.

She returns the apple to the bowl. 'Thanks, I'm not hungry.'

For a moment he looks at her, the flannel held against one cheek, his teeth as white as the cloth, his eyes black- rimmed. Then he tosses the cloth into the sink. 'We'll have a drop to drink then.' He opens a cupboard and takes out two tumblers, a lemonade bottle filled with elderberry wine and a bottle of Irish whiskey.

'I always have a drop of something warming before I go out at night,' he says as he places the bottles and glasses on the table, 'but I dare say a young girl like you isn't used to the strong stuff.' He fills her glass to the brim with purple elderberry, and half-fills his own with whiskey.

'This is a treat, Olwen,' he says, pulling out the other chair. 'A visit from you.'

'There's something I want to ask you about.'

Bryn lifts the tumbler, drinks, sets the glass down and wipes the back of his hand across his mouth. Then, looking at her from under his eyelids, he says, 'You're the spitting image of her. It fair breaks my heart sometimes.'

Olwen is shaken. She has been gathering her nerve to speak of her mother – trying, too, to subdue the anxiety she feels, alone in this house with Bryn Brewen, who has placed himself now between her and the kitchen door. Foolishly, she has sat in the far chair when she should have chosen the other, nearest the door, where she could make a run for it if he turned nasty.

But what use, really? Looking at his powerful arms and lean poacher's body, his starved eyes, she sees he would catch her, if he had a mind to, before she even reached the passage.

'Why do you say that?' She hears her voice quiver. 'My mother was blonde. I'm dark.'

'Aye, you don't have her colouring. *Silver* hair, she had, not blonde – I never seen the like – and blue eyes, same as the old man. But in the face, you both take after her.'

'Both?'

'You and Alice take after Gwen. When I moved here – I was renting the house in them days and working full time at the pit – it was Gwen I was drawn to, Alice being just a little girl to me. I took a fancy to Gwen, and I felt sorry in my heart for her, too, the life she had with John."

'What do you mean? What life?'

'Go on, you know very well. He treated her like poison, didn't he? Like she had some disease he might catch if he got too near. He was all for Alice, just as he was all for you after. So I had it in my head that I might comfort Gwen – don't look at me like that, now. Ever since you were a little 'un, you been looking at me with big eyes, like I'd eat you up. It's not so strange, a young bachelor having feelings for a good-looking woman unhappy in her marriage.'

'Did you . . .' Olwen lowers her eyes to the apples, a bowl of gems in the evening sun that streams through Bryn's window.

'It never came to nothing. Gwen wasn't that sort. Besides, pretty soon Alice started to come after me, and then I forgot all about your granny – and everything else as well, even my own sense and safety.'

'My mother came after you?'

'She did, though she was a bit of a girl, just fifteen, and me well into my twenties.'

'How did she come after you?'

'Just making eyes to start with – in the lane when we passed, or behind her father's back when I was over there borrowing a tool or asking some garden question. John and me got on better in them days, before the bomb went off. I think he felt for me a bit, a young man on my own, just like he was when he came south. Except, soon I wasn't over there to borrow or ask advice. It was to see Alice.' Bryn empties his glass, fills it again to the half, and sits back in his chair. He folds his arms across his chest and looks at her.

Disconcerted by his unusually straight looks and easy speech as much as by what he tells her, Olwen looks away. Outside the window, in the kidney-bean arbour, suffused by the setting sun, scarlet flowers, like lipsticked mouths, pout in the spaces between the distended pods. In the pane she sees Bryn's reflection, tinted in red, gold and green, like a figure in stained glass. She gazes at his golden shoulders.

After a silence during which she sees his reflection raise the tumbler several times, he speaks again.

'I tried to keep off Alice. She was a kid, I thought . . . and then there was John . . . he'll kill you good as look at you, I told myself, if you put a hand on the girl. But *she* wouldn't keep off me. After a bit she took to mitching from school and coming to my house when John was at work. She'd pretend to go off to the bus in the mornings, to fool Gwen, and then double back and tap on my door. I was on the night shift – they always put the young fellers on nights – so she knew I'd be home. After the first couple of times I just left the door on the latch so she could come straight upstairs and into bed with me.'

Olwen turns her head from the window and stares at Bryn. He stares back, a light in his black eyes like the sheen on anthracite, a ruddy colour in his face, put there by the sun or the whiskey . . . or, perhaps, by some strong emotion his story evokes. She has always thought him grave and grey. Now there is nothing of the tomb about him. His wiry hair, a great bush behind, springs in tendrils over his ears and forehead. The round, shiny muscles in his arms, the shadow of chest hair under the cotton vest, suggest a vitality that makes her blood race. At last she sees what her mother saw in him.

'She'd stay with me all day and leave just when the school bus would be getting out here. Not every day she didn't come – once, sometimes twice a week – and I never knew which days the fancy would take her. She was a wit-wat thing, changeable as the weather. Some days she'd come prancing up the stairs full of love and sunshine. Other mornings I'd stand at my bedroom window and see her marching down the lane to catch the bus, her face stormy, and for all the thought she gave me then I might as well not be born. Black moods she had, even as a girl.

'When I hadn't seen her for a bit, I'd be raging. She liked that. Liked to keep me burning. "Have you missed me, Bryn?" she'd ask. "Come into this bed," I'd say, "and I'll show you." But she wouldn't come to me straight off. She'd tease me first. "Watch me," she'd say and strip off all her clothes. When she was naked, she'd turn her body about in the sun, throwing her hair back, sticking out her breasts and her behind, saying, "You can only look today. You can't have." Sometimes I'd let her play her game out, thinking, "Wait till you're in this bed, lovely. I'll show you a trick or two." Other times, though, I couldn't wait, and I'd jump from the bed and swing her up onto me, and then we'd dance a fine jig all around the room. She liked that too. She'd wriggle like a tadpole, pretending to struggle, just to make me do it harder.'

Bryn speaks as if he's eating, ravenously, not giving the words to Olwen but devouring them himself, and the images they create of a naked, skittish girl who rides him as he gallops, a lusty stallion, round and round the cottage bedroom.

Olwen sees the images, too, and they make her giddy. Perhaps it's his voice, honey and whiskey, or the tale he tells, exotic as the *Arabian Nights*, that makes her drunk, for she hasn't touched the elderberry.

She leans towards him, close enough to see, in the failing light, the chest hairs that prick through his vest, a pattern of black dots on white; near enough to catch the faint, lingering scent of shaving cream on his skin, the flavour of whiskey on his breath.

'What else did you do?' she says.

Her question draws him back. As his eyes focus on her, his face alters, becomes covert again. 'Tongue ran away with me. I shouldn't be saying such things to a young girl.'

'I'm older than she was. I'm nearly twenty.' Her words,

spoken in a whisper, drop into the small space that separates her from Bryn like a *billet doux* tossed into his lap. She hears the invitation in her voice and recoils, shrinking back into her chair, her face on fire. 'I only meant –'

'I know what you meant.' He is looking at her with narrowed eyes, his face stern, as if he rebuked a child. 'But *she* wasn't a young girl, except in body. And besides, I'm a man of forty-eight now, with more sense in my head than I had then.'

'So what happened? Did my grandfather find out?' Olwen's voice is stiff. He's rebuffed an advance she never intended to make, and she feels a fool twice over.

'The school found out first. She'd been writing notes in her mother's hand and they caught on. Did it once too often, I expect, though teachers were lax in them days, and families bigger, so girls were always taking days off to help in the house. They sent the truant officer round. John didn't make much fuss about the mitching. She told him she'd taken days off to ride horses over at the farm and swim in the Wen. To my mind, he liked that, for she was showing him she rathered his ways to the teachers'. He didn't hold much with school himself, and he had no wish for her to be a scholar. Still, she had to go every day after they found her out, so she started coming to me at night instead. I managed to change to the day shift with a lot of bother and a cut in pay. I didn't like it much, though. Our times were hasty – she had to be back in bed before John rose at five – and riskier, of course. "Look," I said to her, 'let's tell him, and let's get engaged proper." But she wouldn't hear of it. "I daren't tell him," she'd say. "He'd kill me." "We can run away then," I said, but she wouldn't do that neither. What she wanted – she wanted him to find out. That's what I've concluded, looking back over the years. She never thought of being with me permanent – just used me to get at him.'

Bryn stops and pours the last of the whiskey. He sits back in his chair, silent, and stares at the window. The fading light patterns his face and vest with the black, crisscrossed lines of the lattice so that he is divided into small white squares like a dislocated figure in a surrealist painting.

Olwen waits, but he merely sips the whiskey and sighs. 'Get at him for what?' she says at last.

Like an actor hearing his cue, Bryn resumes his story. 'She wanted him to find us out all right. I see it now. After a bit she wouldn't come to my house. Instead, she wanted me to meet her at her gate. "I won't come if you don't fetch me," she said. So I'd go, telling myself, "The worst is that I'll have to fight him, and if I have to fight him for her, I'm prepared." But at the gate, she'd play up, kissing me and clinging to me, in full view of the house. "Come on," I'd say, "let's get out of sight," but she'd make excuses to stay there, where he'd only have to look out of the window to see us. "Do it to me here," she'd say, "I can't wait," or, "I'm afraid to go with you tonight, Bryn." She wasn't afraid, not her. I was the bag of nerves – not fearing for myself, mind, but scared I might lose her in that daft game. I *did* think she wasn't all there. She was acting like she'd flipped her lid, but I wasn't put off by that. Mad or sane, I'd have taken her – being mad myself in those days.'

Twilight has cast deep shadows about the room and Olwen can no longer see Bryn's features, only the furry outline of his head. Darkness transforms him – or makes him truly himself. She thinks of pictures she's seen of ancient Egyptian animal-gods, stories she's read of werewolves and incubi. On the wall behind him his shadow looms, gigantic, jagged, as if hewn from rock, his hair a wheel, wiry tendrils protruding like spokes. From the dark mass of his face the long scar gleams like woad.

'How did you get that scar?' Olwen says. 'You were knifed, weren't you?'

'How do you know that?' Bryn's voice is tranquil, whiskey-smoothed. 'Do you have the sight?'

'I saw it.' She feels her hands quiver and fastens them to her knees, thrusting her body forward, closer to him. 'I've had . . . visions.'

'Oh?' He lifts his glass and tips back his head to drink. 'Visions, Olwen *fach*, or dreams?'

'I've seen things at night, when I couldn't sleep . . . down in the garden.' Olwen moves her right hand from her knee to grip the edge of the table, near his glass where he might cover it, if he wished, with his own. 'I saw my mother in her blue dress . . . my grandfather, too –' Her voice rises to a wail and she grips the table tighter. 'They frighten me, the things I've seen –'

Bryn takes her hand in his and rubs it. 'You're cold as ice.'

'Take my other hand, too.'

'Yes. There, see, I have them both.'

Her fingers tremble. 'Will you hold me?'

'No, Olwen. This will do.' His thumb rubs her knuckles, too hard for comfort. 'Listen, now, let me tell you –'

'Why won't you?'

'Listen to me –'

'The day of my grandfather's funeral you held me. It was you who pulled me back. And ever since I was a little girl, you've looked at me as if –'

His hands on her wrists are like a vice. 'Shut up! Pull yourself together. Do you want to hear the rest of the story?'

'You talk to me as if I were a child. You don't look at me that way though.'

'Olwen!' His voice is harsh as a blow. He pushes her back in her chair. The slats dig into her spine like a reprimand. They puncture her will and she lets go. 'Tell me, then,' she says, yielding to the pressure of his hands. 'I do want to know.'

He slumps into his own chair, as if he were fatigued. First he drains his glass, then he says, 'One night I came to the gate and he was waiting, not her. I didn't know it was him at first, though the moon was full. He had her long cloak on, that she used to wear on chilly nights, and a silver wig he must have picked up at a jumble sale, or the devil knows where.'

The scene flashes up again. Olwen sees the figure emerge from the delphiniums. Where it had crouched for cover, no doubt, waiting for its prey. She sees it move across the grass, its odd, shuffling gait. No wonder he stumbled. What she had seen was the limp, accentuated by the hindrance of the long cloak, his disguise.

'A blind fool I was, to be taken in. When I got close enough to reach out my arms . . .'

Bryn shudders. Olwen, too, flinches, seeing the knife's swoop, the blade clear and sharp as moonlight.

'. . . He slashed me with a blasted kitchen knife! Tried for my heart, but I was too quick – I had some wit left – and he only ripped the skin off my face.'

Bryn raises his hand to his cheek and lays his palm over the scar. 'Must have been insane, to dress up like that. To be willing to murder me and swing for it. No wonder she was that way. Got it from him . . .' He lifts the empty glass and sets it down again. '*Jawl*, the blood was pouring from me and I was near to passing out, but I got myself home.'

The figure in her mind turns and lifts its face to the window, where Olwen watches. She sees the ogre-face of his anger, his thwarted will, as he lifts his hand to pull the silver wig from his head. Rising before her now, as she sits with Bryn like a conspirator, the vision seems a warning to her to desist, to let the past lie in its grave. But she can't. If there were ever a moment when she might have stopped, it has flown. The path has closed behind her; she can't go back to the place of not-knowing.

'What happened?'

'Next day Alice was gone. Not a word to him or me. He came to the fence in the early morning and shouted my name till I came to the door. "She's pulled a fast one on both of us," he said. "Hopped it to God knows where. You don't need to fear me. I won't try to do you in no more. Alice already done us both in, looks like."

'I think, just then, he felt almost kindly towards me – because we were both suffering the same. If I'd said a good word to him, we mightn't have ended up enemies. But all I said was, "You bloody bastard, I hope you roast in hell."'

Bryn lifts the empty glass and turns it in his hand.

'He spoke right enough, though, when he said she'd done me in. I haven't been able to touch a woman since, though I've burned. She put the mockers on me in every way, not just with women. I lost my job at the colliery soon after 'cause I couldn't get myself there regular. I haven't done nothing but odd jobs and poaching since she left me.'

'I don't understand,' Olwen says, 'why she'd want to make so much mischief.'

'Because she couldn't forgive him or get free of him. I see it plain now. She was fastened to him like mistletoe to an oak tree.'

'He kept her too close,' Olwen says, remembering Gwen's words.

Bryn laughs briefly, a rough, grating sound like a dog's bark. 'That's a mild way of putting it. He claimed her life, Olwen *fach*, took it over like it was his by right, like it was a debt she owed him.'

'You make him sound like a cruel man,' Olwen says, 'but he wasn't. I know it wasn't like that. He loved her –'

'Oh, he loved her all right. Bound to love something he made himself. Don't the Bible say it's the reason God loves us, because we're formed in His image?' Bryn barks again. 'Maybe that's why so many run straight to the devil. I know I'd rather be a sinner than a slave any day.'

'God is supposed to give us free will.'

'Is He? Well, your grandpa was a bigger tyrant than God then. All those parts meant for other men he filled himself. Her whole life was swollen up with him, so swollen it had to burst – that's why I'll never forgive him, though he's dead and gone.'

Bryn rests his elbow on the table and holds up the empty glass so that it catches the moonlight.

'You seen a firefly trapped in a jam jar, haven't you? You know how it dashes about, bright as a little comet? That's how Alice was, never still, never at rest, a shooting star. He was her god – and her sweetheart and her husband as well.'

He's drunk of course. And so she need not be distressed by his words.

Bryn gets up suddenly and crosses the kitchen to turn on the lamp beside the barrel chair. A pool of yellow light wreathes the empty chair. Beneath it Gelert sleeps, his head and front paws thrust under the seat, within the pool of light, the rest of his long body stretched out in shadow on the hearth rug.

On his way back Bryn stops at the cupboard and takes out another bottle. When he sits down at the table Olwen sees that his face is haggard, as if he had just returned from a night in the Cwm. His ashen complexion and black-ringed eyes, she understands at last, are not emblems of depravity but, simply, the characteristics of an insomniac.

He pours whiskey from the bottle into his glass. 'I hope it's enough light for you? I don't like it too bright.'

'What did you mean when you said he was her sweetheart and her husband?'

'What do you think I mean? They were in love with each other, that's what.'

For the first time, Olwen drinks from the glass he has set in front of her. The sugary liquid revolts her, but her mouth is parched and she drinks again. 'I don't believe you,' she says.

'I didn't believe it either, not till Alice told me herself, later on when she came back from London. When she said it straight out, I had to believe.'

'Did he . . .' Olwen wraps her hands around the glass of elderberry. 'Did they . . .' But the words won't come. She lifts her eyes to Bryn's face and he reads the words she can't ask.

'No,' he says. 'No, Olwen, that's not what I meant.' His voice is like salve. 'When she came to me, Alice was a virgin.'

'Then why do you say they were *in love*?'

'Because each was the ruling passion of the other. He never misused her body, but he pilfered her spirit and wrecked her heart. All those stories when she was growing up, about knights and princesses and love potions and charms – he planted an idea in her mind, and then he made it come true. She had only to speak to receive – dresses by the dozen, fine leather or suede for new shoes, a horse hired for my lady – all that cost a pretty penny – and other things, not bought but invented to please her – a crown of leaves for her head, flower chains from the garden – I seen her decked out like that with my own eyes. First time I saw her, just after I moved here, it was on a July morning. I came out into my garden and looked through the vines and saw her, briar roses and laurel woven into her hair and ropes of buttercups and daisies hanging from her neck, earrings of haw-thorn berries dropping like rubies and sweet peas twined around her waist like a jewelled belt, a girl of thirteen prancing about the garden, loaded with flowers like precious stones, and I heard him call her his heart's treasure and queen of the Cwm. That feller's off his rocker, I told myself, and the child's touched too.

'But what he was doing, he was courting her, and he won her right enough, so no man could have her after, and she could never be a woman, never be anything but his princess.'

Olwen has drained her glass and now she feels nauseous. Sugar coats her tongue and the bitter after-taste of elder sets her teeth on edge. 'She ran away from him, though.'

'She moved her body to another place, but she didn't know how to do anything more without him to tell her. In London she lived a lunatic life, and back again after two years with you wrapped in a shawl. She came to my door first, before going to her own house. "Look, Bryn, I have a baby," she said, "and I don't know what to do."

'"Come in, love," I said, "and I'll take care of you both." She wouldn't, though.

'"I only stopped to tell you," she said. "My father'll look after us. That's why I've come home."

'She thought he'd treat her same as before. I couldn't get over how foolish she was in that way – like a baby herself.

'John made ructions, of course, ranting and raving like a madman, and he wouldn't so much as look at you – not then. I'd stand on my step and hear them and fear for her. I went over and banged on the door the first night, but they wouldn't open up. Gwen came to the upstairs window with you in her arms.

'"It's no use, Bryn," she said. "Go you on home. There's nothing to be done."

'I knew she was right, though it broke my heart. There was no room for me. He was the one man in the world she wanted, he'd seen to that, and he'd rather see her dead than at liberty.' Bryn pauses to drink from his glass.

'Did he?' Olwen whispers.

'Did he what?'

'Did he kill her?' When the words are out, she closes her hand over her mouth.

Bryn sets the tumbler down. Tipping his head towards his right shoulder so that his hair sweeps across his face, he looks at her, like a fox peering through a thorn bush, and runs his tongue across his lips. 'So that's what you've been thinking?'

'Tell me the end of it.'

'Aye, I'm about to. One night, after she'd been here a week, she came to my door shouting, "Bryn! Bryn!" I ran to open up and there she stood in her petticoat, bleeding like a pig. He'd attacked her in the Cwm, but she got away and ran to me.'

'I remember it . . .'

'She had you in her arms when he went for her, for she was leaving and taking you with her. They didn't tell Gwen she was going, for your grandmother would have made a fuss about keeping you, but John, he pretended to go along with it, pretended to be taking her to the station, and in the lane he said, "Let's have one last walk in the Cwm, for old times' sake." She thought he'd forgiven her and went with him. Once he got her deep in the trees, he showed his true intention. Handy feller with a knife, your grandad. He ripped her dress from top to bottom and she fell down. She thought to feel the knife in her heart next, thought he'd murder you, too, but there was no rhyme or reason to him, for what he did, he dropped the knife and plucked you from her arms. Screaming you were, and he wrapped you inside his jacket and said, "Go you on, Alice, to Bryn or to the devil, as you please, but I'll keep the little 'un." And she got up and ran away and arrived on my doorstep with no dress and no shoes, her stockings in ribbons, a little travelling bag over one arm, and a great gash up the other.'

'He *didn't* kill her.'

'He never meant to, I'm sure of it. Couldn't kill the thing he loved – the thing he made. When I brought her in and cleaned her up, they were just flesh wounds she had. Most of the blood was coming from that nasty gash in her arm what she'd done herself, falling on a stump in the Cwm, and that was when she pulled her dress off and ran on in just her petticoat.

'When she was cleaned and dressed, she said, "Now walk with me to the bus stop in case he's still out there.' I did, asking her all the way to change her mind, but she was stubborn as a stone. When I put her on the bus she kissed me and said, "I wish you the best, Bryn, which is that you forget you ever knew me and find a good woman." She talked like that, Alice, like she was in a book instead of the real world. I never saw nor heard from her again. She died by her own hand not long after. John got a letter from a London coroner and he went up and brought her ashes home in a casket.'

Olwen stands. 'I have to go.'

Bryn stands too. 'Just one thing more. I've something to show you – something I've been wanting you to see for years.' He steps past her and opens a drawer in the dresser. 'You never seen a photo of her, have you?' He hands her a flat leather folder. 'Take it to the lamp there.'

Olwen looks at a colour photo, a young woman in a blue dress posing in front of a kidney-bean arbour, scarlet flowers surrounding her. She has blue eyes, a wealth of silver hair, and a lovely, unsmiling face. Her beauty, sapphire and ice, chills Olwen to the bone. She has not inherited Alice's beauty, nor her colouring. Yet in her mother's face she sees her own.

Eighteen

Out of the night, a wind has risen. Pale, thin clouds scud across the sky and the moon is wreathed, like a houri, in floating veils. In the Cwm the trees chatter as Bryn and Olwen pass. Beneath the taller, leafier oaks, the deformed sapling, clearly defined in the moonlight, resembles more than ever a stunted human leaning on a stick, about to step out into the lane and accost them.

'Weather's turned chilly,' Bryn remarks. He has his empty sack slung over his shoulder, Gelert at his heels, for he is going into the woods after he has seen Olwen home.

'Aren't you ever afraid of the Cwm at night?' Olwen asks as they reach her gate.

'Afraid? Why? There's nothing in there bigger than I am.'

Bryn opens the gate and Olwen steps through. He shuts it behind her. She folds her arms on the top bar. 'I didn't mean animals.'

'What then? Ghosts? Stuff like that's all in the mind, Olwen love. More's the pity.'

From the corner of her eye Olwen sees the looming black shape of the toolshed. Behind Bryn the dwarf figure points its crooked finger, shaking in the wind as if palsied. Close enough to touch if she stretched out her hand, the delphiniums sway and mutter. They are surrounded by ghosts. Called up by the clairvoyant moon, they crouch in the garden and on the edge of the Cwm, waiting for Bryn to leave her.

'Only ghost I'm aware of, I carry around with me, like this sack when it's full and heavy. And it don't make no difference whether I'm in the Cwm or in my own house. She weighs on me everywhere. Never shows herself though. She's as flighty now as she was then.'

He speaks of memory, confusing it with necromancy, because, though haunted, he has never seen an apparition — nor ever will. It's not Bryn Alice's ghost seeks.

'Go on in now,' he says. 'It's nippy out here. Do you want me to come with you and turn the lights on?'

'No,' Olwen says. 'I'll be all right.'

'I'll watch till you're inside, then.'

She goes up the path towards the dark house. Beside the front door the laurel bush sways in the wind, its branches parting so that Olwen glimpses, through the broad leaves, the hall window, sheened by the moon. By a trick of moonlight and fluttering leaves, it seems as if a figure glides behind the bush as she approaches. When she is level with the shrub, a faintly bitter yet sweetish aroma seems to emanate from its centre.

'Right-oh?' Bryn calls.

Her hand on the door knob, Olwen turns. He leans on the gate, a tall shadow between the toolshed and the delphiniums, his bushy head like a faun's in the moonlight. She wants to call back, 'No, nothing's right,' so that he will open the gate and come to her, enter the house before her and make it safe.

But if he does that, she knows she will ask him to stay. And if she asks, he might. She is not Alice, but she is Alice's daughter, and Bryn is a lonely man with a terrible longing. Deep inside herself, deeper than her present fear and need, she senses wrongness in her wish to detain him. If she called out to him, it would not be a lover's cry. If he came, stayed, it would not be because he loved her. Tonight, a false attraction has sprung up between them, fed on shared secrets, a shared desire, though not for each other. It is Gareth she wants; Alice, though long dead, whom Bryn hankers for. Yet how easy to hoodwink the receptive heart. She begins, at last, to understand her mother.

'You got a lion's heart,' her grandfather said, long ago in the Cwm when she wanted to pursue the enchanter. Remembering his words, she remembers her purpose. It remains, though her motives have altered. She must meet him again, for without that encounter – once longed-for, now dreaded – she can't proceed. She will be trapped for ever, like Bryn, who has now opened the gate and started up the path.

She raises her hand to stop him. 'I'm fine,' she calls. 'Thank you.'

'Sure?'

'I'm sure.'

'Goodnight, then.' He turns and vanishes into the lane.

Olwen opens the front door and steps into the narrow hall.

Moonlight floods the passage and the staircase. On her left the kitchen door stands open. Willow-pattern china gleams on the dresser, copper pots glint above the stove, familiar objects that fail to comfort. In the dark house they seem like decoys, planted to distract her from whatever lurks in the deep shadows outside the moonshine, or in the pitch black at the top of the stairs.

She closes the front door and flicks the switch beside it. The passage lights up, the Tiffany lamp above her head casting a warm glow on wooden stairs, the shadows withdrawing to regroup on the landing. A few steps and she has switched on the kitchen light too. She returns to the hall, to the door, turns the key in the lock and slides the bolt. Then she goes down the passage to the parlour.

A shape reclining in the leather armchair beside the fireplace freezes her. But it is only a stack of needlepoint cushions Gwen has placed there. Her workbox sits on the footstool where her grandfather rested his bad leg when he read to Olwen.

Olwen flicks on the lamp behind the chair. She lifts the cushions and places them on the sofa, the workbox too. I'll tell her, she thinks, that she can't use this chair to keep things on.

Back in the doorway, she looks at the chair, imagines him, his white hair silvered by lamplight, his pipe smoke curling into fantastic shapes; imagines herself on the rug at his feet, her head resting on his knee.

'Grandfather?' she whispers.

The chair remains empty. The black leather, the austere lines, suggest a sternness she has not observed before. She thinks of how he materialized at the cemetery gates, and in the toolshed, and his refusal to appear now seems like a reproof, a tit-for-tat because she, too, is a deserter.

Repelled by the emptiness of the parlour, the musty scent of old books and unused furniture, Olwen goes back up the passage towards the kitchen. At the door, she hesitates and looks up the stairs. She must climb them, put on the landing light and the lights in the bedrooms. Until she has done that – until the entire house is lit – she will not feel easy.

Standing on the bottom stair, her hand clutching the banister, she looks up. From the darkness above something drifts down, a displacement of air, light as a breath, or the remnant of a breeze from an open window. It brushes her bare arms and she shivers.

Of course, the bedroom windows *are* open, and the night has turned cold. She must close the windows, change her shorts for jeans and put on a sweater. The thought of these practical tasks consoles her and she mounts the second step, the third. On the fourth step, halfway up, she stops, for it seems to her that she can hear breathing above.

But the house is empty. She knows that. It is her own fear that raises goosebumps on her arms and transforms the silence. When the lights are on in the bedrooms, when the whole house is lit, she will feel better.

She forces herself to go on. As she climbs, the breathing grows louder, becomes an asthmatic heaving, as if someone above fights for air. Often during his illness her grandfather, in states of extreme anguish or intense excitement, breathed thus, sucking at the air with gasping sounds. But when she reaches the landing and turns on the light, the noise ceases. The house falls into a profound silence.

'I imagined it,' she says aloud. 'I'm so worked up.'

In her grandmother's bedroom, she finds comfort in the sight of Gwen's possessions. A grey cardigan she must have considered wearing that morning lies on the rose-coloured quilt. On a chair under the window her straw hat sits, the green satin band around the crown a reminder of summer mornings, dew on the grass. The scent of lily-of-the-valley lingers. Olwen shuts Gwen's window and goes on to her own room.

Here the casement is wide open, as she left it, the blue curtains blowing out in the breeze. She turns on the lamp beside the bed then crosses to the window. Leaning out to reach the latch, she looks down into the garden. Against the far wall the row of delphiniums slumbers, lunar flowers, their blossoms lustrous pendants among the velvety folds of leaves. Olwen remembers the twelve royal sisters spirited away each night in their sleep to dance till dawn with elvish princes. Each morning the soles of their slippers were worn out, mystifying the king, their father, for he had set a guard outside their chamber, and barred the window of their turret room. For many nights after reading this tale, Olwen had lain in bed wishing for, and fearing, a similar abduction.

On the grass in front of the delphiniums a solid, square object catches the moon's light, a box with silver tracery decorating its sides and dome-shaped lid. In the same moment that she notices the casket, the toolshed door opens and her grandfather comes out, carrying a spade. He is dressed in his Sunday clothes and best cap.

No joy rises in Olwen at this appearance of the longed-for ghost. She knows too much now to hope for any heart-ease from these visions, but there remains, perhaps, the solace of understanding at last – if she does not shrink, if she is not timorous. She knots her fingers as she studies the anomaly of her grandfather, dressed to the nines, gardening by moonlight.

He is digging up the soil, close to the roots of the delphiniums, carefully lifting shovelfuls of the rich earth so that the clods do not break and their grassy surfaces remain intact. As Olwen watches, he takes off his jacket and lays it on the ground beside the squares of earth and the casket. His white shirt gleams with the metallic brightness of chainmail, his hair flowing over his shoulders, liquid as moonshine. When he takes the casket in his hands and lowers it into the pit he has dug, Olwen fathoms the meaning of the vision. He wears his best clothes because he has just returned from a journey to London – the only time in his life he visited that city, possibly – and the casket contains his daughter's ashes. He is burying her beneath the delphiniums.

As she grasps this knowledge, her grandfather is covering the grave. On his knees, he replaces the top soil and smooths the grass, as gently as he once stroked Olwen's hair . . . and, doubtless, Alice's. Then he bends his head and links his hands, and if she did not know otherwise she would believe he prayed.

Olwen shudders. 'Get up,' she says, her voice harsh, a tone she would never have used with him in life. 'Don't do that, Grandfather. It's hopeless.'

Her grandfather rises, puts on his jacket, and moves to the gate. For a moment he stands there, looking across the lane to the Cwm. Among the trees moonshine shimmers, silver threads on black velvet. He pushes open the gate, crosses Archer's Lane and walks into the woods, into the embrace of the figure that looms and glitters, into the spread sleeve. They merge like shadows, uniting limbs and features like the pieces of a jigsaw puzzle locking together: her grandfather and the enchanter.

As this vision vanishes, another rises. Out of the delphiniums, Alice wafts, a full-blown flower, her hair and dress diaphanous with moonlight, her face and bare arms sheened like pearl. On swift, lucid feet she flits to the gate and stands, as her father did moments before, gazing into the Cwm.

Just where the dwarf tree stood, a grander shape appears, as if the sapling and the trees around it have merged into a black garment of preposterous size, large enough to cover the limbs of a giant. Leaves, too, have meshed and become the clustered curls, large as medallions, in a flowing beard and long, wild hair.

In his enveloping night cloak, his face white and sharp in the moonlight, the enchanter towers, his eyes fixed on the woman at the gate. Though his features seem inhuman, chiselled from stone, his eyes glittering like an Arctic sky, his mouth twisted in the parody of a smile, lustful and mocking, Olwen recognizes him. His face is carved on the rafter above her bed, reproduced in the picture Gareth's mother drew, ingrained in her memory. It's the face of her grandfather, distorted by madness – and by the terrible rapture of total possession.

As she watches, transfixed, the figure moves out of the trees, sweeps across the lane, and – as Alice leaps back, light and nervous as a deer – thrusts open the gate. On the path he stops in front of her mother, who seems, as she stands before him, her hands clasped, her head bowed, slender and breakable as a delphinium flower. Her body sways stemlike in the wind that lifts the enchanter's cloak and spins it like a cyclone. For the second time, Olwen feels pity for Alice. Childlike, helpless, she is a victim not a culprit.

The enchanter slips one hand from the folds of his sleeve and holds it out. At the end of his long, moonlit fingers, scarlet talons glitter. Alice lifts her own hand, mechanically, and places it in his. Olwen expects them now to turn towards the Cwm, puppet and puppet-master, to vanish into the woods hand-in-hand, a parody of the father and daughter they had once – or never – been.

Instead, they turn towards the house, the enchanter, with an almost imperceptible movement of his wrist, directing his ward. Simultaneously they raise their heads. Their eyes, shining, curiously transparent, like the lustre of hoarfrost on a window pane, focus on Olwen. Their bloodless lips part to show their teeth, Alice's small and sharp as a weasel's, the enchanter's long and pointed, wolfish. With fakery, they hope to disarm her, as if their murderous smiles could pass for joy and dupe her into believing they mean no harm.

The moon shines full on their faces, lighting their bladelike cheekbones and ivory skin. Alice's hair, oddly stiff now, wreaths her face like the snappable branches of a thorn bush rimed with ice. The enchanter's black locks have the brittle texture of charcoal. Indeed, despite their unearthliness, both figures seem to lack flexibility or grace, as if their limbs were carved or moulded to resemble human forms. Two waxwork figures, animated statues, they move along the path to the house.

Trapped in their freezing gaze, Olwen watches, petrified. For a reason she can't fathom, they want her too. They are coming for her, coming to claim her as their own. Alice stretches out her left arm, her hand open, as if to reach for Olwen. Her curled fingers appear, at first, threatening, as though they would clutch and tear at Olwen were she to come within their grasp. But then she sees that the expression on the spectre's face has altered. In the moonlight, Alice's drawn-back lips suggest a grimace of pain, her white arm and hand like a drowning woman's casting about for aid. Her lips move. 'Olwen,' she mouths.

Standing at the open window, her palms pressed against the cold ledge, Olwen stares at her mother and feels a pain sharper than fear pierce her. Then she turns her eyes to the enchanter, to his grinning, rapacious mouth and ropey beard, his black, shroud-like cloak, and the pain becomes an icicle, numbing her heart.

'I can't help you,' she murmurs. 'I dare not.'

The figures pass beneath the window. Released from their eyes, Olwen can move again. Her first thought is to secure the house. Did she lock the front door? Perhaps keys and bolts won't keep them out, but she has no other hope. Swiftly, she crosses the room, runs along the passage, leaps the two steps to the landing, and flies down the stairs.

Halfway down she stops. Framed in the long, narrow hall window, like a portrait, Alice appears. Her hands part the laurel bush, its broad, shiny leaves mingling with her silver hair. Her face is a replica of the photo Bryn keeps in his dresser drawer, but wan, colourless, the face of a dead woman. Called up by the enchanter to be his consort, she has risen from her shrine beneath the delphiniums, a wreath of her blue burial flowers on her head, her dress an azure shroud. Her white lips open. She imitates a winning smile – a mother's smile. Her hand beckons.

'Olwen, come,' she says.

The door knob whines. Olwen turns her head and sees, through the tinted pane, the dark bulk of the enchanter. The knob rattles under his hand, but she has shot the bolt and turned the key, and the door holds fast. They can't get in! They have no power to enter the house unless she permits it.

Realizing this, Olwen feels her courage mount. She can stand against them, wait them out till morning . . . and when morning comes, they will vanish, as spectres must. She can escape then, go to her grandmother in Swansea, where they will not – cannot – follow for they are bound to their past, which lives only in this house on Archer's Lane.

The black shape outside the door moves away. The next moment, his face appears among the leaves beside Alice's. He crouches over her, his hands on her shoulders, the scarlet talons like epaulettes, the folds of his cloak falling about her. Side by side like this, and close up, their similarity is striking. Olwen sees that they are, truly, blood relatives of the closest tie. Sickened, she sees, too, despite their waxen complexions, her own likeness in their faces.

And now the enchanter's gaze fastens her. As if she looked straight into a snowfield, Olwen is dazzled. His eyes hurt her, but she can't look away. Like a hypnotist he holds her, sapping her strength, robbing her of her will. Her limbs grow weak, her mind drowsy, as though she had swallowed a sleeping draught. In his eyes she sees visions, towers of ice amid great snow drifts, frozen waterfalls and solidified rivers, a terrible white world bereft of hope. He raises his right arm and his long sleeve unfurls like a curtain across the window, blocking Alice from view. Turning his head, he looks towards the open sleeve, freeing Olwen from his gaze. Olwen looks too, and sees in the star-scattered indigo all that her grandfather described.

'It's like the night sky, soft as velvet, embroidered in the finest silver threads. And in this sleeve he can show whatever the heart wants most.'

Repose . . . tranquillity . . . the vision compels her, and she begins to move down the stairs. She must open the door and step into his embrace. Only in the folds of his cloak, beside her mother, will she be safe from the ice world in his eyes, only there find rest. Her fatigue is so great, she can hardly lift her legs. She must force herself to take the few steps across the hall to the front door.

When she has passed the window, she can no longer see him. His eyes can't follow her. In that moment outside his gaze the spell breaks. Her hand, reaching for the bolt, drops to her side. Terror grips her again, like a rough hand shaking her into wakefulness. If she had opened the door, they would have seized her – possessed her.

But they can't come in.

She must remember that, find a place to hide, a place where the eyes of the enchanter can't reach her. Only till morning . . . it can't be many hours hence.

Upstairs, Olwen thinks, in my room.

Averting her eyes from the hall window, she climbs the stairs swiftly, hearing behind her the beating of the laurel on the pane, the knocking of fists against glass – the sounds of their rage.

Suddenly every light in the house dies.

A thought flits through her mind: It must be like this at the bottom of a coal mine, if your lamp goes out . . .

Still, she keeps moving, her hand on the banister. When she reaches the top stair, the breathing she heard earlier starts up again. Harsh and rasping, it comes, she knows beyond doubt, from the room at the end of the corridor. She reaches the landing and moves one foot forward, searching. Her toe knocks against the first of the two steps leading to the passage and she goes up, her right palm pressed to the wall. In front of her the passage is a tunnel, endless, unfamiliar, a place where she could lose her way and never find the opening she seeks, the entrance to her own bedroom and safety.

As she hesitates on the top step, a door creaks. Although she can see nothing, she knows it's the door at the end of the passage. A second creak suggests that the hand on the knob moves slowly, furtively, its owner aware of her presence, hearing, perhaps, the thud of her heart, loud in her own ears.

He is here too, then, in the house with her as well as outside. Her grandfather has become two persons, his body divided in death as, in life, his soul was split between the good man who nurtured her and the despot. If the tyrant is outside in the shape of the enchanter, perhaps the being inside is benevolent and need not be feared?

She hears him breathe harder now, as if opening the door has taxed him.

'Grandfather?' she murmurs and gropes her way along the wall.

As she goes forward, he moves too. She hears the brush of his long robe against the skirting board, the drag of his lame foot. His breath comes louder, swifter, as if he is anxious to reach her.

Olwen's right hand meets air. She has come to her grandmother's room, where the door stands open. Through the opening, Gwen's lily-of-the-valley scent drifts, faint as a memory. An image materializes . . . herself in this passage less than a year ago, at dead of night, going towards her grandfather as she goes towards him now, thinking to comfort him and seeing the yellow flame leap in his eyes, seeing his lip curl as he lunged for her.

Her feet stop, her raised hand, touching only air, quivers. She holds her breath and listens. At the other end of the passage, silence. He has stopped too. In fact the quiet is so complete, he may not be there. She imagined him, possibly. Or is he waiting in the pit-black passage until she comes close, too close to escape his grasp?

Stretching out her hand, she feels for the wall beyond her grandmother's door, finds it, and moves one step forward. How many steps to her own door? She has never counted, but not more than half a dozen certainly. She takes a second step.

Still there is no sound beside her own heart and the scratch of her nails as they graze the wall. Four more steps and she will reach her room. Once inside she can lock the door and wait out the night. In the small space of her bedroom, made fast from the rest of the house, she will feel safer, enclosed, like a rabbit in its burrow, a bird in the nest.

She takes a third step, her fingers sliding across plaster until they brush the wooden door frame. With a sob of relief, Olwen stretches further, groping for the space into which she can fling herself.

Instead of air, she touches a cold, brittle hand. Emaciated, it still has strength to fasten hers. She screams and tries to pull free, but the bony fingers lock tighter. In a hoarse, mocking whisper, he says, 'Got you, my treasure.' His other hand grips her bare arm, his nails digging into her skin. Invisible, cloaked in pitch, he draws her, resisting, towards him.

Though she can't see him, she knows he looks as he did on that other night, his teeth bared, the yellow flame of greed in his eyes. He will rip her as the collie ravaged the sheep. She struggles, but the gap between them closes until her face is pressed to the rough wool of his robe and she can hear the uneven beat of his heart. His hand slides up her arm to her throat.

A scream rings through the night. Olwen thinks it is her own, but another cry follows. 'Father! Let me in!'

Her assailant stiffens. She senses that he cocks his head, listening. But he still holds Olwen fast.

'Why have you locked me out, Father?'

'Alice?' His voice wavers, his fingers slacken their hold.

'Come, Father! I'm here!'

As if she were merely some obstacle encountered in the dark, he pushes Olwen aside. Down the passage he limps, saying her name, 'Alice . . . Alice,' his lame leg and his good leg beating a discordant tune on the wood floor.

Olwen stumbles into her room, slams the door and turns the key. Her knees give way and she sinks. Clutching the shag carpet in her fists, she sits against the door, tears streaming down her face.

She hears him thump down the two steps to the landing. There he pauses and calls his daughter's name again. His voice chills Olwen, a howl of monstrous desire, crazed, lustful, child-like all at once.

'Here I am, Father!'

The stairs creak under his descent. He will let them in. Olwen looks about the room for a hiding place. But there is no closet or corner where they would not easily find her. For a wild moment she imagines leaping from the window, but it's too high – she would injure herself.

On the table beside her bed something small, bright as a cat's eye, glints in the moonlight. It's her grandmother's keeper, given to her that morning.

Downstairs, she hears a bolt slide.

She springs across the room, snatches up the ring and slips it onto her finger. Too large, the ring slides and threatens to fall. Olwen closes her fingers into her palm. She holds her fist out in the moonlight. Secured, the ring gleams steadily.

'Help me, then,' she murmurs.

Now the house is silent, as if the three downstairs know of her discovery and ponder their next move. Then, softly, stealthily, the front door opens, closes.

Olwen's breath hitches in her throat. They have entered. The ring does not work for her. Rigid, she listens for footsteps on the stairs.

Instead, sounds drift up from the garden. Low voices beneath her window, a rustling of garments in the wind. She crosses the moonlit space and looks out. Three figures move down the path towards the gate. In the centre, the enchanter has spread his long sleeves like wings, one arm over the slender shoulders of her mother, the other embracing the bowed and limping form of her grandfather, looking older, frailer than he ever did in life, even during his sickness. They pass through the gate as if it were mere shadow, drift across the lane, and vanish into the Cwm like mist. Olwen feels relief but no joy. As her fear ebbs away, a deep despair shrouds her heart. He has them both now.

On the edge of the trees, a little girl appears. Long dark braids hang down her back. Her pink dress is familiar, her posture too. Hands linked against her chest, she thrusts her shoulders forward and tilts her head to peer into the Cwm. Watching the child, Olwen understands. She has not escaped. They will come back for her.

Nineteen

Her honey-coloured hair is plaited this morning, looped over her ears, a romantic, medieval fashion suited to her outfit. In a long peasant skirt and white ruffled blouse, the sleeves slipped off her shoulders, Rosamund Miller looks like a figure out of a fairytale – the princess disguised as a goose girl – except that in her hands she holds a white Tupperware container.

Standing in Olwen's kitchen in a burst of mid-morning sun, she says, 'I hope I didn't wake you.' Her eyes, round and innocent as cornflowers, gaze at Olwen's dishevelled hair and rumpled clothes. 'Do you wear shorts to bed? I think that's so interesting! It tells me there's no nonsense in you. It *is* nonsense when you think about it, to have a whole different range of clothes just to sleep in.'

'I was too tired to change last night,' Olwen says. 'Would you like a cup of coffee?'

'I wouldn't mind, though I've had breakfast already with Alun.'

As she crosses the kitchen, Olwen sees by the mantelpiece clock that it is after eleven. Just a few minutes ago Rosamund's persistent hand on the door knocker woke her from the deep sleep she had finally slipped into at dawn.

'Why were you so tired?' Rosamund asks as Olwen pours water into the coffee percolator. 'You didn't go out, did you?'

'No,' Olwen says, measuring coffee into the filter cup, her back to Rosamund.

'I thought not. I've never seen you go out in the evening all the months I've lived here. A bit of a stay-at-home, aren't you?'

Olwen switches on the percolator. 'I suppose so.' Her back still turned to Rosamund, she stares into the shiny aluminium surface of the coffee pot, at her own distorted image, a pale elongated face, its features freakishly enlarged, an immoderate mouth, excessive eyes, a deluge of tangled hair: a mask, a parody, an aberration, like the faces that stared at her last night through the hall window . . .

'Did you have a visitor, then?'

'What?' Olwen swings round. 'What do you mean?'

Rosamund laughs, a brief, surprised 'huh' sound. 'I don't *mean* anything, dear. I just wonder why you were too tired to put on your nightie. And why you slept in so late. Look, I brought you some muffins.' She puts the Tupperware container on the table and pulls out a chair. 'Fresh baked and stuffed with blackberries. There are so many blackberries in the lane, have you noticed? I can't stay long. I promised Alun I wouldn't.'

Olwen brings to the table two willow-pattern plates, two knives and the butter crock. 'Thank you.'

'Oh, don't mention it. Alun was out till after eleven last night. Some school meeting. On a Friday, imagine! Barbaric, isn't it? To keep myself busy I made muffins, a ton of them, more than we can eat in a week. I gave some to Aunt Flindy, too, and I left some on Mr Brewen's doorstep. Will he return my container, do you think? I never see him about. For heaven's sake, Olwen, sit down. You're making me edgy.'

Olwen sits opposite Rosamund and folds her arms on the table.

'I waited up for Alun last night. I always do. And about ten o'clock I strolled down to the gate, just to see if he was coming, and while I was standing there I thought I heard voices in the lane, so I stepped out. I looked up the lane, and do you know what, I saw two people outside your gate. I thought it was you and . . . a friend . . . so I went back into my house. I didn't want you to see me and think I was prying.' Rosamund pauses, lifts her eyebrows, perfect arcs, pencilled a darker shade than her hair.

Olwen says nothing.

'When I was inside, it struck me that it might have been Alun, that he might have come up to see if you were all right, you know, with Gwen being away. But of course it wasn't Alun because he didn't get back for another hour, as I told you.'

'No,' Olwen says. 'Alun didn't come here last night.'

Rosamund sighs. 'I'm so restless when he's not at home. Being married is wonderful, but it's work too. You have to work hard to meet each other's needs, keep each other happy. Do you know, Olwen, I have an entire wardrobe full of night clothes, from full-length gowns fit for a dance to little bits of things that are – well, that are pornographic, to be honest! Men are so weird, you see, when it comes to sex. They have fantasies they like you to act out, and most of them have to do with the clothes you wear. Looking is as big a thrill for them as doing it.'

'I think the coffee's ready,' Olwen says. She gets up to get away from Rosamund. This is their first meeting since the dinner party, their third since the Millers moved in, but Rosamund talks as if they are old, intimate friends, making Olwen, who has never discussed sex with anyone, embarrassed and uneasy. As she carries the cups to the percolator she thinks, if I were to talk about it, it wouldn't be like this, nor with her.

For there is something repellant in Rosamund's tone this morning, something in her knowing, confidential smile that suggests trickery. But perhaps Olwen's mind is too weighed down by the horrors of last night – Alice's spectral simpering as she parted the laurel, the enchanter's smirk as he unfurled his sleeve – and so she weaves an imaginary significance into Rosamund's foolish chatter.

Yet there *is* a difference, in the way she talks, the way she looks at Olwen, a kind of frenzy beneath the self-assurance, shocking, out of place, like a glimpse of torn and unwashed petticoat under an expensive skirt. Why is she afraid? For she is afraid, Olwen sees that now. Whom did she see last night when she looked for her husband? Olwen and Bryn, or the other two? Did the enchanter turn his glittering eyes on her as she stood in the lane – or is it Olwen herself Rosamund fears? Because I am so strange . . .

In the aluminium of the percolator, her reflection acquiesces and mocks her:

> Mirror, mirror, on the wall,
> Who is maddest of us all?

Olwen tilts the coffee pot, fills the cups, and carries them to the table.

'No sugar, thank you,' Rosamund says. 'I've given it up. Olwen, I have one outfit that drives Alun out of his senses with lust. No, I don't want a muffin. Help yourself. Do you mind if I smoke instead?' She draws a pack of cigarettes from her skirt pocket.

'No. I didn't know you did.' Olwen slices and butters a muffin.

'Officially, I don't. I'm supposed to have stopped. Well, health and odour and all that – there's no argument in its favour, is there? I couldn't disagree with Alun. But old habits die hard, that's what he doesn't understand. And I *enjoy* it. So I have one on the sly now and then.' She lights up. 'Don't tell him.'

'Why would I? Smoke as much as you like.'

Rosamund inhales deeply. 'I was telling you about this outfit I have. It's a black transparent chemise with matching bikini pants, all see-through except where he *really* wants to see.' She touches her right nipple with the tip of her index finger. 'A black rose here.' Her finger circles the nipple, 'and here.' She repeats the motion on her other breast. 'With a red sequin in the centre, and the bikini pants have a rose in front, too, with red sequins etching the petals. The thing is, the roses are flaps you can lift up without taking off the panties or the chemise.'

Olwen puts down her half-eaten muffin and stares at Rosamund.

'And what Alun likes to do, he likes to lift the roses and look at just those parts of me, and then he likes to touch me there, where I'm naked, but still wearing the outfit.' She waves her cigarette and laughs. 'He's just like a little boy playing peek-a-boo, but to him it's *so* erotic! Men!' She shakes her head and dips her hand into the Tupperware box. 'Are they good? I'll just try one. Half of one. Will you share it? You don't have to watch your figure. You're so thin, Olwen. Of course, you know all about it, don't you?' She slices a muffin and reaches over to place one half on Olwen's plate. 'That's why you wear shorts and tight jeans all the time. In a different way, they're just as sexy as a peep-through nightie, aren't they?'

'I've never thought about it like that.'

'Oh, go on!' Rosamund spreads butter thickly on the half muffin and takes a bite. 'You attract Alun, I suppose you know?'

Olwen pulls at a loose thread in the sleeve of her cotton shirt. 'Rosamund, I wish –'

'He told me you flirted with him when he came to mend the gate.'

Olwen's head snaps up. 'No!'

She wants to tell Rosamund that she has never flirted, that even the simplest exchanges with young men are hard for her, let alone the intricacies of flirtation.

'It's all right, Olwen,' Rosamund says. 'I'm used to it. It's one of the penalties I pay for marrying a charismatic man. And I know he probably started it. Alun enjoys flirting, but it's quite harmless. He doesn't mean anything by it.' She dabs at the crumbs on her plate and presses her finger to her tongue. 'It's only a problem when a woman takes him seriously – and you wouldn't do that. You have too much sense. Discipline, Alun calls it. He thinks you're *too* disciplined. There's a lot hidden underneath that wants to come out, he says.' She draws another cigarette from the pack and leans forward. 'The thing is, he adores me. You can see that, can't you?'

'Yes,' Olwen says, 'anyone can see that.'

'So . . . did he tease you about getting together?'

'No. He was anxious to get back to you, Rosamund. He said he didn't like to be separated from you for long.'

'That's right. That's what you have to remember. He couldn't part from me.' Rosamund strikes a match. 'Anyway,' she says, pausing to light her cigarette, 'you like the doctor's son. I saw him drive you home once. I was in my upstairs window. You had a row, didn't you? Rows are nothing. All lovers have them. I saw his father drive your grandmother off yesterday morning, too. Gwen's wonderful for sixty, isn't she? I hope I look like that when I'm her age.' She stands up, brushing crumbs from her skirt. 'We'll be moving in a month or so. Alun has a teaching job in London. Isn't that great? I think so. We're not suited to country life at all.'

'I'll walk you to the gate,' Olwen says.

On the path, Rosamund admires the flowers. 'Our garden is all grass. I'd like to have flowers, but I don't fancy all the work. And when you're renting –'

'Come and pick a bunch whenever you like.'

Rosamund touches her arm. 'That's sweet of you. You know, if we weren't leaving, you and I would be friends, I'm sure.'

At the gate, she says, 'I'd ask you to dinner tonight, but we're invited out ourselves – a colleague of Alun's at Pont Ysaf Grammar. Well, bye, Olwen. We had a nice chat. It's good for women to get together. I don't have many women friends now I'm married, though I used to have tons. Maybe in London . . .' And she is off down the lane, her skirt swinging about her shapely calves, her bare shoulders glinting in the bright sun.

Back in the house, Olwen sits at the table with a second cup of coffee and wonders, is love always like that? Like her grandfather's and Rosamund's – protective and self-interested, stifling lover and beloved in a jealous embrace? If she and Gareth were lovers, would she behave so? She remembers how she felt at the Mountain Inn when he put his arm around Myra Talbot. Sandpaper had scraped her nerves. That searing pain was jealousy – and rage.

Remembering distresses her and she thinks, instead, about her grandfather. But that too is painful. Seeing him as a man who demanded exclusive love, who tried to create it, first in her mother, then in her – reduces him, making him, she knows, less than he was in reality.

Yet it seems true that, when love is snatched away, denied, the lover becomes obsessed, filled with turmoil, like an empty conch shell in which the crash and roar of the distant sea can still be heard, though it is only a deception, a trick of the senses and of memory.

She thinks of Bryn Brewen, who can't love again – as if the passion and desire he once felt have eaten up the gentler emotions, leaving his heart depleted. Other people cross her mind: Aunt Flindy, widowed; Morgan Pryce, undesired; her cousin, Gwyneira, perpetually jilted – all of them victims of love. And she must also exclude herself from the list, she who rejected all others to cleave to her grandfather, and who wished to die when he left her. Is love worth all this pain? Could one not find another, less arduous path through the world?

But then she thinks of Gwen, standing at this table where she now sits, in her spring-green dress, smiling shyly, hopeful as a girl, her hazel eyes warm with pleasure when the doctor appeared in the doorway; Gwen, whose first love was destroyed, ready to love again at sixty.

If I have discipline, Olwen thinks, I inherit it from her. And perhaps it is discipline, an austere enough quality on its own, that, when linked with passion, nourishes love. Looking into the garden, she believes it is so. A disciplined yet passionate gardener, she has brought the garden into bloom.

'Just go on opening,' Dr Lloyd said. 'Naturally.'

Olwen clears and washes the breakfast dishes. When she opens the kitchen window to shake the crumbs from the tablecloth, the fresh air billows in so exuberantly she is taken by delight. It's as if she had opened the casement to find a lover who leans over the sill to surprise her with a kiss and a posy. Pleasure makes her light-footed, light-hearted almost, as she goes through every room in the house opening the windows she had secured the previous night. When she is done, the cottage is regaled with perfumes, as if the garden itself had come inside – as it should, of course.

Back in the kitchen, she takes Gwen's wicker basket and scissors and goes out to cut flowers. Roses, gladioli, phlox, some of every kind she gathers, save the sunflowers and delphiniums which, by their height and proportions, exclude themselves from selection, unfitted for any setting save the soil they spring from. Like her grandfather, they spurn the inside of houses.

When the basket is full she carries it indoors, brings vases for the flowers, and fills every room with blossoms. On Gwen's dressing table she places a tall vase of gladioli, elegant, stately flowers to honour her grandmother's strength, and in recognition of her own debt to Gwen's saving power. It was she who saved Olwen as a baby, her courage and goodness that sprang last night from the keeper. Olwen had slept with the ring on her finger, a tiny wad of tissue paper tucked into the band to hold it fast, taking it off only when she woke to morning sun and Rosamund's knocking. It lies now in a handkerchief in her dressing-table drawer, waiting to be altered. An heirloom, a treasure, when it fits her properly she will wear it always.

In the parlour, near her grandfather's chair, she sets a bowl of carnations and forget-me-nots, and in his sick-room the first chrysanthemums. Last, she carries a vase of red roses to her own room: for love, she thinks.

Going through the house with flowers, she is struck by its warmth and cheer. On this sunny afternoon all the memories that issue forth as she opens doors are tender, poignant. She doesn't want to leave the cottage, only to live in it peaceably again.

Finished, she bathes and dresses. Under her denim shorts and white shirt she wears the silky white bikini Gwen bought for her the last time they were in Swansea and which she has never yet worn, regarding it at the time with distaste – the distaste of her grandfather. She brushes her hair and lets it loose about her shoulders. Ready, she takes the pictures from her dressing table drawer and lays them on her bed to look at them.

She understands them now, and, she believes, the woman

who drew them. Her models, of course, besides Gareth himself, were Olwen's own mother and grandfather. She must have seen them together – in Pont Ysaf perhaps – or more likely, wandering about the countryside, perhaps many times, perhaps once only – a chance meeting on the old Roman road on the other side of the Cwm. Whether once or often, they had struck her imagination, for in their faces she had seen what was most to be feared: possession, jealousy, an absence of control. Later – much later – when she was a mother fearing for her son, she made pictures, parables, to show him what in life he would have to confront and overcome.

Through the generosity of her son, Olwen has the pictures now. Perhaps Gareth no longer needs them? The thought is comforting, but wrong, she intuits. Surely it must take years of struggle to win the battles they depict, to reach that state where, immune to the enchanter, one may risk enchantment.

Replacing the pictures in her drawer, Olwen leaves the room. She goes out of the house and down the path. It is late afternoon. In the cool of the day she strolls along the lane towards the river.

Long shadows of trees lie on the grass in the little copse above the Wen Pool. The scent of blackberries, ripe, redolent, permeates the air. Going down the slope, Olwen sees that the pool is empty and her heart sinks. Perhaps he has come and gone already, she has left it so late.

Standing on the mossy bank, she looks down at her own reflection in the water where she has never swum. Today she will. She strips off her clothes and lays them on a rock, then lowers herself into the pool. It is so cold it snatches her breath away. Shivering, Olwen ducks, immersing herself to the shoulders. When the first chill wears off, she strikes out, swimming overarm, the stroke her aunt and her grandmother taught her.

It's hard work. Accustomed to the buoyancy of the sea, she soon grows short of breath in the unhelpful water. Pulling herself up to rest, she finds she is out of her depth. The Wen, she understands, has no gradation. She is over an abyss. Panic seizes her and she sinks. Down through deepening layers of green she goes, the water like thunder in her ears. Breathless, she feels the urge to struggle, though she knows she should be still, unresisting. Her head throbs and her nose hurts. Then, just as she feels her lungs will burst, her feet touch gravel. The Wen is not bottomless, of course. It is not even as deep as she feared. Her soles bounce off the gravel as if it were a trampoline, and she rises swiftly, the water helping after all. She breaks the surface and, gasping, using her arms wildly, swims on. At last she reaches the other side, grasps the long, tough grass there, and hauls herself up onto the bank.

'You're not in shape, Olwen!"

As she climbs out of the water onto the grassy slope, she sees him on the opposite bank, a white towel rolled under one arm, his thumbs hooked into the pockets of his faded blue jeans. She stands facing him, her breath coming sharply, her hands clutching her hips.

In a striped T-shirt, navy on white, his hair tousled by a breeze that ripples over the Wen, he has a nautical air – the young sailor on leave from his ship. The image excites her, conjuring possibilities – as if they were strangers meeting for the first time, by chance, in some exotic place. If they had met like that, she would still be drawn to him, instantly, powerfully, knowing at once that he was the one she wanted. Or so she believes, looking at him now across the Wen Pool. The thrill she feels wipes out resentment (his words are teasing) and humiliation (he saw her defeat), and she is breathless not from fear and effort but because he has come – by chance or on purpose – and, like her, he is surprised by, and glad for, the meeting.

'I was wrong,' he says. 'You're in perfect shape.'

As his eyes rove over her body and the familiar look comes to his face, she feels her breasts swell and press against the silky cloth of her bikini.

'I saw you go down. I'd have come in for you, but you bobbed up again and carried on . . .'

His eyes and his voice are at odds. Entranced by what his eyes say, Olwen doesn't answer.

'Shall I come over and tow you back? Olwen? You *are* coming back? You're not waiting for me to go away, are you?'

'I'm coming. Stay there.'

She lowers herself into the pool again. Treading the gravel, she measures the distance to the opposite bank, reminding herself to save breath so that she will not flounder in the middle. She knows she's not a stylish swimmer, but under his gaze she wants, at least, to appear competent. Gathering her courage, she strikes out.

This time the crossing is easier. As if she lies, again, on the crossed hands of her aunt and her grandmother, she feels borne up. He is there, ready to aid her. ('We won't let you drown, Olwen.') Knowing this, she needs no help. When she lifts her head, thinking she has reached the centre, she is close to the bank. Gareth kneels at the water's edge, his hands stretched out.

'Great,' he says, unwrapping the white towel and draping it over her. 'Practise a bit and you'll be an expert. You have a strong stroke, only you don't use your arms to your best advantage.'

Looking up at him as he closes the ends of the towel across her body, she sees that he is nervous. Beneath his left eyebrow, the tiny scar quivers.

'I stopped at your house on my way here. I thought you might like to go out.' He shrugs his shoulders, drops his hands to his sides. 'Well . . . you say something for a change. I'm just talking.'

His eyes, green where one looks for blue, are the colour of ivy – of jealousy? Will he be a generous or a jealous lover? She holds out her hand to him, but he makes no move.

'Once bitten, twice shy. I've been bitten more than once, remember.'

'I came here to look for you.'

'Tell me what to do, Olwen.'

'Let's go to the stone,' she says.

As soon as they pass through the willow curtain, they are in each other's arms. Olwen hooks her wet body to his, her dampness seeping through his cotton T-shirt so that he is wet too and their bodies stick. When he bends his head to kiss her, his hair, falling across her face, has the texture and scent of spring leaves. Rough denim grazes her thighs as he supports her, leaning on him, and she feels him rise against her stomach, hard and supple as the branch of a young oak.

Gareth draws her down onto the warm, white stone, large as a bed, unfastens the bikini top and spreads his hands over her breasts. In his palms, her nipples spring up, in his mouth, her tongue cleaves to his, and as though buoyed on waves, her body becomes pliant, weightless. When he lifts her thigh, it's as if she were floating, lifted on water.

Nimbly, he unzips, pulls back the slip of silk between her legs and enters her.

Olwen cries out, 'Don't!' and tries to pull away.

His arms fasten her. 'I must. I can't stop now.'

For a moment, she hates him. He hurts her deliberately and cares nothing for her pain. Then, suddenly, the sensations alter, the pain disperses. She feels it ebb away under his thrusts, as if he massages and heals her. Spurred by desire, she closes over him, swift currents rising to suck him into her. She is the pool now, he the diver. She makes him wet and slick so that he may plunge easily and penetrate deeper. No longer herself, she is the vortex that swirls inside her and demands him. Grasping his shoulders, she pushes down, hard and fast.

'Slower,' he urges. 'I'm on the edge. Keep still a minute, Olwen.'

But she can't stop, and with dizzying pleasure she feels him rush to her centre. He shudders . . . and lies still.

It's over, she understands, her delight drowning in disappointment. She wants more, but it's over. Inside her, he is a spent swimmer, inert, floating. Tears blur her eyes. How is she to bear this?

As he slips out of her, Gareth pulls her close. Trembling, Olwen lies in the crook of his arm.

'It was too soon for you. You didn't feel anything.'

'Yes,' she says. 'I did. I felt a lot. I still do.'

He lifts her hair to stroke her neck. 'That's what I mean. You didn't finish. Only I did. It was all too quick, from the start.' He runs his hand down her back to her waist, then up again, to caress her shoulder. 'I should have taken more time. We didn't even undress. I wanted you, you see. I have for a year. You know that.' As he talks, he moves his hand over her body, making patterns on her skin, his fingers as tender as his voice.

'Kiss me,' she says.

He puts his mouth on hers and Olwen closes her eyes. 'I still want you,' she says, as they lie with their mouths touching, his breath entering her. 'More now than I did before.'

'You know what I've felt then,' he says, and presses his hand hard against her back when she tries to draw away.

'I'm not crowing. I'm just telling you. This is how it is. We'll do it again, Olwen. Will you let me stay with you tonight? I want to sleep with you.'

'Yes,' she says. 'Yes, I want to. Can we do it again now?'

His arms tighten around her. He thrusts his tongue into her

mouth and locks her legs between his, turning so that he pulls her on top of him. Happiness swells in Olwen like laughter. It's never over, she understands, never finished. These are just words people use; like all words, inadequate. For there is no completion in the way he moves under her. As she rises over his body and slips her hands up under his shirt to press her palms against his skin, she knows that they merely paused.

At that moment, as she arches over him, she feels it – the sweep of a garment, soft and cool as velvet, across her back. Olwen cries out and springs away from Gareth. On her knees, her hands flat on the stone, crouching, she looks about. For a moment she seems to see a cloaked figure looking at her through the trailing branches of the willow. Then Gareth sits up, puts his arm around her, and the figure vanishes . . . or, perhaps, was never there. Behind the willow tree, the dark gathers, casting long shadows across the stone, cold and smooth as marble beneath her hands and knees. Olwen shivers and moves further into Gareth's embrace.

'What is it?' he says. 'What happened, Olwen?'

'It's freezing,' she says. 'Let's go home.'

In the copse Olwen dresses swiftly. Evening has come on apace, and the dark shapes of trees and bushes clustered about the Wen make her uneasy. Transparent in daylight, the pool has assumed an opaque aspect now, a black mantle cast on the ground, sombre and still, scattered with sequins, reflections of the first stars.

'I've never been here at night before,' Gareth says. 'It's eerie, isn't it? Remember the story of King Arthur and the Lady of the Lake?'

'She gave him the sword Excalibur,' Olwen says, gazing down at the Wen. 'There are lots of stories like that in Welsh legends – fairy women rising out of lakes.'

'Looking at the Wen now, I can believe those stories. It seems haunted.'

'I'm ready,' she says. 'Let's go.'

Gareth tucks the towel under one arm and puts his other arm around Olwen's waist. 'You came to me out of the lake.'

'I didn't give you a sword though.'

'Yes you did.'

Twenty

As they cross the field and go down the lane, Olwen cannot rid herself of the conviction that they are watched. Yet each time she looks over her shoulder there is nothing behind them save the lengthening shadows.

They go through the garden gate and past the crouching toolshed, the wraith-like delphiniums. When they enter the house, she locks and bolts the door.

'What frightened you outside?' Gareth says.

Olwen shakes her head. 'Nothing.'

In the bright kitchen she recovers. The flowers on the table, Gwen's copper pots above the stove, the paisley armchair and the brass fire irons cheer her.

'We'll have something to eat,' she says and crosses to the fridge.

Standing beside the table, Gareth watches her. 'I felt it too,' he says.

'There's cold ham and cheese. We can make sandwiches.'

He comes to her, puts his arm around her shoulders. 'Am I still invited to stay the night?'

'What will your father think?'

'He won't wait up.'

'And in the morning?'

'Sundays, he sleeps in. It's his only chance.'

'You had it all planned, did you?' She holds out a plate of sliced ham.

'No, I only hoped. I always have.'

Olwen takes a slab of Caerphilly cheese, a jar of relish and the butter crock from the fridge. Balancing these in her hands, she moves away from Gareth to the table. 'Will you bring the bread from the bin, please? And two plates.' She takes a knife from the table drawer. Gareth comes with the plates, the ham, and a cob loaf.

'A simple supper,' she says, slicing the cheese. 'I expect you're used to something more elaborate. Do you have a girlfriend in Oxford? A lot of girlfriends?'

He pulls out a chair and sits. 'You have the wrong impression of me. That's the only trouble between us. If you have another knife, I can cut the bread.'

Olwen hands him a knife from the drawer. 'It's just that . . .' She has meant to tell him that he's so beautiful, so graceful, he must enchant every woman who sees him. Instead, she says, 'I know you've slept with women before.'

'Yes. Do you mind?'

Is it different with me? she wants to ask. Do you prefer me to the others? Will you love me?

'I don't know,' she says. 'There's only milk to drink, or water.'

'Don't you have coffee?'

'Yes, but it would keep us awake.'

'Tonight we're not going to sleep much, Olwen. I'll make it, shall I?'

Olwen, buttering the bread he has cut, pauses to smile at him. 'This is nice,' she says.

'Not as nice as it will be.'

As they eat, he says, 'Down by the Wen . . . we didn't take care, you know. I'm sorry.'

'It's not your fault,' she says.

'We should take care now. My car's at the end of the lane. I can be back in a few minutes.'

'You did plan then.'

'No, not really. I . . . just happen to have them there.'

'Oh.' For other women. He keeps condoms in his car so that he can make love to other women at the end of an evening out. In Oxford. But he started before that, of course. He has made love with Pont Ysaf girls, girls she knew at school – Myra Talbot, perhaps.

Gareth covers her hand with his. 'Look,' he says, 'from time to time it happens that –'

'It's all right,' she says quickly. 'I don't want to know. I never thought you were waiting for me.'

'I was waiting for you. I didn't know if I'd ever be with you, though. You see, I couldn't be a monk in Oxford, not knowing whether –'

'Let's not talk about it now. I'll come to the car with you.'

They go down the garden path holding hands. Yet she feels distanced from him now. Shadows of other women have risen between them, and they dim the bright hope she has carried all day in her heart. Faces of women she has never seen flit across her mind – and they are all lovely, confident, seductive.

In the lane she looks over Bryn Brewen's gate to his house. Every window is dark. He is in the Cwm, of course. Last night she sat in his kitchen, and when he walked home with her she had wanted to call him in. I was afraid, she thinks, that's why. But she remembers, too, another feeling . . . it wasn't only fear that tempted her.

A light burns in Aunt Flindy's parlour. The old woman must be sitting in her rocker . . . doing what? Listening to the radio, dozing, carping at Cinders? How does she pass the time house-bound and without company? Olwen thinks of the masses of framed photographs. Aunt Flindy does have company – she is visited every night by ghosts who spring from her memory. How terrible, to be alone like that. And how thoughtless she has been, never giving the old woman a kind word, never sparing an hour to sit with her.

Olwen moves closer to Gareth, pressing her arm against his. 'Do you believe in ghosts?'

'Yes,' he says. 'I think so. A long time ago, when I was a kid, I used to see things. My father told you about that, didn't he?'

'The people in your mother's pictures. The enchanter and the girl on the horse.'

They are passing the Millers' cottage. Behind the bedroom curtains a red light glows. Olwen has a bizarre vision of Rosamund in costume, in many costumes, performing erotic dances for Alun as he sits cross-legged on satin sheets. Does she enjoy it, or is it simply what she must do to keep him in love?

'The girl in the picture looks like you, Olwen. You must have seen that – the resemblance.'

The entrance to the Cwm, a black tunnel, lies on Gareth's left. Olwen holds his hand tightly as they pass it. 'When did *you* see it?'

'Not till last summer, the night of the dance.'

'Yet we'd been going to the same school for years.'

'I know. That's what amazed me, when I realized.'

'You'd never looked at me before that night.'

'I'd seen you at school –'

'But you'd never *looked* at me. I had to dress up and wear make-up – all of that – to make you look at me.'

They have reached his car. Gareth leans on the bonnet and links his arms around her waist. 'Are you upset?'

'I had to put on an act so you'd notice me.'

He pulls her against him and she rests her head on his chest. 'I noticed you, though.' Beside her cheek, she can feel his heart pulse.

'Olwen . . . that night. It wasn't an act. The other way around, I think. More like a transformation. As if you'd disguised yourself till then. You didn't want to be noticed before. Am I right?'

Is his heart constant or changeable? She slides her hand under her face, so that she can feel the beat beneath her palm. As a child, discovering bird nests in the Cwm, she had never been content simply to gaze. She had wanted to snatch an egg and crush the shell, feel the tiny, live bird in her hand. Only her grandfather calling, 'Don't touch, mind,' had restrained her, reminding her that if she broke the egg she would kill the bird.

'Besides, Olwen, it wasn't just the way you looked – though it could have been just that in different circumstances – but you looked like *her*. And you had the same quality that I remembered . . .' He lays his hand on her head. 'I don't think you understand. You think it's the old story, a fellow being drawn to a pretty girl. It was more like seeing a ghost. I was torn. Part of me wanted to run a mile – get as far away from you as I could.'

'But you asked me to dance.'

She can see him now, crossing the school gym, oblivious to the people who stood between them, though some said his name and some tried to waylay him . . . coming to her where she stood by the wall – as if she had him on a string. She had smiled at him, that was all, and he had left his friends and come to her.

'You had – have – this quality that draws me. Compels me, I should say.'

'What quality?' She arches her fingers and runs them over his chest. Touching the soft cotton of his T-shirt is, to Olwen, as intimate and thrilling as any embrace they have shared that day. She will never tire of touching him, she believes.

'Intensity,' Gareth says. 'When she stood by my bed, she

didn't move or speak at first, yet I felt this tremendous power surging from her, I remember, and I was caught up in it. That's what frightened me so much. Not seeing a ghost, but feeling so overwhelmed . . . as if she had me in thrall, like in the old tales. You know the story of Kaye and the Snow Queen?'

'Yes,' Olwen says. 'The Queen enchanted Kaye, and then she turned his heart to ice.'

'Well, I felt enchanted – but it was fire not ice. And I felt the same when I saw you at the dance. I looked at you and you smiled, and I was back in the dream. I had this illusion, Olwen, that your hair and dress swirled and flowed – you were all motion and energy, like a current – and you swept me across that room, your eyes and your smile pulling me in. But in fact you never moved, did you? You kept as still as she did.' He laughs briefly. 'I've never spoken like this before. I sound besotted, don't I!'

'Gareth, let's not stay here.' She releases herself from his arms. 'We should go back now.'

'Just a minute, then.' He opens the car door, takes something she does not see from the glove compartment, and slips it into the pocket of his jeans.

As they go up the lane, arms entwined about each other's waists, Olwen senses his presence. Hidden among the trees, he moves beside them, matching his step to theirs, his malice permeating the air like the smell of decay, as if they walked through a cemetery where all the ghosts had risen. But he's *my* ghost, Olwen thinks – he shan't have Gareth too. And she feels resistance and will surge in her. The pictures were wrong in one essential detail. It is she, not Gareth, who must battle the enchanter.

'Those pictures weren't an omen,' she says, her voice strong, defiant. 'Your mother didn't see into the future – not in the way you've believed. The girl she drew was my *mother*, not me. When your mother lived here she must have seen her and my grandfather and remembered their faces. They must have made an impression on her, so that she could reproduce them exactly, only exaggerated – the enchanter's beard and locks she invented – and she gave the girl dark hair though my mother was blonde.'

Gareth is silent.

Olwen presses his waist. 'It's true. I've seen a photo, so I know it's my mother in the picture.'

'I've been mistaken then –'

'Yes, there's nothing to dread – no omen, no curse, nothing supernatural. We're just ordinary, normal. It's a coincidence.'

He shakes his head, and she sees that he will not be easily dissuaded. Perhaps he feels disappointed, for she is telling him that there is no magic, no mystery, linking them – accident has brought them together, not destiny. Like her, he is a romantic; they have been raised on romances. What if romance is all that binds him to her?

'There's still something more,' he says. 'Why would she choose *your* family, Olwen – why *their* faces when there were so many, more recent, she might have used? And why should I see those apparitions – and then come here and meet you? Is that all coincidence?'

They have come to the garden gate. Shining in moonlight, the twisted tree on the edge of the Cwm points its long knotty finger at her. Rage sweeps out of the woods, and hatred. She is on the verge of committing an unpardonable offence – for she intends to take Gareth into the house again, into her bed, into herself . . .

'There is more. But will you let me tell it tomorrow?'

His face, lit by the moon, is troubled. He does not want to let go of questions that must have obsessed him for a long time, and he is tenacious, she understands . . . like his father.

Lifting onto her toes, placing her hands on his shoulders, Olwen kisses the scar beneath his eyebrow. 'Tomorrow, Gareth. Please?'

His expression alters, desire leaping in his eyes. He pulls her into his arms.

'Come!' she says urgently. 'Into the house!'

Light and perilous as a skiff, the narrow bed leaps and tosses on a turbulent sea. Joists straining, sheets streaming, it races through a hurricane, cresting tidal waves, plunging down cataracts, spinning on crosswaves, threatening always to capsize and pitch the sailors overboard. Beneath, a bottomless ocean swells and churns.

So it seems to Olwen, as Gareth thrusts deeper and faster. He has lifted her body clear of the mattress and she has no anchor save him. She wraps him with her arms, her legs, so that she will not be swept away. Water streams about them. She feels it on her eyelids, in her hair, slippery as seaweed, and in the slickness of their limbs as she slides under him, losing her grip.

'Don't let me go,' she says, repeatedly, as the waves peak. 'Hold on to me, Gareth.'

At first he heard her, answered her, his voice soothing. 'It's all right, love. It's all right. I've got you.'

But now he doesn't hear. He lets her go, and Olwen cries out as the sea snatches her and she is hurled away from him, borne off on a giant wave that will surely dash her to pieces. She screams his name . . . but he is gone . . . only the wave lifts her. Thrown clear of Gareth, of herself, of all moorings, she feels weightless and lost, until she careens from the height – and drowns indeed – but in a whirlpool of ecstasy, the first pure bodily delight she has ever known . . .

Ecstasy . . . even as her mind forms the word the feeling dissolves. As she tries to grasp and hold it, her body arching in pursuit, it scatters and slips away, leaving in its wake a recollection, an image: herself, a child, wading into the Swansea sea at night, her cupped palms scooping water as she tries to capture the phosphorescence that tinsels the surface of the ocean. Her skirt bunched in her hands, Aunt Pridwyn follows, saying, 'You can't catch it, love. It's just lights. It has no substance.'

Through calm water, Olwen swims back to the shore of herself. Gareth's arms close around her. He pulls her down onto damp sheets and she lies quiet, anchored against his body, held fast.

'I felt it,' she says. 'I had it, Gareth . . .' She searches for words to tell him. 'I went so far, I was afraid, and then –'

He laughs softly. 'And then you came. I know, Olwen.'

He has withdrawn from her, but she feels him still hard against her thigh. 'You didn't, though –'

'Not yet.' He nuzzles her neck beneath her ear. 'I want it to last a long time tonight.' Olwen moves her hand down to enclose him. He is slick and resilient. Her circled fingers slip up and down the length of him, and she thinks of rings, possession, power. Just minutes ago he rode above her, navigating the storm, controlling her, judging, she realizes, the moment to let go, to let her fly out on the wave. Now the balance has shifted. He gives himself up to her, all his wishes centred on her hand, what it does to him as her fingers marry his ridges. It's a heady sensation for Olwen, too thrilling almost to bear. If she spoke, he would come into her again at once. He longs to, she senses . . . waits only until she is ready, until she tells him.

'Be inside me,' she says, 'again.'

In the eye of the hurricane, Olwen rests, her head on Gareth's shoulder, her arms around his neck. He sits in the window seat, one leg stretched out on its ledge to support her weight as she lies across him and he moves, infinitely slowly, inside her. They have brought pillows and folded a sheet there, made it another bed. The scented night breezes cool their heated bodies and moonlight streams over them. The window is flung wide, so that they are perched almost in space, on one side of them only air and the drop, should they move too violently, into the garden far below. So their love-making is precarious. But Olwen is not afraid; risk intensifies each caress she gives and receives.

Beyond Gareth's shoulder the dark Cwm rises. Olwen gazes at the black trunks of trees, the glittering foliage, leaves iced with moonlight, and knows that a watcher there could see her naked body entwined in Gareth's embrace. She does not care. This is right. This is as it should be. And she raises herself to kneel over her lover, stretching her body, tossing her hair back and tilting her chin at the trees.

In the Cwm nothing appears in response to her challenge. No sound rises from its depths, no faces peer among the branches. It is simply a wood at night, the only predators, the fox, the owl, the poacher and his dog.

Slowly, gently, taking her unawares, Gareth brings her again to pleasure. This time it is a deep, joyful merging she feels, for he meets her, swims with her. Like a pair of dolphins they make a graceful arc together and leap over the final wave.

Olwen drops her head on his chest. Gareth lifts her as he stands up. 'I'll carry you to bed.' Astride him, Olwen looks over his shoulder . . . and sees, on the edge of the Cwm, the woman in blue and, beside her, holding her hand, a waiflike child with a pale face and heavy, braided hair. Frail as flowers under the great oaks, they stand looking up at her.

Twenty-one

In the early light the face on the rafter is hard to see. Lying on her back, Olwen studies the whorls and cracks in the wood until she can distinguish the knife cuts. Even when she makes them out, they no longer form a recognizable composition. Now she must remember and invent the tilted eyes, curved mouth and swirling hair. Otherwise, the marks are merely ornate scratchings on the warped surface of the beam. Is it only the poor light, or has the carving faded, as furnishing fades and loses its pattern from too much exposure to the sun?

Or is it her response that has changed? Objects, scenes – people – can appear to possess attributes that depend, in fact, more on the gazer than on their own actuality. She has realized this, watching Gareth sleep. His hair tousled on the pillow and falling in tendrils over his forehead, his eyelids pale in contrast to his tan, he seems to her trusting, innocent – qualities she has not noticed in him before and which, perhaps, are not his. The scar beneath his eyebrow is a naked place, stark now that his green eyes can't deflect her gaze. Nothing is whiter, purer, more fragile. Looking at it, she seems to penetrate to her lover's core, to that hidden place where he is unclothed and vulnerable. In love with him, and after a night of loving, she sees, possibly, a reflection merely of the deep tenderness he has evoked, an image of her own fragility and the frailty of their connection, breakable as a bird's egg.

When the pleasure and pain of gazing became unbearable (already she wonders, what will he feel when he wakes, what tomorrow, in a year?) Olwen turned her head away to decipher nicks in the rafter. The face, when she finally restores it, has lost all suggestion of animosity – of power – as if, at last, it has caught up with the man who shaped it, altered like her grandfather, whose ghost she saw, crumpled, helpless, halt, beneath the cloak of the enchanter.

And it comes to her suddenly that this day is Sunday, that there is a thing she must do, a promise to keep. Today she must go into the Cwm, find and free her grandfather if she can . . . and Alice, too. They are her ghosts. If she abandons them now, she will jettison herself. She has a debt to pay – to Alice who gave birth to her, to John who raised her. Despite them, yes – but also because of them – she lives and loves Gareth.

Olwen slides from the bed, crosses the room on tiptoe and takes her clothes, jeans and a shirt, into the bathroom where she washes, dresses, plaits her hair. Before going downstairs she looks into her room, sees that Gareth has not stirred. Beside him stands the small table, in the drawer of which lies the keeper wrapped in lace. She starts to fetch it, then changes her mind. Gareth might wake and want to go with her. No help then – neither from the ring nor from her lover. What she must do, she must do by herself.

By the kitchen clock, it is just after seven. She has hardly slept, yet she feels alert. Quickly she makes and drinks a cup of coffee, eats a slice of buttered bread, and writes a brief note: 'I've gone into the Cwm. Please wait.'

Then she leaves the house and walks out under a chill, pale sky where the sun is a transparent circle, a white-gold ring glinting behind the morning mist. Wrapped in fog, the garden seems insubstantial, the laurel bush and the chestnut tree rising out of the billows like the weird, wavering shapes in dreams. Mist drains the flowers of colour and bleaches the grass as it sweeps across the garden like the furred hem of a long winter cloak.

Approaching the toolshed, Olwen sees the little window glitter through the vapour that shrouds the tarpaulin. An old, decrepit dog who sleeps with one eye open, the shed holds no terror for her now. It saddens her merely, as if it really were an aged dog she has loved and must soon put to rest.

Opposite the shed, ranged along the wall, the delphiniums seem to fade and droop under the weight of the enveloping fog. Close up, she can see the faint brown stains on the blossoms. Their season is almost over; soon their petals will fall like confetti on the grave of her unwed, unburied mother.

As she shuts the gate on the garden, Olwen looks up to the window of her room, thinks of the young man in her bed, and feels the twin rivers of hope and fear flow into her heart and merge there. How many people have stood at windows, looking out or looking in on what they longed for and could not possess? Alice, trapped in her father's house, gazing out on the mirage of freedom; Bryn, loitering in the lane, hoping for a glimpse of her; her grandfather lying in his sick-bed, seeing the bright shape of his daughter down in the garden; Aunt Flindy, widowed, abandoned, an eternal watcher, confusing memory and vision; Morgan Pryce, who manages to keep in motion the scenery beyond his windows, as long as he sits in the driver's seat, only to go home each night to a house with no view. And Gwen, years spent behind the windows of her loveless house . . . and Olwen herself –

I must be kind, Olwen thinks, to those who are left. Kindness will keep her from windows shut fast, or open only on despair. Perhaps.

Starting down the lane, walking beneath the great oaks, she thinks, when I come back, I'll do better. Instantly another thought grasps her, colder than the morning air. Is it possible that she *won't* come back? She shivers and quickens her pace. Too late now for doubts, choices. If she is ever to choose again, she must first go through with what others have already planned for her.

She reaches the entrance to the Cwm. Leaves blown down in Monday's storm fill the ditch. In the woods, mist winds about the tree trunks and hangs from the branches in giant cocoons. Olwen crosses the ditch then pauses. Along the path she must follow, mist drifts and billows like pipe smoke, twisting into fantastic shapes. Elongated or puffed distortions of the human form gyrate on the air for a moment, then disperse and flit away into the woods as new spectres rise up. The path teems with wraiths, swaying, dipping, vanishing, as if the enchanter has called up his minions to frighten and deter her.

Yes, he is here, watching to see whether she will proceed or falter. He crouches perhaps behind one of the hawthorn bushes, loaded with scarlet berries, the colour of his nails, or perhaps he lies in wait behind a broad tree trunk, ready to ambush her if she steps further into the woods.

At the far end of the path, beyond the vaporous dancers, the mist becomes an opaque white curtain suspended from the high, interlocking boughs of an oak and an elm. Surely that is his hiding place. Like a puppeteer, he stands behind the curtain directing the mad ballet to tease and daunt her so that she can go neither forward nor back.

Then, as she hesitates, her will floundering, a different shape materializes. A memory, sprung from the hawthorns, unfurls like a canvas, driving away the spectres, and Olwen is back in an earlier time, in a long ago summer morning.

Coming into the Cwm with her grandfather, she sees, up ahead, a hawthorn bush shaking violently, as if to uproot itself. Pulling at his sleeve, she cries, 'Grandfather! Look!' Not knowing whether to feel delight or fear, she clutches at his jacket sleeve and hops up and down. 'What is it? What's it doing? Shall we run away?'

'Quiet now,' he says softly. 'Don't make it more agitated than it is already.'

At first she thinks he means the bush. Then, as they go towards it, he says, 'Something's trapped in there. Hisht, Olwen! Stop bouncing like a ball.'

When they reach the bush, he gives her his walking stick to hold and bends to part the thorny branches. Deep in the heart of the bramble, Olwen, looking under his arm, sees a blue jay thrashing wildly. Her grandfather reaches in. His hands close over the bird. Olwen sees the creature grow rigid, still as death, as he grasps it. When he pulls it out, his hands are covered in long, red scratches. Cupping the bird in his palms, he shows it to Olwen.

'It's dead!' she wails.

'Not her! She's faking. Frightened out of your wits, aren't you, my beauty? Have a look at her, Olwen, before I let her go.'

Olwen looks at the lovely sky-blue feathers, the smooth, milky head, and the tiny, sharp eyes, which she sees are alert and watchful. She stretches out a finger to stroke the plumage. Then her grandfather flings up his hands and the bird soars from them, streaking away through the high branches into the blue sky.

A fierce emotion grips Olwen. More acute than anything she has felt before, it courses through her body and hurls her out of herself, so that she is merely a voice, crying, 'Grandfather!'

The Cwm flings back the echo of her voice . . . and its own silence. The mist has completely dispersed and filtered sunlight gilds the path. Olwen feels the sun's warmth on her bare arms. Deep in the green recesses of the woods, far from the place where she stands, a bird begins to sing, blithe, indifferent . . .

Everything in the Cwm is indifferent, no love or hatred here, only the instinct to survive. The bird her grandfather freed felt no gratitude, no obligation. Rabbits, foxes, badgers, struggling in Bryn Brewen's traps, feel pain, terror, but the steel teeth that hold them and the man who sets the traps are not distinguished. And when her grandfather happened on one of Bryn's contraptions, the released animal scurried or limped away, not recognizing him as rescuer, scenting only the human, the enemy in him. To distinguish, to reason, to synthesize – these are human abilities and human tasks.

Olwen walks into the woods. On either side the leaves hang down in dense tiers. In their stillness they resemble the ornate foliage sculpted on ancient buildings. Remembering old stories, old pictures, she imagines, in the gloomy places among the leaves, the stone heads of griffins, the stone eyes of basilisks. Other eyes watch her too, she is sure, eyes she has seen many times in dreams and once in reality, glittering like a winter sea, or gleaming like polished ebony. Changeable in colour, they are fixed in their expression – always malicious, always implacable. She has looked into these eyes and, almost, they vanquished her.

But now Olwen is stalwart. Strengthened and cleansed, she walks the path with a firm step, her body straight as a lance, certainty buttressing her heart. Today she will find them – her grandfather, her mother, and the one who keeps them earth-bound, chained to his will by sorcery. She has only to go forward to the clearing. Appearing and vanishing, like the set of a play, the clearing will be there, the actors too. They are waiting for her.

A sudden breeze rustles the foliage, startling her. It slips out of the trees and comes upon her softly, like an unexpected companion, lifting her hair and caressing her skin. Playful, teasing, the little wind cavorts along the path. Olwen follows it . . . and there is the glade, a silent grassy space, a perfect circle, like memory, insubstantial, shifting like emotions, the substances of which it is made.

Quiet, sheltered, an enclosed courtyard, the glade is massed this morning with goldenrod, foxgloves, wild thyme. In the centre stands a mound of stones, like a ruined fountain or a crumbling altar. Olwen touches the stones, turns one over in her hand. Smooth and sun-warmed, faintly marked with bluish-green, it has the texture of a finger nail.

The air is heavy, musky. There are no birds, only stirrings in the trees on the other side of the glade. The woods are deeper, darker there, the trees growing close, tangled creepers and the thorny stems of dog roses filling the spaces between. This is a part of the woods she has never seen before, and Olwen senses that she must go there. He has shifted the location, wishing to draw her deeper into the Cwm, meaning to confuse her with new scenery, unfamiliar terrain. She crosses the glade and enters the woods again.

In here there is no path to follow. Instead she must thrust her way through dense vegetation beneath crowded branches that obliterate the sky. A yellowish gaseous glow perforates the branches at intervals, showing the snaky outlines of creepers and the thick fronds of ferns that ripple along the forest floor like giant iguanas. All colours are subdued: peat-brown, dark moist green, the greyish-white of fungi. Olwen pushes forward through the netted undergrowth, stumbling over broken branches and the rotting carcasses of fallen trees. It is very cold, and the scent of decay permeates the air.

She is aware suddenly that she is followed. A branch snaps behind her. Glancing back, she glimpses a flutter of blue amid the dark foliage, a flash of silver, the sweep of a cloak, the colour of midnight, as it is pulled out of view behind the bole of an elm. Just ahead there is another break in the trees, another clearing, the grass as dark there as the mouth of a well. On the far side stand two birches, their branches intertwined, and between them another tree, stunted, leafless, paler even than the birch barks.

Close behind her, her hidden companions whisper – quick, uneasy sounds, like the conferring of relatives at a death-bed. Leaves rustle as they creep nearer still, feigning stealth . . . for they want her to hear them, of course. They want her to turn round, and the enchanter is one of them. He exerts his will now to prevent her from entering this glade. As if he spoke, the air grows weighty with prohibition. She feels it close in like an invisible wall. As if he has spread his great cloak and prepares to swoop, she feels stifled, weakened.

Swiftly, before these sensations can take hold of her, Olwen steps out of the trees and hurries across the clearing. When she reaches the centre she stops short. For now she sees that the thing between the birches is not a shrivelled tree. It is the half-naked body of a man, trapped in the branches, his outstretched arms fastened at the wrists with creeper, tough as ropes, looped around the trunks of the silver birches.

His trousers are torn, mud-spattered, stained with moss and bark, as if he has worn them through a long and arduous journey. A piece of cloth hangs down from his right knee and Olwen can see his calf, permanently scarred and bruised, yet strangely beautiful, rainbow-coloured. White hair curls profusely on his naked chest and floats like thistledown about his head, sunk onto his breastbone.

Her followers leave their cover and come beside her. There are three. Olwen does not look at them. Instead, she moves towards the figure in the trees. Her companions move with her, matching their steps to hers. As she gets closer, she sees that the body of the imprisoned man is covered in welts, the lacerations of thorns and nettles. Like her, he has tried to penetrate the forest. Beneath the cuts and scratches, his skin is grey, lifeless.

Now her escorts glide in front. Turning to face her, they spread their arms, as though to make a fence and cut her off from the prisoner. She looks up at them and terror grips her. They are more striking – and more hideous – than any creatures she has seen or imagined.

Tall as young trees, they seem to have stepped from the pages of an old book of myth and magic, a queen and her champion, and their dark chaperone. The woman's blue dress has a high, narrow bodice and flowing skirt. Her silver hair is piled into a netted headdress that ends in an ivory-coloured cone. Sapphires sparkle at her throat, matching her long, tilted eyes in colour and brilliance.

The young man wears armour. Light flashes from his breast-plate and sword hilt. The emblem on his shield is wrought in rubies, a rose pierced with a thorn. His flaxen hair curls to his shoulders, his eyes burn like the woman's. In their faces and colouring Olwen sees the strong resemblance, penetrates their disguise, and recognizes her mother . . . and her grandfather as she has never seen him, youthful, dazzling . . . as he wished to be, perhaps, for his daughter.

Their lithe bodies and perfect features are flawless, yes. But their faces are pallid and blank as paper, as if they are cut-outs, creations, merely, of the enchanter.

Taller than they, broader and stronger, like an elm beside

willows, he wears a deep black robe embroidered with stars, half moons, and the symbols of astrology. Wonderful at first glance, but as she looks harder, Olwen sees that the silver threads are tarnished with age. His hair is thick and shaggy, his beard brittle and black as charred bones, a wolfish cast to his features. In his taut, yellow face, his eyes glitter with the sharp, colourless light of diamonds.

Slowly, warily, Olwen steps towards the enchanter. Forcing her eyes away from his piercing gaze, she fixes them on the pale outstretched arms behind him. Still she feels his terrible, silent animosity weaken her as she struggles on, lifting her heavy feet, trudging as if through a swamp. When she is level with him, he thrusts his arm in front of her. The long sleeve falls like a curtain and she stares into deep folds, black and silver like the night sky.

Against this backdrop, a scene materializes: she sees the garden of her grandparents' house, sees her grandfather, healthy and brown, one foot on the rim of a shovel, his hands gripping the wooden handle as he drives the blade into the earth. And Olwen sees herself, a child, playing near him, her plaits bouncing as she hops over numbers chalked on the stone path.

Her body stirs with a sensation slow and subtle that both excites and enervates her, an urge to let go, to slip into the folds of the shining sleeve. Live currents shoot through the silver threads, as lightning streaks across the night sky, and the cloak seems to spin and flare, a force rushing out of it into her veins, sapping her resistance.

Suddenly, Olwen feels a cold hand on her shoulder, cold lips press her cheek. 'Turn away from the sleeve,' her mother whispers. 'Don't look there. Go on . . . go forward.'

On Olwen's other side, the young knight's gauntleted fingers touch her hair, a caress as ephemeral as memory. 'Save yourself,' he murmurs. 'Save us all.'

Turning in response to his touch, Olwen looks into his shield and sees reflected beneath the pierced rose the tableau in the enchanter's sleeve. As she gazes at this double image, old, half-remembered lines of a once-loved poem drift into her mind, 'And moving through a mirror clear . . . Shadows of the world appear.'

'You have a lion heart,' the young knight says. 'Resist reflections.'

228

' "I am half sick of shadows!" ' Olwen cries.

In the shield-mirror, her grandfather turns his head to look at her. The child looks too. Neither smiles, and she sees that their faces have the same waxen quality as her watchers.

'Why, they are dead!' Olwen says.

Beside her, Alice sighs and presses her shoulder.

Then Olwen sees something more and is startled out of her trance. The child is not herself but Alice, flowers wreathed in her hair and looped about her neck. She, Olwen, does not figure in the idyllic scene displayed in the enchanter's sleeve. It is a hoax, a deception. She has no part to play, for the roles were cast before her birth. She is, at best, a stand-in. To step through the velvet curtain, to return to that time, would mean entrapment forever in a substitute life.

Yet . . . they depend on her, too. Alice grasps her shoulder, more like a child than a parent. The man imprisoned in the trees is helpless, in need of rescue. This is her role then – to protect them, and herself also.

Olwen looks up into the eyes of the enchanter. At the same time, she raises her hands and presses on the arm that holds the magic sleeve aloft. The glitter in his pupils almost blinds her, as if she looked into the reaches of a mountain glacier. But even as the needle-sharp rays stab through her skin, she feels the arm sink. Power flows into her limbs. She is invincible now, for she has no secret longing, no forbidden desire. At last she is free of enchantment. And he knows this. Heavy, ashen eyelids droop over his eyes. His arm falls like a broken bough.

Olwen steps past the enchanter to the twin trees and begins to unwind the creepers that bind the lifeless form. As she works, the ropes fall and rot away of themselves, the wounds fade, his body stirs. As she takes his arm, the man lifts his head and murmurs, 'Olwen, *cariad*.'

'Come, Grandfather,' she says, 'it's summer again,' and they go together down a path that opens now beyond the birches, a path as broad as an avenue, stretching away into sunshine.

Olwen looks back . . . in time to see the enchanter spread his cloak for the last time. Into its indigo sleeve the puppets glide, the knight and his lady. He wraps them up, a showman packing his bag of tricks, swathes the cloak about him, lifting one arm to cover his face . . . and becomes a massive, dark shape, a fire-blackened tree trunk. For a moment he holds this posture. Then,

229

as all dead things must, he disintegrates, evaporates, merging into the shadows cast by the live oaks and elms. The glade in which Olwen confronted him vanishes like mist. Behind her only trees, vines, undergrowth – only the Cwm. And, running through it, the familiar path winds towards Archer's Lane.

As they walk, her grandfather begins to move away from her, relinquishing her support. When they come out of the woods into a wide meadow, he goes in front. He does not limp and he has no cane. At the far end of the meadow, a low hill rises, washed in sunlight. He signals her to stop. Holding himself proudly, a man in his prime, his hair shining, he crosses the flower-strewn field, weaving a path among the headstones, and climbs the hill.

At the summit he pauses and holds his cupped hands to the sky. As Olwen watches, his arms make a wide, sweeping arc and something blue flashes out of his fingers and soars into the air.

Spry in his Sunday suit, his hair clouding under his grey cap, John stands suffused in sunlight on the brow of Cefn Heights, his face turned toward Olwen. Then he doffs his cap and twirls it jauntily, smiling and bowing, playing the dandy for her, as he did on long ago Sundays when they dressed in their best to walk in the Cwm. Olwen glimpses the cap's blue silk lining and her heart lurches.

'Go on, Grandfather,' she murmurs. 'Please.'

As if he hears her – or perhaps, simply because he is able – John strides across the golden grass and, without a backward look, vanishes on the other side of the hill.

Olwen goes through the woods, along the well-known path she has walked since childhood, no breaks in the trees now, no ephemeral glades or magic circles springing up in front of her. With no actors, no scenes to play, the stages have vanished behind leafy curtains. Her only company in the Cwm are its natural inhabitants, the birds and the small, shy creatures.

Soon she sees the lane in front and the roof of the Millers' cottage. Remembering Gareth, she grows anxious, eager. Is he waiting, or has he gone? Does he stand at her window or pace the garden, agitated by desire and love? Or is it embarrassment, regret, he feels, for words spoken but not meant? Olwen quickens her pace, the need to know speeding her towards the house on Archer's Lane . . . towards her future, bright and unpredictable as the sun, now fully risen out of the morning mist.

GITA MEHTA

Raj

Born a princess into life as it has long been led in the Royal House of Balmer, Jaya Singh must grapple with history if she is to fulfil her role as the guardian of her people. For momentous changes are sweeping across India as her great civilisation heads inexorably towards the bloody struggle for Independence from the British Raj.

Torn between tradition and the ideals of Mahatma Gandhi, Jaya becomes the politically aroused leader who will guide her Kingdom through a treacherously shifting world until the moment when palace and country can triumph over their destiny.

Not since *Gone With the Wind* have fiction and history been so compellingly interwoven.

'Easily the year's best novel' *Daily Mail*

'Mehta's talent is as sharp as a laser beam'

Sunday Times

DOMINI TAYLOR

Siege

By the author of the major BBC TV serial *Mother Love*

Besieged by terror
Rented for the summer holidays by the impressively extended Kemp family, the remote fortified farmhouse seems a perfect choice.

Yet the idyllic hilltop fortress withholds powerful secrets. And inexplicably hostile villagers and a near-fatal accident threaten to stretch already fragile relationships to breaking point – then set in train a kaleidoscopic nightmare of events that subject the family to death, devastation and overwhelming terror . . .

'A tense psychological thriller . . . Master of Menace, Taylor tightens the screw without mercy'

John Nicholson, *The Times*

A Selected List of Fiction Available from Mandarin

While every effort is made to keep prices low, it is sometimes necessary to increase prices at short notice. Mandarin Paperbacks reserves the right to show new retail prices on covers which may differ from those previously advertised in the text or elsewhere.

The prices shown below were correct at the time of going to press.

☐	7493 0003 5	**Mirage**	James Follett	£3.99
☐	7493 0134 1	**To Kill a Mockingbird**	Harper Lee	£2.99
☐	7493 0076 0	**The Crystal Contract**	Julian Rathbone	£3.99
☐	7493 0145 7	**Talking Oscars**	Simon Williams	£3.50
☐	7493 0118 X	**The Wire**	Nik Gowing	£3.99
☐	7493 0121 X	**Under Cover of Daylight**	James Hall	£3.50
☐	7493 0020 5	**Pratt of the Argus**	David Nobbs	£3.99
☐	7493 0097 3	**Second from Last in the Sack Race**	David Nobbs	£3.50

All these books are available at your bookshop or newsagent, or can be ordered direct from the publisher. Just tick the titles you want and fill in the form below.

Mandarin Paperbacks, Cash Sales Department, PO Box 11, Falmouth, Cornwall TR10 9EN.

Please send cheque or postal order, no currency, for purchase price quoted and allow the following for postage and packing:

UK — 80p for the first book, 20p for each additional book ordered to a maximum charge of £2.00.

BFPO — 80p for the first book, 20p for each additional book.

Overseas including Eire — £1.50 for the first book, £1.00 for the second and 30p for each additional book thereafter.

NAME (Block letters) ....

ADDRESS ....

....

....